DARKER

BY

FOUR

JUNE CL TAN

HARPER TEEN
An Imprint of HarperCollinsPublishers

ALSO BY JUNE CL TAN:

Jade Fire Gold

HarperTeen is an imprint of HarperCollins Publishers.

Darker by Four

Copyright © 2024 by June CL Tan

Library of Congress Control Number: 2023937637
ISBN 978-0-06-328384-8

Typography by Catherine Lee
24 25 26 27 28 LBC 5 4 3 2 1

First Edition

Content Note

Please note that while this work of fantasy draws inspiration from a real-life cultural park, Haw Par Villa, and the author's experiences with folk religion as a member of the Chinese diaspora community in Southeast Asia, this book should not be taken as an authoritative or singular source on any religion or culture. Nor should it be used as an educational reference for the mythology of gods and the underworld; the metaphysics of yin and yang, and qi; historical or modern Taoist and Buddhist practices; or Chinese spirituality in general.

"Hell" and "the underworld" are used interchangeably in this book as equivalents of "dìyù" (earth prison), which is the traditional name for the realm of the dead in Chinese mythology and folk religion.

Please also be aware that this book contains themes and/or mentions of death, parental death (flashbacks), child abuse (inferences), panic attacks and anxiety (including one episode that is briefly described), alcohol consumption and alcoholism, and fantasy violence.

To all the readers who supported Jade Fire Gold—
you made this book possible <3

Love is simply the name for the desire and
pursuit of the whole.

—Plato
Symposium

Five Four

The boy stands alone on the roof of the tallest skyscraper in the city, a thin slice of darkness against the glowing lights. He could be eighteen, twenty-eight, or anywhere in between.

He turns up the collar of his wool coat, creating a stiff funnel around his pale neck, hiding the delicate silk choker he wears. Fastened by a discreet silver clasp, it's a black gash across his snow-white throat like an irrevocable scar. Bright and bloody, his pocket square peeks out from under his coat, a splash of blood on his inky suit. All this expensive fabric molds to his form like a second skin, yet it is hardly adequate protection against the cold. Fortunately, temperature has little effect on this boy. He merely likes to look sharp.

And, considering his profession, it is only respectful.

Raking a hand through silvery-white hair, he stares into the distance, sadness softening his blade-sharp features. This isn't the first time he has haunted this roof. He likes it up here. The solitude reminds him of another place he haunts in his own world.

Everything here is more alive, though.

From his vantage point, he sees the regular blinking of red and green and headlights snaking along roads stretching far into the distance. Electronic beats vibrate from well-lit stores, discordant against the honks of impatient drivers battling wayward pedestrians. The boy squints at the neon words shrieking the latest financial and political news underneath digital billboards on towering buildings, then lowers his gaze to the streets.

Humans. Scurrying like ants.

The city is a jarring melody of chaos, but he hears the song of its soul. The yearning inside him grows. He does not belong here—he never did, and maybe, he never will.

But perhaps the threads of fate are weaving a new tapestry tonight.

The boy waits, breathing in the familiar scent of the city, the mellow warmth of life filling his lungs. But as always, camouflaged in shades of charcoal and smoke, the taint of death lurks in a way that only he can understand.

He waits and waits a little more. Waits until the city softens, slows, slumbers. Until it dreams.

He tilts his head as if a distant voice were whispering to him through the wind, his eyes shifting to his watch. It's an ancient-looking timepiece with a pitch-black face and gold gears. He closes his eyes and takes a breath. A moment later, the minute repeater engages and a series of chimes, like that from an old grandfather clock, sound.

Five long ones. A pause. Then more chimes. Each a short chirp.

Once, twice, thrice. Four times.

Five, four. Wu, si.

It is time, he thinks, opening his eyes. Time to finally forget her.

The boy straightens and looks up at flickering stars in heaven. Then he steps forward to the edge of the parapet, puts one foot out in the air—

—and disappears.

1
Nikai

Nikai's stomach started to growl as he thought about the meal he was planning to eat at Kuu Bar after work: warm rice, pickled vegetables, and a crispy pork cutlet deep-fried to golden perfection. There was food back in the underworld, but it wasn't as good as what one could find in the human realm.

His stomach grumbled again, but he ignored it. It was best to look like he was doing his job. Dressed in pristine white suits, the other Reapers of the Fourth Court were hovering around the pile of distorted metal stretching across one of the expressways of the human city. The aftermath of the thirteen-vehicle pileup had summoned them, and they were counting casualties like good worker bees.

Nikai, however, was *Head* Reaper, which allowed for privileges such as daydreaming about food. But he wouldn't get to eat that coveted meal unless he hurried the task along.

He surveyed the scene. Shattered glass caught the light of the streetlamps, and the scent of burning rubber had a base note of human blood. Sounds of human pain assailed his ears. With a calm exhale, he let it all slide past him.

As he watched, the human survivors began to pull themselves from the wreckage. He wasn't worried about them. Over the years, he'd learned to focus on the dead rather than the living—they couldn't see him anyway. *Time*, however, was his concern. The Reapers had to collect the souls immediately, for the Blight could appear at any time. Drawn by the negative energy of newly departed souls, the supernatural virus infected them, turning them into vicious monsters.

Nikai knew his team had to hurry. He approached a new Reaper who had just joined his team. She was a bespectacled young woman with an enthusiastic manner about her. He wondered how she'd become a Reaper, but he knew better than to ask.

"You should read the death notes tonight," he said. "You need the experience."

"Yes, sir. Of course, sir." The new Reaper clicked her heels together, taking the tablet from him. She pursed her lips, sifting through the death notes with her stylus. Each slide had a photograph of a person, their name, a time of death, and a cause of death.

Nikai remembered a time when death notes were actual pieces of paper the size of poker cards. He was new and wide-eyed then, eager to do his job right, just like this Reaper beside him. But as the centuries went by, simultaneously slower and faster than expected, the work became grimmer and grimmer.

Probably why we're called grim reapers, Nikai thought wryly. He hated the word *reaper*. It sounded like they were harvesting the living, waiting until they were ripe before hacking away at their lives. In truth, a Reaper's job was to guide souls into the afterlife, where they would reside in one of the Ten Courts of Hell until their individual cycle of reincarnation was up.

Ushering. That was a better term. Nikai was an usher, not a reaper. Ushering made more sense. Ushering was kinder. Although tonight, ushering was downright bleak.

Of the fifteen souls that needed to be collected tonight, six were children.

Adult souls were a pain. Filled with feelings of regret and rage and sorrow, they argued and pleaded and cried and screamed. Because of this, most Reapers preferred collecting the souls of children. But Nikai would rather take the souls of a hundred adults over a child's any day.

A flicker in his peripheral view drew his attention.

A young man with silvery-white hair had appeared from nowhere.

The new Reaper fumbled her stylus. "Y-Your Majesty," she said, lowering her head.

Nikai assumed she hadn't seen any of the Kings this close before. He hadn't expected the Fourth King to drop by either. The Kings had better things to do than carry out the menial labor of collecting the souls of the dead. Instinctively, Nikai straightened his tie. Four was all about making a good impression; thankfully, Nikai had worn his sharpest all-black Head Reaper suit tonight.

"Greetings, Four," he said, smiling at his boss.

The new Reaper's eyes darted between them, no doubt surprised to see King and Reaper on such informal terms.

Nikai's chest swelled with pride. A hierarchy would always divide them, but Four saw him as a friend, and that was enough. Four had found him, a lost soul destined to wander in limbo for eternity with no chance for redemption or reincarnation. He'd given Nikai a purpose. A *home*. Four was his friend. His family.

Four nodded back absently. He was staring hard at the wreckage in front of them. A mysterious crease had notched itself between his dark brows, too faint for a passing observer to detect, but Nikai knew his friend well. Four was troubled, and he seemed to be waiting for something—or someone. But who else could be coming here?

There was another flicker, and the King of the First Court appeared.

One's stiletto heels clicked sharply on the tarmac, the sound echoing in Nikai's ears even as sirens pierced the night. The patent fuchsia of One's shoes matched their bright pink lips, both pops of color vibrant against an emerald pantsuit that accentuated their curves and edges. A single jewel shaped like a dewdrop hung around their neck, catching Nikai's eye as it flashed an impossible spectrum of colors. Their pixie haircut was ironic; One was hardly a delicate fairy.

Nikai's peacock-blue hair flopped down as he bowed low to the First King. Next to him, the new Reaper's breaths grew short. Meeting two Kings in one night—no wonder she looked like she was about to pass out. Already the air around them felt heavier, darker somehow, as if someone had thrown a blanket over a lamp. Nikai knew it was the two Kings' spiritual pressure that was making it so.

The new Reaper squeaked, "Your Majesty."

"Good evening to you both." One's smile was so radiant Nikai had to blink away.

His cheeks were burning. He was never able to meet One's eyes directly, always blushing involuntarily as he did now. They were, after all, the *first* of the Kings. They were beautiful. Intimidating, sure. Possibly even frightening. But beautiful nonetheless.

Four seemed unsurprised by One's arrival. Was this who he was expecting? But instead of speaking to him, One walked over to a blue taxi in the middle of the pileup and lowered themself to peer into the shattered windows.

Nikai's thoughts of an easy evening and delicious dinner were slipping away. The Kings of Hell never showed up for soul collections. Four's arrival had interrupted the Reapers' work, but at least it was the Fourth Court's Reapers who were on the scene, and he *was* their King. But for One to stop by as well? It made no sense. And with two Kings present, all Reapers were standing at attention instead of doing their jobs. Time was ticking; the Blight could strike at any moment.

But One was still scrutinizing the taxi with narrowed eyes.

Curious, Nikai turned his attention there. The driver was alive, but Nikai sensed the gradual severance of a soul from another mortal in there. The passenger was about to die.

But there was something else.

Another heartbeat. Another flutter of spiritual energy inside.

The new Reaper sensed it, too. "A baby," she whispered.

That heartbeat was slowing as the feathery soul struggled inside its mortal body. But even as its tether was weakening, Nikai could feel there was something different about that soul.

He was about to go closer when One gestured to Four. "A word, Brother," they said, and walked to the side of the highway.

Four nodded at his Reapers. "Carry on with your work." The Fourth Court Reapers inclined their heads briefly and went back to their duties. "Come with me," he told Nikai, who followed obediently to where One was waiting.

One threw a questioning glance at him.

"You may speak freely in front of Nikai," Four told them. His tone left no room for debate.

Nikai smiled reassuringly. He was discreet. As Head Reaper, he had to be. Though it felt like Four simply wanted him around now to annoy the other King.

"Why did you call for me?" Four asked.

"The soul of the woman in that taxi will leave her body soon, but since it has not been collected, it is not too late for you to return it to her," One replied.

Nikai swallowed his shock. It wasn't his place to question any of the Kings, but what One was suggesting—saving the life of the woman and thus, her unborn child—was absurd. Didn't the ancient tenets forbid the Kings from interfering in human affairs?

Undisturbed by One's request, Four was a picture of calm. "I have no reason to do anything," he said, his grin crooked and taunting.

Nikai stared at the shiny buckles of his well-polished shoes. He didn't want to be caught up in a feud between Kings.

"I only need the woman for the birth of the child," One said, "and it looks like that could happen in a matter of hours. You can have her soul back after that. The timing will be of no difference to you and your Court."

"If the child is meant to live, it will," Four replied coolly. "Death is our dominion; life is not ours to give. You know this." He brushed the lint off his coat, his smile widening to reveal his canines. But there was no humor or amusement in it. "And as I was once told, the red threads of fate are not beholden to us."

7

He's upset, Nikai thought, seeing through Four's smile. But it wasn't anger Nikai sensed, but something closer to regret.

One's expression softened. "No, Brother, fate does not owe us anything," they said gently. "But I am here because there was a sign from the skies tonight. Did you see the green light heading east? The spirit trail of a dying star has appeared, which means an anomaly has occurred in the human realm. I followed that green light, and it pointed me here to this child. The child may be valuable to the mortal realm, chosen for a greater purpose, and so, it must live."

Four regarded the taxi.

Nikai stared too. The feathery soul inside *was* different, but he didn't have the words to explain why. It was like looking at a shade of blue and not being able to give its exact name, only understanding it was different from all other shades of blue.

"Anomalies are rare," was all Four said.

"Then you should know how important this is," One said. "I saw the dying star's spirit trail with my own eyes. I am certain of what it is. Fate wants this child to live. Why else would the child be here in the jurisdiction of the only King who possesses the means to intervene?"

One nodded at the black-and-gold watch on Four's wrist.

Nikai didn't know much about the timepiece, just that it was a mysterious underworld artifact and that Four always wore it on his person. The Kings collected such artifacts during their travels, storing them for safekeeping. Four's watch was said to have the power to intervene in the sacred and inevitable cycle of life and death.

"You know as well as I do that this artifact is not to be used lightly, for the consequences could be dire. The last time . . ." Four trailed off, his expression darkening.

The last time? Nikai couldn't believe his ears. As far as he knew, the watch was never to be used.

"It will not be like the last time," One assured. "*This* time, fate has determined the child shall live."

"I do not trust fate," Four said, a note of bitterness creeping into his voice.

"Fate binds us, connects us through past, present, and future. Our trust or distrust plays no part. It simply is," One said.

Four turned to the taxi again. As he stared, Nikai caught a look in his eyes. It was hopeful. It was greedy. It was the look of someone driven to desperation.

Four blinked and it vanished.

"I will help you," he said. "The woman can live on borrowed time, but I expect something in return for my labor."

"Surely you are not proposing a deal between *us* over a matter decided by fate?" One laughed, but Nikai saw tension in the angles of their shoulders. Deals with the Kings were not to be taken lightly, especially when they were between each other.

"Not a deal, but if my artifact is to be used, then it is only fair that I be rewarded for my efforts," Four said in a reasonable tone.

One relaxed. "What would you like?"

"I heard you recently came into possession of another artifact. I am merely curious to have a look at it."

"Of course." One ran a hand over their pendant. A thin willow branch with verdant leaves appeared in their other hand. "I am still examining its arcane properties, but it seems there is a vast power in this."

Four took the branch, twirling it between his fingers. "I have some expertise in this area. Perhaps I could examine it back in our realm?"

There was a beat of hesitation before One said, "Do take good care of it, and if you should discover anything, inform me. I expect its return to my kingdom in a few days."

Four slipped the branch carefully into his coat pocket.

Then he touched the face of his watch and closed his eyes.

Silently, Nikai counted the series of chimes that followed.

Five long ones followed by short chirps. Once, twice, thrice. Four times.

Five, four.

Wu, si. A peculiar chime, Nikai thought. The numbers were almost homophonous to *no death* . . . or *my death*.

Something in the taxi *moved*.

Four opened his eyes. "It is done."

"Good." One touched their necklace briefly. "Thank you, dear brother. I shall not forget your kindness tonight." They brushed Four's cheek with a gentle hand.

The air shivered, and they were gone.

The crease between Four's brows returned. Deeper this time.

"Is everything okay?" Nikai asked. "Will you be in trouble for helping—"

"Nikai."

The Reaper stilled. Something about the way Four had said his name troubled him. It seemed so final.

"Yes, My King?"

There was deep affection in Four's gaze when he squeezed Nikai's shoulder.

"Four?" Nikai said, confused.

"I am going to see the stars, my friend."

The Fourth King turned on his heel and vanished into the dark.

Nikai let out a long breath. The entire situation was out of the ordinary and left a funny feeling in his stomach.

"What was that about?"

He jumped in fright. The new Reaper had snuck up behind him.

"Sorry, sir," she said, sheepish. "I was just curious. Two Kings appearing—"

"Nothing to be curious about," Nikai snapped, with more sharpness than he'd intended. "If anything, this is way above your pay grade. I suggest you keep everything you saw and heard tonight to yourself. Have you finished reading out the death notes?"

The new Reaper looked contrite. "Yes, sir. I've an update, sir. It seems two of the humans survived after all."

"That happens sometimes. Must've been a glitch in the system," Nikai said smoothly, hoping none of the Reapers would guess what had really happened.

The new Reaper's face brightened. "It was the woman in the taxi and her baby—they're alive. I have deleted their death notes according to our protocol." Nikai kept his expression impassive as she continued, "The other souls we collected are ready for transportation."

"Good. Come on then, let's wrap this up."

Nikai returned to the souls awaiting their journey to the afterlife. The ambulances had arrived, but the human paramedics were oblivious to the underworld beings who were working by their side. The souls seemed calm enough, and there was no sign of the Blight. But it was best to be cautious.

Quickly, Nikai pointed two fingers to the ground. A circular symbol with intricate characters lining its edges appeared, glowing a pale green.

There were three ways into the underworld: through the Gates, through a portal that tore through the fabric of time and space, or through soul collection. The first was the most common, and the second was the most dangerous. The third could only be carried out by a Reaper.

Eyes closed, Nikai prayed for a smooth journey and recited the incantation that would send them all to Hell.

It was much later when Nikai was finally done with his Reaper duties—well, almost done, there were always reports to be filed and emails to be sent. But that could wait; he needed to see Four. The exchange between the two Kings earlier had left him out of sorts, and he had questions for his friend.

Nikai expected Four to be in the throne room of the Fourth Court doing what he'd come to think of as *King things*, such as settling a petty dispute between some souls or listening to the Librarian complain about the lack of resources devoted to the Archives, but the throne room was empty.

I am going to see the stars, my friend.

Nikai knew exactly where to find his King.

He went outside, whistling jauntily as he climbed the hill to the Garden of Tongues. At midnight on the seventh day of each month, the Garden hovered between the underworld and the mortal realm for a few precious minutes. You could sit and look up at the blanket of inky sky above with its pinpricks of scattered light.

Stars. They were the same ones the humans could see.

In all the years Nikai had been a Reaper, Four always came here whenever the worlds were aligned, just to see the stars. Nikai never understood why the view captivated him so, but there was a melancholy about Four that was loud and pressing when he was here. Yet it was a hollow sound, dull and empty, like a piece of him was missing.

Nikai checked his watch when he finally got to the top of the hill. Seconds to midnight. Just in time. He entered the Garden, but the place was deserted. Strange. He had been so certain that he would find his King here.

He glanced around the empty garden again. Where was Four?

A noise behind him made him turn. Someone was scrambling up the hill, footsteps heavy, panting loudly.

It was the new Reaper from earlier.

"Nikai!" she cried, running to him.

"What's wrong?"

"He—he's—" The Reaper choked on her words.

Nikai held her shoulders. He could feel her trembling. "Calm down; tell me what's wrong."

A sob caught in her throat. "It's Four . . . he's *gone.*"

2
Rui

"Stop!" Ada hissed. "We have to put up the barrier first."

Rui shook her head at her best friend and schoolmate. "Not until we're closer to the nest." She took a step, and Ada hissed again.

"We agreed to go on my cue."

"We can dawdle, or we can go on offense," Rui snapped, tightening her grip on her swords. "I'll take down the Revenants myself."

"You and what army?" Ada sniped back. "It's a *nest*."

"I said, *myself.*"

"Gods, Rui. Are you trying to make up for yesterday? When I kicked your ass during our spell-casting session?"

"You got lucky. Don't forget who holds the top score on—"

"*Children*, kindly stop shit-talking each other." The strong baritone of Ash Song, their proctor, crackled over the speakers of the Simulator. "You're supposed to be on the same team."

Ada chirped, "Yes, sir."

"Whatever," Rui muttered at the same time.

"I heard you, Cadet Lin," Ash said, sounding unamused. "Get rid of that crappy attitude or I'll make sure your application to the Guild gets mysteriously lost."

Rui rolled her eyes.

It was an empty threat. As her evaluator and mentor at Xingshan Academy, Ash might have some say in her final assessment when she graduated, but Rui was the best all-round cadet the Academy had produced in her cohort. Even Ash couldn't deny that fact. More importantly, the Exorcist Guild couldn't afford to lose any promising cadets. Not when the Blight had been running rampant in recent years.

As the supernatural virus attacked, more Revenants formed, and more

Exorcists were needed to vanquish them. Problem was, not everyone was born with a strong spirit core and a high level of yangqi like Rui or Ada. Not everyone could train to be an Exorcist. As far as Rui was concerned, it meant she was *valuable*. In a year, she would graduate with top honors, join the esteemed Exorcist Guild, and rise in its ranks.

That was the plan. Unless she got killed first, of course.

"*Roo-ee*, tell him you're sorry," Ada whispered urgently under her breath. "You don't have to mean it."

Rui sighed. Ada was right. It was best to stay on Ash's good side, considering he was a descendant of the illustrious Song family. His grandfather was Head of the Guild, and rumor had it that Ash was on track to follow in his footsteps. Ash's lineage was peppered with famous names; his father was a hero who died battling Revenants . . . while Rui was descended from a family of nobodies: a deadbeat dad and a mother who was long gone from this world.

Rui kept her distaste down and coated her tongue with a layer of sugar. "My apologies, Captain." *Long live the Song Dynasty*, she added in her head.

"Accepted," Ash said. Rui could hear his obnoxious smirk. At twenty-two, Ash was already a Captain—the youngest Exorcist ever to be made one. No wonder his ego was the size of a small whale. "Carry on," he instructed. "Cadet Senai, on your lead."

Ada nodded. "Yes, Captain."

"Make sure you watch the clock, kiddos."

Rui glanced at the blinking LED numbers on her training watch.

4:09

4:08

4:07

Today's simulation training program was set in a cargo terminal of a port. Huge metal containers were stacked like toy blocks, one on top of another, creating narrow zigzagging lanes to form a maze. In four minutes, the simulated moon would peak and the yin energy in the area would shoot up. Revenants siphoned yinqi to grow more powerful. If she and Ada didn't move quickly, the tables would turn, and they'd become the hunted.

"You ready?" Rui asked.

"Let's do this," Ada replied, pulling out a talisman. She was the superior protective spell caster between them.

Rui was the attack dog.

As Ada whispered the incantation, the yellow paper in her hand began to smoke, and the red ink on it disintegrated. The air seemed to split. A glowing dome rose above them, sealing off the perimeter—a barrier spell.

Ada signaled with her fingers. *Your three o'clock.*

Rui moved right. Ada split left, her bright magenta ponytail swaying as she went. Soon the shadows swallowed her up and Rui was alone.

A trickle of unease grazed Rui's skin. She had woken up this morning with a strange buzz in her head. Something was different today. Maybe it was because it'd been exactly four years since—

She stopped in her tracks, ears pricking.

A soft mewling was coming from where Ada had pointed, disturbingly similar to a baby's cry. Rui knew she was in a simulation program, but the hairs on the back of her neck still stood.

There.

A faint silvery wisp floating against a rusty metal container like a slime-track left by a snail. It was something no ordinary human could see. But for those like Rui, who had cultivated their spirit core and spiritual energy, the spirit trail of a Revenant's yinqi was clear as day.

Rui drew a deep breath, clearing the meridian pathways in her body. Her limbs relaxed, and her yangqi condensed. At the next inhale, she crossed her arms and swung her swords outward, emptying her lungs quickly.

A familiar, feverish eruption flooded her mind and body. Crimson light shot from the dual swords in her hands as her spiritual energy infused the weapons. They lengthened, the tips of the blades transforming into jagged edges like a lightning bolt.

She grinned.

Yin versus yang—this was how you fought a Revenant. Revenants fed on the yang energy of humans, but this same energy could be refined into magic and used to kill the dark creatures.

Feeling the thrill of magic pulsing with each heartbeat, Rui spun her swords, striding confidently forward. This sense of power, of absolute control—it never got old.

As she rounded the corner, a flash of magenta moved closer from the opposite end.

Ada. She had stopped in front of a metal container with a big hole punctured in the middle.

The Revenant nest had to be in there.

Question was, how many monsters had already formed? The mewling from inside grew louder. Something like feet scuttled.

Rui adjusted her swords, bracing for whatever was coming.

Several Revenants crawled from the nest. Their hairless bodies and heads were a mottled gray like they were afflicted with disease, which wasn't far from the truth. They varied in size, some as large as a tall adult human, others smaller like children. Some stood on their legs while others crawled on all fours, their scraggly limbs spiderlike.

Ada leaped forward first, her wicked-looking whip lashing out as she twirled. Not to be outdone, Rui homed in, swords ablaze. The first few Revenants were easy game. A quick slash here, a light skewering there. The creatures shrieked, vanishing into puffs of acrid smoke and cold air.

Blood pumping, Rui continued her assault, advancing toward the nest, taking down every Revenant that emerged. Adrenaline sang in her veins. *This* was what she lived for. The fight. The kill. The moment of glory.

"Pace yourself," Ada warned.

"I've got lots of spiritual energy to spare." Cocky but true. Rui *did* possess an unusually high amount of yangqi. She only wished it hadn't cost her mother's life to discover this.

"This is too easy. I'm barely breaking a sweat," Ada said, swatting another Revenant with her whip. "Something's up."

"We've trained for years; we're good at this."

But at the back of her mind, Rui knew Ada was right. Although they were seniors, they were still cadets, and they had only done neighborhood patrols under the watchful eye of a mentor. This training program was testing their readiness for an *actual* Night Hunt, a dangerous expedition where Exorcists raided Revenant nests across the city.

The other senior cadets who'd gone through this simulation were sworn to secrecy about the details, but they had returned to the dormitory a little green around the gills, exhausted from expending their spiritual energy. One of their classmates, Teshin Mak, had slept for two days straight.

So far, the test *was* too easy.

There·was a loud beep.

Rui swore under her breath. The zeros on her watch were red. They'd run out of time.

The moon shone bright above them.

Ada shot her a grim look. "The real test is starting."

She'd barely finished her sentence when an unearthly howl echoed.

A diaphanous humanoid form emerged from the nest. Slowly, its shape filled in, solidifying into a woman with dark eyes and long hair. Unlike any of the other Revenants that had come before, she looked too human. As human as the Revenant that—

"Watch out!" Ada shouted.

The Revenant clawed at Rui's face.

Rui dodged. Barely. Snatching a talisman from her sleeve, she yelled out the incantation. Something tugged in her spirit core, and the paper lit up in flames. Crimson spirit ropes appeared next to her, sparking as she channeled her magic. She pointed. The ropes shot through the air, wrapping around the Revenant. A strong burning smell wafted in the air as the Revenant screamed.

Rui ran forward with her swords, and the screaming stopped.

"Poof," she whispered. Each dead Revenant dulled her pain. It was like medicine, an opioid she was addicted to.

Across from her, Ada was shooting qi-infused spikes from a one-handed crossbow. The spikes burned holes in the incoming Revenants, destroying them immediately. Teshin's experimental weapons didn't always work, but the crossbow was more effective than Rui had expected.

But the Revenants coming for Ada were normal ones, or what Rui had come to think of as normal. No human faces. No human expressions. They were ghoul-like things that couldn't speak intelligibly and possessed no emotion other than the desire to feed.

The Revenant woman that had just attacked Rui was different.

She heard a gasp.

A young boy was crawling to Ada. Was it Rui's imagination or did he look like Aidan?

Ada lashed her whip. The deadly metal hook at the end stabbed a hole in the chest of the little Revenant boy.

Ada pulled hard, a wretched cry bursting from her throat.

The boy exploded into smoke and cold air.

Ada's face was bloodless, her hands shaking as she stared at the empty spot where the boy had stood.

Rui ran to her. "Are you okay?"

"I'm fine," Ada said, but she looked on the verge of tears. "Let's get the rest of them." She sped off without another word.

Rui started to follow, but something stopped her in her tracks.

Behind you.

She spun around, swords raised, expecting another Revenant.

But instead—

One of her swords fell to the ground with a clatter.

It *was* another Revenant. Except . . . how could it be?

Rui had seen his face again and again in her nightmares: the twist of his sneering lips as his eyes watched her hungrily, the heavy set of his jaw, the scar running down his neck where the curls of his dark hair ended.

He was even wearing the same clothes from that night—jeans and a shirt with blue stitching.

Her mother's screams filled her ears, and the scars on her legs itched. She was fourteen again, attending a mundane school like any other normal kid.

It had been a full moon that night. There was political talk of a curfew in those days, but it hadn't been implemented yet. It was late, but Rui had insisted on making a detour to the Night Market for some rock candy. It was her birthday, and she wanted her treat. She didn't know she had a strong spirit core or that her high yangqi could attract Revenants more easily. It had never happened before.

So when a man approached her mother and her for directions on a quiet street on their way home, Rui didn't give it a second thought, even though she felt a weird jolt when she saw him. After all, Revenants were supposed to be grotesque creatures; they didn't look human.

Then the man bared his teeth and lunged.

Funny how a split second can change a life forever. Her mother was gone, and Rui's life was upended. If her mother hadn't given in and brought her to the Night Market, if *Rui* hadn't thrown that tantrum . . . her mother would still be alive, and Rui wouldn't wake up every morning hating the person she saw in the mirror.

Now, the Revenant wearing the face of her mother's murderer was staring back at her.

Hot tears burned her eyes. She had trained for this very moment. Trained to kill this bastard if she set eyes on him again. Fourteen-year-old Rui had promised her future self this reward when she enrolled at Xing-shan Academy.

But eighteen-year-old Rui stood still. Frozen in fear.

The Revenant smiled. "Remember me?" He grabbed her neck, cold fingers digging into her flesh. "I wonder if you're as tasty as you smell."

Something sharp pierced her skin.

A chill set into her bones.

No, she screamed in her head when the realization dawned. The Revenant was *drinking* from her, sucking her spiritual energy dry. Was this what her mother felt when she was dying? Was this the fate she had saved Rui from?

"Rui!"

The air exploded with light.

Ada was fighting her way over.

"He's not real, Rui! We're in a simulation—focus!"

Rui blinked.

Focus. The Revenant wasn't real. None of this was real. The only thing real was that her mother was gone forever. Anger roused her strength. This was her chance to kill her mother's murderer. Even if he was an image, even if he wasn't real, she had made a vow.

She dug deep, reaching for whatever spiritual energy she had left. Light flickered near her hand.

The Revenant lifted his head from her neck. "What are you doing?"

"Killing you," she spat, and swung her arm.

Crimson light flashed.

Cold air gusted, and she fell to the ground, landing awkwardly on her shoulder. She was spent. Empty inside. As her vision blurred and the world dimmed, she heard Ash's mocking voice over the speakers.

"If this were the real world, Cadet Lin Ru Yi, you would be dead."

3
Rui

Ignoring the healer's pleas to stay, Rui left the infirmary after she woke and went straight to Teshin to ask for a crossbow. She'd seen what the small contraption could do and was itching to get her hands on one. The next hour was spent alone in her dorm room, familiarizing herself with the weapon and stewing in anxiety as she waited for Ada to tell her if they had passed the test.

The answer came in the form of a knock on the door.

Rui sprang out of bed. "Did we pass?"

"Obviously not." Ada stepped in, her eyeliner looking more smudged than usual. She kicked off her shoes and flung her navy school blazer over the chair. "I got swarmed after you fainted. Couldn't kill all the monsters by myself."

"Did they drink from you?" Rui asked, rubbing her arms. She couldn't shake that feeling from earlier, like she was drowning in ice water.

"No," Ada said. "When it was clear you were out like a light and I wasn't making any progress, Ash stopped the program. I told you to pace yourself, Rui. We aren't endless wells of spiritual energy. There's a limit to our abilities, even yours. You should've listened to me—remember what we talked about?"

"Hunting Revenants is a team sport," Rui said morosely, crawling back into bed. She wrapped her blanket around her head. Working with others wasn't her strong suit, and she was picky about who she spent time with. It was a bad trait to have if she wanted to be an Exorcist, but she knew better than to rely on other people. Sooner or later, everyone would disappoint. It was only a matter of time. That was humanity in a nutshell.

The bed dipped as Ada climbed on.

Rui felt a poke at her ribs, and she stuck her head out of the blanket. "I'm sorry. I know you wanted to pass the test on the first try."

"It's okay," Ada said, the corners of her mouth curling. She never stayed upset with Rui for long. "At least we get another chance at beating the program, and we'll be more prepared now that we know what the test is about."

"Facing our deepest fears?"

Ada nodded. "It's a low trick, even for Ash. I can't believe he programmed it that way. That Revenant looked exactly like Aidan, and I"—she drew a shuddering breath—"I blew a hole in him."

It was easy to kill a Revenant when it looked like an inhuman creature, when it was something terrible and *other*. But if Aidan, the real Aidan—the sweet, unmagical brother Ada adored—if he were ever turned into a Revenant somehow while still looking like himself, it would be Ada's job to kill him.

Because he'll no longer be Aidan. He'll be a monster, Rui reminded herself.

Ada fiddled with the pleats on Rui's skirt. "That last Revenant you killed in the Simulator before you fainted . . . who did he look like?"

Rui got up.

Fingers skating over the hangers in her closet, she pulled out a navy military-style coat with light gold buttons and the emblem of the Academy embroidered above the breast pocket. She laid the coat at the foot of her bed and rummaged for a sweater.

"The Revenant that killed my mother," she said at last, her voice slightly hoarse.

A furious noise erupted behind her, and Rui found herself enveloped by a sudden tangle of arms and the scent of green apple.

"That horrible no-good piece of—I can't believe Ash did that to you. It's bad enough he scheduled the test for today, of all days." Ada made another angry sound.

Rui nudged her away. "I'm trying to get dressed."

"Why!" Ada exclaimed, hands flailing. "Why did they program those weird Revenants into the test? Revenants can't speak, and they don't have faces or personalities or—"

"*Hybrids* can speak, and they look human," Rui said.

Ada sucked in sharply.

Officially, Hybrid Revenants did not exist. But every cadet had heard the rumor. Hybrids looked like humans and behaved like humans. They could be someone you loved, but then they'd try to kill you. Most cadets thought it was an urban legend.

But Rui knew better.

"I know what you're going to say, Ada. You're going to tell me they made the Revenants look human to catch us off guard and test our mental strength. You're going to tell me they didn't do it because Hybrids actually exist. But just because there haven't been any solid reports of Hybrids that we know of, it doesn't mean they don't exist. I know what I saw that night."

Ada squeezed her hand. "I believe you, you know that. It's just . . . the Blight doesn't infect humans."

"Maybe it does, and we don't know it yet."

"Maybe. How did Ash even know what that jerk looked like?"

"He must've asked around," said Rui. "The Guild questioned me after my mom died, remember? I told them what I saw, even drew a sketch."

Not that they believed her in the end. They'd said she was delusional, that she'd been so scared she'd imagined things. *Didn't stop them from recommending me to the Academy.*

"It would explain why the Exorcists are having a hard time lately," she said out loud. "Why there've been so many Night Hunts suddenly. The Revenants are different now, they're—"

"Rui—" Ada began.

"Look, I don't want to talk about it anymore, okay?" Rui raised her voice, then felt bad for raising it. She didn't mean to take her frustration out on Ada. It bothered her that the Simulator could conjure up the

Revenant's exact face from a lousy sketch she'd drawn four years ago as a kid. Was it even possible? How else would Ash have known if not from her old records?

She wriggled into her jeans and got her coat, wincing when her arm caught in the sleeve.

"Is it your shoulder?" said Ada. "You landed so hard on it. Let me help."

Rui was careful not to make a sound when the pain flared up again as Ada guided her arm. Instead, she clucked her tongue and finger-gunned. "I'm good. The Academy healers are amazing, remember?"

Ada didn't look convinced.

Wrapping a thick utility belt around her torso, Rui slid her talismans and new crossbow securely into their compartments.

"What are you doing?" Ada said. "It's not time to get ready for our rounds yet. You should get some rest. In fact, maybe you should sit out tonight's shift. Someone else can cover you; it's just a routine patrol."

Rui shook her head. "I'm not missing out on any training."

Even though the cadet patrols were routed away from known Revenant nests to keep the cadets safe until they were ready for actual Night Hunts, they still ran into a lone Revenant now and then. Rui wasn't giving up the possibility of killing one tonight.

"I'm catching the next shuttle off the island," she told Ada.

"Are you going to the temple again? I thought you paid respects to your mom yesterday."

"I'm checking on my dad." The lie slipped out smooth and easy like melted butter. Rui wasn't going to see her father. Today was a day neither of them acknowledged in the other's presence. If her mother was the link that bound them together, her death was what tore them apart.

"Guess I'm spending the afternoon working on my Student Council campaign by my lonesome self. I was counting on your help, *Rooroo*." Laughing, Ada flicked Rui's uneven bangs into her face.

Annoyed as Rui was by the abominable nickname, she couldn't help but smile. It was *her* fault to share it with Ada in the first place, and Ada was only trying to lighten the mood. She seemed to understand when to push Rui and when to step back, and that understanding was why they were best friends.

Many at the Academy marveled at their odd little friendship. Questioned it, probably. Rui questioned it herself sometimes, wondering how she lucked out on her first day at the Academy. She had loitered awkwardly outside the classroom, convinced she didn't belong because she knew nothing about Exorcism or magic. She'd turned and ran, only to collide with an impish-looking girl with cherry-red hair. The girl saw through Rui's scowl, understood the fear living inside, and decided they would be friends. And that was that.

"Why are you looking at me like that?" Ada asked now with a curious smile.

"Nothing," Rui mumbled, turning away. They'd dated for a whirlwind month last year before Ada called it off. The split was amicable. Sometimes, though, a tiny part of Rui wished they'd never broken up. But just because she loved her best friend, it didn't mean she was *in love* with her. In fact, Rui was starting to think that love—*romantic* love—wasn't her thing. It was a sham. One party always got hurt, either by the other or by circumstances. Her father had loved her mother more than life itself and look where that got him.

She stuffed her weapons into her sword bag and slung it over her shoulder. "How's your Council president campaign coming along?"

"Messily. There's still so much to do."

"People will vote for you; they'd be a fool if they didn't. You're a natural leader, and you get along with everyone. Don't sell yourself short."

Ada made a face as she grabbed her blazer and slipped her shoes back on, but Rui could tell she was pleased.

"We'll find out soon enough when they count the votes next week. See you at tonight's patrol. Don't be late or Ash will have something mean to say, and oh"—Ada paused by the door—"tell your dad I said hi."

There was something odd about Ada's expression. Like she knew Rui was keeping secrets. But she bounced out of the room, and Rui was alone again.

Rui stood in silence, nails scraping the ragged skin around her fingers. Maybe one day, she could share everything with her best friend. All the secrets. All the lies.

But for now, the less Ada knew, the safer she would be.

4
Rui

A pathetic drizzle greeted her when Rui stepped out of the subway into the beating heart of the city. Barely grazing her skin, the rain got in her eyes anyway. She swiped her face irritably and squinted. Against the late autumn sky and rainwater-colored buildings, a gleaming knife-shaped tower rose in the distance.

The headquarters of the Exorcist Guild.

Her fists curled. One day. She would make it there one day.

Keeping her earbuds on and avoiding any eye contact so no one would speak to her—or worse, ask her for directions—Rui jogged diagonally across the traffic junction. A barrage of angry honking followed her. Everyone who lived long enough on these city streets knew that pedestrian lights were more guidelines than rules, but it didn't mean the drivers liked it.

The news tickers on buildings were flashing.

FULL MOON TOMORROW NIGHT . . . LOCKDOWN STARTS AT 2100 HRS . . . ALL RESIDENTS TO REMAIN INDOORS UNTIL SUNRISE . . .

The introduction of the curfew had been met with little protest. Staying in every full moon or whenever there was a Night Hunt was a small price to pay for safety. But what would the headlines say tomorrow? Bodies had been turning up in alleyways or sprawled out on sidewalks in plain view in recent months. Cold and hard. Eyes bulging, mouths O-shaped like they'd been gasping for air. No signs of physical injuries were ever found on them. People without magic couldn't see Revenants, but the corpses were evidence enough that Revenants could see *them*, and worse, kill them.

Rui folded her coat over her arm, tucking the Xingshan emblem out of sight. The rumblings of a blame game had started in the media. *The New Generation of Exorcists: Gifted or Entitled? . . . Can the New Generation Save Us or Are We in Trouble? . . .* That was the flavor of some of the recent headlines and opinion articles. Xingshan Academy and the Exorcist Guild were revered institutions, but their reputation depended on their perceived competence.

Rui wasn't too worried just yet, but she didn't want anyone to notice her either. Not where she was going. Without her Academy coat marking her, she was another face in the crowd, easily overlooked among these bustling streets.

She veered off the main avenue, thinking about the text message she'd received earlier in the day. Something about a new job and a request to stop by when she was free. She turned up the volume of her music, ignoring how her pulse had tripped over itself when she thought of the person who'd sent it.

Not long after, she reached a neighborhood hidden between high-rises. The drizzle had stopped, and the sun showed its face. Rui shook the droplets from her coat and brushed damp hair out of her eyes.

MORT STREET

The lettering on the street sign was scratched up, and the area less snazzy than the tourist traps and landscaped parks Rui had left behind. Dandelions sprouted from cracks along the potholed road, and graffiti scrawled across the one-way street sign. She bent and picked a flower. She blew on it, coming close to making a wish but deciding at the last moment that maybe she no longer believed in such childish things.

The row of shophouses at the end of the road had a neglected look. Their windows were shuttered, and some of the doors were boarded up. Even the mosaic tiles on the five-foot way separating them from the street had chipped off to reveal dusty cement. But, defiantly, a familiar-looking two-story building stood out from the tired field.

Painted in bright shades of burnt orange and red and alabaster, the shophouse was a cheerful shout among the bland beige. It was distinctive, just like the mage who lived there. Round red paper lanterns hung across the awning, swaying in the breeze like a welcoming wave of a hand. Zizi lit them at night, along with random fairy lights he had strung across the gate for no discernible reason.

As Rui approached, her eyes followed the seafoam swirls etched into the pillars of the shophouse. The murals of old gods inked onto the facade seemed to come alive. She could hear her mother's voice asking, *Do you think this place has a story, Ru-er?*

There used to be more neighborhoods dotted with colorful buildings like these when Rui was little. She'd go on walks with her mother on weekends when her father was busy with his research work. They would explore the less-trodden parts of the city, where old temples appeared in corners, their roofs decorated with stone dragons, their grounds rich with tales from the past. Rui loved stuffing her face with mung bean pastries and walnut cake from the mom-and-pop bakeries they would pass, and she'd make up stories about the places and people she saw.

But over time the city razed its history to the ground, erecting new titans of tomorrow wrought in steel and glass. The city of her childhood was moving on, but some part of Rui was stuck in the past, afraid that her memories of her mother would fade and disappear, just like these old neighborhoods.

Her chest twisted painfully. Her mother would have loved Zizi's quaint little shophouse.

Enough.

She wasn't here to mope about the past.

After making sure she was alone, she slipped through the gate and into the front courtyard. People came to see Zizi for one reason or another. People who were willing to pay a pretty penny under the table for spells to be tested, talismans and charms to be written, magical objects to be authenticated, and so on. Zizi provided all kinds of services, and his clients were all sorts of characters—characters that an Exorcist-in-training should not be seen with.

Although it was common knowledge that there was a black market for magic and the supernatural in the bowels of the city, such dealings were technically unsanctioned by the authorities. The Guild Council was tasked with keeping an eye on things, but they kept that eye half-closed, balancing the line between moral high ground and pragmatism. Most of the time, people who dabbled in everyday magic, mages like Zizi, and places like the Night Market were left alone unless they stepped over the line. No one was foolish enough to cross the Guild Council.

Rui knew she was playing a dangerous game here. If Zizi ever got into trouble with the Guild, it would mean that *she* was in trouble, too. The Guild's arms were long and its grip tight enough to choke off anything it considered threatening to its cause or reputation. But Zizi covered his tracks well, and he was the only one who could help her.

Heaving a sigh, she opened the door to the shophouse.

Sandalwood incense shot through her nostrils, and her eyes watered from the smoke. Coughing, she flung the windows open. The breeze ruffled the stacks of hell money lining the shelves; they were fake bank notes used as offerings for ancestral rites. Sunlight filtered through the skywell, spilling onto the stone fountain in the middle. The water shimmered and gurgled. But there was no sign of the mage.

Rui hollered, "Zizi? *Zee zee!*"

She ripped off her earbuds and stomped through the length of the shophouse to the small room at the back. It opened out to a whimsical rear courtyard surrounded by climbing vines. A tree stood in the center, its opulent lilac-blue and purple flowers cascading from hanging branches. It wasn't the season for wisteria, but Zizi kept his tree in bloom all year round with magic because he liked the colors.

Zizi himself was draped on a chaise, lounging in that annoyingly insouciant manner of his. His eyes were closed, and he had headphones on. An unlit cigarette dangled precariously from his mouth. Rui had never seen him smoke, but he was never without a cigarette. It could've been a nervous habit, but Zizi was the least anxious person she knew. Sometimes, he'd hold the cigarette between his fingers, brandishing it around when he talked. Other times, he'd stick it behind his ear, and Rui had to resist the urge to pluck it off.

She leaned in. "Zizi!"

He sat up with a jolt, swearing loudly. His eyes were glazed. Had he really been asleep? She had thought he was pretending.

Blue-and-white-striped pajamas hung on his lean frame, dotted with small red hearts. Rui spied the edge of a tattoo creeping out from the low dip of his top. When Zizi caught her staring, he pulled his favorite black bat-winged cardigan close and buttoned it like a fussy grandmother.

Rui didn't actually know if it was his *favorite* cardigan. But he wore it so often she'd assumed so. She did ask him once why he was in pajamas all the time. He'd expressed surprise, as if there were an obvious answer. *They're comfortable*, he said, his tone so cutting she never questioned him about his sartorial choices again.

"I was sleeping, Rooroo," Zizi grumbled now.

There it was again. That gods-awful nickname he'd come up with in a moment of affection after Rui had successfully traded a spell for a boring-looking teapot he'd lusted after for months. It had been cursed to brew any tea into delicious poison, and he was planning a soiree with the less desirable elements of the underground magic community.

She gave him a sour look. "I'm here."

"I can see that." Zizi grinned in that off-kilter way of his. Rui imagined a charming serial killer might look like this before they made their move.

"Well?" she said. "What job do you have for me?"

"A client showed up a few weeks ago with a rather curious request, so now I've a spell that needs testing."

"What kind of client?"

Zizi shrugged. "Don't know, don't care. Didn't like the smell of that one. But hey, business is business, and they offered me a good price."

31

His reputation depended on his discretion. Rui knew she wasn't getting more out of him. She scanned his expression, searching for clues. There were none to be had.

He looked like . . . well, he looked like how a *Zizi* might look. Dark wavy bangs shadowed his gaze, skimming his granite cheekbones. His nose was a dagger, his jaw freshly chiseled, and his otherwise vulpine face tempered by his eyes. They were mono-lidded and fringed with thick dark lashes, the irises an impossible blue like the hottest part of a flame. Rui had always thought they were kind eyes, and they were the first thing she'd noticed about him four years ago.

A bright searing light had exploded when the Revenant touched her that night. The force flung her against a fence, driving a piece of barbed wire into her leg. She'd passed out. When she finally woke, the Revenant was nowhere to be seen. She was lying on the street, weak and in pain, the blood from her leg seeping into the cracks on the ground, every muscle in her body hurting as if she'd been rammed by a truck. Too distraught to move or call for help, she had lain there, staring numbly at her mother's cold body.

A pair of eyes appeared. Light in the darkness. A boy her age. Scrawny, dark-haired, wearing checkered pajamas and that off-kilter grin.

Don't be afraid. I'm here, he whispered, and took her hand.

Rui thought she was hallucinating from blood loss. But the boy was real, and he saved her.

Present-day Zizi cleared his throat loudly. He was taller now, his frame filled in with sinewy muscle. But he was still the same boy she had met four years ago: his head tilting at an angle whenever he looked at her, his eyes alit with curiosity as if he'd stumbled into a wondrous new world.

He brushed his earlobe with his fingers. It was an unsubtle gesture.

Rui cracked a reluctant smile. Instead of his usual silver hoop earrings, he was wearing the ones she'd gotten him as a joke. They were plastic cartoon ghosts dangling from short silver chains. The ghosts had pink dots on their cheeks—*blushing* ghosts. He'd called them childish, but he wore them from time to time.

Rui sighed to herself. She was wrong. He wasn't a charming serial killer. More like a Doberman puppy that had grown too large to be cute. Trained to be a guard dog but one that still loved playing fetch with an old squeaky toy.

Beaming, Zizi spread his arms.

Rui ignored him. She turned and went back into the shophouse, listening to the lazy flapping sound of Zizi's flip-flops as he followed her.

"No hug?" he called from behind as they entered the kitchen.

Rui heard his pout. "We don't hug."

Zizi swiveled in front of her. "Did I agree to that?"

She elbowed him away. He laughed and leaned against the kitchen island, stretching languidly. She tried not to stare as his pajama top rode up, exposing a strip of smooth skin above his hip.

"You're extra grouchy today," Zizi said. "Did something happen at school?"

"You should've left the windows open," Rui said, looking around. "Where's Mao? Please don't tell me you kept her inside with all that incense smoke."

"Is that what you're unhappy about?" Zizi called out in a higher register. "Mah-aaooo."

There was a tinkling sound.

A dark ball of fur bounded into the kitchen. Mao jumped onto the marble island, purring as she headbutted Zizi's arm. He scratched the black cat's head affectionately. "See? She's absolutely fine. Does my favorite apprentice feel better now?"

Rui cradled Mao in her arms. "I'm not your apprentice. I'm a Xingshan cadet."

"It's tragic that those knuckleheads got to you." Zizi never failed to remind her of his disappointment that she had joined the Academy.

Burying her face into Mao's warm fur, Rui grumbled, "Why do you keep mocking the Academy?"

"You know why," Zizi retorted, ticking off his fingers as he spoke. "First, the Academy is connected to the Guild, and those elitist jerks think they're better than everyone else because the normies depend on them for security. Second, the Guild wants to control how magic is used, so they force kids to join the Academy, where they get indoctrinated and molded into mindless little soldiers. Magic should be free; magic should be explored. We need to experiment and forge a new way forward if we want to get rid of the Revenants for good and—"

"We *don't know* if we can ever get rid of the Revenants for good," Rui interrupted. "They exist because of the Blight, and no one knows what it is exactly or how to stop it from spreading. The fact is, everyone does depend on Exorcists to keep them safe, and I'm far from a mindless little soldier. The Academy doesn't force us to do anything. You would know this if you'd bothered to enroll."

Their eyes met. The darker pair challenging, the lighter ones amused.

Life for people with high yangqi was full of danger. Rui didn't have to say it. Zizi knew that. Revenants were drawn to him the same way they were drawn to her. If he didn't know how to defend himself, he'd be a sitting duck.

There were two ways to learn magic: the Academy or the underground magic community. The Academy and the Guild promised glory and respectability—and vengeance—everything Rui craved. She had made her choice, and Zizi had made his a long time ago.

Zizi ticked off another finger. "Lastly, the Academy uniforms are an eyesore."

"Then why are you hanging out with me?" Rui muttered, setting the cat on the floor.

"You're useful."

She flinched.

But she *was* undeniably useful. After Zizi saved her, Rui discovered he'd lost his parents when he was young and had been adopted by his grandmother, who ran a bakery. He'd moved out early to run his own business, and soon, Rui found herself beta testing his possibly dangerous and very illegal talismans and magical items. In return, he paid her a pleasant sum of money that covered the living expenses her Academy scholarship did not.

Zizi wasn't without his uses either. He had access to information sources that Rui lacked. It was purely transactional between them, or so she told herself in the beginning. Somewhere along the way, it felt like things had changed between them.

"Also," Zizi was saying, "for reasons yet unknown, I do enjoy your company despite the fact that you're so grumpy."

Rui wasn't very good at accepting compliments, especially ones that came unexpectedly from Zizi. *Purely transactional*, she reminded herself. He only wanted her around because she was useful, and she was only around because she needed money and information.

"Where's the spell you want me to test?" she asked.

Zizi bobbed on his feet. "In due time. But first, coffee."

Rui slid eagerly onto the barstool by the kitchen island. The Academy's brew was a standard mild roast, practical and terribly boring. But it was convenient and free, and most cadets drank it before training to give themselves an extra push. But while caffeine sharpened the senses of those who could practice magic, their sensitivity to the ingredient meant that an over-caffeinated cadet or Exorcist was a danger to themselves and their comrades. The crash would hit too hard, and the drop could come at any time.

Crash or not, Rui never turned down a chance to drink Zizi's coffee. It was special. Sometimes, it was mellow like a quiet dusk. Sometimes it was a vibrant dawn, full of promise. He could tease out exacting flavors from the beans and transform them into a feeling the drinker needed at that very moment. It was, frankly, kind of magical.

She was still feeling the effects of Ash's test. Fatigue coursed through her body, and her shoulder ached. Maybe she should have stayed in the infirmary as the healer advised, but with the boost from Zizi's coffee, Rui was sure tonight's patrol with the other cadets would be a breeze.

Zizi pottered around, scooping coffee beans into a grinder. The rings on his slender fingers sparkled, but Rui's attention was drawn to the new silver bracelet next to the other fraying black and red threads he always wore around his wrist. Was it a present from someone else? Her stomach clenched. She wasn't quite sure why the new piece of jewelry felt so offensive.

She wrenched her eyes away from him and stared at her phone.

Zizi glanced up. "Anything interesting in the news these days?"

Rui scanned the screen. There was an op-ed about how the Exorcist Guild needed to refocus on the central business district and the wealthy Tin Hill neighborhood instead of spreading its resources too thinly—and equally—across all areas. Rui dismissed it. Rich people liked to complain, and she didn't think they ought to. There was also a report on a recent successful Night Hunt, which was countered by an article about the rising death toll in the city due to Revenant attacks. Tucked at the bottom of the page was an update about the long-delayed reconstruction of the Outram subway station.

"A gas pipe in Outram burst last night, right by the old subway station," she summarized. "The explosion shattered half the ground-floor windows of the new office tower they're building. Good thing it happened at night and the workers weren't there."

"The tower with the horrific spiral design?" Zizi said, barely paying attention. "That's not very interesting."

"*I* think the tower's design is cool—it looks like some kind of stairway to heaven. Anyway, the incident's pending an investigation. Do you know anything about that?"

Zizi gave her a blank look. "Nope. Why would I?"

"Really?" Rui said, skeptical. "Your *friends* haven't been using that subway station for something else?"

As the city grew, new subway lines and stations were built, and the old ones closed. Left unused, the underground magic community took over. The Guild left them alone because of the unspoken promise that they would keep the subterranean network of tunnels clear of Revenants and other undesirables.

"Really," Zizi said. "Outram Station's been abandoned for decades, but there was always talk of reconstruction, and with the new buildings coming up around it, the place is off-limits for us."

Us . . . that makes me one of them, Rui couldn't help but think, remembering again how she and Zizi were on different sides of the magical community divide.

She chewed on her lip. "Heard anything else lately about Hybrids?"

"Unfortunately not."

Disappointment, painfully familiar, thickened in her chest. For four years, she'd trawled through public records of Night Hunts, reading every case file she could get her hands on. But there were no reports, no records of any Revenant that bore a resemblance to a human. Like the Guild said, Hybrids did not exist.

But no record meant no capture and no kill.

The Revenant that murdered her mother—the one that looked human—was still at large. Rui was sure of it. If she could find him, if she could *kill* him, maybe the hole in her chest would disappear. Maybe her father would be well again.

"Here you go." Zizi set a cup of coffee in front of her, his fingers flicking the air.

Rui wasn't sure if he was casting a secret flavoring spell or saying a dramatic *voilà* in his head. Both were equally plausible. Closing her eyes, she took a long sip. As rich velvet glided over her taste buds, a cozy warmth spread through her limbs, like she was curling up on the couch with her favorite book on a rainy day.

When she opened her eyes, she saw Zizi adding spoonful after spoonful of sugar into his own drink. He preferred his coffee funeral style: too black and too sweet. It was the traditional coffee served at funeral wakes when descendants stayed up for consecutive nights as a sign of respect for their ancestors. The same coffee Rui had drunk at her mother's funeral.

At the sixth teaspoonful of sugar, Rui lost her restraint. "You know that's going to kill you someday, right? I bet all that sugar is making your migraines worse."

"I didn't think you cared, Rui. I'm touched," Zizi said, half-sarcastic. He smiled and dropped another spoonful of sugar into his coffee to make a silly point.

"I merely tolerate you," she said. "Now show me the spell you need tested."

Zizi's lips twitched with amusement. "So tiny, and yet so bossy."

Rolling her eyes, Rui followed him to the coat closet in the hallway. Inside, there was a leather trench with fancy silver epaulets, a leopard-print faux-fur midi coat, a garish orange poncho, and a plain black jacket that looked completely out of place. There wasn't much room, and they were standing close enough to touch.

Something fluttered in Rui's stomach, catching her off guard. Maybe she needed food. Maybe she needed a nap. Groaning inwardly, she grabbed the thing in her stomach by its neck and wrung it dead.

Zizi nudged a pair of spiked boots aside and raised his right leg a few inches from the ground. His slipper fell off.

Rui sighed. "Why isn't the button up here so we can press it with our fingers like normal people?"

"Because it is a *secret* button," Zizi replied with a sideways glance and a lifted brow. "And because I am not, by any measure, a normal person."

Deliberately, he brought his big toe to the bottom corner of the closet and pushed a button so camouflaged that Rui wouldn't have known it was there if she hadn't witnessed this ridiculous act of his so many times before.

Something whirred like gears locking into place. The back wall slid open.

A large room with softly lit panels on the walls revealed itself. Scores of rectangular yellow paper hung down from the ceiling like leaves on a weeping willow. Talismans. Some had red calligraphy already written on them—completed spells—while others were still blank. The dimness of the room concealed several large pillows and a fluffy blanket, which Rui knew were in the corner.

This was Zizi's spell lab. It was so different from the spell labs at the Academy. *Those* looked more like the science laboratories in a mundane school.

Humming a pop song from the previous decade, Zizi retrieved his slipper and flip-flopped in. He meandered around, plucking a few talismans like they were ripe fruits.

He spread them out like a deck of cards on the single glass table in the corner of the room. "May I interest you in some spells? Standard stuff— barrier spells, binding spells—the usual incantations will do. I made a few extra the other day. Thought it might come in handy for you."

"Are they free?"

He gave her a little bow. "For you? Absolutely."

Rui swiped the stack off the table just as her phone began to buzz. She ignored it and focused on her haul, carefully folding the papers in half before sliding them into her pocket. Talismans were nifty little things to have around, and having fresh ones meant she didn't have to go through the trouble of making them herself or signing them out from the Academy's spell labs. Besides, she wasn't very good at calligraphy, and skillful penmanship was the difference between an effective spell and a total dud.

"Take a look at this," Zizi said, showing her another talisman. "It's a spell that separates a Revenant's spiritual energy from its form for a short period of time, rendering it completely vulnerable. I finally finished it last night. If it works, it might be my best work yet."

Rui ran a finger down the talisman. She didn't recognize the complicated characters written on it. Most of the spells she tested were devised by Zizi. The unorthodox way he used magic befuddled her. He'd been experimenting with it since he was a young child, and the trauma of his magic manifesting too early in life had resulted in his unusual eyes. Sometimes he went too far in his experiments, and they triggered migraines that consumed him for days, leaving him curled up on the floor in the dark.

Once, Rui found him lying motionless in the rear courtyard. Eyelids fluttering, blue irises so dark they were almost black, as if he were trapped between worlds, unable to crawl his way out. She had never felt fear the way she had in that moment, and she was close to tears when he finally roused.

"So? What do you think?" Zizi was watching her carefully with a smug, expectant look. He wanted to be praised.

Rui wasn't good at giving praise. "Is that why you were snoozing earlier?" she asked instead. "Because you stayed up all night again?"

"That was a beauty nap."

"I guess you do need one."

"You wound me," Zizi said, a hand on his chest.

Rui shot him a scathing side-eye. He didn't look wounded at all. He was so melodramatic it was hard to take him seriously sometimes.

"Is it even possible to separate a Revenant's yinqi from its body?" she asked. As far as she knew, yinqi existed throughout a typical Revenant's body, keeping it alive. There wasn't a concentration of it in one spot, and she'd never heard of a method that could pull all of it out.

"That's what you're going to find out," Zizi said. "This is the spell I need tested. Be careful when you cast it. Theoretically, if there's contact between two bodies, the spiritual energy may transfer."

Rui's phone buzzed again. Who could be calling her?

"Are you listening, Rui?"

She stopped fidgeting. "What did you say?"

Zizi repeated slowly, "When you're testing this spell, do not touch the Revenant and do not let it touch you. There's a minuscule chance that if you do, its spiritual energy may mix with yours, and its hunger will possess you. Do you understand?"

"Yeah, yeah, I got it. Don't touch the scary monster."

"*Rooroo.* Be serious."

"Don't call me that. Like you said, it's a minuscule chance, right?"

"A minuscule chance is still a non-zero chance."

"Do you think I'm incapable of casting it properly?"

Zizi took the cigarette from behind his ear and flipped it between his knuckles. "The spell needs to be tested. You're the tester. So, you test it."

"Answer my question," Rui persisted. "Are you doubting my abilities?"

"I'm just . . ." He looked at the talisman, then back at her. "Call it superstition or whatever, but it's been four years, and today's your . . ." He broke off with a sigh.

Today's your mother's death anniversary. Today's your birthday, a day you stopped celebrating four years ago because you almost died. Today's . . .

Rui didn't know what he meant to say.

"Well, I'm not testing it today," she said. "I'm going on patrol with the other cadets tonight. And you're being silly . . . Have I ever failed to test a spell properly for you?"

"You better do a good job then," he said. "If it works, it'll be extremely valuable. I could sell it to the Guild for a ton of money and retire to the countryside with Mao."

"Convenient how you hate the Guild, but you'll take their money."

"A boy has to eat."

"So does a girl. Double my fee."

Zizi made an unhappy face.

"I'll have to find an actual Revenant to test it on. This is beyond the scope of what I normally do. It carries a higher risk. Double my fee."

"You drive a hard bargain."

"I am the best."

"Fine," Zizi said, caving quickly.

Rui smirked. "Good."

Zizi smirked back. "All this negotiation is making me hungry. Why don't you stay for a while? We can get sushi."

Rui's pocket was buzzing furiously again.

"Hang on." She pulled out her phone.

5 missed calls. 4 voice mails.

They were all from the same number.

She punched in the password for her mailbox and held the phone to her ear. A woman's voice. Rapid-fire words. Concern and irritation.

Your father . . .

Rui felt her chest squeezing.

"Something wrong?" Zizi asked.

"Nothing. I have to go," she mumbled, grabbing the new talisman. Ignoring his questions, she hurried from the room and ran out the front door.

5

Yiran

Four boys sat in a circle by the swimming pool on the roof deck of a swanky condominium. Expensive cologne wafted, hiding the after-school musk of teenagers and exhaust from the city streets below, while the late-afternoon sun glistened off limited-edition watches on tanned wrists and hair shiny enough to rival that of a shampoo model's.

We look like an ad for people who take tropical vacations in the dead of winter, Yiran thought. It wasn't far from the truth, he supposed, glancing at the cabanas around them, presumably added to give a cheesy sense of ambiance despite the season.

He picked at an uneven patch at the hem of his cashmere sweater-vest, rolling the fabric into a tiny ball between his fingers. He was bored, bored, bored. Bored with the scenery, bored with the noisy traffic, and bored with . . . everything. Mostly though, he was sick of waiting for his opponent to decide his next move.

"Hurry up, Cheng. We haven't got all day." Yiran flicked the ball of cashmere at his schoolmate. "Do you want another card or not?"

Nicholas Cheng tugged at his collar. "Give me a sec. I need to think."

"It's just math." Yiran yawned. A wide, satisfying stretch of the jaw.

Cheng polished his glasses with his shirttail and put them back on. "Okay, hit me."

Yiran flipped the next card and slid it toward him. "Nine of diamonds, for a total of"—he looked at Cheng's other two cards—"twenty."

Cheng looked relieved. "I'll stay with what I've got."

"As you wish, Nicky boy. Theodore, my friend?"

Theo threw his cards down with a grunt. "Stand."

"Good choice." Yiran glanced to his right.

The last boy, Sweets—nicknamed for his love of candied jellies—shook his head. "I'll take my chances with eighteen."

"Dealer's turn." Yiran assessed the two cards in front of him. His five of hearts was open for everyone to see. His other card was face down, but he knew what it was. "Ta-da—four of spades."

Sweets raised his eyebrows. "Yikes."

Theo cracked his knuckles, casting a look at Yiran that said, *That's rough, buddy.*

Sensing an impending victory, Cheng relaxed.

Yiran stretched his neck. Five and four. It wasn't promising. Blackjack *was* a game of math. Simple to understand, trickier to execute. Luck and a player's appetite for risk went hand in hand, but Yiran didn't care about the win. The thrill of the bet was enough to keep him going.

He reached for the deck and drew a card. "Two of hearts. Total of eleven."

Theo snickered.

Edging closer, his face slightly pale, Cheng tapped the table. "It's not over yet. Hurry up, take another card."

"Aren't you enjoying the suspense?" Yiran teased.

"You have to take another card. The rules—"

"I know my own house rules." Yiran slid a finger over the smooth surface of the topmost card of the deck. His chances of winning had gone up with the last draw. There was still no guarantee of a win, but maybe today was his lucky day.

He flipped the card over.

Cheng smacked his forehead, the sound as final as the game's result.

Yiran smiled. "Twenty-one. The house wins."

Sweets let out a low whistle. "Nice. King of spades."

The dark king, Yiran thought out of the blue. His smile suddenly felt forced. The game had ended. There was nothing left to look forward to.

Theo and Sweets handed over their stacks of twenty-dollar bills without hesitation, but Cheng was still clutching his face.

"Pony up, Nicky."

"But I—"

"Shh." Yiran held a finger up. "You knew this might happen when you said you wanted in. My game, my rules."

Cursing, Cheng removed his watch. "My dad's going to kill me. He got this for my sixteenth birthday—it's worth more than your freaking car."

"No one's interested in your sob story, darling."

Muttering under his breath, Cheng handed over his watch. Yiran heard the word *asshole* and possibly something worse. Grabbing his bag from the deck chair, Cheng left in a huff.

Sweets whistled, peering at the watch Cheng had left behind. "Collector's edition. That boy's got some nerve. What are you going to do with it?"

"Same thing I always do," Yiran replied, shuffling the cards.

Which was nothing at all.

The treasured possessions he won from his schoolmates were piled up in the corner of his wardrobe. Useless trinkets he never touched. He thought about selling them from time to time. Never got the energy to go through with it. Rumor at school was that Yiran funded his lavish drug-filled lifestyle with the sales of his winnings. It was insulting; he would never ingest a drug intentionally. He couldn't bear to relinquish control of his own mind, not when his grandfather controlled everything else. But he did relish the myth of the person Song Yiran *could be*, even if it was far from the truth.

"Your babysitter's here."

Yiran looked up. Theo was pointing to a man in a tidy black suit who had appeared by the entrance of the roof deck. The man wore a pair of generic sunglasses over his generic face. His head was slightly bent, a hand by his ear like he was listening to instructions from his earpiece.

Yiran shoved the pack of cards and Cheng's watch into his messenger bag.

"Hey, Robert," he called out.

He didn't know or care if the man's name was Robert. His grandfather's people were all the same to him. An endless stream of men in black suits who chaperoned Master Song's precious grandson. Well, *chaperone* was a euphemism, and Yiran wasn't precious. His grandfather was merely afraid Yiran would besmirch the reputation of the esteemed Song family and the Exorcist Guild.

The man in the suit approached. "It's time to head home." He added, "Er shaoye."

It was lip service. The honorific was used, but the man didn't lower his head by even an inch. Yiran got the message: he wasn't worthy of real respect.

"It's still early. I don't have to be home yet," he said. But his feet were already moving. No one kept the Song patriarch waiting.

The man kept in step with him. "Master Song wants to see you before dinner. It'll take thirty minutes in this traffic to get back to the mansion."

"I can do it in fifteen."

"Master Song instructed me to drive."

"My car—"

"Has been towed."

Yiran almost dropped his bag. "What? But I—"

"Will get it back eventually, I'm sure." The man's face was impassive, but it wasn't difficult to guess what was going through his head. *Spoiled brat. Good-for-nothing. Bastard grandson.* He didn't have to say it out loud.

Yiran knew.

The pin on the man's jacket glinted. An Exorcist. Few Exorcists lived to a ripe old age and most stayed with the Guild until injury or death caught up with them. But there were some who left earlier to work for the city's upper crust as part of their security detail. Yiran found them to be tenacious babysitters.

He glanced over his shoulder.

Theo had lain down for a nap. Eyes locked on his phone, Sweets waved a vague farewell.

Irritation scratched at Yiran's throat. As sons of some of the city's most influential people, they were precious too. Just not in the way that constrained their lives. He was envious of them, and he hated that.

He turned to the man in the black suit. "Let's go, Robert. The old man won't be happy if I'm late."

"Appreciate the favor, Robert." Yiran slammed the car door shut.

Traffic turned out to be clear and they had made good time, and maybe the man wasn't that bad after all. He'd agreed to stop at the gates to the estate instead of the front door—as long as Yiran promised to go to the study right after he cleaned up. A direct summons from his grandfather meant Yiran was in trouble, and he wanted time to clear his head.

Old ginkgo trees lined the winding driveway. They were silent sentinels, watching as Yiran made his way up to the mansion. Their leaves had turned with the season, and the path was a glorious explosion of gold and yellow. It reminded Yiran of the day he first arrived.

It had been a crisp autumn morning, the sun warm and gentle on his face. He was barely six years old, clinging onto his mother's legs, hiding his face behind her skirt. He was a sickly thing then, shy and small for his age. Catnip for bullies at school.

Yiran's breath had caught at the sight of Song Mansion, and he fell desperately in love with it. He'd stared in wonder at the terra-cotta tiles on its curved roofs, the jagged stones in the quadrangle courtyard in the center of the cluster of buildings, made smooth in places by footsteps.

The first thing he'd noticed inside the house were the doors. There were so many of them, mostly locked. Intricately carved with symbols and fantastical animals and figures, they felt like portals to different worlds. It was the first time the word *magic* rang loud and clear in Yiran's head. He'd thought he was the luckiest boy in the world when his mother told him that *this* was where he would be living from that day on.

Then she left and he never saw her again. And in time, he understood that a house could never love him back.

Now, Yiran dropped his bag onto his bed, splashed some cold water onto his face, and changed out of his school uniform into something fresh.

Made sense to present his cleanest self since his best wasn't good enough.

Minutes later, he was standing outside his grandfather's study, one hand raised and the other straightening his shirt. His heart was starting to pound.

He knocked. Two quick raps, the way he'd been trained to do.

His grandfather's voice trailed out. "Come in."

Yiran exhaled through his mouth and twisted the doorknob.

Once inside, he bowed low. "Zufu."

Despite his age, Song Wei was an imposing man. His wide shoulders showed no signs of hunching, and his stride was firm and purposeful when he got up from his rosewood chair and walked over. Trimmed neatly at the sides, his hair was a regal mix of black and silver, and his eyes were keen as they took in his grandson's appearance. Leisurely, he circled Yiran like an eagle setting its sights on prey.

Yiran resisted the urge to fidget.

"Commissioner Senai called earlier. Apparently, you've broken the traffic laws. Again. That makes it five times in two months that the Commissioner himself had to step in to clean up your mess."

Another circle.

"And now, *I* owe the man because he has to make sure that *you* don't have to appear in front of a judge in court."

Another damned circle.

"You should know better."

Yiran stared at his feet. His socks peeked out from under his house slippers. The socks used to be white. Now they were a shoddy gray, scuffed at the heels with little tears in the fabric. He should have put on a different pair before coming here.

"Never forget that you are a Song," his grandfather said. "Whatever you do or don't do will always be tied to our family and the Guild. Have you seen the headlines lately? Do you know what people are saying about us? How many times have I told you the Guild's status is only secure because we provide something people need? We pay for this dearly, sacrificing our lives so that everyone else—everyone who is weak—can be safe. What will happen if they decide we're no longer doing our jobs well? That we're redundant? Or worse, that we are *dangerous*?"

His grandfather spoke softly. Yiran wished the old man would raise his voice, that he would shout at Yiran and get it over with. But that wasn't his grandfather's style. Song Wei knew the power of the quiet before a storm, the unsettling anticipation of what was to come.

"Do you understand what I'm saying?" his grandfather asked, his voice almost a whisper.

Yiran nodded. Exorcists were accepted by the rest of society because their magic worked against the Revenants. But if that ability to wield magic came from the very thing the Revenants desired, would a world without such people be safer? For the sake of his half brother and grandfather, Yiran hoped no one would try to find out.

"What do you have to say for yourself, boy?"

Keeping his gaze lowered, Yiran counted to eleven, letting his breath trickle out slowly. In the past, he would attempt to answer, but no answer ever placated his grandfather. Perhaps a satisfactory answer did not exist, and Yiran had given up trying. Even a stubborn dog will learn who its master is, and what it must do to get fed.

"I've told you to get your act together many times, but it seems my words have gone unheeded. You've had your chances. Pack your things. You're leaving this place."

Yiran must've heard wrong. His grandfather couldn't be kicking him out over a silly traffic violation, could he?

"What does . . . *leaving* mean?" he asked, throat tight.

"There's a private academy two towns away. You will keep up your attendance and your grades, and you will graduate. I don't want to see you back here unless I ask for you."

Why are you doing this to me? Yiran wanted to yell. *Why did you take me in only to throw me out?* But he stayed silent and contained his anger. Because deep inside, he knew why. He was never really a Song. Never truly part of the family. He'd been living here for the past twelve years like a parasite, and today, his grandfather was finally culling his infected stock.

His grandfather settled onto his chair and picked up his reading glasses. "You leave tomorrow morning. Someone will drive you." He opened a ledger, licked his thumb, and flipped a page.

Yiran knew he was being dismissed, in more ways than one. Even as his mind protested, his body had given up. His head lowered and his spine curved to complete the bow.

"Yes, Zufu."

Yiran barely made it down the hallway before sinking onto the cold floor. He would be in full view of the servants if any were to walk by, and they would know something had happened between him and his grandfather again. But he was past caring about what the staff thought.

Eyes closed, he lay there, feeling the scrape of the hardwood floor against his scarred fingertips. One more year of high school and he'd be off to college. No big deal if he left earlier. It wasn't like he'd miss Sweets or Theo. Not much, anyway. They were friends by convenience, thrown together because of family connections. Loyalty played little part in their friendship. But Yiran had chosen the two of them, hadn't he? And they had chosen him.

His grandfather wasn't giving him a choice.

"Why are you lying on the floor?"

Great. The golden boy of the Song family had found him.

"I'm resting."

Ash made a sound between a laugh and a snort that was somehow still charming. "I didn't know you'd be home."

Is this really my home? Yiran wanted to ask. But he kept his mouth shut and his eyes closed.

"Come on, get up."

Yiran felt a nudge at his leg. He sighed and opened his eyes.

Looking at Song Lan Xi was like looking into a funhouse mirror, except *Yiran* was the distorted image. His half brother went by the moniker *Ash*—a nod to the gray hair that sprouted prematurely from his head because of his extraordinarily high level of yangqi. But it didn't matter what he chose to call himself. Unlike Yiran, Ash wore the Song family name well and he strode through life with the ease of someone born to succeed.

He was everything Yiran was not and could not be.

Sometimes, when the nights grew long and lonely, Yiran found himself hating him. He hated Ash's confidence, his guts, his swagger. He hated that their grandfather loved Ash more, and that Ash was the only connection Yiran had to their dead father. He hated that Ash would lay his own life on the line to protect his family. Most of all, Yiran hated not knowing if he would do the same in return.

"I didn't see your car in the driveway," said Ash. "Did you crash it again?"

The accusation pushed Yiran to his feet. Two months ago, he had the misfortune of crossing paths with a jaywalker. The girl had suddenly appeared at the intersection with her head turned in the wrong direction. He'd swerved to avoid her, ramming into a fire hydrant. But his grandfather took one glance at the missing fender and broken headlight, and it was all that mattered.

"I told you it wasn't my fault the last time," he said.

"Okay, okay. I believe you," Ash soothed. "So why are you home early?"

He doesn't know about my exile. Yiran pushed his hair out of his face, mumbling, "Zufu sent someone to pick me up from Theo's. He wanted to talk."

Ash glanced down the hallway, a shadow crossing his face. "What did Yeye want to talk about?" He didn't address their grandfather in the formal way Yiran did. He didn't need to.

"Nothing," Yiran replied. Ash would find out from their grandfather anyway. "I've homework to do. See you at dinner."

"We won't be having dinner with you. Yeye and I have things to discuss."

Yiran picked at a loose thread around his shirt button. He didn't know whether to be relieved or angry. His grandfather and Ash never included him in their secretive meetings where they discussed matters concerning the Exorcist Guild. Why would they? He wasn't one of them. He didn't have magic and he couldn't see Revenants, let alone catch or kill one.

Ash noticed his mood. "I'll be back late tonight if you want to talk," he offered.

"Are you going on a Night Hunt?"

"You should stay in tonight." Ash patted Yiran on the back. It felt like a noncommittal answer.

"Some kids at school were talking about the rising supernatural homicides," Yiran said, hoping that Ash would share more with him for once. "It's getting bad out there with the Revenants, isn't it?"

"Negativity sells. The media loves to exaggerate the bad stuff. It's all clickbait—don't worry about it." Ash spun on the spot, stopping with a picture-perfect pose—clever smirk, eyebrow raised, and a finger pointed at Yiran. "I'll see you later."

Fists curling, Yiran watched as Ash went in the direction of the study. As expected, Ash had brushed him off again. Yiran wasn't an Exorcist. Couldn't even qualify to be a Xingshan cadet. He didn't belong in that world.

He forced himself to walk away before he could be tempted to eavesdrop.

Despair hung in his room like an axe waiting to fall. Yiran pulled out his largest suitcase. He stood in front of his wardrobe, still in disbelief that he was leaving this place. Possibly for good. He stared at the crap he'd accumulated from his schoolmates. Was this how he'd been wasting his life?

There was a knock on his door.

A hesitant voice said, "Er shaoye?"

Auntie Kimmie.

"Dinner will be ready soon. I told the cook to make your favorite soup dumplings."

She knows. Yiran heard it in her voice. He couldn't face her. Not now. The housekeeper cared for him like she would her own child. She was the one who dried his tears in those early years when he missed his mother, the one who had tended to his wounds all the times his grandfather had tried to figure out what was wrong with him.

"Thanks, Auntie. I'll eat later when I'm hungry." Yiran listened for her footsteps to recede. He couldn't leave without saying goodbye, but he couldn't handle her tears either.

He snatched the first thing he saw on his hangers and threw it on the bed. His hands and arms moved in a frenzy of yanking and throwing, until throwing was the only thing he did. Finally, he fell face down on the clump of clothes.

An electronic tune came from his back pocket.

Yiran pulled out his phone and lay on his stomach, frowning at the two faces that showed up on the screen.

"What do you want?" he asked, not bothering to hide his foul temper.

"We were going to the Night Market for supper, but they're calling a Night Hunt later tonight. Ruining my plans again," Theo whined. "I'm so sick of the stupid curfews."

"What does it have to do with me?" Yiran grunted without an ounce of sympathy. With Theo's family connections, it wasn't surprising he got the news of the Hunt early. But Yiran was peeved that Theo got confirmation *before* he did from his own Exorcist half brother.

"Theo's sleeping over at my place tonight," Sweets said. "We're doing movies and the new RPG game that dropped yesterday. *And* I broke into my dad's stash." He held up a bottle of expensive-looking whiskey. "You interested?"

"You know I don't drink."

Theo laughed. "You grounded, er shaoye?"

"Screw you."

Yiran hung up. Sometimes, he thought, he hated his friends, too.

He tossed his phone aside and rolled onto his back. Resentment throbbed against his skull. It wasn't his fault he was born a bastard. Wasn't his fault his father died and his mother abandoned him. Wasn't his fault the powerful magic of the Songs had skipped him for some reason, leaving him a dangling, rotting leaf on the family tree. Just another mouth to feed and clothe.

A sudden thought tickled his brain.

The Night Market would still be open before curfew. If Yiran skipped dinner, he could make it there in time. He sat up, excitement coursing through his veins, the thought slowly building into something else. It was a wild plan, but he was hanging from a dry branch; all he needed was a spark to burn everything down.

And tonight, he was going to find a flame.

6
Rui

The higher you climb, the harder you fall.

If that were true, then Matthias Lin's plummet from grace was a meteor that shattered her world, Rui thought, as she stood in front of his apartment.

The loan sharks had done a thorough job this time. Obscenities splashed across the door in angry red paint. Even the grille gate was not spared. At least they hadn't hung a pig's head.

Yet.

Rui turned to the middle-aged woman who was standing at the door of the neighboring apartment. "Thanks for calling me, Auntie Chen. I'm so sorry for the trouble. It won't happen again."

"Young people shouldn't make promises they can't keep," Auntie Chen said, one hand resting on her generous hip. "I know you're a good daughter, Rui, but these ah long don't care about the law, and your father is—"

"I'm *really* sorry," Rui repeated, knowing full well apologies often meant nothing. Just ephemeral words to absolve the offender. "Don't worry, Auntie Chen, the loan sharks won't bother you. They know you're not involved."

Auntie Chen shook her head, muttering about *ah long* and *irresponsible fathers* as she retreated into her home.

Rui kept a penitent smile on her face until the door was shut. She fished for her keys, hands trembling as she jammed the right one into the padlock. She failed twice before the stubborn thing finally gave and the notches fell in place.

The grille gate opened with a loud creak. Thank gods for this piece of junk. With enough brute force, the loan sharks could have easily busted through the wooden door, but a steel gate was a different matter. The new apartments didn't have this extra layer of security anymore. Good thing her father lived in one of the older constructions where rent was cheaper.

The shoebox apartment looked like a typhoon had hit it. For a moment, Rui thought the loan sharks had broken in after all. But the mess was familiar. Empty takeout food cartons were strewn over the small dining table, dirty clothing spewed onto the chairs. The cheap window blinds were torn, the couch was askew, and fluff was coming out of some cushions.

Rui wrinkled her nose at the smell coming from the kitchen.

When was the last time she visited or saw her father? Was it late spring? She'd been busy with training, and frankly, it was easier to pretend he didn't exist. They'd moved here after her mother died. The living room was once partitioned to create enough space to squeeze in a single bed to fit a teenage girl. Not long after she'd enrolled in the Academy, Rui petitioned for a permanent room there all year round. She left this dump, scrubbing all traces of herself from it. She hadn't planned on returning today, but maybe the universe was warning her not to lie to Ada again.

"Dad?" Her voice sounded small to her ears. The same way she'd sounded when she was a frightened child expecting to find someone passed out on the floor, or worse, lying face down in a pool of their own vomit.

"Dad?" she called out again, maneuvering her way through the clutter to the bedroom. It was messier than the living room. Stacks of medical journals, their pages torn and yellowing, piled up on the floor. Old photographs and half-crumpled papers with her father's chicken scratch handwriting on them spread across the desk and unmade bed.

Rui stuck her head into the bathroom.

A man was sitting on the floor with his legs sprawled out. His khakis were wrinkled, and there were food stains on the sleeves of his T-shirt. He was staring into space, as if his mind were a million miles away, fixated on something else.

It was unnerving to see herself in his features. Her wide-set brown eyes were her mother's, but she shared the same slightly upturned nose as her father and an angular jaw that slanted to a narrow chin. It frightened her sometimes to think they might share more than a physical resemblance.

Once a prominent researcher and doctor at the city's top hospital, Matthias Lin was now a shadow of himself. He had crumbled after his wife died, and the subsequent accusations of malpractice along with his increasingly erratic behavior did nothing to help his case. He wilted, faded into nothing, his skin stretching too tightly over his bones. It hurt to look at him, and Rui stopped looking a long time ago.

She was different. She fed on her grief, thriving, blossoming like a vicious weed nourished by the hope of vengeance.

"Baba," she said.

Her father looked up with a start, his face lighting up when he recognized her. "What are you doing here, Ru-er?"

Rui startled. Only her mother called her that. "Auntie Chen told me what happened," she said. "Are you okay?"

Her father sniffed and rubbed his eyes, picking his glasses up from the bathroom rug. The black wire frames sat crookedly on his nose. Rui wondered if he could see through the clouded lenses. She made a mental note to clean them for him.

"Are they gone?" he asked tiredly.

She nodded. "They left a present on the front door. I'll get some paint and cleaning supplies from the store."

Her father strained a smile. "No need. I have some leftover paint under the sink. I'll do it."

How many times had he repainted the front door? Now that she was here, it was clear that her father needed more help than a paint job. But her stubbornness returned. It was *his* fault things were the way they were. She couldn't solve his problems for him. Carefully, she sheathed the sharp edge of anger that had long overcome guilt and worry.

"I've nothing planned until tonight's patrol," she said. "I can stay and help with the door."

Her father's smile became less strained, and he patted the spot next to him. "Will you sit with me for a while?"

Rui sank to the floor. The chill from the tiles seeped through her jeans, bringing gooseflesh to her skin. She couldn't remember when she'd last sat with her father or paused long enough to share a moment—or anything—together.

"How's school?" he said. "How's my miracle child doing?"

Miracle child. Rui's mother used to tell the story of how she'd gotten into an accident while pregnant, and how she had been in danger of losing her baby and her own life. But the paramedics arrived in time, and Rui was born, albeit prematurely. Her miracle child.

"I'm fine," Rui said, staring at the mold at the edge of the shower curtain. "How much do you owe them?"

Matthias Lin's head drooped, like a puppeteer's string had loosened and he no longer had the strength to hold it up. "You don't have to worry about that."

It took her every effort not to yell at him. "As long as no one gets hurt," she said monotonously, unclenching her hands.

"No one will get hurt," he said.

Empty words, empty promises. Empty everything. Rui was sick of it.

She was about to get up when her father did the strangest thing. He took her hand in his. Squeezed it. His hand felt warm and big and safe, like she remembered from when she was a little girl. For the briefest of moments, she let herself believe that everything was fine. That Matthias Lin was the larger-than-life doctor who wanted to save the world. The man she'd looked up to and had wanted to be like when she grew up.

"You know I miss her, too, right?" her father said softly.

Rui swallowed the lump in her throat. It was the first time in a long time that he'd acknowledged the loss of his wife.

Rui leaned against him, resting her weary head on his thin shoulder. *I know you do,* she thought, and squeezed his hand back.

7
Yiran

Yiran pulled up across the entrance to a busy street, wild thoughts in his head buzzing like a swarm of wrathful hornets. He hadn't paused to think twice since stealing a car from the family garage and driving to a place he knew he shouldn't be visiting. There was still time to back out, to sneak the car home without getting caught. Or, if he *were* caught in the act of returning, there was still a chance to grovel for his grandfather's forgiveness.

But years of pent-up rancor had calcified in his chest, clogging any path to rational thought. If he was being forced to leave the city, he was going to do it his way by sending a parting gift to his grandfather.

Yiran turned the engine off and got out of the car, slamming the door shut. Popping the collar of his leather jacket, he locked his jaw and walked into the Night Market.

Smoke ribboned against the indigo sky, and the air smelled charred and sweet from incense and burning hell money. Red plastic plates and bowls filled with fruit, cooked rice, and steamed meats lined the sidewalk—offerings for hungry ghosts and spirits. There were so many stalls, selling everything from street food and ingredients for potions to antiques and allegedly magical items. The place was a delirious explosion of noise and color, busy with different dialects singing the same song of trade.

Unlike his friends, Yiran had never been to the Night Market before. No Song family member or Exorcist of good repute would be caught here, and Yiran's mother had never brought him when he was little. He stared curiously at the people milling around him.

On the surface, the merchants and customers looked like ordinary people. Noisy aunties, uncles smoking smelly cigarettes, younger people dressed in the latest trends, kids and elderly folk too. They were normies, like him.

But there were also magic practitioners to be found at the Night Market. Not practitioners like the Exorcists. The other kind. The kind who would get Yiran into more trouble if he was caught consorting with them.

Trouble was exactly what he sought.

He stopped at a stall selling an array of talismans. It was larger than the rest and parked in front of an old shophouse with red lanterns. The lanterns had black markings, a sign that there was a magic practitioner living there. *Mages.* That was what they were called.

Red lantern good, white lantern bad. Theo's dad had said that once when Yiran had asked him about the Market. Mr. Wang was a shrewd businessman who didn't mind resorting to some lucky charms and the like. But he would never go further than that by dealing with actual rogue mages who supposedly dabbled in *sorcery*—magic that was absolutely forbidden by the Guild. Those were the white lanterns.

The middle-aged woman at the talisman stall looked up from her wares, squinting at Yiran through her cat-eye spectacles.

"Looking for a charm to help ace your studies, shuaige?" she asked, chewing her toothpick. "Or something that will get your crush's attention? Auntie Lian has everything you want." She fanned a bunch of charms in front of Yiran and plucked one out. "This one's popular. Sold it to an office girl last week and she got asked out on a date right away. I'll sell it to you for half-price—you can't get it this cheap anywhere else. Here, take it!" She grabbed Yiran's hand and pressed the intricately folded red paper into his palm. "Burn it and drop the ashes into a drink of your choice. Coffee, plain water, juice, anything is fine. Stand in front of the cute girl you like when she's drinking it, and she'll think you're the handsomest boy in the world."

"I'm not here for that, auntie," Yiran said, dropping the red paper onto her table.

"Works on cute boys, too," Auntie Lian said with a twinkle in her eye. "Don't be shy, go after what your heart desires."

"Maybe some other time. I'm here for something else."

"Oh?" Auntie Lian peered up at him over her glasses, taking in his clothes and person. "What exactly are you looking for, my dear?"

Yiran flashed a charming smile. "The secret menu."

To his chagrin, she burst out laughing. "Where do you think you are? A fast-food restaurant?" She pointed at the line of stalls. "Have your pick, all the street food you want is there in the open. We don't have a secret menu, or any secrets here."

"That's not what I mean, you know that. I'm looking for actual magic." When the woman gestured at her charms, Yiran scoffed. "No offense, auntie, but I don't need help pulling anyone—him, her, or them. This face card never declines."

He had dated enough people to know this was a fact. But the dates had been casual, lacking in some way, physically attractive people Yiran knew he was supposed to be drawn to, but who somehow left him feeling lonelier. Deciding that the void inside him could not be filled by a person, he stopped bothering a year ago. He used discretion as an excuse, silence as implication, and everyone assumed he was scoring anyway.

His friends, on the other hand, had no issue sharing their exploits openly, but Yiran couldn't grasp the concept of treating another human being as a trophy. This difference and his disinterest made him wonder if *he* was the problem, if his lack of magic wasn't his only defect.

Auntie Lian's salesperson face shuttered. She made a sucking sound through her teeth and spat out her toothpick. "No offense taken, young man. Like I said, there's no secret menu in the Night Market. Whatever kind of *magic* you think you're looking for, it's all in these charms and amulets."

Yiran pointed at the shophouse behind the stall. "How about the mage inside? Can they help me? I can be generous." He pulled his sleeve back to reveal Nick Cheng's watch.

Auntie Lian's eyes bulged. "How generous?"

"Whatever it takes." He glanced down the line of stalls. "I can also take my business elsewhere. I'm sure there're other mages around—I'm not picky."

He started to walk away.

"Wait." Auntie Lian lowered her voice. "What exactly are you looking for?"

"A spell to capture something."

"What kind of something?"

"Something valuable. It would be a feat that will make me famous in some circles," Yiran said, pulse racing.

He thought Auntie Lian would tell him to get lost, but she popped another toothpick into her mouth and made a gesture with her hand. From the shadows, a barrel-chested man appeared.

"Show him in," Auntie Lian said.

The man led Yiran to the front doors of the shophouse.

Yiran stepped across the threshold, unsure of what to expect. He found himself in a large empty parlor with a single wooden table in the middle. It was old and rickety, with two chairs beside it that were just as old and rickety.

The barrel-chested man grunted.

Yiran sat down.

Seconds later, an older gentleman in a white mandarin-collared tunic and black flowing pants appeared. His bald head was tattooed with symbols that reminded Yiran of birds in flight.

He sat down across from Yiran, a genial smile on his lined face. "How may I help you?"

"I wish to purchase a spell."

"Can you cast a spell?"

Could the mage not sense that Yiran was a normie? Yiran watched as the mage's eyes traveled to the small white scars on his fingertips. He retracted his hands from the tabletop quickly, keeping them out of sight on his lap. He felt silly for doing so, but something about the mage's expression puzzled him. The mage wasn't just curious about Yiran's scars, he was *disturbed* by them.

"No," Yiran replied. "I can't cast it myself. It'll have to be a spell that will work regardless of that."

A slow nod. "You wish to capture something that will bring you fame. What is the object you seek?"

"I want to catch a Revenant."

"You mean you wish to *kill* a Revenant."

"No. I want a spell that can help me lure one in and immobilize it. I want it alive." The words sounded outrageous to his own ears. But this was Yiran's parting gift—one last spiteful hurrah, a monstrous middle finger to his grandfather. He stared at the mage. "And I want everyone to see it—even the normies."

The long silence that followed his words was damning.

The old mage stood abruptly. "See him out. Tell Lian to screen our customers with more care. We are not in want of money."

Yiran jumped out of his chair. "Do you have a spell like that? Can you make a Revenant visible to everyone?"

The old man ignored him and retreated into the alcove.

"Wait—let go of me!" Yiran shoved the barrel-chested man away.

The man grunted, his brows meeting in a dangerous line.

Throwing him a dirty look, Yiran straightened his leather jacket. "I can walk out myself."

He strode out the door and turned left toward another stall, but the barrel-chested man blocked his way.

"Look, buddy," Yiran said, raising his hands. "Let's forget about what just happened, okay? I'll get out of your hair. We're good."

The man glared. "*Out* is the other way."

Yiran's hand curled into a fist. *It's not worth it*, the cool-headed part of him cautioned. He wanted to throttle that voice. But he knew it was right.

"Fine. I'm leaving," he said, moving backward.

The man didn't budge. Just stood and stared. Finally, Yiran turned on his heel. Lian caught his eye as he passed her stall again. She winked.

Cursing, Yiran walked on.

He'd messed up. What was he thinking, coming down here? His plan seemed so amateur and childish now. He *knew* that, and yet he'd let his anger get the better of him, the way it always did when it came to his grandfather. He had nothing to show from this gamble, and there was hell to pay when he got home.

He stood outside the Night Market, staring at the red plates of offerings on the sidewalk.

Once, when Yiran was small, before he'd ever been to Song Mansion, his mother told him the story of a boy who'd accidentally kicked the plates of offerings meant for hungry ghosts. From then on, the boy was plagued by spirits who haunted him until his last days for messing with their meal. Yiran had been frightened by that story, and his mother soothed him by telling him that—

Why are you thinking of her? he scolded himself, shoving that memory away. His mother had made it clear she didn't want him in her life—why else would she leave him at Song Mansion without even saying goodbye?

Yiran lashed his foot out, connecting with a bowl by the sidewalk. Rice spilled everywhere. Finding satisfaction in destruction, he kicked another plate. Oranges rolled onto the road. He pulled his foot back for another round.

"What do you think you're doing?" said a voice behind him.

He turned and saw a girl with choppy bangs and a giant scowl on her face.

8
Rui

"What do you think you're doing?" Rui asked the tall boy who was kicking the offerings left on the sidewalk near the Night Market. She had taken a shortcut on her way to the meeting place for her patrol and was passing through the neighborhood. She didn't expect to encounter a vandal.

The boy shot her an irritated glare, his dark brown eyes flashing. He reminded her of someone, but she couldn't put her finger on it.

"Mind your own business, Darcy."

"My name isn't Darcy. Those are offerings. Don't you have any respect for the dead?"

The boy laughed derisively. "They're *dead*. Why would they care about stale rice and old oranges? Don't tell me you believe in wandering spirits and ghosts and all that nonsense?"

Rui opened her mouth, decided he wasn't worth her time, and closed it.

He jerked his chin up at an angle, the corner of his lips curling into an almost sneer. "Go on, run along."

His expression reminded Rui of another pompous jerk. "You're Ash's brother," she realized.

The boy recoiled. Whether it was out of surprise or something else, Rui wasn't sure. *Song Yiran.* That was his name.

Now that she knew who he was, it was clear that Yiran's resemblance to Ash was more impressionistic than technical. One of his ears stuck out. Just a fraction. It ruined the symmetry of his face. Still, like Ash, Yiran was remarkably good-looking. But unlike Ash, who had *golden boy* written all over him, there was something about Yiran that felt . . . missing. Like a painting left unfinished because the artist had gotten distracted by a grander idea, or a bonsai tree pruned by an inexpert hand. Whatever it was, it made him a lesser copy of his older brother.

But both the Song grandsons possessed the air of having been born into money. Yiran's blue jeans were carefully constructed to look worn at the knees, and a weathered black leather jacket hung over his light gray hoodie. Nothing too fancy. But she knew if she turned everything inside out, the tags would be designer.

Yiran wrinkled his nose like he smelled something foul. "How do you know my brother? Are you one of them?"

It took Rui a moment to realize he meant *Exorcist*. "Not yet. I'm a cadet at Xingshan."

"Same thing, Darcy."

Rui had heard stories about the younger grandson of the Head of the Exorcist Guild. Most of them were unpleasant. If this current attitude was anything to go by, she wouldn't be surprised if all the rumors were true.

"First of all, my name is *Rui*. Second, I'd rather be one of them out here protecting people than an arrogant brat disrespecting the dead." Was it wise to insult a Song? Probably not. But Rui wasn't in the mood to care. The visit to her father's had left her out of sorts, and the failed simulation test chipped away at her temper.

Yiran rolled his eyes. "Whatever, *Darcy*."

Hackles rising, Rui readied another insult.

A deafening siren blared.

Yiran covered his ears.

"It's a Night Hunt. The Exorcists are hunting Revenants," Rui shouted above the noise.

"I know what a Night Hunt is," Yiran said with unconcealed scorn. He walked off without another word.

Jerk. Rui jogged in the other direction. She couldn't wait to complain to Ada about Ash's bratty kid brother. Hopefully, she'd never have to set eyes on him again.

The siren continued for another minute before silencing. It was weird that a Night Hunt would be held so close to the cadets' patrol route. Since the cadets were still in training, the two routes never crossed. But the sirens covered a large area. Maybe the Hunt wasn't taking place anywhere near the route itself.

Rui checked her weapons and talismans, making sure they were secured and within easy reach. Zizi's special talisman was tucked inside the inner pocket of her coat. A secret, much like everything else they shared. She hadn't thought about how to successfully test it, but it was something for future Rui to figure out. She had told Zizi she would do it, and she needed the money for her father's debts.

The meeting place was empty, the row of eateries were closed, and the area was deserted. Rui stared at a sign outside Gojo's Café listing the many flavors of bubble tea, wondering if her father had eaten the simple dinner she'd cooked for him before leaving the apartment.

Pacing down the street, she buttoned her coat, wishing she'd thought to bring a scarf. The night was unusually chilly for autumn, and the sounds of the Night Market seemed far away. The disquiet she had been feeling all day grew.

Four years. Four. *Si*. It sounded like *death*.

Gods. She shook her head. She was being superstitious.

Ten minutes went by, and no cadet showed up. There was no sign of the Exorcist mentor assigned to the team tonight either.

Rui pulled out her phone and tapped the screen. "Pick up, Ada," she groaned after the tenth ring.

Finally, a voice groggy with sleep mumbled, "Hello?"

"You're sleeping? Why aren't you here for the patrol?"

"I was taking a nap. The patrol's been called off—didn't you know? I thought you'd come back to campus from your dad's." Ada sounded wide awake now. "They called a Night Hunt out of the blue, and the territory extends to Tangren Quarter, so they ordered our patrol group to stay back on campus. Some strange Revenant is running wild. Didn't you get the message?"

Rui's heart skipped a beat. "Strange Revenant? Is it a Hybrid?"

There was a slight pause on Ada's side. "I think they meant it was a stronger Revenant or something. You're not thinking of going after it yourself, are you?"

Rui didn't reply.

"You have to come back," Ada said. "All cadets must be inside the dorms. You can't defy orders. What time is it—we've roll call in less than an hour."

Rui cursed. "I'm on my way."

She hung up and opened Apparition—the Academy's app for communication. With everything that was happening at her father's, she'd forgotten to check it. Sure enough, there was a message repeating what Ada had said.

There was also a text from Zizi.

Sushi was great but I ordered waaaay too much as usual. Wish you stayed to help.

The text ended with a GIF of a ghost bearing a resemblance to the earrings she'd gifted him. A tiny word bubble appeared at its mouth with one word: *boo*. Zizi must have meant it when he said he enjoyed her cantankerous company.

Or maybe he's just weird, her brain pointed out. *Both could be true*, her heart argued. *Stop thinking about him*, she chided herself. This was no time to ponder what Zizi might or might not have meant. She had to get back to the Academy.

As she turned, a distinctive smell wafted in the air, like flowery perfume mixed with something rotting. Her hands went to her sword bag.

A Revenant was in the area.

Miasma pressed down, growing heavier by the second. Rui knew she had to leave, but her feet moved toward the scent. The Revenant was too near to the Night Market where the crowd was, and she didn't know if they'd evacuated yet. There was no sign of the Exorcists. What if they were late?

Some strange Revenant is running wild. . . .

What if it really was a Hybrid? What if it was *him*? She was near the scene of her mother's murder exactly four years ago. . . . It felt like too much of a coincidence.

Rui made up her mind. She had her talismans and her weapons. She would get to the Revenant first, she would kill it before—

A scream ripped the night apart.

9
Rui

A woman was running toward Rui. "Help! A monster!"

"You can see the Revenant?" Rui said, incredulous. The woman looked like a normie; she *couldn't* see Revenants. Unless— "Does it look human? Where is it?"

"Around the corner. The boy is trying to f-fight it."

"What boy?"

The woman started to sob incoherently. Her fear seemed to seep into Rui as she clung on to her.

"Never mind," said Rui. "Get away from here."

She pried the woman off and sprinted ahead, but the sight that accosted her was so surprising she stopped in her tracks.

Song Yiran was holding up a baseball bat. In front of him, a Revenant backed up against the wall, its ghoul-like features twisted in confusion.

"What the hell are you doing?" Rui shouted at him.

Yiran yelled back, "I'm trying to kill it, obviously."

"With a *baseball bat*?"

"That's all I had in my trunk."

Their loud voices agitated the Revenant. It snarled, limbs flailing toward them.

"Move!"

Rui shouldered Yiran out of the way and loaded Teshin's crossbow with metal spikes.

She set her sights.

Now.

Her aim was true. But when the spikes hit the Revenant, their crimson light fizzled. They fell, tinkling uselessly on stone, the dissonant music rattling her. Why wasn't the magic working?

The Revenant pounced.

Rui leaped out of the way. Cold sweat broke across her forehead as she thought of her next move. No time for barrier spells. If any civilian was foolish enough to wander into the area, they'd have to fend for themselves. Quickly, she pulled out a talisman and cast a binding spell instead.

Spirit ropes wrapped around the Revenant. This time, the crimson light burned into pallid flesh.

Relief was sweet. But that moment of respite was short-lived.

The Revenant screeched, scratching at its throat as if trying to tear its skin apart. Within seconds, it broke free of the binding spell. Clearly, it wasn't an ordinary Revenant.

This was the Revenant Ada warned her about.

The smell of rot in the air was increasing, and with it, an acrid sulfur stench that burned Rui's nostrils. Something strange was happening to the Revenant. She watched in horror as its mouth opened in a silent scream, expanding wider and wider. Until it gaped beyond reason. Until it looked like the monster was swallowing itself whole from the inside.

From that chasm of a mouth, something else crawled out.

A newborn creature with distorted limbs and bulging eyes. Its long black hair writhed like snakes and its hungry dark eyes had a reddish tinge. Its gray and bloated face was morphing into a *woman's face*.

A Hybrid? But it didn't look like one. It looked like an evolutionary mistake, trapped between human and monster. The creature arched its spine, flinging its head upward at the night sky. It let out a piercing cry, and violet tentacles burst from its back.

The light from Rui's blades flickered as she shuddered at that awful, unholy sound. She had never seen a Revenant like this before. Not in real life, not in her textbooks. She could hear Ash's sardonic voice in her head. *This is why Exorcists work in teams.* But there was no time to call him or Ada or Zizi or anyone else for backup. She was the only thing standing between this hungry monster and certain death.

She exhaled, and her crimson blades grew stronger and brighter. Spite was a powerful motivator; if she killed this Revenant by herself, she could rub it in Ash's face.

"What the fuck is that thing?"

Song Yiran was still standing a few paces away, transfixed by the terrible sight of the monster.

"Why didn't you run when you had the chance?" she yelled. His presence was a distraction. She had to keep an eye on his safety.

"I don't run," Yiran said, jaw hard.

Rui glared. Didn't he understand she had no time for his bravado nonsense? "Then shut up and don't get in my way."

She faced the Revenant again, shooting a few energy bolts at the creature's torso.

The Revenant dodged. But it was moving slowly now. Was it unused to its new form? If it had less control of its new body, she could take advantage of that. She shot another series of bolts at one tentacle as a test.

The Revenant screeched. Scorch marks pitted its flesh.

Rui grinned. From the way they burned, she guessed the tentacles were filled with yinqi. They were her target. But she had to get closer.

She leveraged off the side of the building and catapulted into the air. As she sailed over the Revenant, it reared, bottomless eyes following the arc of her trajectory. Before she began her descent, Rui rotated her body and thrusted both arms out, certain of her strike. She felt her blade slicing through flesh and twisted some more. But just as her other blade grazed another tentacle, her right shoulder popped.

Pain shot through her nerves. She had practiced this move a hundred times. Maybe it was a hundred times too little. Maybe it was the morning's injury that affected her technique. Or maybe it was plain old fear. It didn't matter.

She had missed.

A tentacle shot out from nowhere, slamming into her ribs. Air gusted from her lungs, and she felt something crack. She couldn't breathe.

Couldn't scream. Her swords clattered onto the ground, metal ringing like a death chime.

The tentacle wrapped around her. The ground shrank as she went up, up, up, her legs dangling like a rag doll's. She didn't want to know how far the drop would be. Or if she would live to feel it.

The Revenant brought her close to its monstrous face. The stench of rot and sulfur was overpowering. Against her will, Rui whimpered.

Something pricked her neck. A fog clouded over her mind.

The Revenant started to *drink*.

It was a hundred times worse than what she had experienced in the training program. Her head lolled back toward the night sky. *The stars are out tonight.* It was a strange thought to have in this moment. But the bright spots in the sky were turning black. She was getting weaker, her mind drifting off to somewhere quiet . . . somewhere dark.

"Let go of her!"

I don't run.

"I said, let go of her!"

The tentacle around her loosened.

Rui's lungs filled with air. Her vision focused. She saw a figure jumping up and down on the ground below.

Something whizzed past her ear.

That foolish boy had traded his baseball bat for rocks, and he was throwing them at the Revenant. As if that would do anything at all. A misguided rock shot past her head. How good—or bad—was Yiran's aim?

It didn't matter what he did. Rui couldn't move a muscle, couldn't string together a coherent thought. It was over. The Revenant was going to suck her dry. She was going to die tonight, just like how she was supposed to die exactly four years ago. Fate merely held its cards close, letting her believe that she was safe, that death would not come for her.

Get a grip on yourself. This is not how it ends. Zizi's voice—or maybe it was her father's—spoke in her mind.

Baba.

If she died, what would become of her father? There would be no one to take care of him. No one to make sure he stayed alive. No one who would care if he died.

She couldn't give up. Not like this.

Gasping, she reached into her coat, fingers inching for the flimsy piece of paper in her pocket.

Another rock bounced off the Revenant's torso. It didn't do any damage, but it did distract it. For a moment, the creature forgot about Rui. It lifted its head and growled at Yiran.

Rui twisted. Her shoulder screamed in pain. But Zizi's talisman was in her hands. She started the incantation with a shaky whisper.

Nothing happened.

Hope faded.

Then—at the corner of the talisman—light flickered.

Rui's chant grew louder as she thanked all the gods in this world and the next. A few more words and her spell would be complete—but her chant became a yell when the Revenant flung her into the air.

Free-falling, she crashed into the canopy of trees, unable to brace herself. Branches scratched her face and hands. Something pierced her side, tearing through fabric and flesh.

The ground struck her hard. Jolted her teeth, shook her bones. In a daze, she struggled up and felt her ribs. Her fingers met with something warm and wet.

Blood. A lot of it.

"Are you all right?" Yiran's form came into focus. For some reason, he was holding one of her swords. He paled when he saw her bloody hand. "What happened to you?"

"The Revenant threw me in the air—were you not paying attention?" Every word she said to this imbecile was a waste of effort and time.

"There's so much blood," Yiran said, looking faint.

All Rui wanted was for him to hand over her weapon and get lost. She tried to stand, but her legs buckled. "Give it to me." She tried to grab at the sword in Yiran's hand, but he held it away, afraid she might hurt herself. She swiped at him again.

"Stop moving—you're injured."

"Shut up, I've got to kill—"

A howl turned both their heads. The Revenant was shuddering violently, swaying from side to side.

"Listen," Yiran said. "I'm going to pick you up and make a run for it."

Rui's head was muddled with pain, but she forced herself to concentrate. "No, it'll chase us. We can't lead it to other people, and you can't outrun it if you're carrying me. Just go."

As suddenly as it started, the Revenant's tremors stopped. It crawled toward them, tentacles trailing behind like misshapen limbs.

"*Go,*" she repeated.

"Don't be ridiculous. I'm not leaving you like this."

Yiran faced the Revenant, shielding her. What was he thinking? He couldn't fight it. Not without a spiritual weapon.

Something caught her eye. The talisman. A small piece of it was stuck on her sleeve. The Revenant had thrown her before she could finish Zizi's spell . . . Would it still work if she finished the incantation?

Theoretically, if there's contact between two bodies, the spiritual energy may transfer.

"Spiritual weapon," Rui whispered to herself, an absurd idea forming in her mind. That was the key. She couldn't kill the Revenant in her current state, but with her weapon and a boost of *her* spiritual energy, maybe, just maybe, Song Yiran could use her sword. There was only a slim chance her idea would work. But what other choice did they have?

She seized Yiran's hand, dragging him down to her. They locked eyes. He didn't pull away from her, and she didn't let go.

In one breath, she recited the rest of the incantation.

The last bit of talisman lit up.

Please.

Seconds ticked by like an eternity. Rui was suddenly hyperaware of her splintered ribs, the blood trickling from her side, her own shallow breathing, and the sound of the Revenant dragging its body along the gravel path.

And *him*. The boy who was staring at her in wonder.

The spell hit.

Energy vibrated through her blood like an electronic hum of tiny needles pricking and biting. Heat spread through her body—followed by a piercing cold, like ice burning in her veins. The hum rose to a crescendo, screeching like nails on a chalkboard as it went back and forth between Yiran and her. A song that only both of them could hear.

With no warning, it stopped.

They stared at each other, breathless.

Rui was shivering. But although Yiran's face had gone pale, an ethereal glow emanated from him. It disappeared as his hand warmed in hers, and the same unusual heat radiated off the rest of him.

Yiran was first to speak, his voice hoarse. "What was *that*?" He jerked away from her, a hand on his own chest like he was checking for a heartbeat. "What did you do to me?"

"I'm saving us." Rui nudged his cheek so he faced the Revenant. "You have to kill that."

"Fuck."

"Exactly. If you want to stay alive, do as I say. Raise my sword."

Yiran held her sword up, a skeptical look on his face.

"Now, go."

"Go?"

Rui didn't understand why he was so confused. "You've got a boost of my yangqi; use my sword. Channel your magic and kill the Revenant."

"But *how*?"

When she stared back at him, just as flabbergasted as he seemed, Yiran swallowed. Even in the subdued light of the streetlamps, she could see a flush spreading across his cheeks.

"I was born with a normal spirit core," he confessed, looking wretched.

"You're a normie?" How did she miss that earlier? She focused on him, but it was too late. Whatever energy she sensed from him now might be a result of Zizi's spell. "Isn't every Song born with a powerful spirit core?" she said, desperate for it to be true.

Yiran hung his head. "Every Song but me. I don't have magic."

I don't have magic.

His words were a death knell. They were going to perish after all. Word on the street was that Yiran hadn't enrolled at Xingshan because Song Wei had lost his only son in the war against the Revenants, and he wanted at least one grandson to be out of harm's way. She didn't know it was because he was incapable of magic.

But something had happened between them because of the spell. Rui was sure of it. She *felt* different. Hollow, like something was missing from her.

"It doesn't matter," she said, hoping she was right. "The spell might've still transferred some of my spiritual energy to you. But it won't last long and it's our only chance. We can do this—*you* can do this. Breathe in slow, focus on how your breath moves in your stomach."

"But—"

Rui gripped his hand, speaking as calmly as she could. "Trust me. Ground yourself and breathe. Feel your vital force, your qi, circulating through your body. Feel the energy. Let it flow over you like a wave."

"Okay, breathe," Yiran repeated. He inhaled and exhaled.

Soft crimson light shimmered from his hands. For some strange reason, the light looked like it was pouring out from the small white scars on each of his fingertips, as if he'd been cut dozens of times, the cuts healing and tearing and healing again. Rui had never seen anyone channel magic directly from their hands before, but relief rushed through her.

They had a chance.

"You're doing good," she said. "Run your hand over the blade, that's right, like that."

The entire sword in Yiran's hand lit up with crimson light.

He fell back in surprise. Rui choked on a hysterical laugh. It felt like her chest was about to explode.

Zizi's spell worked. It *worked*.

Yiran gawked at the glowing sword in his hand. "What—*how*? This is impossible."

"Focus," she hissed. "Keep breathing."

"Okay, okay."

As Yiran kept the rhythm of his breathing, the blade transformed, its light brighter than before. The blade wasn't shaped like a lightning bolt. It was bigger and thicker, curved like an outsized saber. A nagging voice in Rui's head questioned its appearance, but there was no time to think about it.

"I can't cast any protection spells for you. You only get one chance," she told Yiran. "Use me as bait. Approach the Revenant from behind and cut off its tentacles."

"Cut off?"

With an exasperated grunt, Rui pointed at the weapon in his hand. "See this? Sword, tentacle, chop."

"Sword, tentacle, chop," Yiran recited. He gave her a tentative smile. "It'll be fine, right?"

Without waiting for an answer, he sprinted off into the dark.

Rui propped herself up on her good elbow, ignoring the pain pulsating through her body. When Yiran was out of sight, she grabbed a rock and threw it at the Revenant.

"Hey, asshole, I'm right here!"

The Revenant raised its head at the sound of her voice. Shambling closer, it made a sorrowful sound, almost as if it were crying. But Revenants didn't have emotions . . . did they?

Something flitted behind it.

Yiran. He approached the creature with a natural predatory agility, like this was something he was born to do. He raised his arms. Rui held her breath. The blade of crimson light flashed.

A howl echoed through the night.

Flesh smoked as a deep cut emerged across the Revenant's back. But Yiran's strike had missed most of its tentacles. Helplessly, Rui watched as the Revenant lunged at him. He twisted just out of reach, but not before the Revenant hit his arm. His sword flew to the ground, landing a distance away.

Yiran sprang back and dropped to one knee, bracing himself with a hand.

It's going to kill him. Rui had sent him to his death. What was she thinking?

But Yiran got up. He looked undaunted and more determined than before. He angled his body as if he were escaping to the right. The Revenant shifted in anticipation. Cutting left, Yiran slammed a shoulder into its body.

The Revenant smashed into the fence. Without wasting a second, Yiran ran and dove for the sword. But the crimson blade had vanished, and the sword looked like an ordinary sword, the metal dull and silver.

"It's gone," Yiran shouted to Rui.

"It's not," she said, keeping an eye on the Revenant. One of its tentacles was caught on the wires of the fence, but it was pulling itself free. "I don't feel my spiritual energy returning, which means the spell's still working."

"I can't—my grandfather tested me—"

Even from a distance, she could sense Yiran's doubt. "The past doesn't matter. The spell's working. You have magic—use it."

Yiran shook his head. "I can't do this."

"You just did it," Rui insisted. The Revenant was pushing back on its deformed feet, snapping its head this way and that. But Yiran stood frozen, staring at the sword in his hands as if he were off in some faraway place. Rui dragged herself closer to him, pleading, "Trust me, you can do it."

The Revenant was close. Closer.

Desperation shoved her. "Song Yiran—I believe in you, dammit!"

The sharpness in her voice snapped Yiran out of his daze. His eyes went to her for a moment, and she saw something flicker in them. Whatever it was, it gave her hope.

But as Yiran ran toward the Revenant, the blade of his sword stayed dull.

Heart in her throat, Rui whispered, "Channel your magic. *Do it.*"

Just as the Revenant's tentacles grazed his arms, Yiran slid his hand down the blade.

Light flashed.

The Revenant screamed.

Something pungent and wine-colored sprayed through the air.

Yiran spun and sliced again. The Revenant's tentacles flopped onto the ground with a wet sound. Lunging with a triumphant yell, he pushed his blade into the Revenant's chest.

The creature shuddered for a few moments, but it didn't vaporize the way Rui had expected it to. Its body hardened, turning gray. Then it crumbled like a sandcastle, bits of ash scattering everywhere. In moments, all that was left was smoke and dust and that acrid sulfur stench.

Rui fell back onto the grass, dizzy and nauseated. The annoying boy had done it. He killed the Revenant. *Of course he did. He's a Song*, she thought as black spots filled her vision.

Footsteps drew close. Warm hands slipped under her and lifted her up.

"What are you doing?" she said, barely able to speak.

"We need to get you to a hospital."

"No hospital." She pushed her bloody palms against his chest, but Yiran held her tight.

"I'll bring you to my grandfather. He'll know what to do."

"Not him, not the Guild." Rui couldn't show up at the Guild like this. She would have to explain what happened. The illegal spell she used, the transference of spiritual energy, going after a Revenant by herself—the evidence was damning. She would get kicked out of the Academy. She would lose everything. "No Guild. Put me down, I'm fine."

"How are you fine? Look at yourself."

"You don't understand. Put me down right now. I don't need your help."

"Shut up and listen," Yiran growled.

Rui blinked hard.

Yiran came into focus. He was licking his dry lips. "I don't know what you did to me. I'm not even sure if I want to know, because it feels like there's a fire inside me and I'm going mad. But I know you're bleeding to death, and you need help. You're an Exorcist. I'm bringing you to my grandfather."

His hair was flattened to his forehead, neck slicked with sweat, eyes wild and frantic. Rui was pressed close enough to sense his heart beating too quickly. He was barely holding it together. She could not let him fall apart.

She swallowed and tasted blood. "Mort Street—bring me to Mort Street."

10
Nikai

Nikai dangled his long legs from one of the swings in the Garden of Tongues. It had become a habit of his to come here to see the stars the way Four used to. But tonight was special.

It was the same night Four had vanished exactly eighteen years ago.

Ever since his King's disappearance, Nikai's life as a Reaper had been in disarray: soul collections went poorly, he was stuck in bureaucratic perdition writing reports about the increasing number of Blighted-souls-turned-Revenants, *and* he had a new boss to report to.

The Tenth King had been tasked with overseeing the Fourth Court while the search for Four continued. Ten was a nasty piece of work. He had an uncouth appetite for torture and relished any challenge in which he had the upper hand. It pained Nikai to bow to his rule, but all of that was the least of Nikai's worries.

Hell itself was falling apart.

It had started with the little things—errors in death cards, system glitches that sent souls to the wrong Courts—small annoyances that one could take in stride. But soon, the edges of the underworld began to fade. Bits of landscape turned gray and colorless, crumbling away. Buildings and other infrastructure followed, succumbing to the ravenous dark. Souls were not spared either: they, too, disappeared into the Nothing.

Except it wasn't *nothing* that they became.

Nikai would know. After all, he'd been trapped in the Nothing once.

Dread crawled up his spine, a familiar specter that appeared whenever he thought of it. The Nothing was a difficult thing to describe. You had to see it, be *inside* it, feel the sheer terror of the place where all hope was sucked out of you.

Once confined to the limbo space between the human realm and the

Tenth Court, the Nothing was now growing, like a hungry, insatiable beast. No one could stop its steady creep. The cause was simple: the power of all ten Kings was needed to keep the balance between the spirit and human realms, and the Nothing in its original confines, but the underworld was short one King.

Four.

It's not your fault.

Words Nikai had repeated to himself for eighteen years. Words he was repeating to himself now as he clutched the cold chains of the swing. Just like before, those words did nothing to assuage his guilt.

After Four's disappearance, the other nine Kings had come together to search for their missing brother, taking turns traveling to the far-flung corners of their realm, where no Reaper would survive and no soul could exist.

But no trace of Four was ever found.

All the Kings knew was that One had unwittingly enabled Four's disappearance by lending him an artifact in the form of a willow branch, and Four had used its power. For that momentary lapse in judgment, One was confined to their palace, never to step out of their throne room. It wasn't fair, Nikai thought. He'd been witness to the incident, and he knew One had no idea that Four had planned to steal the willow branch to use it. But someone had to bear the blame, and the burden fell on the First King.

The only other clue was a cryptic message Four had left with the Lady of the Pavilion, an immortal who tended to Wangyi Lake.

Those who seek me shall never see me.

No one knew why Four had left the message with her, nor what it truly meant. It was assumed to be a farewell taunt, and that Four had found a way to hide himself somewhere in the vast and mysterious regions of the underworld that did not appear on any map.

Nikai had been interrogated too. But to his shame, he was of little help. As days turned into years and the Fourth King did not return, doubt mushroomed in Nikai's mind. Why did Four give up his throne? Perhaps

Nikai didn't understand his friend at all, or perhaps, they'd never really been friends. Still, Nikai refused to believe his King was gone forever.

Sighing deeply, Nikai wiped his eyes with his handkerchief.

Seconds later, the clouds parted and the stars emerged.

Nikai sat on the swing, taking in the conjunction of the realms. He wondered how many humans were looking up right now, marveling at the same night sky as he was in the underworld.

Nikai remembered a time when he and Four were sitting right on these same swings. Nikai had been thinking about how humans liked to wish upon stars, as if the celestial bodies of hot gases had the power to change fate.

What would you wish for? he'd asked Four.

To see the stars forever, Four said, a childlike sense of awe blossoming on his face. *How about you?*

Nikai had shrugged, making up something trite. He didn't like hiding things from his friend, but some wishes were dangerous.

"To see the stars forever," Nikai said out loud to himself now. What had Four meant? How could one see the stars forever? It was certainly impossible in the underworld, apart from these few precious minutes once a month. But in the human realm, one could see the stars every night, he supposed.

Nikai kicked his legs in the air, urging the swing higher. A stray thought crept into his head. Did *he* ever gaze at the stars when he was human? Had he *been* the sort of human who would gaze at the stars?

An unexplained longing crept into Nikai's chest, a desire too treacherous to consider. When he was granted the chance to leave the Nothing, he'd made a choice to forget everything about his mortal life or why he'd been sent there in the first place. He'd drunk the tea. He'd let go of his past life forever. It was pointless to think or feel too much. His mortal memories would never return.

Hell was his home now.

Time to get back to work. Nikai pushed himself off the swing and straightened his suit.

As he made his way nimbly down the hill, something made him pause. He glanced back up at the sky.

The clouds were curtaining, hiding the stars once again. But a strange light peeked through. It grew bright, brighter, its edges a blurred green. It was hurtling eastward across the night sky.

The First King's voice rang in Nikai's head, *Did you see the green light heading east? The spirit trail of a dying star has appeared, which means an anomaly has occurred in the human realm.*

Nikai was afraid to breathe. Something was happening in the human realm at this very moment. He kept his head and made a note of the coordinates of the dying star's spirit trail, then sped down the hill as if a pack of wolves were nipping at his heels.

Fate was intervening, the same way it did just before Four had vanished. And Nikai was determined to witness it once again.

11
Yiran

Yiran kicked at the front door of the weird-looking shophouse. Scattered thoughts flew through his mind. Did he just kill a Revenant? Did he have *magic* now? No. It couldn't be. This couldn't be happening—but the girl in his arms was proof that something did happen. An image of her surfaced in his mind: lying in the passenger seat of his car, blood fanned out on cream-colored leather like vicious angel wings.

The car. There was so much blood on the leather seats. What was he going to tell his grandfather? Maybe he could pay someone to clean it first or—

He swore loudly. If his arms were not full of bleeding girl, he'd slap himself. Why was he thinking about a freaking car when the girl was slumped against him, silent and still? *Is she dead?* asked his good-for-nothing brain. He shushed it and kicked the front door of the shophouse again.

"Open up!"

Light leaked from the window shutters. Yiran heard an eclectic selection of swear words as someone fumbled with the doorknob.

"You better have a good reason for waking me up. I was having the funniest dream about talking pandas."

The voice was low and scratchy with sleep, and it belonged to someone much younger than Yiran had expected.

Haloed in the light, a shirtless boy slouched against the doorframe. One of his eyes was shut, the other barely opened and startlingly light-colored. There was a tattoo on his chest above his heart: two butterflies hovering together, as if in a dance.

Stifling a yawn, the boy raked the dark mess of hair off his face and peered out, finally seeing what or *who* was in Yiran's arms. Something fragile sparked like lightning across the boy's face, and like lightning, it vanished quickly, chased by a thunderous rage.

He lunged wildly. *"What did you do to her?"*

Moving back, Yiran said through his teeth, "It wasn't me—it was a Revenant."

Anguish ripped from the boy's throat. "Give her to me."

Yiran hesitated. The boy had a look in his eyes, a desperate kind of helplessness that sought a violent release. Yiran wasn't sure if he could trust this beautiful, untamed creature. But the girl had said this boy was the only one who could help.

"No, we shouldn't move her too much. She lost a lot of blood." Yiran pushed past the doorway, bumping a shoulder meaningfully against the boy's chest.

Inside, he looked for a place to lay the girl down. The shophouse wasn't what he expected. It didn't look like a retail space; it looked like someone's home. If that someone was partial to sandalwood and lemongrass incense, left stacks of funeral paraphernalia on their bookshelves, and indulged in half-finished paintings of people with distorted faces caught either in the throes of ecstasy or extreme fear.

Yiran blinked away from a disturbing painting of a woman crawling out of a crab, her limbs bleeding with what looked like fresh red paint.

The boy with the pale blue eyes motioned at a chaise. Carefully, Yiran lowered the girl onto it.

Her eyes fluttered open and focused on the boy, who had knelt beside her. "Zizi?"

"Don't be afraid. I'm here," said the boy named Zizi. He brushed the girl's bangs aside, tucking the longer strands behind her ear.

The girl struggled to breathe. "Not afraid . . . you fool."

The gurgling sound from her throat turned Yiran's stomach. He whispered to Zizi, "Is she going to be all right? She's not going to . . . you know . . ."

"I can hear you, *fool.*" The girl closed her eyes and coughed. Blood trickled down her chin. "Not going to die yet. Sorry to . . . d-disappoint."

Zizi shot Yiran a scathing look. Then he leaned over the girl like he was about to put his arms around her, but all he did was whisper something in her ear. There was a pause before she nodded.

"Look away," he said to Yiran.

"What?"

Zizi narrowed his eyes. "I said, look away."

Too exhausted to argue, Yiran faced the wall, trying his best not to stare at a portrait of a man with dark hair and blue eyes dressed in something that looked suspiciously like a garbage bag. Maybe it was a portrait of Zizi's future self. Maybe it was a commentary on the state of the environment.

Behind him, fabric ripped, and the girl hissed in pain. Gradually, the air crackled like the beginning of a storm and the room grew hot.

Yiran tugged at his collar. His adrenaline from earlier was gone, and he was drained and lightheaded. He wiped the sweat from his forehead only to realize he was burning up. There was a new sensation crawling over him, like something was *moving* in his veins. It was the same feeling he had moments after the girl had cast her spell.

Magic, whispered his fast-beating heart.

His soul shivered.

This was magic. What he'd just witnessed was magic. And now, some form of it was inside him too. It was the *thing* in his veins, brought to life by the spell the girl had cast.

It was the strangest feeling.

To his grandfather, Yiran was a constant reminder of the shame that someone carrying the Song family name could be born without the ability to do magic. It hurt. Yiran never showed it, not even to Ash. He played it off like he was relieved he didn't have to train at the Academy and was happy to waste his days away doing nothing.

Truth was, he yearned.

But he had always been the other. A sad, pathetic intruder looking into a world where he wasn't allowed to exist. A boy who fell in love with a mansion and all its locked doors.

Tonight, one door unbolted. All he needed to do was to push it and walk through. But he was afraid he would find himself still unworthy.

The girl's scowling face appeared in his mind. What was her name? *Rui.* It was a pretty name. The owner of the name was pretty in a way that reminded him of a wildflower bloom in the desert. His chance meeting with her had left him with the impression that she had a sizable chip on her shoulder and believed shouting was an effective way to communicate. Yiran wanted very much for her to survive her injuries.

Impulsively, he turned around.

Zizi was kneeling with his hands over Rui, blocking her from Yiran's line of vision. A mysterious glow radiated from the boy, illuminating him. Lines of black ink, sharp like a knife's edge, ran over pale skin from his scapula down toward his narrow waist, ending at the small of his back. Swooping and looping, the dark curves were at once delicate and cruel.

Feathers.

Yiran was reminded of the bloody imprint Rui left on his car seat. He stared, fascinated. There was something so real about the tattoo that he wouldn't be surprised if Zizi suddenly sprouted real wings, like a sullied angel cast down to earth.

Zizi shifted, and Yiran glimpsed his face. His eyes. They were not pale blue like before, but eerie black pools of nothing. A shiver skittered across Yiran's skin.

Rui made a small sound. The tension in her body released, and her head tipped back onto the armrest. Color returned to her face, and her breathing sounded less labored.

Whatever Zizi did to save her, it was nothing short of miraculous. Was he a healer? Yiran had heard of healers. The term made them sound like people who specialized in herbs and exotic tea, but he knew that some of them were Exorcists too. Yiran didn't think an Exorcist would be living in a place like this, which could only mean that Zizi was from the underground magic community.

The glow from Zizi faded, and the temperature in the room dropped back to normal. Slowly, that precious new thing in Yiran's veins dissipated and he was left with a hollowness he'd never felt before. He heaved a lungful of air, trying to fill himself up. He didn't want to lose that feeling of being complete. Of being *enough*.

Zizi got up, palms rust red, the bare skin on his torso blood-dappled like an avant-garde painting, looking as if he might have tumbled into the world exactly this way: fully formed, bloody and bare, eyes naked like a winter's lake.

"I've done all I can," he said quietly. His eyes were blue again. Deep emotion lingered in them, and Yiran knew immediately that this boy would go to the ends of the earth for the injured girl. "I thought we agreed you would look away."

Yiran tilted his head toward Rui and saw why Zizi was making such a fuss. He averted his gaze as Zizi threw a large silk shawl over her. Scrounging around, Zizi pulled out another slinky piece of fabric from between cushions. He put the pajama top on and buttoned it up like it was the normal thing to do in a situation like this. Like he left pieces of clothing all over the house so he could dress and undress at varying intervals.

He tucked a cigarette behind his ear with care and gestured at Yiran as if he was beckoning a puppy. "Come along."

With some uncertainty and much irritation, Yiran followed. The kitchen was a menagerie of coffee beans stored in an assortment of mismatched jars and decorated with instruments that looked like they could be used to conjure up a frothy cup of latte with some light torture on the side.

"Sit."

Yiran didn't appreciate the condescension in the other boy's tone, but he was tired. He got onto the barstool and propped his elbows onto the counter.

Zizi rinsed his bloody hands under the tap and puttered around. He threw a handful of coffee beans into a mortar and pounded them furiously with a pestle. Yiran wasn't versed in the intricacies of barista work, but he couldn't fathom why Zizi wasn't using the electric grinder instead.

Zizi seemed to sense Yiran's question. "Helps me think," he said, giving the beans a particularly hard smash.

"Is she going to be all right?" Yiran said.

Zizi put his pestle down, staying silent for a few seconds.

"She will be," he finally replied, a catch in his voice. "Her spiritual energy is at the bare minimum, but that's not quite it. It's like she turned into a *normie*, which doesn't make sense at all. If a Revenant drank that much from her, she would be dead, she wouldn't be like this. And if the Revenant didn't drink that much, Rui would have recovered some of her spiritual energy by now and still be able to do magic. But . . ." Zizi shook his head. "I found new signs of magical trauma in her spirit core. What happened? Did she cast a spell on herself?"

"I'm not entirely sure. . . ." Yiran pulled out one of the swords he'd retrieved earlier from Rui's sword bag. He tried to remember that buzzy feeling. Tried to reach the magic that was supposedly in him now.

He didn't feel a thing.

The gnarly hand of desperation gripped his throat, tight enough to choke. *Did you really think it was going to work? Did you really think you could do magic? You are nobody. You are nothing.* He wanted to stomp the voice in his head out. He wanted to strangle whoever it belonged to.

But he was afraid the voice was his own.

Zizi tapped the counter impatiently. "You were saying?"

Ignoring him, Yiran thought of Rui. She'd been so certain when she taught him how to use her weapon, so certain that he could do it.

Song Yiran—I believe in you.

It was a cringeworthy thing to say. He didn't even know if she'd meant it. But somehow, it worked.

He centered himself, trying to grasp the feeling he had when he fought the Revenant. His body had seemed to know what to do and how to do it before his mind did. *Instinct.* Like that of an animal or anything in the natural world. Pure and unbridled, before the mind could intercept it with doubt.

A soft crimson light shivered from the blade. It was neither solid nor deadly, more like a dribbling afterthought. But it was enough to silence the taunting voice in Yiran's head. The magic he had displayed wasn't impressive. But it was something. Big things grew from somethings.

Zizi knocked the sword out of Yiran's hand, catching it before it fell to the floor. He set the sword aside on the counter with careful reverence.

"How are you able to use Rui's spiritual weapon?" he demanded.

Yiran rubbed his arm. "What exactly is a spiritual weapon?" He knew some Exorcists carried swords, but he'd never seen Ash with one, and it wasn't until tonight that he saw one in action.

"Anyone with magic can use common weapons. But spiritual weapons are highly specialized conduits that you can infuse with your own qi," Zizi said, still looking perplexed. "Your spiritual weapon feels right in your hands, like it's a part of you. It's normally a bladed weapon forged from the purest steel, but sometimes it's something else altogether. The form reflects the practitioner's character and skill, and once a weapon has been claimed, it's bound to the individual. No one else can use it—unless . . ."

He grabbed Yiran's wrist, turned Yiran's palm face up, and placed his own hand over it. Yiran sat still as a statue. The peaks and valleys of the other boy's palm were a treasure map he couldn't read. But it seemed like Zizi found an answer in his.

"Gods." Zizi dropped his hand and backed away.

"What's wrong?"

"If Rui cast the spell I think she did on herself . . ." Zizi slammed a fist onto the counter. "This is bad. Your qi levels are through the roof—did she touch you when she cast that spell? Did she transfer her spiritual energy to you?" Zizi clutched his head. "Dammit. She's going to be so mad at me."

Yiran hid his relief. For a moment he'd thought Zizi would tell him it was all a farce and that what he had done with Rui's weapon wasn't magic. But it was real. He *did* have magic.

"I was able to kill the Revenant and save our lives because of the spell she cast," he said. "Why would Rui be mad?"

"If her spiritual energy hasn't reverted to her by now, it might mean the transfer is somehow permanent. I'm not sure if I know how to fix it." Zizi cursed again.

Of course. Rui would want her magic back. Who wouldn't? Except Yiran wasn't sure if he wanted to give it back. If he had magic, maybe he wouldn't be sent away. Maybe he'd never have to see the disappointment in his grandfather's eyes again. No one needed to know the source of his newfound magic.

Would Rui wake up with that haunting emptiness Yiran felt earlier? He pushed a pang of sympathy away. It didn't matter. She wasn't his business, and he didn't intend to make her so. The world he longed for was finally within his grasp. The magic swimming in his veins, the girl lying half-dead in the other room, this boy with extraordinary eyes—they were the key to holding on to it.

But first, he needed to cover up tonight's mess. He didn't know much about the Exorcist Guild, but he did know it didn't take kindly to magic practitioners who flouted the law. He remembered Rui's reaction when he'd said he wanted to take her to his grandfather and the Guild.

"Rui's an Exorcist, isn't she? She could go to the Guild for help. Maybe they'll know what to do," Yiran suggested in a helpful manner.

"Rui isn't one of *them*," Zizi corrected, looking irked. "She only trains at Xingshan Academy."

"That's just semantics. She's going to be an Exorcist."

"I don't want the Guild involved in this." Zizi's tone was as sharp as the line of his jaw. "I don't trust them, and they don't like people like me."

Yiran hid a smile. As he suspected, Zizi was part of the underground magic community. The spell had to be his, which meant he couldn't tell anyone about what had happened because he'd get into trouble. And if the spiritual energy transfer was somehow permanent and could not be reversed . . . *finders keepers.*

As if catching on to what Yiran was thinking, Zizi sized him up. "You're Song Wei's other grandson, aren't you?"

Yiran winced, a familiar twitch in his gut. He was always Song Wei's grandson. Always Ash's little brother. Never his own person.

"How did you know?"

"You look like a Song, and I've heard about an anomaly in the family. You may possess high levels of qi now, but the spirit core you were born with seems sadly ordinary, so I figured you're the other grandson."

An anomaly. That was what he was. Yiran smiled, implying he couldn't care less about what Zizi said. "I'm well aware of my spirit core and its limitations."

Zizi clucked his tongue. "Are you? See, that's what I'm not getting. How are you holding on to so much spiritual energy? A person must be born with a naturally strong spirit core to do that, and they'd have to cultivate it in order to do magic. But despite being a weak ass, you're somehow pulling it off." He paused, gaze sharpening on Yiran. "I guess my real question is, why didn't you die during the transfer?"

Why indeed. When Yiran was younger, he found articles in the dodgier sites on the internet that shared stories of people with mediocre cores trying to increase their qi. They always failed. You could strengthen your core through training, make it more resilient, but you couldn't expand its capacity. Besides, his grandfather's experiments had made it clear that Yiran couldn't change *what* he was.

Yiran shrugged. "Apologies for my strong will to survive. It's a product of my upbringing."

"Have you ever felt unexplainable energies around you?" Zizi said, twirling his cigarette.

"No."

"Are you sure?"

"Like you said, I'm ordinary. I was born without the ability to practice magic. I can't sense anything."

"Why do I find that hard to believe?"

"Would you like me to swear it on my father's grave?" Yiran snapped.

An odd look crossed Zizi's face as he stuck his cigarette back behind his ear. "Sorry about your dad."

The words were an unexpected punch to the gut, painful because of how gently and kindly Zizi had said them. For one, there was nothing about Zizi that suggested he was gentle or kind. Yiran could only assume he'd meant to patronize. For another, everyone knew of Song Liming and how he'd gotten himself killed in typical Song fashion—heroically.

Yiran had never asked Ash anything about their father. It was bad enough Yiran never knew the man, but knowing him through the lens of someone whose life he'd been part of since birth would be impossible to stomach.

Zizi resumed his battering of coffee beans. A few broken bits jumped out of the bowl, arranging themselves haphazardly on the counter. Yiran picked up a piece, turning it around with his fingers.

"You know what?" Zizi said in between his bashing. "Never mind. I don't care about you. I'll just have to figure out a way to fix this so Rui won't hate me."

The jagged edge of the coffee bean dug into Yiran's fingertips. "I thought you didn't know how to reverse the spell?"

Zizi grinned. "Nothing is impossible. And *I* am very gifted."

Yiran didn't think anyone could look so shameless. "The spell Rui used—it's one of yours, isn't it? That's why she said she couldn't go to the hospital and that's why you don't want the Guild involved. You broke some magical rule."

"Rules are for cowards who have no vision," Zizi replied tartly.

Ordinarily, Yiran would agree. But this was a matter of family pride.

His grandfather might not think so, but Yiran was still a Song. Or at least, he was trying to be one. The Guild was doing their best to ensure that society didn't run amok with people who used magic to harm others. Rui had dragged him into her spell without asking for consent. Sure, she had a good reason to: it was their only chance to stay alive. But it didn't change the fact that what she did was wrong. A Xingshan Academy cadet in cahoots with a mage . . .

He flicked the coffee bean. "I assume the both of you want to keep tonight a secret?"

Neither of them missed the subtle threat in Yiran's question.

The blue in Zizi's eyes chilled. He came around the counter, lips twisting into a nasty grin. "I get the feeling we're not the only ones who want to keep this quiet, Song er shaoye."

His use of the honorific grated on Yiran's nerves. "Says the bloody wizard who sold a girl a dangerous and illegal spell he can't undo."

"I am a *mage*," Zizi sniffed. "I didn't sell the spell to her, and she wasn't supposed to cast it on herself."

"She didn't have much of a choice. She was injured, and the Revenant was going to kill us."

"And for some reason she chose you, of all people, as her savior? Why were you even there?"

Yiran forced himself to look the other boy in the eye. "I had a fight with my grandfather. I got angry and thought I could capture a Revenant alive."

Zizi laughed. "That may be the stupidest thing I've ever heard in my life."

Yiran's fists wanted to yell hello to the other boy's face, but he kept them by his side.

Zizi didn't seem to notice the change in Yiran's expression. Or maybe he didn't care. He went on, not bothering to soften his scorn. "Guess it must be hard, growing up as a Song without magic, especially with your father and that slimy protégé brother of yours. It's not surprising you have granddaddy issues."

Something in Zizi's words crossed the line. It wasn't because he was wrong.

The first punch grazed Zizi's hair instead of his nose as he ducked. The second punch was too slow and missed entirely.

Zizi shifted. In an instant, Yiran found himself on the floor, coughing from a blow to his stomach.

Zizi shook his hair off his face. "Stay down. I don't want to hurt you."

Yiran scoffed. "You got lucky."

Quick swipe at the legs, and Zizi stumbled forward. This time, Yiran's punch caught him on the cheekbone. Before Yiran could bask in satisfaction, Zizi shoved him against the counter. The edge of the island dug painfully into his spine, but he scuffled for a chance to get another jab in.

"Stop," Zizi hissed, gripping Yiran's arms.

Yiran found himself pinned down on the counter, his back arched as he tried to throw the other boy off. But Zizi was stronger than he looked, Yiran gave him that.

Zizi's shirt hung loose, tickling Yiran's neck as he leaned in. "I get one hit to your face because you tried to ruin my prettier one, and then we're square and this ends."

Out of the corner of his eye, Yiran caught a metallic flash. His fingers found what he was looking for. Warmth pulsated through him, a flurry of energy spreading to his fingers.

He sneered. "I don't like your terms, *wizard*."

He shoved Zizi off. Exhaling, he started to run a hand down the blade of Rui's sword.

"Stop! You can't use it!" Zizi shouted.

"Says who?" Yiran grinned as the blade began to glow.

"You could die."

Yiran wavered, his hand stopping mid-blade.

Zizi looked dead serious. "You're untrained and your spirit core is bloated with qi. It's unstable. Any time you try to use magic, you're straining it, forcing it to do something it's not meant to do. If your core breaks, you die."

"This isn't something to joke—"

"Do I look like I'm joking? Put. The. Sword. Down."

Heat was flaring inside of Yiran. His surroundings seemed to throb against him. What if Zizi was telling the truth? Was magic worth the price of his life? Fear flooded his brain. He didn't know the answer. Wasn't prepared to find out.

Shakily, he placed Rui's sword back on the counter and shallowed his breath. The heat inside him began to cool.

Zizi pinched the bridge of his nose. "Thank gods. Please don't do anything so stupid again," he said.

Relaxing, he winked at Yiran—and threw a punch.

12
Rui

Something incredibly soft was nuzzling her cheek. The warm weight on her chest was . . . *purring*?

Rui cracked one eye open. A black paw with pink toe beans was zooming in. She closed her eye with a sigh. But Mao continued to tap on her nose, until finally, Rui gave up on sleep.

She nudged the cat off and tried to sit up, yelping as pain pierced her shoulder and ribs. The pajama top she had on was two sizes too big and printed with tiny colorful cupcakes—totally not her style. Hazy memories seeped into her mind: the Night Market, the Revenant, Song Yiran's desperate voice speaking to her as he ran all the red lights racing to Mort Street . . . She'd slipped into darkness, only to be greeted by pale blue eyes when she regained consciousness.

Heat crept up her neck when she remembered Zizi asking for permission to remove her sweater so he could tend to her wounds. There'd been no time for modesty. Better to survive and live with the mortification of him seeing her in a bra than die on his ridiculous chaise. At least it was the nice lacy bra Ada had given her for her birthday.

Gingerly, Rui unraveled the bandages around her ribs. A new scar had formed on her side. Pink and tender, it looked like it was weeks old instead of a few hours young. Her light brown skin was pallid, and she could see the faint tracing of green and blue veins. Teeth chattering, she rubbed the unpleasant gooseflesh on her arms and wrapped the blanket tightly around herself. A faint scent of strawberries and mint wafted from the sheets. It was a scent that lingered around Zizi.

Was this *his* room?

A shiver went down her spine, though this time it wasn't from the cold. She came to the shophouse often enough, but she'd never been up on the second floor, let alone Zizi's bedroom.

The walls had paintings of broken clocks against surreal landscapes with deserts and azure skies. Old film posters with yellowing edges hung next to them, and colorful geometric ornaments and other bric-a-brac lined whatever horizontal space in the room that wasn't the floor. Clothes covered the length of the love seat by the window, and books lay carelessly everywhere, like Zizi had been reading a dozen different ones at the same time. Rui spied some titles on philosophy, history, and astrophysics, and one odd-looking book that had a plain white jacket and red lettering on its spine—*The Eleven* by J. Hesina.

The clutter felt deliberate. Like it was a show for someone else.

Rui sank back into Zizi's bed. Her heartbeat elevated. *It's just a bed*, she chided herself. A mattress, a thing with coils and foam, nothing more. It wasn't even a comfortable one. She looked up with a sigh. The ceiling was painted like a map of the night sky, a rich indigo with thin white lines joining white dots into varying shapes. If she were an astrologer, she'd know the constellations, but stars never held her interest. They were too dangerous, like dreams that could cut you if you tried too hard to touch them. How often did Zizi lie here, pondering his false heaven?

Something rattled against the nightstand.

There were seventeen missed calls, seven voice messages, and twenty-four unread texts on her phone. They were all from Ada.

ARE YOU ALIVE?!?! shouted the last text.

The light shining through the window shutters told her it was mid-morning. She'd been absent from campus the entire night. Ada had to be out of her mind with worry. But a Zizi did not exist in Ada's world, and neither did a Rui with ties to the underground magic community. Rui wanted to keep it that way. How could she tell Ada about being attacked by the strange Revenant from last night without explaining who Zizi was and the work she did for him?

Rui had to lie again. There was no other way around it. That was the problem with keeping secrets. Sometimes, you had to tell a lie. To cover that up, you told another lie, and then another and another, until the lies became the secret itself.

Rui placed her phone back on the nightstand next to her sword bag. As her mind came up with various excuses to hide the truth, she started to feel out of sorts. It wasn't her injuries; those were physical, cuts and tears that would heal.

Something else had changed. There was a wrongness *inside* her.

She closed her eyes, searching for that place of quiet where her magic resided. Her fingers twitched. Her breathing grew strained.

There was nothing. Just the beat of her heart.

The spell she'd cast was supposed to be temporary, and the transfer of spiritual energy would last minutes. Why did her qi feel so out of flux now? Why did she feel so . . . hollow? Was it because the spell was meant for Revenants, and not humans?

Zizi. He would know what to do. He could reverse the spell. It was simple, wasn't it? Child's play for someone like him. Everything was going to be fine. Everything *had* to be fine. As if her thoughts had summoned him, there was a soft knock on the bedroom door.

"Rui?"

"Yeah?"

Zizi poked his head in. He had twisted his bangs back, securing them on top of his head with a metal hair clip. Rui wanted to remove it, let his hair spill over his eyes. She lingered a moment too long. Suddenly, he was looking at her looking at him.

Rui blinked away and pretended to yawn.

"You're awake," he said, stating the obvious.

"Mmmff," she agreed from inside her blanket fort. "You can come in."

Zizi flip-flopped into the room with a big mug of coffee in one hand. He placed the mug on the nightstand and sat on the side of the bed. Rui wished she had brushed her teeth or at least rinsed her mouth. There was a bruise blooming on his left cheekbone.

"What happened to your face?"

"Nothing."

Rui cleared her parched throat. "Will the spell wear off soon?"

Zizi's face did a complicated thing. He was angry and upset and afraid all at once. "Don't freak out, but your core is damaged. There're signs of deep magical trauma. Layers of trauma, not just from last night, but from before."

He meant the night her mother was murdered. She'd never found out how she managed to scare the Revenant away.

"So it'll take a while for me to heal, but can't you reverse the spell first?" If she couldn't train, it would mean postponing her retake of the simulation test.

Zizi mumbled, "I'll explain everything downstairs."

"Okay." Rui shivered. "I'm freezing. Is this normal?"

The taut line of Zizi's mouth didn't match the softness in his eyes. "Why don't you take a hot shower before you go down? Bathroom's that way. Towels are inside, and your sweater too—I couldn't figure out how to mend it, but at least I got the stains off with some scrubbing."

"You washed my sweater? By hand?" Even if he meant nothing by it—and Rui was certain it meant nothing—the act of him taking care of her clothes felt oddly intimate.

"I figured you'd need it when you woke. It was gross, all that blood and dirt. Of course, you're more than welcome to keep the lovely top I chose for you."

"Ha ha. Thanks."

Zizi made a face. "Your boyfriend's still here, by the way."

Rui gave the blanket an indignant kick. "Song Yiran is not my boyfriend."

"Why not? He's cute and he's filthy rich." There was a challenge in Zizi's tone. But Rui couldn't figure out what the challenge was or what it meant.

"He's not that cute."

Zizi seemed pleased with her answer. "Did you know he has violent tendencies?"

"He's just a coddled rich kid. He's soft, like mochi."

Zizi scrunched his nose. "Tasteless. Sticks to your teeth."

Despite herself, Rui laughed. "I met him for the first time last night. I don't even know him. Anyway," she sighed, "I'm taking a break from dating boys, girls, and anyone in between. I don't have time for a relationship."

Zizi gave her a peculiar look. It was brief, but for some reason it made her remember that he was also a boy and, thus, on her do-not-date list.

She pulled the blanket back around her. "Why don't you go downstairs? I'll be there soon."

He nodded and left the room.

Rui picked up the cup of coffee, downing half of it in one gulp. Hot liquid scalded her tongue, but it was nothing compared to the revolting taste in her mouth. She tried not to gag. It wasn't coffee; it was some medicinal concoction that tasted like dirty roots and mud.

"Why didn't he warn me?" she groaned, dragging herself to the bathroom.

The rush of water soothed her body, and gradually, the pain eased. But when she finally got out, the chill in her bones remained. Her sweater was still damp, so she put on the fluffy white bathrobe instead. A tiny, pasty-faced human with bedraggled hair stared back in the mirror. She pinched her cheeks, trying to get some color back into them.

Feeling utterly sorry for herself, Rui shuffled to the top of the stairs. She could see Yiran curled up on the floor next to a bookshelf. His face was covered by his leather jacket, and his hoodie had patches of dried blood. His clothes must've gotten stained when he carried her to his two-door coupe and sped her here. Typical rich boy. It wasn't surprising he had a license and his own car. A nice one, too. She hoped she'd bled all over his expensive leather seats.

In the kitchen, Zizi was smashing coffee beans with a pestle, the sleeve of his bat-winged cardigan flapping as his arm went up and down.

A groan came from under the leather jacket. "Stop it, I'm trying to sleep."

Zizi continued to bang away.

Yiran scrambled up, eyes bloodshot, hands itching for a fight. He spun around, looking for something to grab, finally settling on a stash of paper. He threw it in the air.

The floor was littered with hell money. The face of a bearded old man wearing a grand black hat with wingtips glared up at Rui from each rectangular piece—the mythical King of Hell.

She sighed. Yiran sure had a knack for disrespecting the dead.

Zizi glowered. "You're going to pick up every single one of those and stack them back properly on my shelves."

Yiran threw his jacket across the room. It landed with a satisfying splat. "Make me."

Zizi raised his pestle in a throwing motion.

Yiran answered by rolling up his sleeves.

Sighing for the innumerable time, Rui lumbered down the stairs to save the fools from themselves.

"Glad you're getting to know each other on such an intimate level," she said.

They turned at the sound of her voice.

Zizi laid his pestle down and adjusted his cardigan.

Yiran had the decency to look a little guilty. He hooked his thumbs into his pockets. "Did we wake you, Darcy—uh, *Rui*? How are you feeling?"

There was a cut on his lip, the abrasion spreading to the side of his mouth. Rui suddenly had an idea of how Zizi got that bruise on his cheekbone.

"I feel like crap," she replied. Then, grudgingly, "Thanks for bringing me here last night."

Yiran rubbed the back of his neck. "Yeah, well—"

"You didn't tell Ash or your grandfather about this, did you?" she cut in. She didn't want him to think she was excessively grateful or anything. He was just a stranger who was holding on to something of hers.

Yiran shook his head.

He looked so miserable that Rui almost felt sorry for him. He was probably in trouble with his grandfather. The Head of the Exorcist Guild wouldn't be pleased that his grandson had gone to the Night Market. But that was Yiran's problem. Not hers. He'd made a choice to be there. She wasn't going to be a scapegoat for some rich boy's mistakes.

She steadied herself against the counter. Her limbs felt heavy, and she longed for a hot drink to warm her body. But she didn't want Zizi to worry, and she couldn't let Yiran think her weak. Not when she needed him to do what she wanted. She straightened. Rest and sleep could come later.

"We need to talk about what happened last night," she said.

Everyone in the room knew her statement translated to *We should all agree to tell the same story to anyone who asks.*

She stared resolutely at Yiran, continuing, "I was in Tangren Quarter because I didn't see the text from the Academy about the canceled patrol. On my way back to campus, I ran into a Revenant. You were at the wrong place at the wrong time. I killed the Revenant and saved you." She pointed a finger at Zizi. "*You* will reverse the spell and transfer my spiritual energy back right now. Everything falls back into place. End of story. No one outside this room needs to know what actually happened."

"Did the Revenant really have tentacles?" Zizi said.

"Why do you care?"

"Professional curiosity."

"They grew from its back, and all its spiritual energy was concentrated there. After it was killed, it didn't vaporize into smoke. There was a—a kind of body. It became like stone or a statue, and then it crumbled into dust."

"That's weird."

"But it didn't look human. I don't think it was a Hybrid." Rui bit back her disappointment.

There was a snort from Yiran's direction. "*Hybrid?* Come on, they don't exist."

Rui ignored him. She didn't owe anyone her past or her pain, especially not Song Yiran. She leaned close to Zizi, asking in a low voice, "Will you speak to your friends about this?" She couldn't help feeling like a hypocrite. She'd asked many favors of him through the years because of his connections, and yet she'd made a choice to stand with the Exorcist Guild.

Zizi nodded. "Why don't you take a seat? I'll make you a hot drink." He must've noticed how pale she was, how she was shivering under the enormous bathrobe.

Rui gave him a small smile and curled up on the old leather armchair in a corner of the parlor by the window, a place in the shophouse she'd come to think of as her special spot. Sunlight streamed in, and she held her hands up to warm them.

Yiran yawned. "You know, I could use some coffee."

"There's a joint two blocks south," Zizi told him. "Heard their cappuccinos taste like dirty dishwater. Why don't you give that a go?"

"I'm already here, and you're making *her* a drink."

"Because it's *her*." Zizi gestured at the front door. "No one's stopping you from leaving."

"You're so immature."

"You accused me of being a witch," Zizi said, looking gravely insulted.

"Wizard," Yiran corrected. "Witch, sorcerer, mage—what's the difference anyway?"

"Look, clowns," said Rui, drawing on her shallow well of patience. "I think we have more important things to worry about than terminology. Zizi, make him a cup." After a beat, she added, "Please."

"Maybe he shouldn't be drinking coffee. We don't know if it'll affect him negatively because of what happened."

"What does coffee have to do with anything? If you don't want to make me one, I'll do it myself." Yiran reached for the coffee machine, but Zizi smacked his hand away.

"It's a stimulant, more so for magic practitioners than normies. With all that energy circulating inside you now, you might go off the rails. The crash will be terrible and dangerous."

"You're kidding me," Yiran said. "My brother drinks coffee all the time."

"That's because he's Ash Song," said Rui. Yiran seemed to accept that reasoning, which made her wonder what Ash was like as a sibling. "So, about the other thing, we're in agreement with my story, yes?"

Yiran shrugged. He was rubbing his fingertips together. Rui stared at the small white scars on them, suddenly remembering how they'd turned luminescent the night before after the spell hit, like magic was leaking out of his fingers themselves. Rui wasn't sure what that meant, and she wondered how he'd gotten those scars.

Zizi's voice interrupted her thoughts. "There's one other thing we should discuss. With all that spiritual energy, Mochi's spirit core should've burned out, but it didn't. Look at him, he's perfectly fine." Zizi seemed a little disappointed.

"Maybe I'm special," Yiran said, sarcastic. "It was your spell. Shouldn't you know what went wrong?"

"Magic is complex."

"Is that wizard speak for *Oops, I made a mistake but I'm too pigheaded to admit it*?"

Zizi ignored him and walked over to hand a cup of hot chocolate to Rui. She accepted it gratefully, taking a few comforting sips.

"You should lay low until we find a way to fix this," she said to Yiran.

"Or I could kill some Revenants."

"You're joking."

"No. I'm not." There was steel in Yiran's eyes.

"Why do you want to kill Revenants?"

"Why do *you* want to kill Revenants?"

"Because—" Rui stopped. She didn't owe him any explanation. Didn't owe him anything. The magic *belonged* to her. And she needed it back. She whipped to Zizi in frustration. "Reverse the spell right now."

Zizi didn't say a word. Didn't even turn to look at her. Instead, he tossed some coffee beans into the grinder and switched it on. The obnoxious clacking and whirring of the machine filled the kitchen.

Yiran paced, clenching and unclenching his fists.

"Is something going on?" Rui asked, sliding to the edge of her seat.

Neither of the boys answered.

Cursing loudly, Zizi switched the machine off with a slap and came to her again, getting down on his knees as if he were proposing or begging for forgiveness. Rui had an inkling it was the latter.

"I shouldn't have given you that talisman."

"We made a fair agreement. I said I would test it for a price."

"It didn't have to be *you*. It's just that you're the best, the one I trust. But the spell was dangerous, and I knew it. I shouldn't have asked." Zizi looked disgusted with himself. "I'm sorry."

They were two simple words. But he'd never apologized to her before, and she didn't know how to react.

"I'm sorry," he repeated, looking distraught.

"I'm not mad at you," she said softly. "Reverse the spell and everything will be fine—"

"Just say it," Yiran burst out. "Tell her or I will."

"Tell me what?"

Zizi stood up, the words rushing out of his mouth. "I'm not sure if I can reverse the spell. The impossible happened, and it seems like the transfer became permanent, or at least that's what it looks like for now."

Rui slumped against the chair, not quite understanding the words she just heard. *Permanent?* How could that be? But she couldn't deny it. Her spiritual energy felt different, lacking in some way. She'd ignored the hollow feeling since she'd woken in Zizi's bed, hoping it was nothing, hoping it was a figment of her imagination.

But it wasn't.

She choked back a sudden sob. How could she live without magic? It gave her a sense of purpose and duty, knowing she could have her revenge, knowing she could do more with her life. She'd lost something four years ago and found something else. Magic had filled the void left by her mother.

She was suddenly frightened, not because she felt empty, but because she wondered if the emptiness had been there all along, and magic had been a flimsy bandage she'd wrapped over a wound that was still festering.

"I can't do anything now," Zizi said, "but it doesn't mean I can't fix this eventually. It's just too dangerous to attempt anything until you heal completely. Even if I had a way to reverse the spell, doing it now could kill you." He glanced at Yiran. "He looks fine, but his core can't handle this much spiritual energy for long. It could burn out at some point."

Rui didn't think she could feel any worse. "Are you . . . are you saying that I can't get my magic back unless my core recovers fully, but if we don't get my magic out of Yiran as soon as possible, he might *die*?"

Yiran was lying on the floor now, shielding his face as if he were hiding from the world.

"Did you know this already?" she asked him.

Yiran drew a shaky breath. "Yes."

Four years.

Death had come calling on her doorstep again, right on schedule. This time, *she* was its instrument. She had cast the spell, flicked the switch on Yiran's life. And she might lose her magic forever.

Rui shivered. It felt like the cold would never leave her. No one said a word. The seconds stretched, silent and unbearable. She lifted her hand, cautious, not quite sure of what she wanted to do. Lightly, she tugged at the red string around Zizi's wrist, feeling the tension in the frayed thread. She slipped her hand into his, the back of hers nestling against his palm.

His pale blue eyes were questioning. She'd never reached out to him like this before.

Help me, she thought. She felt his fingers curling over hers, warming her chilled skin.

"There's another problem," Zizi said, somewhat reluctantly. "Mochi has a strong spiritual presence now, which means he'll be more vulnerable to Revenant attacks. He must learn how to manage it."

Zizi was right. Yiran had to train, he had to cultivate his spirit core, learn how to use magic. It was his best chance at survival. But he couldn't go to the Academy, not while she was there.

"He could come here," she said to Zizi. "You could teach him the basics to stabilize his core."

Zizi dropped her hand. "I can't get tangled up in Song family business. Think about it, he's from an Exorcist family—they'll want him at Xingshan."

She knew he was right, but she couldn't help feeling betrayed. *How about me?* she wanted to ask. She had lost her means for vengeance; she had lost her purpose. Couldn't Zizi help her out with this one small thing? She glared at him, but deep down, she knew she was being selfish. She was asking him to risk himself for her.

"Don't you think I should be the one deciding this?" Yiran groaned from the floor. "Stop talking about me as if I'm not here."

Before anyone could reply, there was a loud knock on the front door.

The three of them jumped.

Yiran's eyes flicked between Zizi and Rui. "Should we get that?"

Zizi shook his head. "Probably someone selling something. They always leave sooner or later."

"Open up!" The visitor was banging on the door now.

Yiran stood up. "That sounds like—"

"Open up!" repeated the voice from outside. "This is an official visit from the Exorcist Guild. Unlock your door."

Zizi straightened his pajama top, a grim look on his face. "Seems like we have an unwelcome guest."

13
Yiran

Ash Song stepped into the shophouse, a paper cup in one hand and a long coat slung over his arm. He was dressed in his noncombat Exorcist uniform—a sleek black suit and slim tie, with a small red lapel pin to identify his Captain status.

"This was not the combination of people I was expecting to see." He eyed the trio suspiciously, his gaze pausing on the dried blood on Yiran's clothes.

Yiran tensed. Ash couldn't sense that he was bearing magic stolen from Rui, could he?

"The blood—" Ash began.

"It's not mine," Yiran said quickly. "I'm not hurt."

"Good. I've been looking for you all night."

"How'd you find me?"

"The tracer on your phone Grandpa had installed," Ash replied, his frown growing deeper and deeper as he took in the paintings in Zizi's parlor. He sipped his coffee. "I tracked it to this neighborhood and saw the coupe parked outside."

Yiran caught Rui giving Zizi a look that said, *Are you kidding me?* Zizi waggled his eyebrows in reply.

They don't know what it's like to have a grandfather like mine. Yiran couldn't believe that Song Wei had snuck a tracer into his phone. His grandfather didn't trust him at all.

Ash frowned at Rui, who stared back brazenly as she tightened the belt on her bathrobe. "Cadet Lin Ru Yi, while it would be inappropriate for me to comment on any cadet's personal life and make judgment on their"—he side-eyed Zizi—"choices, I do think you can do better. Please put on some proper clothes and get back to the Academy. Cadet Senai has been screaming her head off about your absence, and I'd like to shut her up."

Pink blossomed on Rui's face. "Zizi's not my—we're not—"

Grinning, Zizi threw an arm around her shoulders, visibly tickled by Ash's assumption. "Oh, come on, I'm sure we can all agree Rui looks absolutely ravishing in my old bathrobe."

Yiran wished he had punched Zizi harder. "How do you know each other?" he asked, looking between Rui and Ash.

"He's my mentor at the Academy," Rui said, jamming a good elbow into Zizi's ribs. He yelped and let go of her. "You've got it all wrong, Ash. I saved your little brother's life last night. That's my blood on his clothes."

"I see." Ash nodded. "So the preliminary reports are accurate. I heard there was an incident with a Revenant and someone from the Academy was involved. In that case, thank you for your service. Put on some proper clothes and get back to the Academy. By the way, you're under probation. Flout the rules one more time and you'll be suspended."

"What? Why?"

"All cadets were ordered to stay in their dorms last night. You didn't follow that order, ergo, probation. You know how it works."

"But it was for a good reason."

Ash took another swig from his coffee cup and placed it on a side table. Zizi frowned at the cup.

"You are free to make an appeal to the Discipline Committee, Cadet Lin. I'm only here to retrieve my brother."

Rui folded her arms, sullen but resigned.

"Let's go home, Yiran."

Ash wasn't going to question Yiran about his whereabouts the night before or why the coupe was parked outside when Yiran had lost his driving rights. Not in front of two strangers, anyway. Ash might have slipped up with his revelation about the phone tracer, but the real dirty laundry was kept in the family. That was the Song way.

Yiran wasn't doing things the Song way today.

"Rui saved my life, and possibly the lives of others in the area," he said. "Shouldn't she be commended instead? I'll talk to this committee of yours, I'll tell them what she did."

Rui and Zizi swapped skeptical looks. *They would be right to distrust you.* Yiran shook off his guilt.

Ash was paying attention now. It wasn't every day that Song Yiran stood up for someone else. "Best to keep your nose out of other people's business, Xiao Ran," he said, using the diminutive of Yiran's name to signal his status as the elder.

"This *is* my business," Yiran said, heated. "I don't know what your reports say, but I was there last night when the Revenant attacked. I'm an eyewitness, and—"

Ash brushed him off. "You can tell me everything when we get home."

"Wait, listen to me—"

"We're leaving. Now."

Oxygen seemed to leave the room as Ash stared at Yiran coldly. Yiran wondered if this was the look he gave his subordinates when they said or did things he disapproved of.

Zizi's eyebrows had crawled up his forehead. He was obviously enjoying this messy family drama unfolding in front of him. Two punches. Next time, Yiran would deliver two punches to that pretty, smirky face.

"I'm not leaving until I have my say," Yiran declared. "Rui got hurt while trying to save me. We ran into this wizard after our fight with the Revenant and he said he could heal her, so we came here."

"Mage," Zizi said, bowing with a flourish. "Yes, I am their savior."

As Yiran expected, Zizi played along. Rui looked like she wanted to stab herself in the eyeballs.

Gaining steam, Yiran went on. "The warning for the Night Hunt came too late. I'm sure the stallholders at the Night Market will tell you the same. There were no Exorcists in the area when the Revenant appeared— only Rui. She's the reason why I'm still alive, and why no one else was hurt. If word got out that she was being punished for doing the right thing . . ." He paused for effect.

Immediately recognizing what Yiran was getting at, Ash changed his demeanor from irritation to understanding. Yiran could see his half brother's brain ticking. This was a potential public relations disaster for the Guild, and if the Night Market and the underground magic community got involved . . .

Now for the final nudge.

"Why weren't the Exorcists there?" Yiran asked. He made sure to sound curious and not accusing. "Was it a miscalculation?"

Ash twisted to Rui with an urbane smile. "It seems my brother feels a debt of gratitude to you, Cadet Lin. And rightfully so. If your case is considered by the Discipline Committee, I'm sure they'll take all evidence and testimony into account. Although on second thought, probation might be too harsh considering the circumstances. As your mentor, I will put in a word myself to have it removed."

Rui gave Yiran a small nod. *Good. She thinks you're helping her.* He grinned back. Sometimes, he thought, the only way to lie was to tell the truth.

"One more thing."

All eyes fixed on Yiran. Rui was frowning now.

Yiran raised his hand. His fingertips were glowing.

Rui jerked forward, but Zizi held her back. Thankfully, Ash was too stunned to be paying attention to anyone or anything else but Yiran.

Ash kept staring, mouth agape. "Is that . . . ? That's . . ."

"Magic," Yiran finished. "I can do magic."

His fingertips glowed brighter, the crimson light deepening. The scars on his fingertips tingled. Yiran didn't remember this happening last night. Heat rose in his chest. The light flickered.

He felt a sudden stab of pain in his fingers.

Out of the corner of his eye, he saw Zizi shooting him a warning look. *Enough.*

Yiran let his breathing go back to its natural pattern, and the crimson light disappeared. His display had lasted a few seconds, but he felt exhausted. Zizi was right; he needed to learn how to control his newfound power.

Ash dropped his coat and wrapped Yiran in a bear hug. When he let go, his eyes were suspiciously wet-looking. "This is—this is amazing. But *how*?"

"I don't know. It happened suddenly last night during the Revenant attack. I didn't think it was possible either, but you saw what I just did—" Yiran darted a quick glance at Zizi. "I guess it must be some sort of anomaly."

Zizi coughed. "Perhaps his fight-or-flight response triggered something. The mysteries of the human body, am I right?"

Rui fired Zizi a look of betrayal, which he pretended not to notice. But again, she didn't say a word. Yiran had bet on her silence, guessing she'd have no choice but to go along with whatever he said so her own secrets would not be exposed.

Ash straightened, suddenly businesslike. "You seemed to have skipped some steps in this—from a surge of spiritual energy to that display of magic—we should be careful." He pulled out his phone. "We need to tell Grandpa at once, and we need to get your vitals checked right away. Magic shouldn't be coming out from your hands like that."

Yiran nodded along.

"You'll also have to learn to protect yourself, and you'll need a spiritual weapon." Ash slid his blazer back, revealing the pearl handgrips of the two pistols tucked into his holsters. "Like this."

"Those are your spiritual weapons?" Yiran said, a touch of awe creeping into his tone.

"*He* would bring a gun to a sword fight," Zizi muttered from behind.

Suddenly nervous, Yiran said, "Let's tell Grandfather in person."

"Right. Come on, let's go." Ash was vibrating with excitement again.

"Yiran," Rui said in a sickeningly sweet voice, "before you leave, can you show me where you left my swords?"

Her sword bag was next to the bed. It was bright red in color. She couldn't have missed it when she woke.

"Give me a sec, Ash." Yiran followed her to the stairs at the other corner of the parlor, aware that Zizi was watching them like a hawk.

Once they were upstairs and out of earshot, Yiran said, "What do you want?"

Rui grabbed his collar and slammed him against the wall. Pain went up his neck to the base of his skull. He was surprised by how strong she was, given her current condition. Was it a result of training?

Her arm was pressed against his throat, one knee rising dangerously between his legs. She leaned in, breaths coming up hot against his cheek. He could see the shadows under her eyes, the sharp edge of her mouth.

"Just what do you think you're doing? I thought we agreed on our story. You're not supposed to tell anyone you have magic."

"If you recall, I never agreed to—"

Rui's knee slid up.

"Wait, wait, wait—I'm helping you."

"I don't need your help."

"Ash isn't a fool, but he doesn't know you lost your magic," Yiran said. "Nobody needs to know about that part. I'm the only witness to what really happened, and I'm not telling anyone. It's clear you're injured, and you have magical trauma. We can say it's because you fought the Revenant— that's your excuse for not being able to use your spiritual weapons. That's your excuse to lay low. *I* can't do anything to hide my spiritual energy or the fact that Revenants are going to come after me. Like Zizi said, I've to train to protect myself, and I'll do that until we figure something out. If the wizard won't help me, I have to go to the Academy."

"There is no *we*," Rui said stubbornly. But Yiran could tell she was reconsidering things. Guilt was a powerful weapon, and he had made sure to remind her she'd put his life at risk.

"Look, doing it this way takes the focus off you," he reasoned. "I'll hone my skills, learn to protect myself. No one will be the wiser, and you can take the time to recover."

Rui glared in disbelief. "Hone your skills? But—"

"If I train, I might get to do something useful or kill at least one Revenant before we get you your magic back. Why waste the opportunity?"

The pressure against his windpipe lifted. "Your qi levels are already above what your core can handle."

"So?"

"It's too dangerous." A shadow crossed her face. "Did Zizi tell you that apart from the work they put into training, how powerful a magic practitioner gets to be is solely dependent on the spirit core they're born with? With your core, the odds are low that you'll get anywhere."

"I'm alive, aren't I?" Yiran said. "I'm already defying the odds."

"But if you push too hard, you might . . ." She bit her lip, but he knew exactly what she'd meant to say.

"Everyone dies, sooner or later. Might as well go down in a blaze of glory and take some of those bastards down with me."

He'd thought hard about it overnight after calling a truce with Zizi. Was magic worth risking his life? Was the Song family name something to aspire to? For the last twelve years, he'd had a good life, leashed to that name and everything that came with it. It would mean nothing now unless he lived it on his own terms.

Rui was looking at him like she was seeing him for the first time. Her gaze stripped him, layer by layer, until he wondered if she could see the true face behind all the masks he wore for the world. Was it a frightening face, or was it a frightened face? Was it a face he would recognize himself?

She released him. "What do you want from me in return?"

How did it feel, Yiran wondered, to live life this way? When everything was transactional? When everything was a means to an end? He shook off the uncomfortable feeling that they were more similar than he'd thought. It was clear Rui wanted her magic back for reasons that ran deeper than she cared to share. That was another thing they had in common.

"Nothing. I want nothing from you," he lied. "Just lay low and get better."

Her expression changed to something he couldn't decipher. She whispered back, "I hate you. I hate everything about you. I don't know what you're trying to prove to your brother, and I don't care. But I won't let you die."

It's not about my brother, he wanted to tell her. But all he did was smile. She backed into the bedroom and shut the door in his face.

Trepidation followed Yiran as he went down the stairs. Now that he'd said his decision out loud, everything felt more real. More impossible. What if Xingshan Academy didn't accept him? What if, after all this, his grandfather stuck to his guns and sent Yiran away?

Downstairs, Ash was touring Zizi's parlor, sipping his coffee and poking around at the miscellaneous objects lying on the shelves. Yiran hesitated, staying in the shadows.

"I see you're still dabbling in this nonsense," Ash said, stopping in front of a painting. "Self-portrait?"

"Hmm," came Zizi's noncommittal reply. He was sprawled on a chair, one leg dangling over the armrest, idly playing with his cigarette and looking as content as a cat basking in the sun.

Ash pushed aside the hell money strewn on the floor with his foot. "Talent like yours is hard to find. The Guild is short of healers and spell casters. We're too combat focused, and it makes our Night Hunts more dangerous. We need support members in each team. Three is a better number than—"

"I fail to see how this is my problem," Zizi interrupted.

"You should've said yes to me all those years ago. You could've enrolled in the Academy, made a name for yourself. You're Captain material, you know that. Instead, you waste your talent on cheap tricks."

Zizi stretched indulgently, letting out a loud yawn as he unclipped his bangs. "Ever thought that maybe you did a piss-poor job of selling cadet life to me? School's not for me. I'm not one of you, and I don't intend to be. Besides, my grandmother thinks I'm doing fine as it is, and her opinion is the one I care about."

Ash merely smiled. "Perhaps my grandfather will pay your grandmother a visit soon, and perhaps she'll change her mind. He can be rather persuasive."

"Be my guest. But you'll find my grandmother more stubborn than me, Lan Xi."

No one else but their grandfather called Ash by his birth name. Ash didn't seem to mind. Instead, he continued to look intrigued by the tattooed boy. *Why?* Yiran wanted to yell. Why didn't Ash look at Yiran this way? Like he was powerful. Like he could be dangerous. But Yiran had magic now, and he would fight and scheme to keep it, and one day, Ash and his grandfather would look at him differently. Like he was powerful. Like he was dangerous.

"What are you doing here?" came a voice behind him.

Rui was staring at him. She'd changed back into her own clothes and was carrying her sword bag.

"Nothing," Yiran mumbled.

She pushed past, and he followed her to the parlor.

"Am I interrupting something?" she said.

"No," said two voices with varying degrees of conviction.

"Could you drop me off at the subway station, Captain Song?" Rui said. "I should get back to campus before I get into any more trouble."

Ash nodded. "Sure, it's on the way." His phone rang, and he held it immediately to his ear.

Rui glared a goodbye to Zizi. He waved happily from his chair as she trekked out the front door with Ash.

Yiran retrieved his jacket. He was on his way out when a hand wrapped itself around his wrist, pulling him back.

"I need you to do something for me," Zizi said. He was entirely serious.

"You're asking me for a favor?"

"I went along with your little charade earlier. Treat this as payment to keep my mouth shut about your transgression."

"You want to talk about transgressions? You should be grateful I didn't tell Ash about your little spell."

"Then we both have something to hide. Isn't that the best arrangement?" Zizi grinned. "I'm asking for a favor because despite being a little shit, deep inside that soul of yours, you know what's right and that makes you a good person."

Yiran felt his lips curling. "I'll accept that backhanded compliment. What do you want?"

"I need you to watch over Rui. Tell me if you notice anything off about her."

"I don't even know her," Yiran said, surprised by Zizi's request. "We don't run in the same circles."

"Now that you have"—Zizi stuck his fingers up and made air quotes—"*magic*, and you've told your brother, I assume you'll be enrolling in the Academy. Which means you'll be able to see Rui every day. You won't be in the same classes since she's top of her cohort, but at least you'll be on campus."

"She means a lot to you, doesn't she?"

"She means everything." Zizi had spoken so bluntly it could only be the truth. It was a useful piece of information.

"And if I refuse?" Yiran asked, more to needle Zizi than anything. The thought of having to deal with Rui daily sounded exhausting. Although, who was it who once said, *Keep your friends close, and your enemies closer*? Rui wasn't an enemy, more like a petite and noisy rival. If he knew how her recovery was going, he could make his own plans more effectively.

"You still don't get it, do you?" Zizi said. A muscle ticked in his jaw. "Whether you like it or not, the both of you are connected now. You hold something of hers, something that doesn't *naturally* belong to you. If anything happens to her, who's to say you'll survive it?"

Yiran's skin prickled with a strange chill as the mage stared at him, pale blue eyes piercing through dark wavy bangs. He swallowed thickly and pulled out his phone. "I guess this is where we exchange numbers."

14
Nikai

The spirit trail of the dying star had given Nikai hope he didn't dare feel. After seeking his King for so long, each disappointment felt more bitter than the previous. But his trip to the mortal realm last night lit a new fire in him. He'd returned to the underworld, thoughts whirring for sleepless hours as he dissected what he had witnessed between two teenagers. It was an impossibility that convinced him that impossibilities were merely a lack of imagination, and that this new lead he'd stumbled upon might just be the game changer.

A wild theory had sprung in his head, one so irreverent it was almost blasphemous. Nikai knew he had to be *certain* before he could reveal it to anyone else. He needed to investigate one of the teenagers before taking the next step.

But first, he needed to find his new boss.

Nikai's left eye twitched from fatigue as he sprinted. He tapped his security card, listening to the *zap-zap* of doors opening and closing as he slid through. Traveling through Hell required a firm head and a steady stomach, and it had taken Nikai a while to get the hang of it when he was first brought here by Four. The souls had no reason to leave their assigned Court, but the Reapers and other staff commuted regularly.

Hell's architecture was complex: the Ten Courts sprawled out like kingdoms of their own, but some parts were interconnected in different ways. Not too long ago, Nikai had wandered into a gallery in the human realm and gotten enamored with a piece of art. The artist had drawn impossible stairs that went nowhere and everywhere, humanoid figures walking on floors and walls and ceilings, windows that opened to unexpected perspectives. *Relativity.* That was the title of the lithograph. It had reminded Nikai of the underworld.

"Hey, Nikai, where are you rushing to?" a Sixth Court Reaper juggling a stack of files asked as he sped by her.

"Back to the human world," Nikai panted.

"Are you taking the shortcut to the Gates? They haven't fixed the pits yet—watch out for fires."

"Thanks!" he yelled over his shoulder.

At the next corner, he turned sharply and placed his palm on an arched mirror. The glass transformed into liquid, pulling him in and spitting him out on the other side. He tripped, then caught himself, brushing the soot from his navy jacket, glad to have escaped the pits with only a singed eyebrow.

The Gates of Hell stood before him, pearlescent onyx and tall as mountains. Once intimidating, they were now a familiar sight. Nikai centered himself. The trip from the underworld to the human realm was like the drop in a very high roller-coaster ride, and he found it nauseating.

Bracing, he tapped his card, walked through, and appeared in an alley.

Nikai gave his stomach a few seconds to settle as he breathed in the mortal realm's iridescent air. Squinting in morning light that felt too bright for his otherworldly eyes, he walked out into the street. His invisibility veil wasn't up; it required too much energy to sustain it when he wasn't on soul collection duty. But even with his peacock-blue hair, he passed so easily for a human that no one gave him a second look.

The humans were going about their daily business as usual, oblivious that a Reaper was walking beside them. No mortal—not even the Exorcists—knew about the actual existence of the underworld. Sure, humans had their superstitions, their death rituals and inherited customs. But based on his soul collection experiences, Nikai knew they were always shocked to discover that Hell was real.

Unsurprisingly, the humans were also oblivious to the danger Four's absence had put them in. As the underworld faded, consumed by the Nothing, the barrier between the realms weakened. The Blight became more infectious, and it was harder for Reapers to guard the souls they were collecting. More were turning into Revenants. Things looked fine now as Nikai walked in the bright sunshine, but he knew there would come a day when the Exorcists would no longer be sufficient defense for this world.

All the more reason to find Four.

Nikai stopped in front of Gojo's Café, his pulse speeding up as he thought about what he was about to do. With a quick exhale, he neatened his suit and stepped in.

The Tenth King was easy to spot.

He was sunlight glistening in a pool of blood. His flaxen hair shimmered as he brushed his long ponytail off slim shoulders that were accentuated by a formfitting red hanfu with intricate embroidery. Black leather straps crisscrossed his narrow torso, cinched at the waist with metal buckles. His face was a perfectly chiseled heart, lips full and red like ripe cherries. Dark lashes framed his doe-like eyes, his deep brown irises flecked with gold, and a wash of terra-cotta-red eye shadow and a pop of glitter decorated his lids.

He sat in the corner, stripping off a pair of half-palm leather gloves. The delicate grace of his movements reminded Nikai of a fairy-tale princess who needed rescuing—if that princess had a penchant for biting off the head of every suitor who sought her company.

At this early hour, the only human in the café was the orange-haired boy at the counter reading manga. The music from his headphones was blasting so loudly Nikai could hear it.

Nikai greeted Ten with a bow. "My apologies for disturbing you, Your Majesty, but I come with an urgent and important request."

Ten sucked the last tapioca ball in his tea through an oversized straw and chewed it slowly, staring at Nikai as if he were contemplating the universe or, perhaps, a little murder. He held up a crooked finger. The trail of red polish on his nail made it look like his finger was bleeding.

The orange-haired boy at the counter glanced up, lifting his headphones.

"Another cup of the usual—iced oolong tea, no sugar, extra bubbles?"

Ten nodded.

The boy put his headphones back on and disappeared into the kitchen. Nikai longed for some five-spice popcorn chicken himself, but that could wait.

"Hello, Reaper," Ten said, finally acknowledging him. "I was enjoying some alone time. Pray tell, what is so urgent that you could not wait for my return?"

Nikai sat on the plasticky chair across from him. "I need to use the Darkroom in the Archives, and since you're the regent of the Fourth Court, I require your approval on the paperwork."

"The Darkroom is not a place for Reapers. I see no reason for you to visit it," Ten said, his languid manner unchanging.

"But I wish to look into the birth story of a living human," Nikai said, "and the Darkroom is the only place that allows me to do so."

"A *living* human?" Ten's pretty eyes glinted. "Tell me more."

"I followed the spirit trail of a dying star last night to a park in the human realm, where I encountered a Revenant attacking two teenagers—a boy and a girl. The creature was eventually killed. The girl is a cadet at the Exorcist academy and—"

"Exorcist cadets are trained to kill Revenants. How is this out of the ordinary?" Ten cut in, looking thoroughly unimpressed. "Why are you interested in such mundane things, Reaper? It is unbecoming."

"Your Majesty, it was the boy who killed the Revenant. What's more, he is a human without magic."

"Why did you not start with that? I *adore* plot twists." Ten clasped his hands in delight. "So you are curious about the boy?" When Nikai nodded, Ten shifted his head, peering sideways at Nikai as if he knew the Reaper was holding something back. "Why?"

"I saw the cadet casting a spell," Nikai replied, his heart pressed against his rib cage as he recalled what he'd seen. "Her spiritual energy was transferred to the boy, and he was able to use it to wield her weapon immediately—he was able to do *magic*."

"How can that be? You said the boy is a—what is that word?" Ten knitted his brow.

"I believe he is called a *normie* in the present era of human terminology, Your Majesty." Nikai prided himself in keeping up with the times and the casual language of the youths.

"I suppose it is interesting that this normie survived the ordeal," Ten said, "but it is interesting in the way a new bubble tea flavor is interesting for only the first sip. Why are you wasting your time on the petty lives of humans, Reaper?" Ten turned to the group of small children playing at a park across the street. Their laughter carried into the café. "Look at them," he said softly, as if to himself. "Look at these humans, going about their meaningless little lives, finding joy in the silliest of things."

Nikai was thrown by his expression. He'd never seen the Tenth King look so wistful.

But Ten snapped out of it quickly enough. He tutted, examining his nails, condescension returning as he said to Nikai, "I advise you to stay away from the Archives and the Darkroom, Reaper, lest you be tempted. No, I will not help you with the paperwork."

It had been a long shot, but it was the only shot Nikai had. He refused to give up. He knew Ten wanted to be rid of the burden of overseeing the Fourth Court. Only Four's return could guarantee that. And with the Tenth Court in heightened danger because of the Nothing, Ten might just be the only King who would entertain Nikai's wild theory.

"I must enter the Darkroom because this may be connected to Four," he blurted.

"Explain yourself," Ten said, suddenly alert.

"We know Four still exists because the Kings are eternal. But what if we've been wrong about everything else? What if Four isn't in the underworld but *here*? Four told me he wanted to see the stars forever. It didn't occur to me then, but now, I think what he meant was he wanted to see the stars *from* the human realm."

"Here? Among these plebeians?" Ten scoffed. "I want my brother back more than you do, Reaper. But I do not delude myself with ridiculous speculation. Besides, he cannot exist in the human realm permanently. His power tethers him to the underworld. Like you and I, he is bound."

Underworld beings could only stay in the human world for short periods of time, and the ancient tenets did not allow them to exert the full extent of their powers while they were here. Even now, Nikai could feel the threads of his world hovering around him, pulling him back. But if his hunch was correct . . .

"Which brings us back to the anomaly, Your Majesty," Nikai said. "The energy transfer between those two teenagers proves it *is* possible to separate a being's spiritual energy from them and deposit it elsewhere. Four gave up his throne—what if he gave up his power, his spiritual essence, too? You said it yourself, Your Majesty, Four's power binds him to the underworld. If he found a way to separate it from himself, then he would no longer be tied to it. He could've displaced his power, hiding it somewhere in the human world by masking its presence. That's why none of the Kings have found his trace in the underworld."

"And what became of his being? His soul?" Ten countered.

"I believe the answer might also lie in the anomaly," Nikai said, excitement thrumming in his voice. "A vast amount of spiritual energy was placed in the normie boy, energy he is not meant to have. Does it mean he was born able to hold power, but that power was *taken away* from him?"

Ten leaned back against his chair, trembling slightly. Nikai could not tell if it was from anger or shock. The gold in Ten's eyes glinted. "The *boy* . . . You are implying that he could somehow be a form of my brother."

Nikai nodded. "As impossible as it sounds, yes. But there is one flaw in my theory, one question that keeps coming up. Why did Four want to leave in the first place? Why would he do something so drastic? Why would he choose to be human? There must be something pushing him away from the underworld or something he's running from." Nikai's shoulders slumped. "But I can't figure out what it might be."

"Something pushing him away . . . something he's running from . . ." Ten repeated, staring into space. He looked like he was reliving a moment from the past, a moment that had brought him great sadness. Slipping a hand under his crossed collar, he took out a dried-up willow branch. He always kept the branch with him, tucked under layers of fabric right by where his heart would be, if Ten actually had a beating heart.

Nikai stared longingly at the artifact, wishing it'd been left in his custody instead. He'd been the one to discover it in Four's empty chambers. Brown and rotting, its power sucked dry. It was all that was left. But Nikai did not mourn. Mourning would mean he had accepted his friend would never return.

"Foolish, foolish brother, what have you done?" Ten murmured to himself. "All this because of a broken heart?"

Nikai sat up. "A broken heart? What do you mean?"

Ten startled, as if he'd forgotten Nikai was there. He smoothed his ponytail. "You must have misheard me. Do you not know? A King is born without a heart. We do not feel emotions in the same wretched way that mortals do."

But Nikai was certain he had heard Ten correctly.

"I understand what you are saying, Reaper," Ten said, tucking the willow branch back under his crossed collar. "I do not know if what you suggested is possible or true, but I will confer with the other Kings."

"Will you let me know what happens, Your Majesty?"

Ten gave him a look. "Do not forget the message my brother left us: *Those who seek me shall never see me.* He is devious and clever. He might have placed obstacles and safeguards along the way to thwart his discovery. We must be careful in our approach."

"Of course, Your Majesty." Nikai shifted uncomfortably. "And my request?"

"We will visit the Darkroom *together.* Find out whatever tedious paperwork approvals the Librarian needs, and it will be done."

"Yes, Your Majesty. I will do so right away." Nikai inclined his head. He hadn't expected Ten to want to accompany him to the Archives. If Nikai had his way, he'd be conducting this investigation by himself. But it was good to have a King's backing, he supposed.

Plastic screeched suddenly against tile.

Ten had sprung from his seat. He pressed a hand to his temple, wincing. "My Court is calling me. I must return to my kingdom immediately; there is a village in danger." His face was paler than usual. "Let us hope your lead goes somewhere, because I am running out of time."

There was no wind inside the café, but the hem of Ten's robes fluttered with a life of their own.

As Nikai looked on, the edges of red fabric faded into a dull gray, the color leaching from them. *The Nothing*, he thought, shuddering.

"Return with me, Reaper," Ten commanded. He raised a hand.

Nikai squeezed his eyes shut, bracing for the stomach-churning tug that was coming.

The lights in the café flickered.

"Your order is ready, sir," the orange-haired boy called out as he emerged from the kitchen. "Sir?" He glanced around the empty café, surprised to find himself suddenly alone in the place, and that his most regular customer—the beautiful blond cosplayer with the ponytail—had left without his favorite drink.

15
Yiran

Yiran stood in the kitchen, a box of cereal in one hand and a carton of milk in the other. He'd been too excited to sleep. The first day of school always brought about its own kind of anxiety, and he was feeling it tenfold today. Xingshan Academy wasn't just any school; it was his gateway to the world of magic, his key to belonging.

You're going to fail. This magic doesn't belong to you.

Yiran chased the mocking voice away. He couldn't think like that. Opportunity lay in front of him; he had to grab it and make something of it.

He stared out the window, trying to silence his rambling thoughts. Dawn cast its peaceful light over the sprawling garden of bamboo and stone behind the house. As a kid, he would hide in the verdant copse, thinking about his mother, wondering if she was thinking of him too. He turned away. What was the point of fixating on the past when his future was about to change?

Sighing, he leaned against the counter, eating to calm his nerves, vacantly musing about how his tongue knew the cereal tasted the same, but his brain insisted the purple-colored puffs were just a tad fruitier and more exciting to eat than the orange-colored ones.

"For crying out loud, use a bowl." Ash walked into the kitchen, his expression telegraphing his disapproval of his half brother's eating habits. "Didn't Auntie Kimmie make you breakfast?"

Mouth full of cereal, Yiran replied, "She went to the fish market." He paused to dribble a bit more milk into his mouth to get the right crunch-to-mush ratio before continuing. "Are you giving me a ride to the Academy?"

"Can't," Ash said. "I have to be at the Guild headquarters. Paperwork and meetings. Worst part of this job."

"What's the best part?"

"Killing Revenants, terrorizing cadets when I'm on campus, the fans." Ash grabbed his overnight oats from the fridge and rummaged for a spoon. "I have to say the fan club aunties are the best. I've gotten so many care packages with homemade food and tonics. I don't eat or drink any of that—you never know what's hiding inside." He pointed his spoon at Yiran. "But I do appreciate the gesture."

Admittedly, Ash was somewhat of a minor celebrity. There were, after all, collectible laminated photocards with his face printed on them, sold side by side with pop-idol merchandise. Some cards had little hearts drawn on them, others were holographic, and they all focused on Ash's good looks. There were other well-known Exorcists—the Captains, mostly—who got the same treatment, but Ash was the rising star of the new generation. Yiran supposed it was good politics to have a handsome public face when one dealt with unsavory things.

"Drive yourself to school or get George to take you," Ash said, adding a generous spoonful of almond butter and fresh berries to his bowl of oats.

"George?"

"Yeah, George Li. Average height, glasses, wife gave birth three weeks ago. You've met him—more than once."

Yiran continued to stare blankly.

Ash tsked. "Remember what I said? Always know your people. Treat them well and with respect, and they'll be loyal to you."

Yiran had sat through so many of Ash's random pep talks that they were all a blur. Ash meant well, but Yiran had been sleepwalking toward an inevitable dead end before meeting Rui, and any sagely life advice had seemed redundant.

But things were different now. Yiran promised himself to do better. "I'll remember that," he said. "And it'll be useful to have a car at the Academy, I guess, but I'll have to check if I still have driving privileges."

The thought of asking his grandfather for anything soured his mood. His "magic reveal" was a total nonevent. In fact, it felt like someone had thrown a bucket of ice water in his face. Nothing had changed except that Yiran got to remain in the city. If anything, Song Wei had seemed irritated that his younger grandson could do magic. Probably because he expected Yiran to fail at Xingshan Academy and bring more shame to the family.

"Want me to talk to Yeye about the car?"

"Nah, it's my own business."

Ash clapped a hand on Yiran's shoulder. "He *is* proud of you, you know."

"He has a funny way of showing it." Yiran chugged his milk to stop himself from saying more. He wondered if he was being foolish for wanting an old man's approval.

But you're not doing this for him anymore. You're doing this for yourself.

"Damn right," Yiran muttered, taking another gulp of milk.

"I have to go." Ash licked his spoon clean, dropped it into the kitchen sink, and wet his hand under the tap. "By the way, your hair's sticking out." He patted the offending lock of hair down and pulled Yiran into a hug. "*I'm* proud of you. Always have been, always will."

Blinking rapidly, Yiran pushed him away. "Don't be cringey."

"Me? Cringey?" Ash laughed and sauntered out of the kitchen.

A smile tugged on Yiran's lips. He washed his cereal down with the rest of the milk and jogged back to his room to get his suitcase.

The door was slightly ajar when he got to his grandfather's study. He knocked. Two quick raps.

His grandfather opened the door.

Yiran bowed.

His grandfather eyed the suitcase briefly and retreated into the study. He stopped in front of the expansive bookshelf, speaking without turning his head to Yiran.

"I see you're all packed."

"Yes. I'll be back on the weekends unless there's school stuff." His grandfather didn't like waffling, so Yiran got to the point. "May I borrow a car?"

A beat of hesitation. Then a curt nod.

"Thank you, Zufu."

Seconds passed. Yiran twitched uncomfortably. His grandfather was still focused on the bookshelf, but he hadn't dismissed him yet. Yiran wasn't sure if he was supposed to stay or go.

He counted to eleven. When nothing changed, he said, "I guess I better be going then. Don't want to be late on my first day." His laugh jittered.

His grandfather did not say a word.

Finally, Yiran bowed and left, closing the door behind him.

Disappointment frothed in his stomach. He didn't know what he'd been hoping for. A smile? A kind word? Or for his grandfather to simply say, *Enjoy your time at the Academy*? He'd been foolish to think his bastard status would change in the old man's eyes, that maybe somewhere in that cold heart, there'd be room for someone other than Ash.

Yiran snatched his suitcase and went down the hallway, cursing at his own naivete. It was only when he reached the garage that he realized what his grandfather had been staring so hard at. The bookshelf in the study housed the only picture Song Wei kept of his deceased son in the entire mansion.

It was a faded photograph of a young Song Liming in his Xingshan Academy uniform, smiling without a care in the world.

Yiran swerved into the parking lot, pulling into an empty spot with ease. Several cadets gawked at his luxury two-seater as they walked to class. In hindsight, he could've chosen a less selfish car—you could squeeze someone in the back but it wouldn't be comfortable, and he might need to build some social cachet by offering free rides.

He got out in time to catch a boy laughing snidely at his ride, but another cadet threw him a look of interest. Yiran committed his face to memory, making a mental note to look him up. If Yiran was going to fit in here, it'd be best to know where the clique lines were drawn—and where they could be redrawn. With the Song name hanging around his neck like a noose, he needed all the help he could get.

He left his suitcase in the trunk and walked toward the main campus, adding a little extra swagger to his stride. He wasn't just here to learn and fit in, he wanted to impress.

A group of girls settled into step with him. They were younger than he was. Juniors, maybe.

"You're Ash's little brother, aren't you?" one of them asked.

The *little* chafed, but Yiran flashed a winsome smile. "Pleasure to meet you."

"Aren't you too old to be a freshie?" Up close, the girl's cocky eyes and challenging smile told him she thought highly of herself and not a lot about him.

He had misread the situation. Most girls approached him thinking he could give them Ash's number, or that Yiran could pass on a message or a gift. Sometimes girls approached him for him, but the group that was surrounding him and blocking his path now were a pack of foxes around a rabbit's burrow.

Yiran kept his smile. "Chill with the ageism. No one's ever too old to learn."

Another girl with box-dyed red hair said, "Don't expect anyone to take it easy on you, nepo baby. You'll start at the bottom like all of us. Your granddaddy may have protected you for years, but here, we're all equals. We've heard a lot about you, Song er shaoye."

She cocked her head, and the entire posse turned on their heels, leaving Yiran standing alone.

In his old school, boys like Yiran were untouchable princes in their made-up kingdoms. He knew how that world worked, but Xingshan Academy was a different world. The rumors of a decadent lifestyle he'd let run free because it benefited him in the past were coming back to bite him now. He'd have to work doubly hard to earn everyone's respect.

"Go big or go home," he told himself, appraising the grand entrance of Xingshan Academy.

He would show them what he was made of.

The Academy was a stoic collection of gray and green: blocks of buildings, rectangular patches of grass, an oval field lined by a running track, tennis courts to the west of it, a huge lawn to the east, and the dormitories in the south. It seemed disappointingly ordinary on the surface, but Yiran soon found that this wasn't the case at all.

Cadets spilled from classrooms and lecture halls, hurrying back to lecture halls and classrooms, passing him in a flurry of too-loud laughter. Yiran spotted deconstructed blazers and embellished shirts and skirts, along with colorful hairstyles and piercings and tattoos. Uniforms were mandatory at the Academy, and Ash had said it was because the special fabric worked with the cadets' spiritual energy. But apparently it was up to the cadet *how* they chose to wear it, and it seemed like they took their fashion seriously. Everyone wanted to stand out. It made Yiran look stuffy and out of place with his gelled-back hair and neatly pressed baby-blue dress shirt and dark gray pants. He couldn't wait to get his uniform.

In between classes, the cadets practiced their spell casting and sparring in hallways and open spaces with wanton disregard of passersby. After dodging yet another sword thrust too closely as he walked by, Yiran decided that either this was good reflex training or perhaps everyone was testing his mettle.

He was glad the Academy had decided to fast-track him. His schedule accommodated one-on-one foundational and remedial classes, so he didn't have to sit in a room full of first-years, *and* he was able to observe the top senior class when they trained. In time, if he proved himself, he could train with them too. The box-dyed redhead was wrong—some people didn't have to start from the bottom. But Yiran also knew this privilege would be frowned upon by his peers. Still, he needed all the help he could get.

His first-day lectures flew by quickly. The professors were pleasant, if a little miffed they had to reteach their introductory classes to a single student. He ate a late lunch with a senior professor, feigning interest in the man's dull research in case he was somehow useful in the future. After a day of dealing with adults, Yiran was looking forward to finally meeting people his age. It would be his first time observing the top senior class and their physical training.

He headed north of the main gates past the assembly courtyard and bookstore. As he strolled, a bunch of freshmen at one of the designated study areas stared blatantly at him. Thank gods he didn't have classes with these tiny children. He lobbed them a smile. One of the girls giggled, and her bespectacled friend smacked her with a notebook.

It seemed like everyone knew who he was, and everyone was curious.

A modern structure of metal and glass shaped like a seashell rested on top of a small hill. It didn't look like any other building on campus. Yiran scanned his palm by the entrance and walked in. He was early, and it was quiet and empty inside. He went down the glass-paneled hallway to a set of lockers, chucking his bag in one of them. The well-stocked vending machine caught his interest, and he got a mocha frappé to perk himself up. Drink in hand, he approached an unmarked door at the end of the hallway.

A beam of red light flashed across his body, and the door slid open without a sound. The room was enormous. A single touch screen hung on the panel by the door next to a complicated-looking machine with a keyboard and several buttons and knobs.

He was about to nose around when an all-too-familiar voice said, "What the hell are you doing here?"

Yiran turned. He hadn't noticed the petite girl standing in another corner of the room when he came in. She was stretching in her athletic gear, looking irritated by his presence. What luck. *Rui* just had to be in the senior class he was assigned to observe.

She raised her eyebrows at his clothes. "That designer shirt and those expensive shoes on your first day of school?"

"I don't have my uniforms yet."

"Doesn't excuse the shoes. Heard you drove one of your fancy cars."

"For convenience."

"Embarrassing."

"It won't be embarrassing when you're feeling hungry in the middle of the night and you want some soup dumplings from Laodifang." Yiran winked. "You know who to call."

"You're not here on vacation, you're here to train. This isn't fun and games, not when lives are at stake," Rui said, emphasizing her displeasure with her hands. "You can't zip in and out of campus whenever you want. There are rules. Go read your student handbook."

"Has anyone ever told you how bossy you are?"

She gave him a funny look. "Zizi says that all the time."

You hold something of hers, something that doesn't naturally *belong to you.*

Yiran lowered his voice. "Speaking of Zizi, has he figured out a way to . . ."

Rui shook her head. "You'd be the second person to know if he did."

Hiding his relief, Yiran joked, "Guess he's busy pulling rabbits out of his pajamas or dancing in the rain while eating chicken wings."

"Sushi."

"Huh?"

"He likes sushi."

"I guess you'd know. You two are close, aren't you? How did you meet?"

"What are you doing here anyway?" Rui said, ignoring his questions. "Did you get lost?"

"I have permission to sit in for trainings with this class."

"But we're seniors—the *top* seniors."

She sounded indignant. Flattery might be the way to soothe her. "Then I'm sure it'll be enlightening for me. You're the strongest, the best cadet. There's a lot I can learn from you," he said.

"I *was* the strongest," Rui said, her eyes downcast, "and I can't be the best unless I get my magic back."

"Any idea when that will be?"

"Why don't you ask Zizi yourself? Didn't you exchange numbers or something? I saw you whispering together before you left his shophouse."

There was a curious expression on her face, mingled with something else Yiran couldn't decipher at first. It *felt* like jealousy. He couldn't explain it, but he could sense her emotions when he was near her, like they were telegraphed directly to him. Was this the connection Zizi was talking about? Did it mean Rui could read Yiran?

"I think the only person the wizard cares about is you," he said.

Surprise registered on Rui's face. She distanced herself from him, her expression suspicious, like she was feeling the empathic link between them too.

The door slid open.

Several cadets filed noisily in. One of them, a girl with smudged black eyeliner and bright pink hair, was talking about going to the karaoke club. She stopped in midsentence when she noticed him.

"Oh, it's you."

The other seniors sized him up.

Yiran had come prepared. He'd sat Ash down and made him describe every senior cadet he mentored. Yiran recognized some of them now.

The pastel goth was Ada Senai, daughter of Commissioner Senai—the man who had helped Yiran avoid juvenile court. She was also Rui's best friend, and Yiran was intent on staying on her good side. Then there was Mai Lang, a tanned long-limbed girl who came from a family of Exorcists. She had an uncle who was influential in the city. Yiran glossed over a few others until he found the person he wanted to meet.

Teshin Mak.

Resident weapons expert, graduating senior, and the new vice president of the Student Council. Most importantly, Teshin was one of the heirs to the Mak clan. The Maks were famous in Exorcist circles; the best weapons were forged and restored by them.

Rui's dual swords were bound to her and her magic. Even if she did let Yiran use them, everyone would know the source of *his* newfound magic. There was no legitimacy in that. Yiran had to find another way. If the Maks were as good as they say, maybe they could forge a different kind of weapon for him.

Teshin appeared stern, with golden-brown skin and intense brown eyes to match. Both sides of their head were shaved to expose a tattoo of two halves of a circle, broken by a line. The Mak clan's crest. They were looking at Yiran with open interest.

Yiran smiled. He had to find a way to get close to them.

But Teshin wasn't the only one evaluating Yiran. Mai stared boldly, whipping her pin-straight hair back. She had an overwhelming aura of confidence.

"Did anyone know Song Yiran was joining us today?" she asked in a husky voice.

A chorus of *nos* came from the rest.

"There's no training today," Ada told Yiran. "The Exorcist who's supposed to be here can't make it. We're just going to mess around and practice drills."

Yiran shrugged. "I'm sure I'll learn something by observing you."

"Suit yourself." She gave him a surprisingly sincere smile.

Mai sidled over, her smile the opposite of Ada's. "Since we're doing our own thing today, maybe you should participate. Have a sparring session with one of us or something."

"Yeah, go for it," said another cadet. A couple of others voiced their agreement.

Yiran demurred. "I'm here to watch . . . It's only my first day."

"Aww, come on, do it for funsies," said Mai. "I heard you were vice captain of the fencing team at your old school."

Seemed like he wasn't the only one who'd done his research.

"Let's have a duel. We can start the Simulator and use dummy weapons.

Unless . . ." Mai cocked her head, peering up at him through her thick eye-lashes. "Unless you're afraid of getting your ass kicked?"

"I'll do it," Yiran's mouth said before his brain registered. *Dammit.* He'd wanted to stay out of trouble on his first day.

Mai clapped her hands. "Awesome! Rui will fight you."

"I will what?" Rui snorted.

"Seems only fitting if our best shows him what we're made of."

"Rui is still recovering," Ada said, looking worried, "and we're not sup-posed to use the Simulator without a trainer here."

"I've worked the machine dozens of times," said Mai. "It'll be fine."

"It's okay, Ada. Mai knows the programs," Rui said. Rolling her shoul-ders, she lifted her chin at Yiran. "I'm done stretching and warming up anyway. I'll take him."

Yiran had a bad feeling about this, but it was too late to back out now. His pride was on the line. *Go big or go home.* He put his mocha frappé down and moved to the middle of the room. Everyone else but Rui and Mai went to the bench on the side.

Mai typed a string of rapid commands on the control panel. Spinning around, she grinned widely.

"Welcome to the Simulator."

For a split second, the place seemed to contract.

Then it heaved and burst into sunlight. Tall rock formations littered the landscape. The floor was dirt and sand. The ceiling, blue sky.

A desert. They were in a freaking *desert.*

Yiran whistled. It was impressive. Ash had told him about the Simula-tor, but seeing it with his own eyes was a whole different thing.

"Isn't it cool?" Rui said, her eyes suddenly round and shiny like mar-bles. "Everything's fake, but the program tricks your brain into thinking it's real."

Yiran sensed that this place was somehow comforting for her. How many hours had she logged in this training facility? She didn't strike Yiran as someone with a social life.

The ground rumbled suddenly. A butte shot up, shaking sand all over him. He stumbled and came close to face-planting. He caught his balance in time, but the sand bit into his palms like greedy insects. Small pinhole-sized wells of blood formed on his skin.

Yiran wiped his stinging palms on his pants. Blood stained the corner of his untucked shirt. *It's fake*, he reminded himself. But it was still unsettling.

Unbuttoning his cuffs, he started rolling his shirtsleeves up to his elbows. "Sure wish I was wearing something more appropriate for sparring."

Rui smirked. "Pants too tight? Feel free to take them off. You can do this shirtless too; we don't mind."

Laughter came from outside the simulation. The other cadets must be watching them, but Yiran couldn't see them at all. Refusing to take Rui's bait, he folded his sleeves nonchalantly and stretched his legs. He wasn't too worried. The reason why he wasn't *captain* of the fencing team was because he'd lost a frivolous bet involving a frog. He knew his way around a foil, and he was sure he could adapt to the dummy swords. Hell, he'd already killed his first Revenant. He bit back a smile, knowing that Rui would take his confidence as a sign to make things harder for him.

Two swords appeared in the air.

Rui plucked one and gave it a twirl. "All right, try to disarm me."

"Okay—"

Her blade was at his clavicle before he could twitch a finger. Yiran felt its chilly edge testing his skin. Someone in the audience gave a hoot of approval.

"Shouldn't you wait until I've armed myself?" he said.

"Would a Revenant wait to attack you?"

"Touché."

Rui lowered her blade, and Yiran grabbed the other sword. It felt right in his hand, not quite like how he'd felt when he used Rui's sword after the magic swap, but close. Ash had said the Simulator's programs were dynamically adaptive. Was this what he meant?

Rui leaped back, positioning herself for attack. "Ready?"

Yiran had barely any time to inhale before she lunged at him.

She was fast. Lithe and graceful like a deadly dancer who knew a dozen different ways to cut you up. Her moves were unexpected. He could tell she worked more by intuition than technique. If the spell had taken away her magic, it'd done nothing to lessen her martial arts skills.

Yiran parried her attacks, but Rui managed to hit him again and again. He'd trained for years, but fencing had structure and rules. It had etiquette. Right now, none of that mattered. There was no priority to consider. No waiting, no politeness. Just a girl coming at him with a killer instinct and no hesitation. If Rui wanted to hurt him, his shirt would be in shreds and his body carved with wounds.

The ground was another issue. Whenever he fell or braced himself, gravel and coarse sand cut into his skin. Pain signals flooded his brain. It wasn't real, but it *felt* real, and that made all the difference. He didn't like the Simulator. Didn't like things that messed with his mind. But he was developing a grudging respect for whoever had invented it.

"Get up," Rui ordered. She'd knocked his sword out of his hand and tripped him up with a well-aimed poke at the ankles. "I thought you were captain of the fencing team."

"Vice captain," Yiran said, "and we both know this isn't fencing."

"Then you should know there's only one solution to this—stop fencing."

Yiran rose to his feet and retrieved his sword. Sweat dripped down his back, and his shirt stuck uncomfortably to his skin. As he lifted it to wipe his face and chest, he caught Rui glancing briefly at his bare torso.

Yiran grinned. "On second thought, I think I'll do this shirtless." He slipped his top off and tossed it in the corner. A round of wolf whistles came from the audience.

Rui rolled her eyes. "A Revenant's not going to ogle at your abs."

"Good thing I'm not fighting a Revenant today."

"Trying to distract me because you can't think of a better way to beat me? That's pathetic."

"So you admit you *are* distracted?"

Her smile turned dangerously sweet. "Let's find out."

Rui advanced. Something had changed—her footwork twisted rapidly, and her attacks became even more unpredictable.

She was no longer holding back.

Yiran struggled to fend her off. He was getting hit too often, losing his footing and falling over himself like a useless fool. He was embarrassing himself in front of the people he wanted to impress.

There's only one solution to this—stop fencing.

That was the point, wasn't it? This was a *fight*. A brawl. No rules, no etiquette. A Revenant wouldn't give him the courtesy to catch his balance or breath. But before he could think of his next move, Rui came for him.

Yiran dodged her fist, but her leg swung out of nowhere, catching the back of his knees. He lost his weapon and went down on the sand on all fours. Once again, Rui's blade was at his throat.

"We're done," she said, lips curling in satisfaction.

Yiran glared up at her. "Not yet. One more round."

"The outcome isn't going to change, but if you insist."

"I do insist."

Rui shrugged. "Suit yourself. On your feet then."

As Yiran grabbed his sword, someone yelled, "Now for the fun part!"

Mai. He recognized her voice. What the heck was she doing?

Rui frowned, looking equally confused. "What fun part?"

The arena changed into solid ground and concrete walls. The lights dimmed. Nausea churned in Yiran's stomach. He'd been moving so fast the switch hit him hard. He squinted at the shining orb above him. What was the moon doing there?

In front of him, grimy metal containers were stacked on top of each other to form a kind of pattern. A warehouse? No—a maze. Either he had to solve it, or he had to chase something and catch it. *Or maybe something's chasing me.*

He shook his head to clear it. "Rui?"

She was nowhere to be seen.

A silvery trail appeared above one of the containers like glitter scattered across the air, hovering in an unnatural manner. Another trail appeared. Then another. Yiran smelled something. A flowery scent. Not roses, not chrysanthemums. Something more cloying and mixed with the stench of decay. What was that sound? It was almost like a baby's cry. The small hairs on Yiran's arms and neck stood. Something skittered behind him. He spun around. Nothing but containers and darkness.

It's just a simulation. This isn't real, it's not real. Pressing his back flat against a container, he took a few deep breaths to steady himself. But fear had already sunk its talons in him.

A growl.

Slowly, Yiran peered out.

Revenants.

Red eyes, gaping black holes for mouths, slithery seaweed-like hair. One moved its head in Yiran's direction.

His heart skipped erratically. The dummy sword in his hand whirred in response. Was he supposed to channel his magic into it?

Sensing his hesitation, the Revenant crawled closer.

Yiran shifted back.

Wrong move.

The whole group descended on him at once. Deformed creatures snarling and screeching, gray flesh growing and shrinking in blobs around their bodies. There was something grotesquely human about them, like body parts made and remade in the devil's honor.

They weren't real. But the fear crawling under Yiran's skin, the sweat beading across his forehead, the tremor in his legs as he pushed himself to take a step—that was all real.

Heat fanned out in his veins like a nascent flame. He slashed at the

Revenants, but too many were coming at him. The horde of pale, sickly bodies was crushing him. He opened his mouth and let out a scream.

Light burst forth. Bright, fierce, and strong. Yiran stared in shock. The light was coming from *him*. He couldn't tell where the crimson glow started and where his weapon ended.

The Revenants flew off, thrown by some force.

But Yiran had no time to feel victorious. His chest seized; his breathing turned ragged. Broken capillaries splotched on his arms and chest, forming a mottled reddish pattern that made his skin look diseased. Crimson light was still spilling from his hands like rays of the sun.

"Stop!" someone shouted. It sounded like Rui.

The dummy sword disappeared. The Revenants and the maze vanished. The lights came on.

"Stop!" the voice shouted again.

But Yiran couldn't stop. Energy radiated from his body. He couldn't tell if he was breathing in air or fire.

"*Yiran!* Stop it!"

"I don't . . . know how," he rasped. He tried to tell his hands, his body to stop. But they didn't listen. His insides were on fire. He was just so *hot*.

He staggered back, a sudden realization hitting him: if he didn't find a way to end this, he was going to destroy himself.

16
Yiran

A fist crashed into his sternum.

Air gusted out of his lungs. He fell to the ground, gasping from the shock of the blow.

Rui stood over him, breathing just as heavily. "Are you all right?"

"You hit hard." Yiran panted.

"If you say *for a girl*, I'll hit you again." She sounded a little hysterical herself. She crouched down to examine him. The red splotches on his arms and torso were fading. "I hit you to disrupt your breathing pattern to stop you from channeling," she said.

"Quick thinking...thanks." He rubbed his chest, trying to calm down.

They sat side by side, backs against the wall—Rui with her knees drawn close, Yiran with his legs spread out—catching their breaths.

The other cadets gathered.

"What happened?" Mai said, looking frantic. "You weren't supposed to use actual magic in this program. It's not made for it."

"Should've told me that at the start," Yiran said.

"I didn't think you *could* use magic during that program. There must have been a glitch, or maybe I keyed in something wrongly—I'm so sorry, Yiran." Mai wrung her hands.

She's afraid. Probably because, like him, she had her family's reputation to think about. If he'd come to any actual harm, she'd be in trouble for letting the Simulator run *and* for letting an untrained cadet use it. His mind was still hazy, but Yiran realized something: if he covered for Mai now, she would owe him later.

"It's not your fault, Mai," he said, adding dryly, "That was way less fun than you said it'd be, though."

"Don't make a joke out of it," Ada scolded. "We'll have to get you checked out by a healer."

If he went to a healer, everyone would know what had happened. Mai would get into trouble, and while he didn't care about that, he'd lose his hold over her. He shook his head. "I'm okay. I just need to rest for a bit."

"Are you sure?" Mai said, looking relieved.

"Is this yours?" Teshin called out. They were holding the can of frappé.

Yiran nodded.

"You had coffee?" Rui gasped.

"It's just a mocha."

"You're new to all of this. Don't you remember what—" Rui caught herself in time and shut her mouth.

Ada threw a questioning glance at her.

Right, Zizi said this could happen, Yiran recalled. The mage had warned of an unpleasant caffeine crash for someone in Yiran's situation.

"We weren't supposed to use the Simulator. We should still report this incident," Ada said. But she looked hesitant, and the rest of the seniors were starting to exchange worried glances. Nobody wanted to get into trouble.

Yiran's mind was already working. He had an opening.

"But it's my fault," Yiran said. "I shouldn't have drunk the coffee. Don't worry about it, Mai. And I know you're the Student Council president, Ada, but could you let it go? I won't tell a soul." He conjured an image of his grandfather's furious face in his mind so the emotions that arose in him came through in his expression as he looked up at the group of seniors. "I really don't want any trouble on my first day. Can we just forget about it, please, just this once?"

Yiran could tell the seniors were softening. Whether it was out of guilt or respect that he was willing to shield them, Yiran didn't know and he didn't care. As long as he achieved his goal, what did it matter?

"Just this once," Ada said reluctantly. Yiran noted how her word was respected by everyone. "I'll take you to the dorms to rest."

"I'll come with you," Mai said. "I can drop by the cafeteria to get you something along the way."

"Thanks, I appreciate it." Yiran looked at Teshin. "No more coffee for me, I guess."

Teshin crushed the offending can and tossed it into the bin. "You'll need a lot of remedial training to get on our level, but I see potential," they said. "Let's find some time to talk about spiritual weapons. I've a feeling you might be an unusual case."

Achievement unlocked. "Thanks, Teshin. Appreciate it."

Yiran's pulse was still wild, and his insides hurt. But with some luck and maneuvering, he'd managed to turn the situation into something useful. Not bad for his first day.

A weird sensation went through his chest. He glanced at Rui, certain it had come from her. She was stone-faced, but he felt—no, he *knew*—her envy.

Ada tossed him his shirt. As he buttoned it, he caught Rui slipping out the door, her shoulders stiff. He might've convinced the other seniors today, but there was someone else he still needed to win over.

17
Nikai

The ding of the elevator was more baleful than usual, closer to a crow cawing than a musical note. As the car sank down, Nikai whispered a word. The white box in his hand warmed up. Moments later, the aroma of fried chicken rose from it. The doors opened at the bottom of the administrative tower. He exited and crossed the skybridge, taking care not to look down into the abyss.

"Archives, please," Nikai said to the nondescript black door set into the rock wall. A bell chimed. He turned the doorknob counterclockwise and stepped cautiously through.

The melancholic sounds of an erhu floated in the air.

Built like a wooden temple, the Archives were said to hold the birth and death stories of everyone who had ever lived. This was the Librarian's domain.

"Greetings, Nikai," said the elderly sage, placing his string instrument down. His hair was white, eyes a timeless gray, face disturbingly smooth like an egg.

"Have you eaten, qianbei?" Nikai inquired, knowing the Librarian would appreciate this traditional way of address. "I brought you something delicious from the human realm."

"Ah, I see you youngsters have not forgotten the gift of respect," the Librarian commented, taking the box.

Nikai smiled politely. He might *look* nineteen, and in many ways he'd stayed that age in his mind, but technically he was centuries old.

The Librarian sniffed. "Five-spice popcorn chicken. What a delicacy." It was hard to miss his sarcasm, but Nikai saw how eagerly he slipped the box under his table. "How may I help you?"

"I was sent by the Tenth King to access the Darkroom."

"The Darkroom? For what purpose?" The Librarian's snow-white brows twitched. It wasn't uncommon to investigate stories in the Archives. Knowing how souls lived as humans was helpful in managing them. But this wasn't part of a Reaper's job, and moreover, the stories placed specifically in the Darkroom were unfinished. They were lives still being written and sacred to the living.

"My visit concerns the search for the Fourth King." Briefly, Nikai told him about the two teenagers involved in the anomaly. "It's not much to go on, but it's a new lead," he finished.

The Librarian peered at Nikai. "You were Four's Head Reaper, were you not?"

"Yes." *I was also his friend and confidant. Or at least, I thought so.* Nikai laid a neat stack of papers on the desk. "Here is all the paperwork."

"The stories in the Darkroom are exceptionally fragile. It would be a catastrophe if they were damaged by a Reaper who should not be handling them."

"These documents bear the mark of the Tenth King," Nikai said, keeping his smile respectful. "And you are more than welcome to extract the stories for me."

With a soft *humph*, the Librarian pulled out a pair of round spectacles from the pocket of his mandarin-collared tunic and put them on fussily. Stroking his braided beard, he read through the documents, flipping the pages carefully, ready to find fault. But Nikai was prepared. He had quadruple-checked his work before coming here.

He kept his conceit to himself when the Librarian finally said, "Everything checks out."

"Great."

"But where is the Tenth King? These documents permit him to enter. Not you."

"Oh yes, the addendum." Nikai pulled out his tablet and showed him another document. "Apologies. Unfortunately, the Tenth King is tied up at the moment, and I have his permission to proceed."

"I see. He must be busy. I heard an entire village in the Tenth was taken by the Nothing yesterday. Those poor souls, doomed for the rest of eternity and punished for crimes they did not commit in their mortal life." The Librarian looked at Nikai. "*You* are familiar with the Nothing, correct?"

Nikai stiffened. "It's been a long time since I've thought of the place," he lied. "As you say, the Nothing has encroached upon the Tenth Court, and if we do not stop it, the other Courts are next. Speed is of the essence, qianbei."

The Librarian did not take the hint. Instead, he removed his glasses, slowly polishing the lenses with a cloth.

"Did you know Four was the Tenth King's favorite? They were close once, always together and thick as thieves. Even in the early days, Ten was not inclined to laughter, but Four could make him laugh—not in arrogance or spite, but with joy. I imagine the Tenth King feels betrayed by what happened. He must be deeply hurt that Four left without a word."

He isn't the only one, Nikai thought. What was a Reaper without his King? Not much. Not much at all. Resentment fermented in his chest, unexpected and sour. If Four hadn't rescued him, if Four hadn't pulled him out of the Nothing and offered him friendship and a second chance, Nikai would've been—

You would've been left walking in darkness for eternity. You would've been consumed by despair and regret, never to know the light again. Just like the lost souls from the Tenth Court.

Four had saved Nikai. It was the only truth. And now, it was Nikai's turn to help.

The Librarian set his glasses down and fished out a tarnished brass key from his trouser pocket. It didn't look particularly special.

"All right then. Come with me."

Nikai followed him deeper into the Archives, through corridors of bookcases, stretching to ceilings so high he could not see the top. Scrolls upon scrolls lay on sighing shelves, translucent parchment patchy in the dim light of red candles floating in the air. It seemed preposterous to rely on fire for light in a room full of paper. But those papers would not burn, and Nikai felt no heat from the flames.

He licked his lips. An itch was spreading through his fingers.

Somewhere in this vast room, his own story rested on a shelf.

The Librarian spoke. "This place makes an impression on anyone who steps in. Ordinary souls cannot come in here because they cannot bear it. Reapers are not immune to the effects either. The souls keep memories of their mortal lives, but you Reapers remember nothing, do you? Your mortal memories and sins have been wiped away. In return, you stay and serve the underworld. That is why this room tempts you so. You are curious about who you were, what you were. And curiosity is a treacherous thing."

It was.

Whispers brushed against Nikai's ears.

You have been wondering for so long . . . just one peek and you'll find out why you were sent to the Nothing . . .

Don't you want to know?

The whispers clung onto Nikai's sleeves, tugging his hair, pressing down on his shoulders. He couldn't help but flail his arms, slapping at them.

Shutupshutupshut—

The voices stopped.

Nikai breathed out. "I am here to carry out a task, and I will fulfill it without distraction."

The Librarian smiled thinly.

Soon they reached a wooden door with characters etched across the top:
YOU MUST ENTER AS YOURSELF

The Librarian stuck the key into the middle of the door. It melded seamlessly into the wood, and a yawning cavern emerged.

"Welcome to the Darkroom."

Nikai stepped in.

The door behind him vanished, and the abyss swallowed him in.

Memories of another time and place slithered into his mind. A place where his eyes saw nothing but black, his ears heard nothing but silence, where his hands reached out and touched *nothing*. He could almost feel the rough gravel on his bare feet, the tearing of skin as he was forced to keep walking in utter darkness toward a tiny speck of light in the distance. He had gone on for eternity and would go on for another eternity. There had been nothing in front of him and nothing behind him, only that speck of light that kept moving farther and farther away.

Hope.

The light was hope and the lack of it, understanding he would never reach it, but knowing it still existed.

Then suddenly, he'd found himself out of the dark, lying on the ground, choking on air, the rags on his body drenched through. There was mist everywhere, but the gloom still blinded him, and it had hurt.

A young man was staring down at him. He was beautiful, with silvery-white hair and the saddest eyes.

"You are not who I am looking for," the young man had said. "But whether by chance or fate, I have found you. If you come with me, I will make sure you never have to suffer like this again."

He had reached out feebly, and the young man grasped his hand firmly in his.

"I am Four. Do you remember your name?"

He'd tried to mouth something, but the shape of his real name was lost to him. "No," he replied hoarsely.

The young man smiled. "Then I shall call you *Nikai*."

Nikai's knees struck the cold ground of the Darkroom.

Pain pierced his chest, tingling down his arms and legs, spreading to his toes. His heartbeat thumped in his ears, loud as drums. Sweat pooled in his palms. The tingling sensation turned dull, numbing his hands and feet. All he could think of was the Nothing. It was all he could feel and smell and see and taste.

But you're safe now. You won't ever have to go back there again, said a voice in his head. *You're safe now. Four said he would keep you safe.*

But where is Four now? he shouted back at that voice. *That's right—he left.*

Nikai loosened his tie. Tore at the buttons on his collar. Tried to breathe against the fear suffocating him. He couldn't go back to that place again. Couldn't be in the ravenous dark.

He felt a sudden pressure on his arm.

"You are not alone, Reaper."

The Librarian.

The pressure remained firm. Comforting.

Nikai stayed on the ground. Filled his lungs and belly with air, letting it trickle slowly out through his mouth. He repeated this, focusing on the pressure on his arm. He didn't know how much time had gone by, but gradually, his heartbeat slowed.

A subdued red glow had seeped into his surroundings. His eyes adjusted, and he saw pieces of parchment suspended in the air. Words written in black ink appeared on each parchment, then disappeared and reappeared again.

The stories of living mortals.

"Will you help me, qianbei?" Nikai whispered to the dark.

"Of course, young Reaper," the Librarian said gently. "Where do you wish to begin?"

Nikai struggled to his feet. "Eighteen years ago."

Sometime later, Nikai stood in the empty throne room of the Fourth Court, staring at the mirror before him. He wasn't sure if he had recovered from his episode in the Darkroom, but Ten was waiting for his report.

Nikai palmed the glass. "I want to speak with the Tenth King."

Moments later, the mirror flashed, transforming into a screen. Ten's face appeared, filling the entire space and too close for comfort.

"Reaper."

"Your Majesty."

"Did you discover anything in the Archives?"

"Another piece of the puzzle," Nikai replied. "I didn't find anything unusual about the boy, but the cadet's birth story was corrupted. At first the Librarian couldn't retrieve it. He said nothing like this has happened before. What he did manage to salvage was a different story—part of the original. It was a *death* story that got scrubbed, a fate that was changed. The girl wasn't supposed to be born; her mother was in an accident when she was pregnant, and *she* was supposed to die. Years later, the mother was killed by a strange Revenant, and the girl . . ." Nikai faltered.

"What about the girl?" Ten demanded, listening with rapt attention.

"I think there might be a connection between the girl and Four. I—I was there that night. I was there at the accident the mother was in," Nikai said, his throat tight. "Four saved the mother's life so the girl could be born; the First King asked him to."

Ten flared his nostrils. "The girl who cast the impossible spell is the same child that One claimed fate had led them to?"

"It could be a coincidence." But Nikai wasn't so sure.

"Coincidence is merely the universe conspiring," Ten said. "I must see the girl myself. I must speak with her."

"Speak with her? But we're not allowed to reveal ourselves."

Ten stepped back abruptly.

Nikai could see the throne room now. The place was in disarray. Chairs overturned, silk drapes torn, and crumpled balls of paper littering the ornate floor. A black substance smeared against the walls.

"Is everything okay, Your Majesty?"

"Yes, everything is fine and dandy." Ten picked up an empty glass and hurled it onto the floor. It shattered, spraying pieces everywhere. "Is it not obvious? Everything is *not* fine! My kingdom is falling apart, disintegrating before my very eyes. Here I am, trying to fix the problem my damned brother caused, while my useless siblings sit around doing shit. They think the Nothing will not touch them, but they are wrong."

He flung himself onto his throne. "I proposed your theory to the

Council of Kings. Half of them were willing to deliberate on it while the other half refused to even consider the possibility of Four being in the human realm. We are at an impasse."

Nikai's heart sank. "So nothing will be done?"

"On the contrary, there is so much that can be done. The only question is how far one is willing to go."

"I don't understand, Your Majesty."

Ten stared into space, thoughtful, twirling a finger. He got up and moved toward the mirror. Close. Closer. The red splash on his fingernail went round and round, then pointed straight at Nikai.

Something sinister peeked out from Ten's gold-speckled eyes.

Nikai took a step back. Even though they were separated by the mirror and a labyrinth of Courts and kingdoms between them, he did not feel safe from Ten's reach.

"The Second King thinks that if Four got rid of his power to escape and reside in the human realm, then our search comprises two paths: finding the vessel that holds his power and finding the human who houses his soul." Ten shrugged. "Either way, it requires us to operate in the human realm unrestricted by anything."

Unrestricted by anything? Nikai's uneasiness grew. "But the rules—" One look at Ten's expression, and Nikai shut his mouth.

"I have decided that this is *my* investigation now," Ten declared. "I will no longer be hamstrung by rules and tenets, not while my kingdom and my very existence are in danger. I will be working outside the lines, and *you* will be helping me. No one needs to know any of this. Understood?"

Nikai had reservations about the Tenth King's methods, but if it meant getting Four back, surely it was worth it? He nodded. "Yes, Your Majesty."

Ten ran his tongue over his sharp teeth. "Excellent. Now, if you will excuse me, I have a date with a mortal."

The screen flickered, transforming back into a mirror, and Nikai was left staring at himself, a haunted-looking young man with fear swirling in his eyes.

18
Rui

Xingshan Academy was nestled on an island near the southern tip of the mainland. An old mountain range, weathered with time, rose in the distance behind the campus, and the remnants of an old village lay at the base of it. Detached from the city and connected only by a bridge and shuttle train, the Academy felt like another world.

Rui liked it that way.

She'd left the Simulator facility and shut herself in her room. The image of Yiran on the verge of burning out, looking like he was dying, rattled her mind. Soon her own room grew too claustrophobic, and she decided to go to her favorite spot by the water to clear her mind.

The boardwalk stretched far across the edge of the campus where a small park was. Rui sagged onto the wooden bench and shivered in the light breeze. Even though she wore a thick puffer coat and an extra sweater over her athletic gear, her hands still had a bluish hue. Was it a sign that her recovery was going badly?

So far, no one at the Academy suspected the extent of her injuries. It seemed like the blow to her spirit core hadn't taken away her martial arts skills; she didn't have problems sparring with Yiran earlier. But the real problem plaguing her was unfixed. It was wretched to *appear* totally fine when, inside, she'd been broken apart and left to rust. She dug her hands into her coat pockets, sighing to the sea, her thoughts once again going to Yiran.

At first, she'd been surprised to discover that the Academy had bent the rules for him—the one-on-one lectures and tutorials, the observations of the senior class. But in hindsight, it should've been expected. Rui had long understood that privilege and power went hand in hand. She might be the prodigy, but Yiran had the *pedigree*. She had beaten him fair and square during the sparring session, but somehow it felt like she was the one who'd lost. No matter what, the Song name carried weight.

She was miffed at her classmates too. It wasn't that they didn't like her or respect her abilities; it was that they'd accepted Yiran as one of their own too quickly, as if it was his rightful place to be at the Academy. Would they do the same if they knew how he had gotten his magic?

She pulled out a small vial. The tonic inside was colorless and warm on her tongue. Zizi had given it to her to help with her healing. It did restore her strength, but the medicine couldn't hide the fact that she couldn't conduct her spiritual energy with her weapons.

Her pocket buzzed.

"Speak of the devil," she murmured. It was a text from Zizi.

Been hearing some chatter about missing mages. Disappearances in my circles.

Rui texted back quickly. What do you mean?

Unsure. I'm asking around. Anyway, are you feeling better? I'll fix it—promise!

"I'm holding you to it," she said to her phone.

"Holding whom to what?"

Ada had found her.

Rui smiled. "Nothing."

"You look like you're freezing." Ada wrapped her bright pink scarf around Rui's neck.

"Thanks," said Rui, her voice muffled by the soft wool. It smelled of green apples and citrus, the perfume Ada always wore. "How is he?"

"Yiran? I left him in his room an hour ago. He said he was going to nap. He'll be all right. I think it's just first-day nerves, plus he doesn't know the fundamentals. Mai really shouldn't have switched the program on him."

Rui was surprised by her own relief. Maybe she was more worried about Yiran than she cared to admit.

"By the way," Ada said with a broad smile, "we're going for karaoke when there's no curfew to celebrate the new president of the Student Council. Your lovely presence is mandatory."

"Right! I haven't congratulated you yet." Rui hugged her. "I told you it was going to be you. There's no one better for president."

"I did run a good campaign."

"A flawless one."

"If you insist." Ada patted herself on her back. "Good job, me."

"Good job, you," Rui agreed.

"So, karaoke?"

Rui couldn't hold a tune to save her life. "I don't have a choice, do I?"

"Nope." Ada laughed. "I feel like we haven't been hanging out much recently because of your injuries. I'm glad you're feeling like yourself again."

But I'm not myself. Rui wanted to tell the truth, but instead, she rested her head on Ada's shoulder.

"It was amazing to see you kicking that poor little rich boy's butt," Ada remarked.

Rui knew she wasn't being mean. "Why do you call him a poor little rich boy?"

"Because he is one. It's obvious he's been living in Ash's shadow. Having a famous and accomplished older sibling messes with your self-esteem."

Ada had the ability to empathize with everyone. Sometimes, Rui wished she had it too. "You, my friend," she said, "are way too kind."

Ada pointed at a tall figure jogging toward them. "Speaking of Song er shaoye, is that him?"

Rui thought briefly of running away, but it was too late. Yiran was already in front of them.

"Shouldn't you be resting?" Ada said.

"I couldn't nap. Thought I'd take a walk for some fresh air." He looked around. "This is a nice little park."

"You should still get some rest," Ada nagged. She glanced at her watch.

"Crap. I'm about to be late for my first Council meeting as president. I'll see you later, Rui."

She ran off, leaving an uncomfortable space between Rui and Yiran.

Rui wanted to leave, but this was *her* spot. She didn't want to lose it to him too.

"I've something to tell you," Yiran began.

"Shut up and sit down."

She closed her eyes, listening to the sound of the sea for a few long moments. When she opened them again, Yiran was next to her on the bench. Long legs stretched out, he gazed at the water, his lips an angry line. But the lapping waves seemed to soothe him the way they soothed her. The angles of his shoulders softened and his expression turned meditative.

Rui felt a palpable link between them. A kind of weird emotional connection. Like she could feel what he was feeling. It was awful and she hated it. She had felt his frustration when they sparred, his terror when the program switched and the Revenants came after him. She didn't know if it was because they'd shared a near-death experience together, or because his body contained something of hers. But it was there, undeniably so.

She was afraid he might feel it too.

"Okay," she finally said. "You may speak."

Yiran exhaled through his mouth. "I know it's awkward to see me in school and in your class. Don't worry, I'll stay out of your way." Lines rippled between his brows. "I know you hate me."

"*Hate* is a strong word. *An intense repulsive feeling of dislike* would be a more accurate description," she said. "But it was too troublesome to say in that moment, so I stuck with *hate*."

Yiran's mouth formed something between a smile and a grimace.

Rui looked away, picking at the raw skin around her thumbnail. "I'm sorry," she mumbled.

"For what?"

"For getting you involved in this mess. I'm sorry I didn't give you a

choice when I cast that spell. I'm sorry I planted a time bomb inside you."
It was a relief to say it out loud. She hadn't asked him before she held his
hand and changed both their lives forever. Her guilt had festered, and she
wanted to heal the rot. "You should be the one hating me."

"Why would I hate you?"

"Because you could d—"

"I don't hate you, Rui—I could never hate you." Yiran spoke quickly,
like he was afraid if he took a breath, the words would never come out.
"I never knew my father, and I can't say I know much about my mother
either. I think she loved him, but they couldn't be together. When I was
six, she brought me to Song Mansion. I never saw her again. I found out
who my father was that day—some great Exorcist who died protecting
the city. It's weird, sharing your father with the world. It's like everyone
knows him, or they claim to, anyway. I know who he was *supposed* to be,
but I don't know who he really was. I also found out what being a Song
meant. Sadly, I didn't meet expectations, and it's something I'm reminded
of every day."

Not knowing what to say, Rui fiddled with the tassels of Ada's scarf.

"You know what else?" Yiran continued. The tips of his ears were pink.
"My grandfather was going to send me away. I was supposed to leave my
home like some exile. But now, I get to stay because of what you did. You
may think you made a mistake, but it's because of you that I'm still here,
that I get to try again. It feels like a second chance, even if it's just for a
while."

If Rui had her way, she'd snatch her magic back from him right this
moment. But as she sat, feeling the churn of emotions flowing from him,
she wondered if, just for a few more days, she could let Yiran feel like he
was enough.

But it's not fair. He's always had everything. You've had to fight for your
place. She tried to silence that voice, tried not to think about how even if
her mother's murderer were standing in front of her, there'd be nothing
she could do now.

"I'm glad your grandfather was happy when you told him the news," she said, trying hard not to sound bitter.

"Is that what you think happened?" Yiran looked at his shoes, shaking his head. "The old man didn't care. He seemed upset, like I'd gotten into trouble again. Maybe he's afraid I'll embarrass him even more if I suck at this school."

The boy next to her wasn't the Song Yiran who had charmed her schoolmates, but the other boy, the poor little rich one Ada saw. The one who had so little to lose that he would throw his life away so easily.

Everyone dies sooner or later.

His smile had hurt her.

"Your core was burning up earlier, wasn't it?" Rui put her feet on the bench and drew her knees to her chest. "You didn't know what to do, and you were scared, and everything spilled out of control."

"I was afraid," he admitted quietly. He gave her a strange look, like he knew she was also talking about the young girl she had been four years ago.

The chilly wind returned with a vengeance, and with it, the turquoise sea turned stormy gray. A light drizzle came down, the freezing rain prickling their noses and cheeks.

Rui pulled her coat close.

"You should get out of the rain," Yiran told her.

Rui nodded. But she made no move to leave.

"I'm getting hungry," Yiran said. "The barley soup Mai got me was kind of . . ." He searched for the right word.

"Mealy? Soggy? Bland?" Rui suggested.

"It was pretty disgusting, but I'm sure there's proper food at the cafeteria. Why don't you join me? It's warmer indoors."

"What happened to staying out of my way?"

"I'll start tomorrow. Come on, I'll buy you dinner. We can get takeout downtown. Don't you miss riding in my fancy car?"

"We're not supposed to leave campus whenever we want—" Rui caught his smirk. He was teasing her. "Fine, cafeteria it is. They make their fries and burgers fresh, and they have this blue orangeade drink that Ada really loves. I'd recommend those and the mint-chocolate ice cream."

Yiran wrinkled his nose. "Absolutely no on the ice cream. I don't want to eat toothpaste."

"Mint-chocolate ice cream does not taste like toothpaste," Rui protested.

"We can agree to disagree. A flavor of ice cream shouldn't be a friendship breaker," he said solemnly, but his eyes were crinkling.

Were they friends? Rui wasn't sure. He'd revealed something to her, and she didn't know why she was worthy of this trust. They hardly knew each other. But maybe this was how friendships started, someone placing a fistful of feelings in your hand and saying, *Keep it safe*.

She felt a sudden tickle, like a whisper grazing her skin. A brief sense of vertigo hit her, like the world was warping. She blinked hard.

And gasped.

Yiran was motionless, eyes glazed, mouth shaped like the last word he'd uttered. The waves in front of them were frozen, just like the figures in the distance next to the buildings. Rain hung like strands of pearls in the air, and a surreal silence permeated her surroundings. All she could hear was her own ragged breathing.

Had *time* stopped? But how?

Suddenly aware of another presence, Rui turned.

A man was walking toward her, his long robes flowing red like blood.

He smiled and her heart turned to ice.

19
Rui

"Allow me to introduce myself," the man said, shaking out his long silk sleeves like a peacock displaying its tail feathers. "I am Ten, King of the Tenth Court of Hell."

Rui gawked.

The Tenth King looked only a few years older than Ash. His hair was spun gold and tied in a low ponytail with a simple red ribbon that matched his scarlet hanfu—traditional robes from a bygone era. The modern-looking black leather harness wrapped around his waist and the pair of leather gloves covering his fingers and half of his palms stood out in contrast.

Ten raised his chin, looking down his nose at her. "Close your mouth, human. The correct response to my esteemed presence is to grovel at my feet and address me as *Your Majesty*. I will also accept *My King* or *My Lord*, and if you wish to worship me by adulating the magnificence of my physical attributes, you may go ahead."

Rui continued to stare. Convinced she was hallucinating, she pinched herself.

The skin on her arm *hurt*.

Ten was starting to sulk. "I was not expecting you to be so rude."

"I'm sorry," Rui managed, "it's just that . . . you're *real*?"

"As real as you are."

She blinked. "Am I dead?"

"Alas, you are very much alive," Ten said bitingly. "Humans." He sighed, raising an elegant hand to his smooth forehead. "I blame the despicable mortal who had the audacity to try to draw us. And now everyone thinks we look like grumpy old men wearing ugly wing-tipped hats."

Rui collected her wits. If the Kings of Hell were real, and one had come specifically to find *her*, it could only mean she'd screwed up royally, pun intended. She curtsied, painting on a fawning smile.

"You're nothing like the portraits I've seen on hell money, Your Majesty. In fact, I don't think any mortal could capture the gloriousness of your beauty. There is no painting or photograph that could ever match your magnificence." When Ten seemed somewhat appeased by her flattery, she asked, "What brings you here, Your Majesty?"

"I wanted to have a word with you in private." Ten waved a hand at the frozen cadets scattered around the campus. "All of this must be strange, but do not worry, no human shall be harmed."

Coming from him, assurance sounded like a threat. He moved closer to her, graceful as a dancer. But his spindly limbs reminded Rui of a spider weaving its sticky web. She wondered if she was his prey.

"Tell me how you did it, *Rui*." Her name felt grossly intimate in his mouth.

"Did what, Your Majesty?"

"Tell me how you were able to cast such a powerful spell."

Was he talking about Zizi's ill-fated spell? "How did you know about that?"

Ten opened his palms, shrugging. "I am a god. I know many things."

Like any other spell, she had cast it from muscle memory, a reflex honed from years of training.

"I don't know. I just said the incantation."

"How did you create the spell?"

"I didn't—a mage, Zizi—he made it." His name spilled out of her mouth, and Rui's face heated with shame. It felt like she'd betrayed him somehow, but she had a feeling Ten was using his power to make her talk.

"Interesting." Ten removed his leather gloves.

Rui half expected to see claws or something creepy, but Ten's hands were normal. Lovely, really. Long pianist fingers and nails ruby-stained like jewels. *Or blood.*

He cupped her chin.

Rui wanted to pull away, but fear and confusion kept her still like a moth, pinned down and scrutinized by a lepidopterist.

Seconds later, Ten released her. "Interesting," he repeated, enunciating the word slower this time.

"What's so interesting, Your Majesty?"

Ignoring her question, Ten placed his cold hands on her shoulders. "I need your help, Rui. The King of the Fourth Court is missing, and I need you to find him."

"Excuse me?"

"I need you to find my brother, Four. He is missing."

"Four . . . your brother?"

"Yes. Four, my brother. He has been missing for eighteen years." The Tenth King was looking at her as if he thought her dull.

How could a god go missing? It made no sense. And why would Ten come to *her* for help?

Ten continued to stare expectantly.

"I'm sorry, Your Majesty, but I can't help you. I don't know how to," Rui said, very carefully and very politely. He was obviously someone who took offense easily. "I don't know anything about finding missing people. The Academy doesn't teach us that."

Ten sniffed haughtily. "My brother isn't *people*. He is a King."

"If you haven't found him for so long, I don't see why you think I can," she pointed out. "I'm just a human."

"The search was headed in the wrong direction. But now, I believe we are getting somewhere." Ten smiled. It felt like he had too many teeth.

"But why me?"

"You are special." Seeing her surprise, Ten clarified with a short laugh. "I am not complimenting you, not at all. I am merely saying I think you may have what it takes to find my brother. You have been touched by death and escaped its embrace."

"How . . . how did you know?" she stammered.

"Like I said, I know many things." Ten threw a cursory glance at the still-frozen Yiran before turning back to her. "Let us make a deal."

"A deal?"

"Yes, a mutually beneficial agreement. It is simple. You will help me find my brother, and you shall receive something in return."

Rui remembered a story her mother once told her, about a god who owed a human a favor for helping them. If she knew anything about fairy tales, it was that they were all too real.

A favor from a god . . . She could ask for her magic back. For good grades, for money, for her father's health, for him to stop gambling. She could ask for the world, and Ten might give it to her.

He was watching her carefully. "Shall we proceed with this fair exchange between you and me?"

How could there ever be a fair exchange between a mortal and a god? Her mother's bedtime story had ended with the human's downfall.

Rui shook her head. "No deals with devils."

Ten howled with laughter. "But I am no devil." He ran his tongue over his mouth in a way that made her linger on his cherry lips for longer than she wished to.

Then, he cracked a knuckle.

Rui clutched her chest, legs buckling as she gasped for air.

Ten had unleashed something. An invisible force that felt like spiritual energy. Not bright and warm like yangqi, nor dark and cold like the yinqi of Revenants. It was different, way more powerful, beyond worlds and all-consuming.

Rui fell to the ground.

Ten closed in, the light in his eyes greedy. "Would you like to make a deal, my dear?"

Rui did not want—no, she *did*. She wanted to say yes. She felt the word forcing its way up her throat. She stabbed her nails into her palms and clamped her lips shut with all her might. But there were other ways to show acquiescence. The muscles at the back of her neck relaxed, and she felt her head lowering into a nod.

Ten. He's doing this. Fury sparked in her. A god or not, Rui wasn't going to let him take away her choice. She dug in—and pushed back.

The invisible pressure lifted.

For a moment, the world spun. It felt like she'd eaten something foul, the taste making her retch. Slowly, she pulled herself to her knees and hunched over the bench.

"Whatever you're trying, it won't work," she said, breathing heavily. "You can't force me to agree with you."

Ten was looking at her like he'd discovered hidden treasure. "I cannot coerce someone to make a deal. It must be done voluntarily. I was merely testing you for something else. That was less than a tenth of my spiritual power, but you managed to withstand it even in your weakened state. Astonishing—I am impressed, and I am seldom so. You must help me, there can be no other way."

Rui shook her head, more to clear her mind than to disagree.

Ten shifted to Yiran.

"Hmm," he mused, caressing Yiran's cheek. He pinched it. Left a red mark on smooth skin. "It would be a pity if this *normie* were to perish, would it not?"

"Are you going to kill him if I don't help you?"

"Please. I would never be so uncouth," Ten admonished. "Besides, he does not need *my* help. He is like a balloon filled with air, he will just keep expanding. Until one day—" Ten mimed an explosion. "It is only a matter of time."

Guilt roiled in Rui's stomach. She had seen Yiran lose control in the Simulator. Seen how magic lit him up from the inside and burned through him. His life was in peril, and it was her fault. Even if her spirit core healed, there was a chance Zizi might not be able to transfer her spiritual energy and magic back. Rui trusted Zizi's skill, but she'd never seen him so worried before, like he wasn't confident he could reverse the spell. And if Zizi couldn't help, did it mean Yiran would eventually die? Did it mean Rui would have to live without magic forever?

"The boy." Ten's voice cut through her thoughts. "He means something to you."

"He means nothing to me," Rui said. But it only made Ten smile.

"Shall we revisit the terms of my proposed deal? Humans are full of desires. Surely I can offer you something in return that will pique your interest? Money tends to do the trick. But for you"—Ten's eyes turned to slits—"vengeance, redemption, and maybe a little true love?"

"I don't know what you're talking about." Her heart was beginning to pound again.

"You want your magic back, do you not? You want it back so badly it *hurts*. I see through you, mortal. You and your foolish altruism, you and your selfish desires. You think you can save the world, but that is not the only thing your heart wants."

"You don't know anything about me," Rui spat. But there was a tremor in her voice they both heard.

Ten smiled.

Rui's mind darkened. A hazy veil of memories flashed through her mind. Voices familiar and far away echoed in her ears . . . *a little girl throwing a tantrum of tears, whining, persuading . . . her mother, finally giving in. The dark alleyway . . . screams . . .*

A body lying on the street. Cold. Still.

She heard a slippery voice in her ear. "Nothing can bring your mother back. But I can offer you revenge, a chance to make amends and redeem your sorry little soul."

Tears stung her eyes. It was all her fault. Her fault for throwing that tantrum. Her fault that her father was now a broken man. If she hadn't insisted on going to the Night Market that night, her mother would still be alive.

The visions vanished. But doubt and the guilt remained.

Ten looked triumphant. He knew he'd gotten under her skin. "Would you like me to find the one who killed your mother and hand them over to you to do as you wish?" His words shone down like the sun, and the vicious weed Rui nurtured inside her raised its head.

This was what she wanted.

"Are you sure my mother's murderer is still alive?"

Ten pulled his gloves back on with the air of someone who knew they'd already won the fight. "The nature of deals is such that they have conditions that are agreed upon, and each condition must be fulfilled accordingly. There is no deal in which one side is left empty-handed. I would not have proposed that condition if I knew I would fail to fulfill it."

"Then I want more," said Rui. "If I help you find Four, you have to bring me my mother's murderer *and* you have to make sure I get my magic back."

Ten seemed impressed by her boldness. "I could sweeten the deal further—"

"Why?" she said, instantly suspicious.

Ten looked irritated by her interruption. "I might be speaking too soon, but I think I'm growing fond of you, rude little mortal. So I am willing to throw you another bone. Find my brother and, in return, not only will you have what you just asked for, but"—he patted Yiran's cheek—"your friend will also live. Do we have a deal?"

Rui nodded. This time, of her own volition.

"Then a deal has been made," Ten said with a grand gesture.

"Just like that?" Rui had expected a crash of thunder or something, but nothing happened, and she didn't feel any different after making the deal with the King.

"Not everything has to be dramatic, my dear." Ten smiled. "Death's touch connects you to the underworld, and it is that connection that may draw you to my brother."

"*May?* You're not sure of this?"

"All avenues must be explored in this search, and you are but one small tool in the grand scheme of things."

At least Ten was direct with her, and he didn't seem to care about her lapse in honorifics. "Where do I start?"

"My brother is likely here in the mortal realm, and there is a chance . . ." Ten paused, looking repulsed. "There is a chance he may be in the form of a human."

"A human? How's that possible?" This was getting more absurd. What had she gotten herself into?

"You do not need to know the how or the why to fulfill your task. All you need to know is he is in this city, and I think *you* will be able to sense him."

"You have to give me something better than that. The city's huge and full of people. I can't go waltzing down the street, checking to see if I sense a connection with anyone."

"Not just anyone. Remember that this mortal houses the soul of a god—it will not be anyone ordinary."

"It's someone extraordinary?" Rui frowned. Did he mean— "Someone with a strong spirit core, someone who can do magic?"

"That should whittle your field down. Oh, and one more thing—there is another reason you should hasten your search. A little incentive, perhaps."

Ten giggled when Rui made a frustrated sound. She didn't like the imbalance of power between them. How he was stringing her along, how he seemed to know everything, and she, nothing at all. Still, if he could find her mother's murderer . . .

"What incentive?"

"Humans would not treasure life if they knew nothing of death, and death loses its meaning if one never experiences the full spectrum of life. Life and death exist symbiotically, as do our realms. My brother's disappearance disrupted this balance. Our Reapers collect the souls of the departed, and if souls are not ferried safely into my realm, they will linger as spirits in yours, vulnerable to the Blight. What do you think will happen if my brother is not found?"

Rui swallowed dryly. "More Revenants."

"Clever girl. Now you know why you need to hurry." Ten swiped at his arm, as if brushing away invisible hands tugging at him. "Speaking of time, I must leave your world now." There was an off-color tinge to Ten's face, a translucency she hadn't noticed before. He was fading before her eyes.

"Wait! How do I contact you?"

"Focus on your search. I will find you." The specter of the Tenth King wagged a gloved finger, whispering, "Remember, this is our little secret. No one else must know of this or the consequences will be grave. We do not want to alert my brother, or anyone else who may be helping him."

Ten vanished, and the world was in motion again.

"What are we waiting for?"

Rui yelped in surprise.

Yiran was looking at her quizzically. "Are you okay?"

"I . . . yeah," she said, unable to take her eyes off him. He seemed perfectly fine and alive, untouched by any death god magic.

"Well, you're really pale." Yiran shrugged off his jacket and held it over her head. "Let's get you out of the rain and get those fries you were talking about."

He made no move to squeeze under his jacket with her, putting her comfort first. Rui was surprised he was capable of such a chivalrous and kind act.

As they headed for shelter, she pondered over her encounter with Ten. The enormity of her task daunted her. But now, there was a way to get her magic back and have her vengeance. She glanced sideways at Yiran. And there was a way to save this foolish boy's life. Finally, there was some hope in sight.

But first, she had to hunt down a god.

20
Nikai

From his perch in the observation room, Nikai stared out at all eighteen levels of the Tenth Court's administrative area. He could see the souls hunched over computer terminals in their cubicles, heads bent in concentration. But no one could see him.

Some time ago, Ten had redesigned this place to resemble a panopticon—a circular prison with cells going round a central tower. Using a clever play of light, the inmates *could not* see into the guard tower, which stood in the middle, but the tower itself gave the impression of being *all-seeing*. Similarly, Ten's staff and the souls working here never knew if their King was watching them, and so they self-regulated and behaved as if he had eyes on them all the time. It was a stroke of genius.

And it told Nikai everything he needed to know about the Tenth King.

Underneath the tower, the fiery pits of the kingdom were on full display beneath glass walkways, the sight intimidating enough to deter any wayward soul. But the Tenth Court's area of expertise was psychological. There were pitch-black cells that served the purpose of harsher punishments, should judgment call for it. The atmosphere of the whole kingdom was so different from the Fourth Court it gave Nikai whiplash every time he visited, which, thank the gods, wasn't very often.

Today, however, he was here on his own accord.

Nikai paced, irritated. His pager was going off incessantly with messages from the other Reapers. There was just so much to do.

Ten swept in like a river of blood, interrupting Nikai in mid-curse. "I do not recall asking for you."

Nikai stuffed his pager into his pocket. "Your Majesty." He bowed. There was a corner of gray at the edge of Ten's robes by his foot. "I'm aware I have not been summoned, but I couldn't wait. Did you talk to the girl?"

"I did."

"What happened, Your Majesty?"

Ten took his time to answer, circling the room, observing the workers outside in their cubicles. He seemed to enjoy the sight of Nikai squirming in silence, holding in his barrage of questions for fear of being rude.

"I felt a trace of Four on the girl," Ten finally revealed. "It is likely there because he saved her mother's life and, thus, hers. However, there *is* something more to her, but I am uncertain what it is for now."

That's what the First King said that night about the girl. One had said the child could be valuable to the mortal realm . . . *chosen* for a greater purpose. Few had seen One ever since they were imprisoned in their palace; Nikai had not seen them after Four vanished.

"Did you tell the girl Four saved her life?" Nikai asked, thinking the girl deserved to know.

"As you have reminded me, Reaper, we have not found my sneaky brother for so long and we have no idea how he is hiding from us. It would be wise to keep our cards close until we have more information."

"How about the boy? Did you see him?"

"He was with her. I did not detect a trace of Four on the boy, but . . . he confuses me."

Nikai tensed. "How so?"

"I want you to keep an eye on both of them," Ten said, strolling to the window. "Inform me immediately if anything of interest comes up."

"Yes, Your Majesty," Nikai said. Ten had ignored his question about the boy. Was Ten hiding something?

Ten smoothed his flaxen hair. It seemed dull, its luster diminished. How far into the Tenth kingdom had the Nothing encroached? At least there were no signs of it here in the center of the Court yet.

"By the way, I made a deal with the girl."

"A deal?" Nikai exclaimed. How could Ten drop this information so casually?

"Bit of a savior complex, that one. Makes it easier to fool her."

"Fool her?" That bad feeling about Ten taking matters into his own hands returned. If he was operating outside the confines of stipulated rules between the realms, there was no controlling him and what he might do to the girl or any other mortal.

"There are two types of humans: those who run into a burning house to save a cat, and those that think, *It is just a cat*." Ten considered Nikai, a cunning glint in his eyes. "I wonder which type *you* were."

"Did you tell her that deals with Kings are binding across lifetimes?" Nikai asked, refusing to let the conversation derail.

"I do not see why she needs to know."

"You took advantage of her ignorance and desperation," Nikai accused in a burst of courage. "If the deal is unfulfilled, the two parties will remain bonded until all conditions are complete. Did you tell her that before she agreed? What was the deal?"

Ten cocked his head like a bird spotting a worm. "My dear Reaper, who are you to judge when you have sinned as a mortal? Who are you to lecture me on righteousness when you do not remember how you lived your mortal life?"

"Reapers forgo our memories to take on this role. It is a sacrifice."

"A sacrifice? Do not joke." Coming dangerously close, Ten trailed a fingernail across Nikai's throat.

The room dimmed.

Nikai froze. He could feel his insides slowly seizing.

"You call it a sacrifice, but it is cowardice," said Ten. "How easy it is to forget all the terrible things you did when you were alive, to forget the guilt. How wonderful it is to have your slate wiped clean; all you need to do is to serve your King. Who would not want that? Never forget *where* Four took you from." Ten smiled at him, almost innocently. "Why were you in the Nothing, Nikai? Did you look into your past deeds while you were in the Archives? Or do you prefer to pretend that you were one of the good ones?"

A terrible darkness descended in Nikai, a shroud woven with every possible horrific deed he could have committed in his mortal life. This was the Tenth King's power—he pulled your eyelids back, forced you to see the ugly truth that resided within.

"The Nothing traps you for eternity, neither dead nor alive, merely existing," Ten said. "It is pain in all definitions of the word, and it is forever. And now we are all in danger of falling into its abyss." Disdain dripped from his voice as he regarded Nikai. "Let me ask you, Reaper—do you wish to return to it?"

Nikai hung his head, whispering, "No."

"Do you want your King back?"

"Yes."

"Then let me make the deals I need to. Get out of my sight." Ten turned back to the windows.

Nikai bowed and retreated from the room.

He ran down the hallway and ported through several doors as quickly as he could. Back in the Fourth Court and safe from the eyes and ears of the Tenth, Nikai sat in silence at his desk, thinking about what Ten had said.

. . . let me make the deals I need to . . .

Who else was Ten making deals with? He must be hatching his own plans and excluding Nikai. But this was Nikai's search too, and he refused to be left out. He made a quick call to a trusted friend at a different department who owed him a favor.

"I need you to get me access to the logs of anyone leaving the underworld and returning from the human realm—and for both our sakes, be discreet."

21
Yiran

Yiran was bone-tired after two full weeks at Xingshan Academy. He'd been studying and training like his life depended on it. Which, he supposed, it did.

Days were capped with remedial lessons, late dinners, and little sleep, while weekends were focused on physical training. For someone who had spent his life coasting through everything, this was a sea change. Plus, he had no social life to speak of anymore, and the list of unanswered messages from his friends grew longer and longer. At least his spirit core remained stable. The only pressing problem in that regard was his lack of a spiritual weapon. Without one, Yiran felt like a fraud. It reminded him he was only here because of Rui.

He was trying to focus on what Teshin was saying now. The two of them had been huddled in the armory for hours, going back and forth between the spiritual weapons on display.

"—it doesn't make sense." Teshin ran one hand through their mohawk and another hand across the selection of weapons displayed on the touch screen. Their hair became loose and fluffy, making them look less stern. A string of metal rings hung from their belt. An accessory or a weapon? Knowing Teshin, it was both.

"Sorry, I zoned out for a while. Ash made me do a bunch of drills this morning," Yiran said, stifling a yawn. His grandfather hadn't contacted him, but his chirpy jerk of a half brother popped by often enough. "What doesn't make sense?"

"You. You don't make sense."

Yiran stilled. Had Teshin discovered the questionable origins of his magic?

But Teshin was rubbing their eyes wearily, looking like they'd gotten up before dawn to run ten miles too.

"We've tried the swords and sabers, the crossbows and other ranged weapons, even unusual options like the bladed fan and the umbrella," Teshin said. "Heck, we even tried butterfly knives today. Sorry about that one, should've known you'd hurt yourself. It takes a lot of skill to use one of those."

Yiran relaxed. His secret was safe. "Don't worry about it. I haven't had this much fun in a while." He wriggled his bandaged fingers. He'd sliced them open while trying to spin the butterfly knives.

"Those are old, aren't they?" Teshin said. "The other cuts on your fingers."

Yiran shoved his hands into his pockets. He tried to smooth over his expression, but Teshin had noticed his discomfort.

"I'm sorry," they said. "I shouldn't have asked. It's none of my business."

"It's in the past." Yiran couldn't bring himself to say more. He didn't want to remember what his grandfather did to him, even if the old man's intentions had been good.

"The past should stay the past," Teshin agreed. They tapped the screen, and it went blank. "I think we've done all we can here."

Disappointment slammed into Yiran. Despite knowing that a spiritual weapon was intrinsically tied to its wielder, Yiran had secretly hoped to match with a weapon that wasn't Rui's somehow. He wanted so badly to find his own blade, to prove he was his own person.

He forced a smile that made him feel worse. "Thanks for your help, Teshin. Sorry for wasting your time on a weekend. I'll buy you lunch sometime."

"What are you talking about? I'm not giving up," Teshin said, frowning. They glanced at their watch. "We've got some time before our karaoke night. You're coming over to my place. Mom's not around, but my sister is."

"Your sister?"

Teshin flashed one of their rare smiles. "The women in our clan are weapons artisans. Tesha doesn't study at the Academy. She's homeschooled, and she learns the trade instead. She's a genius. I bet she'll come up with something."

And just like that, Yiran's hope returned.

The Mak residence was a sprawling compound of metal and brick. It lacked the sophisticated elegance of Song Mansion and the eccentric appeal of Zizi's shophouse, but there was an earthiness to it, a kind of rustic warmth that made Yiran think of cozy evenings, laughter, and a large family.

Teshin wasted no time in bringing him to the workshop. There were blades in different stages of treatment, and weapons and tools Yiran had no name for. The fire was going, and the place was warm. He shrugged off his jacket and slung it over a chair.

A girl their age was tending to the forge. She wore a long black cotton dress and lace-up boots. Her hair was in a messy topknot, her eyes dark and focused. As they drew close, Yiran saw a clan tattoo like Teshin's on the nape of her neck, disappearing down her top.

She turned at the sound of their footsteps, wiping her hands on her worn leather apron.

"Yiran, meet my sister, Tesha."

Tesha cocked her head. "Is this the weirdo you were talking about?"

Taking an instant liking to her, Yiran grinned. "The one and only."

"Let's have a look at you then," she said, smiling back.

Teshin was her fraternal twin, so she didn't resemble them. But the two siblings had the same quiet confidence, the kind that came with knowing exactly what you were meant to do with your life. Yiran wished he could relate.

"Grab that sword over there—no, the one on the left," Tesha said. "Go on, swing it around. Show me some footwork."

Yiran did as he was told.

"You can stop."

He put the sword down.

"I heard your fingers glow when you channel magic," Tesha said. "Normally the crimson glow of yangqi only shows on a spiritual weapon when it's been imbued with the wielder's magic; that's why you're a weirdo. Give me your hands, please." Her smile disappeared as she examined his palms, then the backs of his hands, and finally, his fingers. "Channel for me."

Again, Yiran obliged. Sure enough, as his breathing pattern shifted, a soft crimson glow lit up around his fingertips. Not wanting to strain his spirit core, he kept it slow and steady, a low-level flow.

"How's your spell casting?" Tesha asked.

"Not too bad—"

"Mediocre," Teshin said bluntly. "He can do better."

"Ouch. Appreciate the honesty." Yiran pulled his hands back.

Teshin turned to their twin. "Thoughts?"

"I think you might be right," Tesha replied, crossing her arms.

Yiran couldn't tell if it was a good sign or a bad one.

Teshin tilted their head, only for Tesha to raise her eyebrows in reply to what they were silently suggesting. *Must be a twin thing,* Yiran thought. A secret language between the two of them.

"Something wrong?" he asked.

"Someone tampered with your meridian pathways," Tesha said. "But you already knew that." The look in her eyes was kind, like she understood what he'd gone through.

For once, Yiran didn't feel defensive, just confused. "What does that have to do with anything?"

"You don't have to tell us what happened if you don't want to," Tesha assured him. "All I'm saying is whatever was done to you might be what's stopping you from matching properly with a spiritual weapon. I think your qi is circulating in a strange pattern because of the tampering. It might also be affecting your spell casting."

A bitter laugh caught in Yiran's throat. The irony wasn't lost on him. His grandfather had tried so hard to extract magic out of him, to insist on something that wasn't there, no matter the cost. No matter the damage. To think that now, when Yiran *could* practice magic, it was the consequences of his grandfather's past actions that were preventing him from achieving what the old man wanted in the first place.

Yiran tried not to spiral. He had come *so* close, and each time he found another locked door he had no key for.

"What now?" he said, feeling helpless. "Do I just . . . walk away from magic? Do I—"

Teshin cut him off. "When I said I wasn't giving up, I meant I wasn't giving up on you."

Yiran stared. It didn't occur to him that Teshin would care that much. That Teshin would care about *him*. *You're just a weirdo, a puzzle to be solved*, he reminded himself.

Tesha rolled her eyes. "Exorcists. They sure love saving people."

"Can you find a way around it?" Teshin asked.

"Normally, I'd say no," she said. "But there's something about you, Yiran, the way your spiritual energy *sprays* out like, I don't know, a fountain, for lack of a better description, that makes me think maybe there's a chance. I think we need to approach this from a different angle."

Tesha played with her lip ring as she gazed into the fire. Yiran could almost see the gears in her head moving, clicking into place as she hummed softly to herself.

"I've an idea that might work, but it's going to take some time for me to get it right," she concluded, her eyes sparkling.

"Told you she was a genius," Teshin said proudly.

"Don't brag about me until I deliver the goods."

Yiran didn't know why the twins were so set on helping him, or why they were doing so without asking for something in return. He wondered if they would do the same if they knew how and where he'd gotten his magic from.

"What kind of weapon are you thinking of?" he asked.

"Not a weapon," Tesha replied, "but something that can bypass the normal methods of channeling. I can't guarantee it'll work though."

Yiran nodded. "Anything's worth a try."

She took his hands in her callused ones again. "In that case, I hope you're good at keeping still—we're going to make a mold."

22
Rui

Based on the information Ten had given her, Rui concluded there were three groups to focus her search efforts on: Xingshan cadets and professors, Exorcists, and the underground magic community.

She started with the most accessible group, interacting with cadets she'd never spoken to previously, trying to sense if there was anything odd about any of them. The cohorts were small, and she went through the rosters quickly, but her masquerade as an extrovert didn't go unnoticed by her classmates.

"You didn't tell me you were interviewing potential dates to the Winter Ball," Ada said one day as they were eating lunch at the cafeteria.

Rui's spoon splashed into her soup. "Potential dates? What are you talking about?"

To her surprise, Ada clapped her hands gleefully. "Yes! Mai owes me five bucks." When Rui continued to stare incredulously at her, Ada explained, "You were suddenly so friendly to everyone, Mai thought you were looking for a date for the Ball, so she started a bet for fun. Of course, I knew you weren't. Anyway, I only brought it up today because I wanted to cash out." Ada hesitated, looking sheepish. "You're not mad at me, are you?"

"I'm not, but I can't decide if I should be insulted you only bet five bucks on me," Rui replied, feeling both amused and dismayed.

It wasn't long before Rui ran out of cadets to talk to. She moved on to the professors and started playing teacher's pet, booking consultations with them on the pretext of improving her studies—*and* she hinted to Mai it was all an effort to get a leg up for her Guild applications. The new rumor spread quickly and bought Rui cover as she went about her investigation.

But despite Rui's efforts, no one at the Academy stood out. She didn't sense anything, and she didn't feel a connection with anyone, only a lot of awkwardness and anxiety on her end. The only person she *did* feel something with . . .

With all that spiritual energy, Mochi's spirit core should've burned out, but it didn't. Look at him, he's perfectly fine.

What if Zizi had a point? Was there something more to Song Yiran she didn't know about? Still, he had been born with a weak and ordinary spirit core. That was a fact. The only reason she felt anything near him was because he had stolen her magic. She relegated him back to the bottom of her list.

Deciding to try her luck in a different direction, Rui waited until the weekend, when she could leave campus, and went to the Night Market.

She stood outside it now, a bundle of nerves, gathering the courage to enter. She'd walked by the area sometimes, but the last time she was actually inside the Market was that night four years ago.

With a deep breath, she stepped forward.

The place looked the same. Rui didn't know why she expected it to be different. Her eyes still watered from the thick incense, her stomach still growled from the fragrant scent of roasted meats, and her ears picked up the familiar tune of haggling between customer and merchant.

Colorful lights hung from the stalls, giving the place a festive feel, their patterns reflecting in the wet puddles on the ground from an earlier rain shower. It seemed like everyone was out in the streets tonight. Rui weaved her way through the crowd, keeping an eye out for anything or anyone who might seem unusual.

A rhythmic sound of metal hitting metal struck her ears, and she stopped abruptly in the middle of the path.

"Watch it—this isn't your grandfather's road." A young girl with heavy eyeliner glared at her and pushed past. A few others threw Rui impatient looks as they carried on, squeezing their way forward.

Drawn by the metallic ringing sound, Rui filtered into a walkway. A kindly-looking old man was standing in the corner with a huge, round metal container propped up in front of him on a table. He worked his tools, using one to hit the other, slowly breaking up a large milky-white piece of candy into smaller bite-sized pieces.

The old man noticed her. "Would you like some dingding tang?"

Rui shook her head, breathing hard. The thought of tasting her once-favorite candy made her nauseated.

It was an unspoken rule for Xingshan cadets to avoid places like the Night Market, where the underground magic community held territory. But Rui had stopped coming here for another reason.

It felt like the scene of a crime. An unsolved murder that haunted her days and nights.

Angry at her own weak-mindedness, Rui walked quickly back into the crowd. But the trip was starting to feel like a waste of time. It didn't seem likely she'd be able to sense anything; it was too crowded tonight, and she was constantly being jostled.

She moved to the sidewalk for air.

Out of the corner of her eye, something blue flashed. She glanced over her shoulder. There was nothing. But she could've sworn she'd felt eyes on her back.

"Something bothering you, meinu?" A middle-aged woman with cat-eye spectacles was gesturing at her from a stall. "A little lovelorn? How about a charm? Auntie Lian has everything you need."

The woman's stall didn't look any different from the dozen others that sold jade accessories for luck, calligraphic couplets on red paper, prayer candles, joss sticks, and charms—real and fake. But the old shophouse behind her caught Rui's interest.

Red lanterns, black markings. Similar to Zizi's. *A mage.* Rui might not be able to sense a connection with anyone with the surging crowd, but there was something else the magic practitioners at the Night Market were known for.

Information.

It would've been easier if she could ask Zizi for help. But he'd try to drag the truth out of her. A mage who was a stranger, someone who was purely in it for money, they wouldn't ask questions.

"I don't need a charm," Rui said politely, "but can you tell me whose shop that is?"

Auntie Lian frowned, as if she'd noticed something. "Who wants to know?"

"Just me."

"You train at Xingshan Academy?"

Rui was dressed in her street clothes, not her uniform.

"I can always tell," Auntie Lian boasted, taking her silence as confirmation. "Something about you young ones—that look in your eye like you think you'll smile in the face of death. Until you see it, of course." She laughed, tickled by her own words. "A mage lives there, but I'm sure you knew that."

"Are they taking visitors? The lanterns aren't lit."

"Maybe, maybe not."

"I might have a job for them," Rui said as if she were confiding.

"What job?"

Rui replied with a winning smile, "It's a secret job, Auntie Lian. If I told you, it wouldn't be a secret anymore, would it? When will the mage be back?"

"Why do you want to know?"

Rui kept her tone light. "Why not?"

"What do I get in return if I told you?"

"Oh, depends."

Auntie Lian popped a toothpick into her mouth. "Are you sure you don't want that charm for your true love?"

Rui widened her eyes, still smiling her sugary smile as she coaxed, "Are you sure you can't tell me anything else?"

"Cheeky thing. I like you." Auntie Lian chuckled, then sobered. "I wish I could tell you, but I don't know when the mage is coming back."

Rui sensed her concern. On a hunch, she said, "The mage isn't missing, is he?"

Auntie Lian's salesy persona vanished. "What do you know about missing mages?"

"Nothing," Rui confessed. "Just that some have disappeared recently."

Wariness trickled into the woman's expression. "Does the Guild know about this?"

Rui shook her head. She wasn't sure if that was the truth, but it seemed better to assure Auntie Lian.

"We haven't seen Master Kang in over a week, and it's not like him to go away without saying anything or leaving instructions."

"Do you have people looking for him?"

Auntie Lian nodded. "We look after our own, not like your kind."

She said it so matter-of-factly Rui lost the urge to defend *her kind*. Rui was still a cadet, and she didn't know everything about the Guild and how they operated. It was likely the underground magic community had a different experience with the Exorcists than Rui had.

"I hope Master Kang's okay, and you'll find him soon," she said, meaning every word.

"You're a good one. Here, this is on me." Auntie Lian pressed a tiny jade rabbit hanging from a red string into Rui's palm. "For luck."

A mother and child came up to the stall to browse, and Auntie Lian turned to them.

Rui took it as her cue to leave. She dropped the lucky charm into her pocket. It was almost time to meet Ada at the karaoke club anyway. Tonight's trip hadn't garnered her the information she wanted, but it seemed like the mystery of the missing mages was getting bigger. She'd have to talk to Zizi about it.

As she took a shortcut through a small alley to the subway station, that weird feeling of being watched came back. She swiveled around.

Again, she thought she caught a flash of blue. But it'd happened so quickly she must've imagined it. After all, she was the only one in the alley.

23
Rui

The karaoke club was throbbing with music so loud it gave Rui a headache. The senior cadets were in a private full-service room with free-flowing drinks, and fruit and dessert to boot. Everyone was letting loose after a long week of training.

Rui sat in a corner, stuffing her face with grapes. There was a burst of laughter from the other side of the room where Yiran was holding court. She hated how well he was getting along with everyone at school. Hated how she could *feel* his excitement like a visceral punch to her gut. His emotions were so distinct and loud whenever he was near it was hard to tune him out.

She made a face that went unnoticed in the dimly lit room as she crushed another grape in her mouth. The sweet fruit did nothing to mask the lingering bitterness inside her.

Ada appeared. "Pick a song!"

"Both brothers are terrible choices, but at least one of them is easy on the eyes."

"What are you talking about? I said pick a song *to sing*."

Oh. Rui said stiffly, "You know I can't sing."

"Neither can Teshin, and they're about to start their third ballad of the night."

They both winced and then laughed as Teshin's off-key warbling blasted from the speakers.

Ada poked her ribs. "So, which Song brother is easy on your eyes?"

"I'm taking that to my grave." Rui mimed zipping her lips, wriggling out of Ada's reach. "Oops, nature calls."

Ada pretended to glare before joining the growing chorus of rosy-cheeked seniors surrounding Teshin as they gave their best-worst rendition of an angsty love song.

Outside the room, the club was marginally less noisy. It was a moonless night and there was no curfew. Just like the Night Market, every restaurant and bar in the entertainment district was packed.

Squeezing past a harried-looking staffer, Rui went to the back of the club. She groaned at the queue outside the restroom and got in line for the long wait.

She was finally done and washing her hands when two young women stumbled in. The shorter one crammed into a stall and slammed the door shut.

"Hurry up," her friend said as she reapplied her lipstick in the mirror. "I called us a cab home."

"But why?" the girl in the stall whined.

"Haven't you heard about the murders? I don't want to stay out too late."

"Don't be a killjoy! The Exorcists will handle it. There's no curfew tonight, and I'm here to enjoy myself."

"Exorcists?" Miss Lipstick made a face, muttering to herself, "I doubt it."

Rui stuck her wet hands under the hand dryer, trying not to scowl at the girl.

"Oh, just hurry up!" Miss Lipstick yelled at her friend above the roar of air.

Rui stomped out of the restroom. She was so annoyed she almost didn't see the lean figure striding purposefully in her direction. It took her a few moments to realize it was Zizi.

Gone were the pajamas he always wore, the ratty flip-flops he shuffled in, and that bat-wing cardigan she had a secret fondness for. Instead, his silky shirt was tucked into a pair of slim black trousers, and he was wearing actual shoes—leather loafers with burnished gold buckles. A black blazer draped over his shoulders, and an assortment of necklaces hung down, accentuating the cut of his neckline. Even his hair looked different.

The waves were slicked back to define his features, making him look older than his eighteen years.

"You're not wearing pajamas," Rui burst out.

"How good of you to notice," Zizi said.

"What are you doing here?"

He gestured in the general direction of the restroom.

"No, I mean, what are you doing in a karaoke club?"

"What do most people do at a karaoke club?"

"Do you even sing?"

"Like an angel. I'd offer to serenade you right now, but my bladder protests."

Resting a shoulder against the wall, Zizi gazed down at her, eyes half-lidded, lips hinting of amusement and something more. Had he been drinking? He was a complete lightweight. Once, after failing to master a spell, he'd drunk half a bottle of hard lemonade and spouted bad, morose poetry about how pretty her eyes were before falling asleep in her lap. They never spoke of the incident, and Rui assumed he'd forgotten about it.

Zizi was swaying on his feet now. "I came here to hang out with some friends."

"You mean criminals."

He grinned crookedly, tapping her nose lightly with his finger. "Boop! Don't forget you're my friend, too."

"Unfortunately." Rui swatted his hand away, her cheeks suddenly warm. She knew they had to be beet red, and she was glad for the poor lighting in the corridor.

"Well, I'm very glad I met you here." He leaned down, lowering his voice. "I have news. Perhaps we can go outside to the alleyway? To talk, not to take a leak."

"I'm with the other cadets," Rui said, suddenly worried that one of her schoolmates or a patron might catch her talking to him. She checked, but no one around them was paying any attention.

Zizi frowned. "You're not afraid of being seen with me, are you?"

"I don't want anyone thinking I might be involved in something I'm not supposed to be."

"Involved in something? Are you sure you don't mean *someone*?"

"What are you talking about?"

His wounded expression vanished as quickly as it came. "Guess I'll have to text you about you-know-what," he said blithely.

If he had information about Hybrids or reversing the spell, she wanted to know immediately.

She grabbed his wrist.

Zizi's eyes widened, but he allowed himself to be led outside. They ducked into an alley, searching for shadows to hide them from the bright city lights. It was always like this with him: the clandestine meetings, the hiding, the moments that felt stolen. It felt forbidden. It felt *special*.

Rui pushed that thought away. "What do you have to tell me?"

"Remember the client who hired me to create the separation spell? I was going to ask him why he needed it. I thought if I found out the *why*, I might get closer to figuring out the *how*. Maybe it'll help me reverse engineer it in a way that wouldn't affect your spirit core and Mochi's."

"Did you talk to him? What did he say?"

"He was supposed to contact me a couple of weeks ago to check if the spell was ready, but he didn't. I tracked him down. Guess what? He's dead. The man lived alone, no family. His neighbor said she heard he died of a heart attack. Seems a tad too convenient, doesn't it?"

"Are you reading too much into this?" Rui wondered. "Maybe the timing's coincidental."

"That's what I thought. But then I found out I wasn't the only one hired to create a spell like this. At least three other mages had similar jobs." Zizi paused, raking a hand through his hair. The slicked-back locks loosened, waves tumbling down to his cheekbones, shadowing his eyes.

He was hiding something. "What aren't you saying?" Rui asked.

He glanced away at the street.

"Zee zee."

"Gods." His shoulders lifted and sagged as he stared at her in a way that made her head fuzzy. "I can't keep anything from you when you look at me like that."

Feeling smug, Rui crossed her arms. "So tell me."

"All three of the mages the man hired have disappeared."

"Is that a euphemism for—"

"I don't know. I don't know if they're still alive or dead. No one has seen or heard from them in weeks."

Was Master Kang one of them? But she couldn't ask that; Zizi would want to know why she was snooping around the Night Market.

"Are there any more mages who were hired but haven't gone missing?" she said instead.

"I'm not sure. I'm still looking into it."

It couldn't be a coincidence. Even if Master Kang wasn't one of the three mages, it only meant there were *four* missing ones.

She looked up at Zizi. His face was as familiar as her own. She couldn't imagine what she'd do if anything happened to him.

"You'll stay safe, right?" she said, a little shaky.

"I will."

"What can I do to help?"

"Nothing. Leave the sleuthing to me and focus on getting better."

"But I can—"

"You can stop by the shop to say hi," Zizi suggested, grinning lopsidedly. "You haven't in forever."

"It's only been a couple of weeks. I've been busy at school."

"Time is a construct." Zizi tried to stand straight, clearing his throat like he was an orator giving a grand speech. "Haven't you heard the saying? *A day feels like three autumns when one is missing one's beloved.*"

Was he calling *her* his beloved? He'd definitely had a drink. Or three. Flustered, Rui latched onto a random thought. "When your spiritual energy is transferred to someone else, does it make you more aware of them somehow?"

Zizi's expression sharpened immediately. "Are you talking about Mochi?"

She couldn't tell if he was peeved that she had changed the topic or that the topic she chose was Yiran.

"I want to know what the separation spell did to us, what it did to me. That's all," she said. "I've been sensing his feelings. It's not very clear—well, it is sometimes if it's a strong feeling. Is that because of what happened between us? Are we connected now?"

Zizi's expression changed. Guilt battled with something else. Guilt won, and the *something else* folded away, tucked out of sight.

He turned away from her, his shoulders taut. "You're both connected now, that much is true." Rui thought he sounded a little sad. "But I'm not sure if it manifests in the form of what you're saying. It makes sense you'll be hyperaware of each other now, but this is new territory. The spell worked in a way I never anticipated. I don't know the parameters."

"How about Yiran's spirit core? He's not having problems at training."

"He's not? That's odd, but maybe—"

Loud voices carried from the street. Rui heard a scuffle, and she felt— *Yiran.*

She dashed out of the alley, and Zizi followed her.

Yiran and a muscular man were having a staring contest on the sidewalk next to the club. Yiran looked like a kettle about to boil over.

The man had a dark stain on his khaki pants, like something had been spilled on him. He slammed a palm into Yiran's chest, and Yiran staggered back.

"Say you're sorry, boy!"

Yiran lunged, but Zizi hooked his arm around him, pulling him back.

"Let go," Yiran seethed.

Zizi held firm.

"I saw you," the man accused. He was clearly drunk and aching for a fight. "I recognize that coat; it was you."

Why was Yiran wearing his Xingshan Academy coat over his street clothes for a night out on the town? He should've known better than to put a target on his back.

"It wasn't me. I didn't spill anything on you," Yiran insisted, furiously struggling against Zizi's grip. "I won't apologize for something I didn't do."

"I think everyone's had a little too much to drink," said Zizi airily. "Why don't we all go home and have a good night's sleep?"

"I don't drink," Yiran retorted. "Let go of me. I can take him."

Rui slipped in front of Yiran, flashing her most disarming smile at the man. There weren't many people outside the karaoke club. She had a chance to contain this before it blew up.

"I'm so sorry, sir. My friend made an honest mistake. Don't worry, I'll make sure the Academy's notified. He's a disciplinary case, you see."

For a moment, the man seemed confused, then he read between her lines the way Rui had intended him to. "Good. Make sure he gets punished."

She forced herself to keep her apologetic smile. "Of course, sir. Our duty is to protect the city and its people. Have a good night."

"At least one of you has some common sense." The man spat. "Freaks."

The three of them froze.

Too drunk to notice the change in the air, the man carried on. "You— the skinny one with creepy eyes—you have magic too, don't you?" He pointed at the three of them. "You're the reason why Revenants attack us. We should lock all of you up and feed you to those bloody monsters."

"What did you say?" Zizi's voice was soft and deadly. He released Yiran.

The man teetered forward. "I called you a freak. What are you going to do about it? Huh?"

Rui was shaking with anger, but she reminded herself that if things went south, the Academy's reputation would be affected.

Yiran looked too appalled to speak. But Zizi's fingers were twitching, and he shrugged his blazer off. He was about to throw a punch or cast a spell on the man. Zizi didn't care about what people thought of his appearance, but he had no tolerance for bigots, and the drunk man in front of them was a prime example of one.

"There you are, darling! I was looking for you."

A woman dressed in black lace draped herself over the drunk man. Her face was lightened by powder, her black hair ran to her waist, and her sickly sweet perfume was so strong Rui wanted to sneeze.

The woman tugged the drunk man's arm. "Let's go. You promised me dessert and I'm dying for some mango snow slush. Leave those kids alone; they're not worth your time."

The man started to grumble, but the woman cajoled him. As they walked away, Rui caught the woman sneaking a glance back at the three of them. An odd shiver went down her spine. There was something unusual about the woman's expression. She looked like she was gloating, like she had a secret nobody knew.

Zizi picked his blazer up from the ground and dusted it off. "That tasteless fool is wrong. My eyes are beautiful."

"I can't believe he said people with magic should be locked up and *fed* to Revenants," Yiran raged.

"It's not the most uncommon opinion," Zizi told him.

"It's not?"

Zizi stared stonily back. "Welcome to the real world, Mr. Lives-in-a-Gilded-Cage. Guess you might not know how some people feel about magic practitioners. Unfortunately, that man isn't entirely wrong. It's a fact that we *are* more likely to attract Revenants."

"That's why the Academy is on an offshore island," Rui said quietly, rubbing her arms. She was feeling the chill in her bones again. "It can be protected more easily from Revenants, but also, if there's a massive attack on us, we're far enough from the mainland that no one else will get hurt when we go down."

Yiran looked sickened.

The door to the karaoke club opened.

Loud music and chatter filled the street as people spilled out. Mai appeared and made a beeline for Yiran, dragging him to the group of seniors who were gathering.

Ada came over, linking arms with Rui. "I was looking for you. It's time to go back to campus." She eyed Zizi with curiosity. "Who's *this*?"

"Nobody," he said. He gave Rui a wink and turned on his heel.

Rui stared at his retreating back. She wanted him to stay. But it was time to return to their respective worlds.

"Is he a friend?" Ada asked.

"Just someone I ran into."

Ada shot her a knowing smile. "Men don't do it for me, but even I know he's objectively hot. Is that why you look like you want to punch him?"

"What?"

"Punch him softly"—Ada said dramatically, fluttering her eyelashes—"with your *lips*."

Rui fought with her own face and failed. It only made Ada laugh harder.

"You're red and I know you didn't drink tonight. I was only teasing, unless—"

"Unless nothing," Rui groaned. "If you say anything else I'm going to throw myself into the garbage truck across the street."

"Okay, okay, I'll stop. It's time to go back; you owe me a song next time."

As Ada led her to the group of cadets waiting for them, Rui looked over her shoulder.

Zizi was standing at the end of the street, staring at her from afar.

She turned away first, a funny feeling in her chest she couldn't blame on alcohol.

24
Rui

Rui removed her lanyard and surrendered her security pass to the receptionist.

"I hope you had an enriching time at our headquarters today, Cadet Lin." The receptionist smiled warmly. "We're always happy to have our most promising cadets over. I'm sure Professor Wong is looking forward to your report."

Rui faked her brightest and most enthusiastic grin. "It was an amazing experience. Thank you," she gushed. She waved a cheerful goodbye and went through the security turnstile.

Her smile dropped once she was outside the modern knife-shaped building. Citing her research on reconnaissance tactics, she had convinced Professor Wong to get her access to a few Guild personnel at the headquarters. She'd requested field Exorcists to interview, but when she arrived, she realized the Guild had only made a couple of paper pushers available to her. They had low spiritual energies, just on the border of being normies. None of them were potential candidates for Four. She'd wasted the morning listening to mind-numbingly boring explanations of the protocol for writing incident reports.

She should've known that, top cadet or not, the Guild would only allow her superficial access to their people and operations. Now she was stuck writing a lengthy essay on mind-numbingly boring explanations of the protocol for writing incident reports.

Time for plan B: using her connection with Ash to get close to actual Exorcists. Problem was, Ash was the kind of smart that could see through a flimsy scheme. She'd have to think things through before approaching him.

Stomach growling, Rui stopped at Laodifang for soup dumplings before going back to campus for the last lecture of her day. She pulled out her phone and dialed Zizi's number. It rang, but he didn't pick up. She'd been trying to get hold of him for the last few weeks. At first, she thought he was busy. But then she remembered the missing mages.

It's Zizi. He can take care of himself, she rationalized. But her heart twinged with worry.

The dumplings, delicious as they were, did nothing to settle her mind. As she headed to the terminal for the shuttle back to the Academy, her skin twitched with the same prickly feeling she had at the Night Market.

A flash of blue behind her. There, then gone again.

Was someone following her?

Rui loosened her limbs, adding a casual jauntiness to her gait. She meandered her way around the next few blocks, stopping occasionally to window-shop, slowly leading her potential stalker to a less crowded area close to a construction site.

When she was sure they were alone, she spun around, kicking up a cloud of dust with her boot.

"Oh! Argh—" A young man was waving his hands and coughing from the dust.

He didn't *look* dangerous; he was wearing an expensive-looking suit and had the kind of face mothers and grandmothers trusted. But a criminal could wear anything they wanted, and a pretty face could hide the darkest heart. A part of her brain wondered what kind of hair dye he used to keep his hair that shade of peacock blue. It was a color Ada would appreciate.

His hair. The flashes of blue.

"It was *you* at the Night Market that night, wasn't it?" she accused, keeping her hand on her sword bag. "Why are you following me?"

The young man looked flustered. "Greetings, Rui." He bowed.

She was briefly dumbstruck by his politeness and immediate admission of guilt. "How do you know my name?"

"I apologize for being sneaky. I wasn't sure how to approach you." He fumbled with something in his hands. The scent wafting from the plain white box smelled suspiciously like fried chicken. He lifted the lid. "Five-spice popcorn chicken," he announced grandly as if he were offering her a plate of caviar.

Rui kept her distance. "I'm not taking food from a stranger. Answer my question. Who are you?"

The young man's brow wrinkled. "In my world, a gift is always appreciated when one is visiting, and we prefer delicacies from the mortal realm. Though I suppose, technically, I am not visiting right now." He closed the box, looking glum.

"That's right, you were stalking—wait—" Rui's brain caught up. He'd said the words *mortal realm*. Which meant— "Are you a King?"

"No!" the young man exclaimed. "I am Nikai, an usher from the Fourth Court."

Rui lowered her arm. Nikai seemed harmless enough, and he wasn't creepy like Ten. There was a touch of formality in his speech, a kind of old-fashioned way of speaking that was rather charming.

"What's an usher?"

"A Reaper, but I prefer to think of myself as a shepherd of souls. I make sure they are collected free from the Blight, and I ease their path into the afterlife. And *you*, Rui, are a future Exorcist. Think of me as your colleague in spirit."

Rui started to laugh, but he looked so sincere she disguised it as a cough. "Is it true the Mirror of Retribution filters souls according to how they lived their mortal lives?" she asked, morbidly curious. She'd been reading up on underworld mythology in a bid to know more about the Kings of Hell, hoping it would help her with her search, and she had found the Mirror particularly curious.

"Humans are very interested in the afterlife. So many theories, so many stories," Nikai said. "The Mirror does exist. Do not worry, the system is fair enough. Those who live righteously are normally sent by the algorithm to work in clerical jobs."

"You have an *algorithm* for that?" It never occurred to Rui that the underworld would have technology.

"We do. Actually, our current enrollment system is an efficient piece of coding set up by a tech prodigy who was sent to the Third Court. He was there for his corporate crimes but got off easy because of his code." Nikai looked disgusted.

"Sounds like corruption extends to the afterlife," Rui said wryly. "And no offense but a clerical job sounds like hell."

"Paperwork is, as they say, the worst," Nikai agreed.

Rui found herself taking a liking to him, and she didn't like very many people. Though he wasn't exactly a *person*, was he? Nikai's milk-chocolate eyes were round and finely lashed, so different from Ten's vicious gaze. But whenever he blinked, his irises turned pitch black for a moment, reminding her of how non-human he was.

"You seem very calm," Nikai observed. "I thought you might freak out upon hearing all this."

Rui shrugged. Escaping death more than once had presented her a certain perspective. "So . . . why are you here? Did Ten send you?"

Instead of answering, Nikai produced something shiny from his pocket and gave it to her.

A piece of glass.

It was small, like one of Ada's pocket mirrors. The edges of the glass were smooth and dull, no sharp points that could cut. Rui flipped it around. The other side was a plain black substance, like a kind of rock. She turned it back and stared at her own reflection. The mirror looked ordinary, if a little bright.

"It's a piece from the Fourth Court's mirror," Nikai said. "It can be used for communication."

Rui was well-versed in secrets. She understood from his tone that he had placed one in her hand.

"Ten didn't send you here, did he?" she said. "You came to find me yourself. You don't trust him."

Nikai paled. "It is not a matter of trust. Ten is a King, and all Kings are dangerous."

But I've already made a deal with him. And she'd been instructed not to tell anyone about it.

"I'm aware you have made a deal with him," Nikai said, as if he knew what she was thinking. "That's why I'm here to help you if I can."

"Why? The deal doesn't involve you."

"Because you're . . ." Nikai seemed to rethink his words. "Because Four is my King and my friend. It is important to me that he is found. Since you're the human helping us, I must do what I can to aid you."

Rui didn't doubt his sincere desire to find his King, but she was also certain he was hiding something. Maybe it didn't matter; if he could help her, the end goal was the same.

"I haven't had much luck," she said. "I'll accept any help you can give." Quickly, she filled him in on what she'd done so far.

"I see you have focused only on looking for Four himself," Nikai said thoughtfully. "My King is clever and—"

"Wait—you said I've *only* been focused on Four himself? What do you mean?" Rui interjected.

"Did Ten tell you it is likely Four separated his power from his soul? That is how he can remain in the human realm for so long."

"No," Rui said grimly, "Ten did not."

Nikai's lips were razor thin. "The Tenth King's mind is a labyrinth few understand. He must have his reasons."

He's being diplomatic, Rui thought. Why didn't Ten provide her with information that would help her search?

"Are you saying I should be looking for Four's power too?" she asked.

Nikai nodded. "If you find his power, it might lead you to him. We believe he has hidden it somewhere in your realm and masked its presence, most likely in a vessel of some sort, something that can hold immense power and protect it."

"He put his power in a *container*?" An image of a plastic bento box with the word *death* written in red on it flashed in Rui's mind. She gave herself a shake.

"A *magic* container," Nikai said, as if that made things any better.

"Which means I should be looking for an object as well," Rui said thoughtfully. "What does the vessel look like?"

"Unfortunately, we do not know. It will be a magical artifact, a relic of some kind, and it can take a form of many things—a chest, an urn, or perhaps a ring or a locket or—"

"Yeah, I get the idea," Rui cut him off, trying not to feel dispirited. Her task seemed impossible, like fishing a needle from the sea. If only Zizi would answer her calls. *He* might know of some magical artifacts in the human world.

"Both our worlds will suffer even more if Four is not found," Nikai said. "It is vital that you locate him."

"What's happening in your world?" she asked, curious.

The box of fried chicken shook in Nikai's hand. "We call it the Nothing, and it devours everything. That is all I can say. But if Four returns to us, the destruction will stop." He brushed his shoulder, an odd gesture, like he was brushing off cobwebs. "I'm afraid I've run out of time in your realm. I must return."

"But you haven't told me how to use the mirror."

"All you need to do is say my name. If anything out of the ordinary happens or if you spot something, contact me." Nikai gave her another bow. "Thank you for helping us."

She bit her lip, squeezing the mirror tightly in her hand. "Thank me when I actually get it done."

"Good luck, Rui."

Nikai gave her a small smile and vanished into thin air.

25
Yiran

"Here, try it on," Tesha said. She was practically vibrating with excitement.

Yiran took the slinky piece of metal she was waving at him. He slipped his right hand in and flexed his fingers. The glove she'd given him was woven from steel, but it was so light and malleable he wondered what witchcraft the Maks possessed. But their trade secrets were that—secrets.

"What do you think?" Tesha looked like she was about to bounce off the walls.

"Fits like a glove," Yiran deadpanned.

Tesha shrieked with laughter.

"She's easily amused," Teshin said, shaking their head.

Yiran made a fist. "How do I use it? Do I . . . punch things?"

"It isn't a *weapon* weapon, but it'll help you manage your qi for now," Tesha explained. "If I did it right, you should be able to cast spells without leaking too much spiritual energy and spiraling out of control."

"Leaking?"

"Mm-hmm. Didn't you know?" At Yiran's look of confusion, she went on, "Teshin told me about the incident in the simulation on your first day at the Academy, and after seeing you channel the other day, we both think that's what's happening. Normally, when you channel with proper technique, magic flows out in a natural and steady state. Your technique is adequate, but your magic is highly unstable—probably because of the tampering. It comes out in bursts and spurts, like there's too much of it." She shrugged. "It leaks."

"With that amount of spiritual energy circulating inside you, it's strange how it took so long for things to manifest," Teshin added.

The Mak twins seemed to know more about spiritual energy and magic and weapons than what Yiran's lectures were teaching him. And they seemed to think that it was his grandfather's tampering that was the issue here. It could well be that, but Yiran knew it was also because the magic he'd been trying to use belonged to Rui and not himself.

Yiran avoided Teshin's curious gaze. "Time to give this a try."

He brought his gloved hand to his chest. On the next exhale, he swept his arm out, fingers spreading, palm facing the empty wall of the workshop.

A shimmering crimson circle half the size of the wall formed in front of him.

He let out a victorious shout. He had never succeeded in creating such a large and stable defensive shield before. He held it for a few more seconds before pulling back. He was growing accustomed to his trigger point—an invisible line he imagined in his head. Cross it and his spirit core would burn. But each time he practiced, he nudged the line forward just a bit.

"He chose a defensive spell." Tesha nodded at Teshin. "Just like you said he would."

"It seemed safer to," Yiran said, turning to Teshin. "How'd you know I would?"

"Logic," they replied.

But Yiran felt there was more they weren't saying. He raised his hand and tried to channel again. The glove sparked, and he yelped as the heat needled his skin.

"Sorry! It's a prototype, so there might be some issues," Tesha said. "It's a chicken-and-egg situation, that's what's annoying." She removed the glove for him and examined it. The weave pattern was warped in some areas.

Yiran asked, "What do you mean?"

"If you matched to a spiritual weapon already, I could leverage that to craft something to stabilize the leak. But if I can stabilize the leak first, I could probably make you a highly customized weapon you would match to. Thing is, stabilizing the leak is the more complicated way." Tesha stared out the window of the workshop at the Mak ancestral shrine, deep in thought. "I'll have to rethink the design," she murmured to herself.

But Yiran had latched on to what she had said. If what Tesha needed was a weapon he matched with, there might just be a way to make that happen.

The last bell was ringing when Yiran got back to the campus. He had memorized Rui's schedule to keep track of her and knew exactly where to find her.

Just as he expected, she was walking out from her final lecture of the day, looking like one of Sweets's blackberry-flavored lollipops. She had thrown an oversized sweater over her school uniform, and wore thick wool leggings tucked into angry boots. Unlike Ada's cheery pops of pink among her darker clothing, black was Rui's only color of choice.

Yiran straightened. She was carrying her sword bag like she always did.

The flow of cadets parted way for Rui as she trudged down the hallway, looking deep in thought. Yiran caught a few looks batted at her, curious ones that made him assume she was respected yet unliked—but only because she was unknown. Sometimes he couldn't help but think they each were two faces of the same coin. Their methods were dissimilar, but equal. He pulled people in and lulled them into a false sense of proximity; Rui simply pushed people out.

He'd intentionally confided in her at the bench by the sea, and she'd softened toward him for a while as he predicted. But her scowl had returned soon enough, and now it was a magnificent one that could sink a thousand ships. It was her go-to expression whenever she looked at him. Yiran was getting fond of it.

He caught up to her. "Hey."

Rui didn't stop for him, so he walked with her.

"What do you want?" she said.

"Is there an Academy rule against saying hi to someone you know for no other reason than saying hi?" Yiran caught a faint smile on her face.

"You ignored everyone else and came right to me. What do you want?"

"How are you doing?"

"I'm fine."

It took a liar to understand another, and Yiran was a very good liar. And it took someone who spent his life pretending to be untouchable to recognize someone else who was performing the same act with a different script.

Rui wasn't fine at all.

She glanced up at him, something furtive in her eyes. "Is that all? I'm in a hurry."

"I thought you were done with class. Where are you going?"

"Zizi's."

Had the wizard figured out how to reverse the spell? They'd exchanged a few brusque texts previously, but he'd gone silent in the last few weeks.

"Something up?" Yiran said lightly.

"I haven't seen or heard from him since that night at karaoke. I've tried calling, but he's not picking up. I'm going to check his shop."

"I can give you a ride there."

Rui shook her head. "I won't take long."

Yiran decided not to push it.

"He told me he was going to sell the spell for a lot of money and leave the city if it worked," she continued, uncharacteristically willing to talk to Yiran today. Maybe it was because he was the only person who knew of Zizi's existence in her life. "The spell worked, didn't it? Even if it didn't work the way he meant it to. What if he aban—" She stopped talking and picked up her pace.

Abandoned.

She was going to say *abandoned*. His mother's face flashed in his mind, but he stuffed the memories back into the vault where they belonged.

"Zizi doesn't seem the sort to bail on his friends." Yiran didn't know if it was true, but he knew it was true in Rui's case. "Maybe he's out on some pilgrimage looking for rare herbs or maybe he'll show up in your room tomorrow." Yiran flailed, putting on his best Zizi impression. "*What's up, Rui? I fell asleep in a cave and lost track of time, but I discovered a way to solve all our problems. By the way, do you like my clown pajamas? I got them for half-price at a sale.*"

"Zizi can't get into the dorms. There's security."

Yiran waved a hand. "Teleportation."

"That's not how his magic works—that's not how *our* magic works. Haven't you been listening in class?" Rui said, exasperated. "We can't vanish into thin air. That's ridiculous, the stuff of fantasy movies."

"I was being hyperbolic. But my point remains, the wizard's not gone forever. He'll come back."

"I hope you're right." She seemed like she wanted to say more, but she pressed her lips together and walked on.

Yiran groaned. "I can't believe you got me to defend *Zizi* of all people."

"Why *are* you defending him? I thought you hated him."

Yiran replied as solemnly as he could, "*Hate* is a strong word. *An intense repulsive feeling of dislike* would be a more accurate description."

Rui finally laughed. She had a lovely laugh. He wished he heard it more. When they both stopped being jerks to each other, that connection from the magic transfer felt . . . comforting.

She gave him a look as if she could tell what he was thinking.

A riff from an indie rock song started to play.

Yiran answered his phone. Rui tapped her foot impatiently as she waited for him to be done. He was doing a bad job of keeping his expression in check.

"Okay, we'll be there." He hung up, his stomach crawling with anxiety. But there was a glimpse of opportunity. A chance to get hold of one of Rui's swords.

"What's wrong? You okay?" she said.

"I hope you have something presentable to wear. You're having dinner with my grandfather."

Rui's mouth hung open. "Tonight? Why?"

"Something about meeting the top student at the Academy and the person who saved me from a Revenant. You can't turn it down." Yiran couldn't imagine any cadet saying no to meeting the Head of the Exorcist Guild.

"Oh my gods, oh my gods," she said, her eyes wide, hands to her head.

Yiran was amused by her reaction. No one was immune to Song Wei's reputation. "I'll pick you up at the station after you're done at the shop-house." He paused. "My grandfather's probably going to ask you about that night."

Rui narrowed her eyes. She understood him perfectly. "We can rehearse in the car."

26
Rui

Rui knocked on the door of the shophouse for a while before impatience got the better of her. Zizi wasn't one for the usual security measures. The simple lock couldn't deter a child. She took two steps back and gave the door a good kick.

The lock broke easily, and the door swung open.

She hesitated. If Zizi *had* security, it would come in the form of spells. Perhaps she had too much faith in him, but she was confident that whatever countermeasures he might have set up, he would've made sure *she*, of all people, could bypass them safely.

She stepped over the threshold, letting out a loud breath when it was clear she hadn't lost an arm or an eye. It was quiet inside.

"Zizi?" she called out. "Mao?"

The wind chimes whistled softly. But there was no cat and no boy.

The kitchen sink was filled with unwashed dishes, and a half-drunk mug of old coffee sat on the counter. Zizi wasn't the neatest, but he always kept his kitchen clean.

The stairs creaked as she went up to the second floor to the bedroom. It looked suspiciously unchanged since the day she'd woken up in it. For a few long moments, Rui stared at the ceiling of stars, wishing for the first time she could name them all.

There were two other rooms left to explore. One turned out to be a walk-in wardrobe full of pajamas sorted meticulously by color, and surprisingly, an assortment of formal wear. Rui tried to imagine Zizi in a tux. She would've laughed in his face . . . if he were here. She inhaled the scent of mint and strawberries and boy, and walked out, a strange twisting in her chest.

Half camouflaged in shadow, the third door was nestled into the wall at the end of the corridor. It was narrower than the other two doors and it had no knob.

Part of Rui wanted to leave it alone. But most of her was too curious. She gave it an exploratory nudge and then, a bigger shove. It held. Whatever was behind that door would remain a secret for now.

She went down to the fake closet, stooping to press the secret button in the corner.

Nothing happened. No gears whirred; no door opened. Zizi's spell lab was out of bounds.

"Where is he?" she sighed.

Zizi never missed her calls. In fact, he hardly went a day without texting her about something or other. This silence was deafening. Three other mages had vanished since they were hired to create a similar separation spell. Could he be the fourth to go missing? She wasn't sure if the three other mages were still alive. What if Zizi . . .

She banished that thought from her mind, sinking down onto her favorite armchair. In some ways, Zizi was her oldest friend. He was *after Mama, before Ada*, a brief time when fourteen-year-old Rui was on the verge of self-destruction. She'd found refuge in a strange shophouse and a stranger boy. Without Zizi around, she felt out of step with everything.

The ticking of the wall clock grew loud in her head. It felt like she was running out of time. She wanted her magic back. She wanted her revenge. But the stakes were higher than that now. Zizi was missing; the Blight was creating more Revenants; and Nikai had said the destruction of the underworld was imminent.

She *had* to find Four's soul or the vessel that held his power. Yiran's face surfaced in her mind, but Rui huffed at the empty room. He didn't fit the bill. He'd been born with a weak spirit core; he couldn't house the soul of a god.

She glanced at the clock. There was still time to go to the Night Market to scout for information. Maybe Auntie Lian knew something about magical containers.

Something red and black caught her eye on her way to the front door. The cover of an instant ramen cup sticking out of the trash. She picked it up, memories flashing.

Last autumn . . . the ghost earrings in her hand—a surprise gift for Zizi—he was working on something . . . an old locket.

Rui dug deeper into the memory. In her mind's eye, she saw Zizi tearing the seasoning packet for his instant ramen with his teeth.

"Are you even listening to me?" he had said. "I've been trying to unseal this locket for three days and it's not happening."

Rui was playing fetch-the-sparkly-ball with Mao. Zizi complained a lot about his work, and she'd grown accustomed to it. "Stop whining and try again."

He'd glared without malice as he paced, twirling his cigarette like a philosopher in an existential crisis. "The client's expecting to see what's in this damned locket tomorrow. If I don't get it done, I won't get paid and I'm going to starve—*Rooroo*, are you really stealing my food in my dire time of need?"

Rui put the chopsticks down. She'd zoomed into his ramen while he was distracted and talking. "It was just a bite."

Zizi looked aggrieved. "It's almost as if you enjoy seeing me suffer."

"Don't be absurd. Are you sure you tried everything? Who did the locket belong to?"

"The client's mother. It was stated in her will for the locket to be given to her favorite child."

"Are you sure your client is her favorite child? Maybe the locket isn't meant to be opened by him."

"Wait," Zizi exclaimed, running to her, "repeat what you just said."

"Maybe the locket isn't meant to be opened by him?"

He gripped her shoulders. "That's it! You absolute genius, I think you solved it. I swear I could—" He stopped talking, looking as surprised as she felt to discover they were caught up in a hug. He sprang back and resumed his pacing.

Rui's ridiculous little heart had raced and raced. What had Zizi meant to say? Hastily, she'd drunk a gulp of soup to drown her flustered thoughts. The spiciness of it caught up with her, and she coughed, regretting her decision.

"If the locket is for the mother's favorite child, then the sealing spell can only be broken by *that* child—not me," Zizi concluded. "There's nothing that I, even with all my astounding talent, can do, because that's not how the spell is supposed to work. Simple but effective." He clapped. "Thank you, Rui. Finish your ramen and get lost. I'm going to call the client over right now."

"You're welcome?" Rui sputtered as Zizi shoved the bowl into her hands and pushed her toward the front door.

He'd phoned her the next day to tell her that the locket had been sealed by a voice spell. All the client had to do was say his name and tell it to open. Zizi had seemed impressed by the cleverness of it.

The plastic ramen cover crunched in Rui's hand now. She dropped it and ran back up the stairs. The third door stared at her with its narrow shape and puzzling lack of hinges.

What if it was sealed by a voice spell? A spell that would open it for the right person. But that person would be Zizi, not her. Still, she had a feeling about it. If she had no trouble breaking into his shophouse, maybe . . .

"It's Rui," she said, feeling more than a little silly. "Let me in."

She placed a tentative hand on the wood and pushed.

The door remained shut.

It's not going to be so easy, not when it comes to him. She sighed. Whatever was behind that door had better be worth the humiliation.

"It's Rooroo. Open up."

Something touched her cheek. Like a kiss from a ghost.

The door creaked open.

Rui shook a fist at it. Amused and aggravated. It had worked, but only because she used that horrible nickname. She was going to find Zizi, and she was going to murder him.

She went in.

There was a cozy-looking futon on the ground with a fluffy blanket, an old swivel chair, and a table with a stack of sketchbooks on it. Unlike the other two rooms, this was small and bare. But Rui knew at once this was where Zizi actually slept. Nothing and everything about him made sense to her.

She slid a finger across the desk. Dust. He hadn't been in here for a while. No one had. On a whim, she swept the charcoal sticks and colored pencils off the sketchbooks and flipped to a page.

Lifelike eyes stared back through unevenly cut bangs. A drawing of a girl's face. Attention had been paid to the way the tip of her nose was slightly upturned, the generous loop of her smile, and the narrow point of her chin. The portrait was detailed, riveting because of how the nuances of the girl's expression were captured in the moment. The rest of the note-book was full of random illustrations of clocks and trees and buildings.

With trembling hands, Rui went through every sketchbook. The pattern repeated. The girl's face kept appearing, sometimes sad, mostly happy. It was as though the artist chose to remember the girl that way: a smile on her face, joy in the crinkled corners of her wide-set eyes. It was clear the artist had spent an inordinate amount of time observing every line and angle of the girl's face, and that this tender obsession had bled into each charcoal stroke.

It was also clear that the girl was Rui, and the artist was Zizi.

The final sketchbook was larger than the rest, and when she flipped to the last page, her breath caught.

Like the drawings before, it was Rui again.

But this Rui was different. Her hair was long, running past her shoul-ders, and her face older. She was standing by an ancient-looking wisteria tree, wearing a purple layered dress that flowed down to the ground. The young woman's hand was raised, like she was reaching out for someone. There was something magical about the drawing, and as Rui trailed a finger down the page, she almost expected it to spring to life. But it was only a sketch. Nothing more. An image of an older Rui in the future, manifested by Zizi's imagination.

"Well, this is creepy," Rui said to the empty room.

But she knew her heart felt otherwise.

The voice spell Zizi had placed on the door must've been a silly joke to himself. He hadn't meant for her to ever see this room or his drawings. He didn't know that she'd come looking, or that she'd figure out how to break the spell.

Rui had entered the room expecting something else altogether. Not this. *This* told her how Zizi truly felt.

She closed the sketchbook and sank onto the futon, hugging her knees close. She didn't know how or what to feel. But a quiet ache was growing in her chest, a longing for something she couldn't describe. Her mother's death had brought Rui magic, and it had also brought *him*.

She was still sitting on the futon when her phone rang.

Yiran's voice crackled from the speaker. "I'll be at the station in five. Are you there already?"

How long had she been at the shophouse?

"I'm on my way," she replied curtly, and hung up.

She threw a last glance at the stack of sketchbooks and walked out.

27
Rui

Rui tightened her grip on the grab handle in the car. She'd heard so many stories of the formidable Song Wei that he'd become a legend in her mind. This wasn't how she wanted to meet the man who possessed the ability to either give her what she so dearly wanted or wrench it away with a simple nod or shake of his head. Without her magic, she felt especially exposed and vulnerable. What if he saw through her secret? What if—no, she was going to this dinner with a mission in mind: access to the Guild. *That* was what she had to focus on.

She chewed on her nails and stared out the window. Buildings upon buildings zoomed by. Ripe peachy sunset hues grazed glass and steel, enveloping the city in warmth. Dusk was settling in.

Soon the imposing gates of the Song estate loomed, the tips of the iron bars gilded gold and curved sharp like an eagle's claws. The path to the house was tree-lined and felt a mile long. At the end of it, Yiran parked the car casually askew by the garage.

Song Mansion was a modern siheyuan. Rui didn't take to it the way she loved Zizi's shophouse, but it was obvious it meant something to Yiran for reasons beyond the fact that he lived here. The look on his face told her as much.

The front doors were painted a traditionally lacquered vermilion and carved with symbols Rui didn't understand. Two stone lions stood guard on either side. Across the threshold, the short path led to a second, smaller set of doors—a spirit screen etched with even stranger symbols.

Everything inside was warm wood and stone and terra-cotta roofs, and the main courtyard had an egg-shaped koi pond and a surprisingly unruly garden. The openness of the layout gave an illusion of welcoming candor. Yet tall bamboo grew from the gray-pebbled perimeter, screening guests from what was likely the private family quarters north of the gardens and courtyards, tucking them away safely from prying eyes and sniffing noses.

Yiran gestured at a cabinet by the wall. "Shoes off, Darcy."

"I'm not a heathen." She glared automatically, but she'd grown used to him calling her by that name now and then. Secretly, she felt it might suit her, but she'd rather walk barefoot over hot coals than tell him.

They exchanged their boots for pairs of woven house slippers. Muttering something about changing his clothes, Yiran left her in the care of the housekeeper, who introduced herself as Auntie Kimmie. She had come out to greet them.

"It isn't often that er shaoye has friends over," Auntie Kimmie said. She was a kindly lady in her early fifties who wore a tidy dress and a camel-colored cardigan with pearl buttons.

"I'm surprised, he seems popular," Rui said, noting that Auntie Kimmie's use of the honorific was affectionate.

"I was worried for him. He hung out with a certain clique at his old school." It was clear Auntie Kimmie didn't approve of that. "I'm glad he's made friends quickly at the Academy. He's very shy, you see."

Shy was not the word that came to mind when Rui thought of Yiran.

"It's good to have him home. It's been a while since I've seen him. He sends me messages from time to time to keep me updated, you know. He doesn't want me to worry; he's such a good boy."

Rui hadn't thought Yiran to be the sort to keep his housekeeper informed about his life.

"Is there anything else I can get you, Miss Rui?"

Rui gestured at the honey cakes and cup of warm yuzu tea laid out on the table. "This is more than enough, thank you."

Auntie Kimmie nodded and left.

Rui slouched back into her default mode of grumpy and tired. She was tempted to explore the place, but Song Wei could be anywhere. She drank her tea, nibbled her cake, and sent a barrage of text messages to Ada, who had made her promise to describe every inch of the mansion.

Shortly, Yiran returned. Freshly scrubbed from a quick shower, he'd removed his contact lenses and was wearing a pair of tortoiseshell spectacles.

"Are dinners here always so formal?" Rui asked, surprised by his crisp shirt and gray sweater-vest.

"Only when my grandfather is present."

Rui looked down at her own outfit.

Yiran had told her to wear her best, and her best was, well, not that great. She had on her cleanest pair of black jeans—more faded gray than black, frankly, and worn at the knees—and her favorite oversized sweater, which, to her horror, was molting at the right sleeve. By force of habit, she'd brought her talismans and weapons, tucked away in an old sword bag that had seen better days. Standing here in this grand mansion, Rui wished she'd borrowed a dress from Ada.

Yiran shifted his weight from one foot to the other. Nervous energy radiated from him. Rui's own anxiety spiked. Curse that empathic link.

"Why are you still sitting there?" he said. "It's time for dinner. Remember what I told you—"

"Speak only when spoken to, keep my voice low, don't start eating until after he takes his first bite, refill his tea, hold my chopsticks the correct way—please, I'm not an uncultured swine, and I'm not auditioning to be his granddaughter-in-law."

There was a long awkward pause as they both processed what Rui had blurted out of annoyance.

As if on cue, Ash glided into the room. Dressed in a pair of black slacks and a taupe cardigan, he looked every bit like the heir to this kingdom.

"Who's auditioning to be my sister-in-law?"

"Shut up," Yiran said.

Rui considered drowning herself in the koi pond.

"Good evening, Rui," Ash said, trying not to laugh. She nodded back. Ash never called her by her first name. "Come along, kids. We mustn't keep Yeye waiting."

He placed a hand on each of their shoulders, steering them to the dining room. The round table was large enough to seat ten, but it was prepared for four. All the cutlery had the family name embossed onto it, but one set of utensils was different from the rest: a band of gold ran across the top of the chopsticks and the handles of the fork and spoon.

Deliberately, Ash positioned himself between Yiran and Rui, placing her to the left of where his grandfather would be sitting. A little too close for comfort, but perhaps better than sitting directly opposite in full view of the Head of the Exorcist Guild.

Moments later, Song Wei entered. He was as tall as Rui remembered and a lot more intimidating. This was a man who could command with a look and condemn with a gesture.

She had glimpsed him once in person. It'd been the last day of her mother's funeral wake, and she was standing outside the crematorium. A black limousine pulled up in the rain, stopping by the side of the road. Rui's father was too distraught to notice, distracted by the principal of Xingshan Academy who'd come to pay his respects and offer Rui a place in the school. But Rui saw the car and the old man in it. He was dressed in white, a sign of respect for the dead. Song Wei never got out of the vehicle, nor did anyone from the Guild approach the Lins that day. Rui never thought she'd be meeting him again in his own home.

His two grandsons bowed. Noting the differences in their postures, Rui did the same.

"Finally, I get to meet the person who saved my grandson from a nasty fate," Song Wei said, his manner transforming from stern leader to charming host.

"The honor is mine, sir."

"Your name is Lin Ru Yi?"

"I go by Rui."

"You must tell me how you defeated that Revenant, but first, let us eat. Lan Xi has to prepare for tonight."

"For a Hunt? The moon isn't full tonight; is it tactical?" Rui asked.

Song Wei's brows lifted, his gaze sharpening. "Observant, I see." He turned to Yiran. "How has school been? I heard you had another training session in the Simulator yesterday." The temporary warmth Song Wei displayed with Rui vanished when he addressed his younger grandson.

Unspoken tension filled the room. Rui squirmed in her seat. Words started coming out of Yiran's mouth like he was a mechanical toy, wound up and set off. As dishes were served, he regurgitated his recent days at school, studiously avoiding eye contact with anyone. Ash nodded along, commenting at the right moments, slipping in a few jokes to lighten the mood.

Rui concentrated on her food. Their weird family charade was too painful to witness. The longer it went on, the more she wondered if Yiran acted the way he did outside his home because he thought it was the only way to be accepted. To be loved.

When Yiran was done, Ash piped up, "No one succeeds the first few times in the Simulator. Accidents happen. And not everyone matches up with a spirit weapon right away."

"You did," Yiran said tonelessly. He squished his rice to the side of his bowl. He'd hardly eaten any of it.

Rui stuffed a clump of enoki into her mouth and focused on chewing the stringy mushrooms. The only spiritual weapon Yiran could match with was hers, but Song Wei couldn't know that.

Ash waved away the tension with the practiced hand of someone who had to do it often. "It's not a big deal. You'll get it right soon."

"Tesha Mak is working on something for me," Yiran said.

Teshin had taken an unexpected liking to Yiran, so it wasn't that surprising they'd recruited their twin sister to help him. But it was the first time Rui had heard of this.

Song Wei made a low sound of approval. "The Maks are good friends to have. What do you think, Rui? Does my grandson have what it takes to be a real Exorcist?"

What a cruel question to ask a stranger. Rui felt foolish, chasing for the approval of a man like him for so many years. "Why wouldn't he?" she said as innocently and brightly as she could. "He's a Song, one of yours. All the Songs are magical prodigies, aren't they?"

Yiran blanched.

Even though she feared she'd overstepped, Rui continued to smile.

To her surprise, Song Wei looked amused. "You're right—he's a Song and he is my grandson. He will succeed on his own terms."

He clapped Yiran on the back. The boy looked stupefied by the small show of affection, if one could even call it that.

After the meal ended, fresh fruit and tea were laid out in the living room. Ash excused himself, and Song Wei switched his attention to Rui again.

"Tell me how you killed that Revenant. I want to hear it straight from the source."

Rui heard a change in his tone. He wasn't curious; he was investigative. She recounted the events of the night the way she and Yiran had agreed to do.

"Interesting," Song Wei remarked after Rui was done. There was a discomforting parallel between the way he and Ten used that word. "I sense your qi levels fluctuating. How is your recovery?"

"Going well," she lied. Song Wei didn't have skill in healing, did he? She hoped he wasn't sensing anything that might reveal her secret. "It's taking a little longer than I'd like, but it is what it is."

"Considering how badly you were injured, the one who tended to you must have some skill when it comes to the healing arts," Song Wei remarked. "Lan Xi mentioned he's been trying to recruit this person, this Zizi."

Rui caught a faint sneer on Yiran's face at the mention of the mage. She was surprised herself. Did the Guild not care that Zizi belonged to the underground magic community? The Revenant situation had to be bad enough for the Guild to overlook it. Or maybe Ash had concealed Zizi's allegiance from his grandfather.

"I'm not sure if Ash told you *I'm* top of my cohort, sir," Rui said as she refilled Song Wei's teacup for him. She ignored the wave of confusion coming from Yiran over the way she was cozying up to his grandfather. "It's been my dream to beat Ash's record. I want to be the youngest Exorcist ever to make Captain."

Song Wei nodded his approval. "Ambition in young people is a laudable trait."

"Thank you, sir." He seemed to like her enough. Time to wrangle access to the Guild, however limited. "Coincidentally, I was at the Guild this morning doing research for my term paper. It's absolutely fascinating how much detail goes into incident reports, I learned so much in the two hours I was there. Have you considered an internship or residence program where top cadets could shadow Exorcists at the headquarters or on the field? It seems like it'll be an invaluable experience." She smiled earnestly. "I'll volunteer to be part of such a pilot program, should you decide to implement it, sir."

"The cadets already participate in patrols," Song Wei said, but he seemed interested in what she had to say.

"But the routes are limited, and we don't get to see much action."

"Is that what this is about? Have some patience, eager cadet. Your time in this fight will come."

"Yes, sir." Rui concealed her disappointment with a humble smile. Song Wei's gruff tone implied it was the end of that conversation. She would have to find another way in.

"I have some business to discuss with Lan Xi," said Song Wei. "The both of you should head back to the dormitories before the curfew."

Yiran stood immediately. "Yes, Zufu."

Rui followed his cue. "Thank you for inviting me over tonight, sir."

Song Wei dismissed them with a nod.

In the hallway, Yiran tugged on Rui's sleeve. "This way."

"But the front door's the other way."

"I left my car keys in my room."

"Ooh, I'm excited to see Song er shaoye's humble abode."

Yiran rolled his eyes.

Several turns later, Rui said, "Shouldn't we be going to the eastern wing?"

"That's where Ash's room is. I sleep here."

The western side of the house was by all appearances as grand and well-furnished as the rest of the mansion. Except they both knew the implication of sleeping here instead of in the eastern side of the house together with Ash. The west wing of a siheyuan was traditionally reserved for family members lower in the hierarchy. Yiran's expression hadn't changed, but Rui could tell Song Wei's snub cut deep.

Yiran yanked off his sweater-vest violently and threw himself onto the king-sized bed.

His room was tidier than expected. Probably because he had a small army of servants. Books were shelved in alphabetical order with smooth, untouched spines. Freshly laundered clothes sat in neat little piles on the dresser, ready to be put away into what Rui assumed was a ginormous walk-in closet next to the bathroom.

The place was filled with all the material possessions and tech gadgets anyone would want. But what Yiran needed was something intangible. This entire evening was a too-intimate look into what was lacking in his life.

Yiran's eyes were closed. Despite the impending curfew, he seemed in no hurry to get back to campus.

Rui rocked on the balls of her feet, considering her conversation options before settling on the most pertinent one.

"Your grandfather's kind of a jerk to you."

A glower bloomed on Yiran's face, only to wilt into a look of resignation. "That obvious, huh?"

She nodded. "You're a different person when you're here."

"What are you, my therapist?"

"It's not like I want to feel what you're feeling," Rui said, frustrated. "It's that silly link we have."

It was the first time she had acknowledged the connection in front of him. Instead of denying it, Yiran shrugged, confirmation that he felt it too.

He punched a pillow. "It doesn't matter. You don't get it."

"Help me get it."

"Why do you care?"

"Because we're friends," Rui replied without thinking. And they were. She was upset about what had happened between them, bitter that he'd found his footing in a space she cherished as hers. But none of this was his fault.

Yiran's throat worked, but he didn't speak, and he wouldn't look at her.

Rui leaned against the desk, surprised to find a stack of newspapers piled up in the corner. She'd assumed Yiran got his news the same way she did—digitally. She flipped through the paper on top.

"What the . . ." Rui took a hard look at the photograph of a man under a report about a string of mysterious deaths in the city. "Look at this." She shoved the newspaper in front of Yiran's face. "This man—isn't he the one who tried to pick a fight with you outside the karaoke club?"

"Looks like the same jackass."

"He's dead."

Yiran sat up. "He's dead?"

Rui scanned the report. "He died the *same* night we saw him."

"Coincidence. Maybe he drank too much."

"Doesn't seem like it. They don't know what killed him or the others. Do you remember the woman he left with? There was something off about her. I felt it. Something like . . ."

Rui stared at the wall.

She remembered the feeling now.

"A Hybrid," she whispered. "That woman . . . she must've killed him."

"That's nonsense. Listen to yourself, Darcy. You can't look at a person and think they're a murderer based on some *feeling*." Yiran scoffed.

"You're jumping to conclusions. Hybrids don't exist."

"My mother was killed by one, and he—*it*—it almost killed me."

A shudder went through Rui in the quiet that followed. She felt Yiran's shock, then his denial.

"There's no evidence that Hybrids exist," he finally said.

"I know what I saw," she said through gritted teeth.

"Fine. *Hypothetically* speaking, if they're real, what exactly are they?"

"Revenants with human traits. They look like us, talk like us, and some theorize they retain all their consciousness and reason. But because of changes in their spiritual energy, they possess the hunger of a Revenant. Which means they're attracted to yangqi, and they attack humans too."

"But the Blight is a supernatural virus, isn't it?" Yiran said. "It only infects spirits and those sorts of things."

"Viruses evolve," Rui pointed out. "The Blight isn't something you can study in normie biology class. You say there's no evidence that Hybrids exist, but there's no concrete evidence that the Blight can't infect humans either."

"I still think you're jumping to—" A loud sound came from the closet. Yiran jerked toward it. "Did you hear—"

Rui silenced him with a finger, drawing a sword from her bag. She might not have magic, but she knew twenty-seven different ways to maim a person.

Yiran grabbed a tennis racket and nudged the door open.

The walk-in wardrobe was a mess of clothes. Rui spotted a limited-edition trainer missing its mate, some sparkly jewelry, a designer bag, an expensive watch in a case, and a bottle of red wine.

Amid the piles of stuff, something moved.

Raising her sword, she gave Yiran a nod.

He swung his racket back.

Now, she mouthed.

But their arms halted in midair.

A sleepy-faced boy was crawling out of the mess. His dark hair was disheveled, and he was wearing a wrinkled T-shirt and a long, scruffy coat.

"Rui?" Zizi asked, his pale blue eyes blinking in confusion. "Where am I?"

28
Yiran

Yiran tossed his racket aside. "How did you get in here?"

"I've no idea," Zizi said. His eyes flickered with a feverish light. "Last thing I remember was falling asleep under my wisteria tree. It's been downhill from there." He sauntered out of the walk-in wardrobe and starfished on the bed. "Nice place you got here. What's the thread count on these sheets?"

"Get off my bed before I use my fists and make you."

Zizi rolled off and settled onto the floor cross-legged. He stared up at them with suspicion. "What are the two of you doing in his bedroom?"

"None of your business," Rui snapped. She grabbed his collar. "Where have you been? Why didn't you answer my calls?"

"Keep it down," Yiran warned. They were too far from the main house for his grandfather to hear anything, but there were servants around the estate.

"He's right," Zizi said. "You can yell at me when we get out of here."

Yiran watched as Zizi unfurled Rui's fingers one by one until her hands unclenched and her grip on him loosened. He did it gently, like he knew she was brittle glass under that steel exterior.

"Were you worried about me?" he asked softly.

Yiran felt Rui's anger disappearing as she scanned Zizi's face, taking him in like a person deprived of oxygen.

"I was," she whispered.

"I didn't mean to worry you."

There was meaning in their voices that Yiran understood. Embarrassed, he walked away, pretending to tidy his already neat desk, certain he'd witnessed an intimate moment between them he had no part in. His fingers hovered over Rui's sword bag. Tempted. She was distracted, but he couldn't hide the bag in front of them even if he took it.

"What happened to your hands?"

Surprised by the shrillness in Rui's voice, Yiran turned. Zizi's fingers looked oddly naked from the lack of rings. But there was something else on them. Stains, like black ink wiped off too late. The lines resembled veining on a leaf, creeping up in a haphazard pattern from his hands to his wrists.

"I don't know," Zizi said. "More of this black stuff appears each time I wake in a different place. It won't come off."

"What do you mean *each time*?" Yiran took Zizi's hand and rubbed it. The black markings stayed on like a tattoo.

"It started a couple of weeks ago. I'd lose consciousness and find myself in a new place with no idea how I got there. I thought I was sleepwalking at first, but it kept happening and it's getting worse. Feels like magic I don't understand."

"Maybe you should see someone about this," Yiran suggested. "If it's a, I don't know, magical illness, maybe what you need is a healer."

"I'm not sick."

"Do you think it's related to the missing mages?" Rui said.

Yiran glanced between them. "What missing mages?"

Briefly, Rui filled him in. "We don't know who really hired the mages to create that spell. But maybe they've decided to target Zizi now," she finished.

"Is it a curse?" Yiran said. "Like a way to get you to them, but somehow you ended up here?"

"I would know if it were, I think." Zizi winced. "It feels like my head's been chopped off and screwed back wrong."

Rui said, "Whatever it is, you need to be careful—what's wrong?"

Blood had drained from Zizi's face, and he was covering his eyes with his hands. "The lights . . ."

Rui ran to the window and drew the curtains. "Turn off the lights! I think he's getting one of his migraines."

Yiran flipped the switch and the room plunged into near darkness. There was a shuffling noise, and Yiran saw the shape of Zizi crawling under the duvet. With his shoes on. Yiran decided to let that go.

"Do you have any medication?" he asked.

A muffled voice came from under the duvet. "Not on me. With everything going on, I think I missed my dose. Maybe you're right; I need to see someone about this."

Yiran lifted the edge of the duvet slightly and peeked in. He could hear Zizi breathing hard.

"What can I do?" he whispered to the shadowy ball inside. He didn't know why he was whispering, but if the light hurt, maybe loud sounds did too.

Zizi whispered back, "Give me your hand."

Something featherlight dropped onto Yiran's palm.

"Light this."

Yiran looked. There was a cigarette in his hand. Did Zizi want to smoke? How would that help his migraine?

Yiran rummaged through his desk drawers and found an old matchbox he'd nicked from some bar. The first match caught fire and fizzled out just as quickly. He struck a second match, and this time he managed to keep the flame going long enough to inhale. Embers sparked. He blew out a puff of smoke, the taste of burning paper and something flowery on his tongue.

"You owe me one for damaging my lungs," he said to the lump under the duvet.

A hand stuck out. "Your lungs are fine; it's not a normal cigarette."

Yiran placed the cigarette between Zizi's fingers.

Zizi muttered something and waved his hand. Smoke curved in the air, hovering unnaturally, as if bolstered by an unseen force. He had written something.

A number.

Nine.

"Jiu," Rui murmured. She'd moved so quietly Yiran hadn't noticed her beside him. "*Jiu . . .*" she repeated, changing the intonation of the word. She blinked. "*To save?*"

"All right, she knows we're coming," Zizi said. He mumbled something else, and the cigarette turned into a neat pile of ash in his palm. "I assume Mochi has a fancy car parked somewhere around here."

"I do have a bunch of fancy cars in the garage," Yiran said, picking up the small trash can from the corner. He guided the other boy's hand and dusted the ash into it. "Who exactly are we visiting?"

Zizi poked his head out from under the duvet. He had tied the sash from his coat around his eyes.

"My grandmother."

29
Rui

Rui peered out the car window and read the small gold plaque on the low brick wall.

"*The Reverie*. Are you sure this is it?" she said, looking dubiously at the ancient mansion on top of the small hill they'd just driven up. Another building rose behind it, more modern in architecture and ten stories tall.

Yiran killed the engine. "That's what the GPS says."

"Doesn't your grandmother own a bakery, Zizi? You told me those egg tarts were from her bakery."

"The bakery inside the hotel. My grandmother owns the hotel, therefore, she owns the bakery." The sash was still around Zizi's eyes, shielding him from Rui's glare. He stepped out of the vehicle and groped the air in front of him.

Rui was surprised to see Yiran going to him and helping him up the stone stairs voluntarily. She followed them, and together they went through a moon gate into an expanse of manicured garden.

It felt like they had entered another world. Whimsical lamps hung from trees, and the air smelled of tea leaves and blooming flowers. There was a beautiful arbor at the mansion's entrance with vines running up and down the stately red brick. The place looked old-fashioned in a mon-eyed kind of way. It never crossed her mind that Zizi was from a wealthy family. He was always scrounging around for a quick buck, tiptoeing back and forth over the line of criminality. She should've guessed from his expensive taste in silk pajamas.

She pushed the heavy front doors open, and they entered the reception.

The concierge looked up. There was a shiny pin of a camellia flower on her lapel.

"Welcome to The Reverie," she said, clearly confused by the trio. "May

I help—oh dear—" Her gaze had settled on Zizi.

"Don't worry, she's expecting me." Zizi removed the sash around his eyes, tying it around his narrow waist. His skin was less pallid than before.

The concierge composed herself. "In that case, come with me, please."

The hall was enormous and lit by a chandelier and a few ornate side tables and plush armchairs scattered across the room. It was just as dim as the reception, giving the whole place a hazy, dreamlike quality.

"Wait here." The concierge went over to a rotary telephone and spoke into the earpiece.

Zizi settled onto the nearest chaise. But Rui and Yiran looked around, curious about everything.

A magnificent ceiling arched over them like a chapel's, and it was painted with murals. Rui counted ten of them. Each mural depicted a scene from someone's dark imagination: mountains and fiery lava pits; strange beasts prowling a landscape of jagged rock and stone; a suspension bridge hanging over a ravine of knives while vicious-looking winged creatures soared in the skies above . . .

A mysterious figure in black robes appeared in each mural, with a hood shadowing their face. Each figure was painted a little differently; Rui wondered if it was supposed to be the same individual. In one panel, the figure was seated on the edge of a precipice, looking down on people crawling over nails and sharp objects. The figure held a stick or a wand in its skeletal hand and a small cluster of spheres floated in front of it, giving a bizarre impression that they were blowing soap bubbles as the hordes of humans below suffered.

"Magic," Yiran whispered.

Rui could feel his awe. She watched as he breathed in, like he was trying to inhale the grand hall and all its beautiful monstrosities into his own body.

He was right.

A layer of magic surrounded this hotel. Not the kind Exorcists wielded, but the other kind. The ceiling shimmered briefly, the paintings coming alive for a split second before going still again.

Zizi's grandmother had to be a powerful mage.

Remember that this mortal houses the soul of a god—it will not be any-one ordinary.

The sound of heels on marble echoed above them.

An elegant lady was descending the grand circular staircase. The soft silk of her turquoise qipao swished as she walked to them, and her graying hair was coiffed into a bun, the ends tucked neatly and hair-sprayed to death. There was a timelessness to her, suggesting she was either not that old or perhaps older than the world itself. With her pinched expression and cold manner, she reminded Rui of the Academy's discipline master, the one who never let anyone get away with anything.

"Madam Meng." The concierge lowered her head and stood behind her.

Rui smiled politely.

Yiran gave Madam Meng a full-on bow.

Madam Meng was unimpressed by either of them.

Zizi waved weakly from the chaise.

Madam Meng's expression softened, but when she fixed her eyes on Rui, it frosted again.

"So, you're the girl," she said pityingly, like Rui was a stray dog she couldn't shake off.

Rui kept her smile, but her stomach curdled. She definitely wasn't feeling *a connection* with this woman.

"This is *Rui*," Zizi said sharply.

"And I'm Yiran," the other boy piped up. "A pleasure to meet you."

Madam Meng pursed her burgundy-stained lips. "I suppose I should thank the both of you for retrieving my good-for-nothing grandson and bringing him back here."

The strand of tiny pearls hanging from her glasses clicked as she lowered her chin and peered at Zizi. "Hmm . . . looks like it's not the usual migraine this time."

"Doesn't feel like it." Zizi showed her his hands.

Her expression changed. "Come," she said with urgency, "you must take your medicine."

Not wanting to let Zizi out of her sight, Rui said, "I'll go with you."

Madam Meng's eyebrows shot up, but Zizi took Rui's hand and didn't let go. Rui felt her fingers winding around his like it was the most natural thing in the world.

"She's coming with me," Zizi said firmly.

"What about me?" Yiran asked.

"You?" Madam Meng said. "You will wait here and keep your voice down. My guests are not to be disturbed. Song Wei will have something to say about you being here—yes, I know exactly who *you* are."

"I'm only here because Zizi showed up at my house out of the blue," Yiran grumbled.

Ignoring him, Madam Meng gestured Zizi toward an alcove at the end of the hall.

"Guess I'll just wait here by myself," Yiran muttered.

Sensing his dejection, Rui let go of Zizi's hand and backtracked. "We won't take long. Maybe you should call Ash and let him know where you are, get ahead of things in case she calls your grandfather."

Yiran shrugged and walked in the opposite direction.

Rui hurried after Zizi and his grandmother. Several turns later, they came to a large room. Glass jars and metal tea tins lined the tall shelves, each meticulously labeled in neat script. Various teapots rested on the long table at one end of the room.

Rui and Zizi waited on the bench as Madam Meng perused the shelves. A tiny bell tinkled. Something black pounced onto Zizi's lap and curled up.

"Mao! How'd you get here?" Rui reached over to scratch the cat's chin.

Absently, Zizi played with Mao's soft ears. He was quiet, his eyes wide and curious as he waited. Rui imagined this was how he must've spent his days as a child, wandering around this old and rambling estate thick with magic, poking his nose into this and that, experimenting with spells and artifacts to satiate his thirst for knowledge.

Armed with an assortment of tins, Madam Meng got down to work. She dusted loose tea leaves into a gaiwan, then tapped on the wooden dragon carved onto the curve of her walking cane. The dragon spat out a puff of pink powder. Rui wanted to ask what it was, but the whole process felt like a ritual she didn't want to interrupt.

After pouring hot water into the gaiwan, Madam Meng capped it with its matching porcelain lid. As the tea steeped, she examined the black lines on Zizi's hands.

"Do you know what they are?" Rui asked.

Madam Meng ignored her.

Zizi held Mao a little closer. "Is it bad?"

"We will speak of the markings later." Madam Meng picked the gaiwan up, holding the lid and cup expertly as she poured, allowing only tea to escape into another smaller cup. "Drink."

Zizi stuck his tongue into the liquid and retracted it with a grimace.

Madam Meng tutted. "You kick up a fuss like a child every time you have to take your medicine."

"Because it tastes bitter every time, and this one's particularly vile."

"It is only by knowing what is bitter that you will treasure what is sweet."

"I've no problem treasuring what is sweet without ever tasting anything bitter." Zizi downed the tea in a single gulp. He grimaced and gagged.

"Now, you must rest. Leave us," Madam Meng said. "I believe the girl would like a word with me."

How did she know? There was clearly more to the old lady than Rui had thought.

Zizi paused at the door, throwing them a cloaked look before stepping out.

"How did you know I wanted to speak with you?" Rui said.

"An Exorcist-in-training wandering around the Night Market looking for a mage? Word gets around."

"Zizi's a mage, and I hang out with him. It's not unusual for me to talk to mages."

Madam Meng removed her glasses. The change was startling, like she had removed a piece of her face, leaving it blank and unsettling. "Then why didn't you go to him first? What are you looking for?"

Rui fidgeted under Madam Meng's scrutiny, torn between the desperate need to ask for help and Ten's command of secrecy. "It's a who and a what," she finally said. "I'm looking for someone who doesn't want to be found. An unusual person, who came into this world through unusual circumstances."

"And the *what*?"

"Something that can contain . . . things."

Madam Meng raised an elegant eyebrow. "Vagueness gets you nowhere. Spit it out if you want my help, child."

"I . . . I can't."

"Then perhaps you should give up your search," Madam Meng said. "Some things are not meant to be found. Some people are better off lost. Some secrets should remain secrets."

Rui clenched her jaw, more annoyed with herself—and Ten—than the old lady and her cryptic nonsense. The bench creaked as she stood. "Thanks anyway. I—"

She gasped. Madam Meng had grabbed her hand, and she was staring hard at Rui's palm.

"I see he has chosen well," she concluded seconds later. She released Rui, who wiped her hand on her jeans. "But unfortunately, you need to stop seeing him."

"Excuse me?"

"I believe I was speaking plainly. I want you to stop seeing my grandson."

Something lurched viscerally in Rui's chest. "Stop seeing him? We're not—" She tried to laugh at the ridiculousness of it all, but instead she felt pain. "We're not dating if that's what you mean. I would never—"

Would you never? whispered a voice in her head. Her cheeks flushed.

Madam Meng's smile did not reach her eyes. "That makes things easy then. Leave him alone."

"But I'm not bothering him," Rui argued. *He likes being with me*, she thought.

"I want a parting of ways right now, before things progress."

"You can't change my mind by rearranging your sentences. Why don't you want me to see him?"

"You do not need to know."

"Zizi's my friend. He saved my life."

"Friends come and go. Make new ones."

Rui fumed. "I'm speaking plainly, too. I refuse to stop seeing your grandson. I'm happy with the friends I have now and see no reason to replace them."

Madam Meng leaned forward, knuckles white from gripping the table. "Your story will not end well," she hissed.

Fear inched down Rui's spine. "What do you mean?"

"Exactly what I said. Just as you cannot change fate, I cannot force your actions. Do what you will. Choose your own path if you wish, but be warned it will be a difficult one."

Before Rui could respond, Madam Meng rose from her seat and disappeared down the dark aisles.

30
Yiran

The grand hall felt colder without Zizi and Rui. Yiran wasn't sure what to do with himself. He stared at the intriguing ceiling, spotting a mural of a man with the head of a horse shaking hands with another who had the head of a bull. Weirdly, they were dressed in business suits and standing next to what looked like a giant arched doorway. Throngs of humans were on their hands and knees, begging to be let through the door. Or perhaps, to escape whatever hell they were in.

Someone cleared their throat. The concierge was still here.

"I've never heard of your hotel before, and I'm pretty sure I know all the famous and exclusive ones," Yiran said, casually picking up an expensive-looking vase. He wasn't sure what to make of the decor of the hotel. It was a mishmash of things from different eras and styles, but there was something beautiful about the eccentricity of it all.

The concierge pried the vase from his hands. "We have an extremely private clientele."

"The rich and powerful?"

"Would you like some tea? Madam Meng is famous for her blends," she replied coldly.

Yiran nodded and she left the room. He pulled his phone out and called Ash, who picked up after the first ring.

"What's wrong?"

"Why is that the first thing you say to me? Where's my, *Hello, dearest little brother, how are you?*"

"Hello, my dearest little brother, are you back at the Academy?"

"No, I'm with Rui."

"Flouting the curfew for a detour date before you go back to campus? I didn't think she was your type."

Shit. Yiran had forgotten about the curfew. "I don't have a type," he said. "I'm calling because I'm at The Reverie."

Caught off guard, Ash made a surprised sound.

Yiran beamed at his own reflection in a glass cabinet. "So you *have* heard of it. Tell me more."

"Why are you there? Did you meet the owner?"

"Madam Meng? Yeah, I did. Why?" His discomfort grew when he thought of the foreboding old lady. Zizi and he had one thing in common: scary grandparents. "I'm here because Zizi needed to be. We, uh, ran into him, and I sort of maybe gave him a ride here."

"How did you run into—wait, never mind. Get back to the Academy and keep your ass in your room. There's a Hunt starting right now."

"Sorry, you must be busy," Yiran said, mentally kicking himself.

"Yeah . . . things haven't been going well for us."

"But you picked up your phone—"

"Because I saw the caller ID, my dearest little brother. I have to go."

"Be safe," Yiran said. But Ash had already hung up.

Yiran spun in a half circle, pondering Ash's slip. What was it about this hotel and its owner that got him so worked up?

There was a clink of china.

"Here's your tea," said the concierge. "You may wait here until it's time for you to leave."

"Can I take a tour? See the presidential suite, perhaps?" Yiran smiled winningly. "Please?"

She was unmoved by his charm. "The garden is open for viewing, but everything else is restricted for non-guests."

Yiran took his drink. The concierge spared him no attention as he sauntered out the front doors.

The night was quiet. Cradling the cup of tea in his hands for warmth, Yiran walked until he found a stone path leading to a bench near the edge of the hill. The city's lights twinkled in a sea of ink. Since the curfew was on, the highways were empty except for the occasional vehicle. He had to get going, but he couldn't leave without Rui. Deciding to check on her in a few minutes, he sipped his tea and sat down, staring out at the view.

Things haven't been going well for us.

Ash had sounded uncharacteristically ruffled by what was happening at the Night Hunt. Yiran was suddenly appalled by how unconcerned he'd been in the past whenever Ash went out on an expedition. He'd grown up with the idea that his half brother and grandfather were invincible. Put them on a pedestal, worshipping them in his own way like small gods.

But they were only human. Fallible and mortal.

Ash will be fine. He was a gifted Exorcist, and his team had his back. The Hunts were meticulously planned to keep casualties low. Ash would be fine.

"You seem troubled."

Yiran jumped in fright and dropped his cup. The grass sizzled and smoked in spots drenched by the tea. He clutched his stomach, wondering what he'd just ingested. It wasn't poison, was it? He felt fine.

"Sorry about your tea," said the little girl who had appeared out of nowhere. She was about eight years old, with a crooked smile and eyes bright with an uncanny cleverness. She did not look the least bit apologetic.

"It's okay," Yiran said. "Are you lost?"

"*I* am not lost." She cocked her head. "Are you?"

"No." He sat back down.

The little girl scooted next to him. Her legs barely reached the ground. She dangled them, kicking the air. She didn't have a jacket or a coat on, just a frilly lilac dress and a matching cardigan that looked too thin for the weather. A sparkly brooch was pinned to her cardigan, and upon closer look, Yiran saw it was in the shape of a skull with a rose covering one eye socket. It was odd, but who was he to judge what little girls liked?

She had to be a child of a guest at The Reverie. Maybe her parents were drinking vintage wine in a classy dining room, and she'd snuck out because she was bored.

The two of them sat in companionable silence. Yiran's thoughts mean-dered back to his friends. *Friends* . . . Were Rui and Zizi his friends? Rui had said they were friends back at Song Mansion. *You're connected by the spell and her magic, that's all. Don't lose sight of your goal,* Yiran reminded himself, annoyed with the part of him that was feeling guilty.

Squelch.

He turned to the little girl. She smiled, puffed up her cheeks, and squished them again.

He wagged a stern finger at her.

She giggled.

The night breeze skittered across the hill, rustling the leaves on the ground and ushering the scent of flowers and tea. The little girl shivered and rubbed her arms. Her face was looking pale to the point of being sickly. Yiran hadn't noticed the bruised circles under her big, round eyes earlier either.

"Why don't you go inside where it's warm?" he suggested.

She shook her head and plucked a rose from a nearby bush.

"Want my jacket?"

She peered at him curiously, considering his offer. Then shook her head again.

"Don't take things from strangers. Bet your mom taught you that." He laughed.

"I don't have a mom."

Yiran wanted to kick himself. "I'm sorry."

The little girl smiled. "Don't be."

His heart twinged. He saw himself as a young boy standing in the mid-dle of the courtyard at Song Mansion, heard the sound of a gate closing.

"It's not that bad," the little girl reassured him. "I still have family."

"I'm glad. I'm Yiran, by the way. What's your name?"

"Seven."

"That's an unusual name. Very pretty."

Seven gave him a toothy grin. "I like you. You're nice."

"Why, thank you, that's a very kind thing to say."

She placed her small hand on his much larger one and squeezed it briefly. Her skin felt like ice. Maybe she *was* ill. He should get her back to the hotel before her family blamed him for letting her catch a cold or something.

"I'm looking for my brother," the little girl said suddenly. "You wouldn't happen to know where he is, would you?"

Why would I? Yiran shook his head. "I'm sure he's probably in the hotel."

Seven scratched her nose and stared into the distance with a faraway look on her face, as if she were listening to the wind. "I don't think so." A different smile appeared on her face. It made her look like a feral fox cub. "Did you know there's a library inside? It's full of stories."

"Aren't all libraries full of stories?"

"It's a *special* library."

"What's so special about it?"

"I can't tell you."

Yiran didn't know how to respond. He wasn't very good with kids. They required patience, and right now, his was wearing thin. It was time to check on Rui and Zizi.

"Why don't we go talk to the nice concierge lady?" he said. "I'm sure your brother's somewhere inside. The concierge can help you find him. I'd go search with you, but I'm not a guest of the hotel, so I'm not allowed in the facilities."

Seven giggled. "Neither am I."

"Sorry?"

"I can't go inside." Seven lowered her voice conspiratorially. "You see, I have to be invited."

"Invited?"

"Mm-hmm."

Seven held up the rose. Except it was no longer red. Color drained from its petals, leaking down its stem like rivulets of blood, pooling in the palm of Seven's small hand. When she looked up at Yiran again, her irises had faded to a light gray and her hair was turning translucent.

He jerked out of his seat. "Who are you?"

But the question that came to his mind first was, *What are you?*

"I told you. I'm Seven. You must have a poor memory."

The pool of red in her palm seeped into her flesh. A flush returned to her skin. Her hair was once again a pretty dark brown and her eyes glittered with life. The circles under them were gone. The gray rose crumbled to ash, and Seven flicked her fingers absently.

"What kind of magic is that?" Yiran said, his voice strained. She was just a child. How was this possible?

She smiled slyly. "It's *not* magic."

"What do you mean it's not—" His phone rang shrilly. Yiran smacked it to his ear.

"Yiran? Are you with Rui?"

"Ada?"

"I checked both your rooms, but no one was there, and I can't get hold of Rui. Come back to campus right now. Something happened—"

"Slow down, Ada. What's wrong?"

"There was an ambush during the Hunt. Exorcists are hurt. Are you with Rui?"

Yiran's stomach did a flip. Ash was part of the Hunt. "Yeah, I'm with Rui. We'll head back now." He hung up and ran a trembling hand through his hair. The night suddenly felt rife with secrets and violence.

Seven's voice spoke from behind him. "It was nice meeting you, Yiran. I do hope your brother's okay."

Yiran froze. "I never told you I had a brother."

Heart thumping, he turned, not knowing who or what he would see.

But the little girl was no longer there.

31
Rui

The hotel was a labyrinth, and Rui found herself wandering in circles. Mao chittered in her arms.

"Can *you* find him then?"

Mao swished her tail.

Rui set her down, and the cat trotted along the next corridor. They passed a statue of a fair maiden holding a pomegranate. The sculpture was carved in fine marble. It was so lifelike Rui could almost feel the fear in the maiden's eyes as she tried to escape from the man-beast holding her in his muscular arms.

Mao stopped outside a set of arched doors with brass knockers in the shape of a lion's head.

"Is he in there?"

Mao slow-blinked.

Rui pushed the doors open, gasping at the sight in front of her.

The indigo ceiling was domed with silver constellations, and floor-to-ceiling bookcases spiraled from the sides to the middle of the room. Light reflected from stained glass windows, casting myriad colors against the walls and floors. A library with a maze of books? Who would have thought?

Entranced, she twirled between the bookshelves, suddenly giddy. The library felt magical in a way that didn't feel like actual magic—not the kind she used to possess, anyway, or whatever disturbing thing Madam Meng had. *This* felt like the minutes before dawn, the mystical time when the sky was a mix of soft blue and orange and the day was new.

She skimmed the books with her fingers, feeling the ridges of cloth and paper. Some looked well-loved with bent spines and wrinkled corners, others brand-new. None had titles of any kind. She slipped a book off a shelf. There wasn't a single word in it, and the pages of the next book were empty too. She repeated her experiment on another shelf of books only to find the same thing. Or rather, nothing. Maybe this beautiful library wasn't a library at all.

Something in the corner caught her eye. A book bound in chestnut-brown leather that showed signs of patina. It was musty-smelling in the way old books were, and when she opened it, she *felt* something. There were no words, but the pages were alive somehow, like the book was a living creature and its story was being written as she stared at it.

Rui didn't know why, but it felt like the longer she left the book open, the more things would escape into the world, and something would go wrong. She shut the book quickly and put it back. Madam Meng obviously disliked her. It was best not to give the old lady more reason to hate her by messing up any part of the hotel. Besides, if Mao was right, Zizi was in here somewhere.

Right in the middle of the room, where the shelves spun a full circle, Rui found a huddled figure on the floor.

Zizi was fast asleep, curled up with a hand under one cheek, knees drawn to his chest.

The sketches she had found in his room hurtled fresh into her mind, and her confusion returned tenfold. If that was how he felt about her, how did *she* feel about him?

Rui knew she didn't want anyone. She was perfectly fine being alone. She didn't want *him*. And yet—

She brushed the tangle of hair off his face and trailed a finger down that dagger of a nose, over the bow of his lips, finally resting her hand on his cheek. Zizi made a soft sound, shifting ever so slightly into her palm.

And in this wordless library, Rui felt her heart stumble and fall.

Zizi's eyes flickered open.

"You found me," he said, voice low and husky with sleep.

"Actually, it was Mao who led me here."

"Sometimes I think Mao is more human than cat." Zizi stretched lazily, more cat than boy himself. He propped his head up on his elbow, observing her closely. "Is everything all right?"

"I got mad at you because I hadn't heard from you for weeks, so I broke into your shophouse," Rui said, pressing her hands to her face. "Sorry."

"Is that all?"

Rui peeked between her fingers. The smirk on Zizi's face told her he wasn't mad about her trespassing. "You need to fix the button that opens your spell lab. It's not working. I tried it."

"That's because it doesn't work. It's just a random button that does absolutely nothing."

"But you use it every time we go in."

"My lab is secured by magic," Zizi said, trying not to laugh. He ducked his head, mumbling, "I've been doing the button thing to annoy you."

"Why?" she said, utterly bewildered.

"It's not my fault I'm an attention-seeker."

"You did the annoying button thing to get my attention?"

"What can I say? Despite being a genius, I'm extremely pathetic when it comes to certain things."

Rui caught the underlying meaning in his words. In this strange library in a stranger hotel full of magic, away from everything and everyone, stripped of duty and burden, all she wanted was the truth. But to get to the truth, she had to stop lying.

"There's something else I have to tell you," she said haltingly. "I went into the room with the funny door. I'm sorry, I shouldn't have intruded."

A faint blush bloomed on Zizi's cheeks, but he looked impressed. "You figured out the voice spell?"

"Yes."

"And you saw my sketchbooks?"

Rui could only nod.

"Did you . . . *do* you like my drawings?" There was a different question in his pale blue eyes.

If he'd asked her the same question another time, she might have had a different answer. But all she remembered was that feeling in her heart when Madam Meng commanded her not to see him again.

"I haven't had much time to consider the details of your work," she replied, "but I think I do."

Zizi saw the other answer in her smile. Laughing, he took her wrist, guiding her down to him. She nestled close, laying her head on his chest. *Oh no*, she thought, listening to the beat of his heart, *this is nice.*

Don't get used to it, was her next thought.

"Does your head still hurt?" she asked.

"I'm fine now. More than fine now that you're here."

A rogue giggle escaped her. She was mortified. Who was this infuriating boy who'd turned her into someone who *giggled* at a line like that? Rui tried to glare. "I can't believe you said that out loud."

"Made you laugh," Zizi said smugly. He twirled a lock of her hair around his fingers and tickled her nose with it.

"I'm changing the topic." Looking at the shelves above them, she asked, "Why aren't there any words in the books?"

"Truthfully? I don't know. I've asked Gran, but she says some stories are meant to be hidden and never told or something ludicrous like that. *I* think it's a place she set up to add to the mystique of the hotel. It's all part of the brand."

Rui doubted that. There was something *alive* in the library.

"This is my favorite place in the whole estate," Zizi confided. "Surrounded by blank pages, the promise of beginnings with endings yet unwritten . . . it's hopeful, isn't it?"

"I never thought you to be an idealist."

"Not an idealist, but a romantic," he corrected. "Speaking of stories, there was this legend I read a long time ago, a creation myth of sorts from an ancient civilization. Want to hear it?"

"Sure." What she really wanted to tell him was that she would listen to him speak all day, that it was what she did whenever she visited his shophouse, when she'd curl up in the old armchair, pretending not to pay attention as he grumbled about his work. Secretly, she'd hung on to every word he'd said. But it was only now that she was admitting to herself why she did so.

Zizi cleared his throat softly. "A long time ago, when the first mortals arrived in the world, they looked weird as heck. Or at least, they'd be weird to us now. Each human had four legs and four arms and two heads, all joined together at the torso, which was spherical, like a ball—"

"Gross."

"Shh—anyway, the gods were afraid the humans would challenge them and defeat them. So the gods struck the humans with lightning, splitting each in half. Not only were their physical bodies separated, but their souls were also cleaved into two. From that day on, each human felt the loss of their matching half. They would weep and bleed from the wound, and they spent the rest of their lives doomed to search eternally for the other half who would make them whole again." Zizi paused dramatically. "The end."

"The end?" Rui repeated.

"That's all the story there was."

"I thought there'd be a happy ending."

"Not all stories have happy endings."

"I know, I just . . . it seems tragic to spend your life that way, searching for the other half of your soul."

"Could be fun, like a treasure hunt."

She scowled. Trust him to turn everything into a joke.

But Zizi was suddenly serious again. "But haven't you ever felt like that? Like you're searching for someone out there who's just *right* for you—someone who completes you."

Rui stayed silent, wondering, maybe even hoping, that somehow she might be that last piece of the puzzle that would complete this boy who was looking back at her with those strange, strange eyes. But it was just a story, and maybe she was just a silly romantic too.

"Since you've confessed your crimes, there's something I've been meaning to tell you." Zizi faced her. "When I saw you that night, I knew."

He was talking about the night they first met. The night he saved her life. The night her mother died.

"Knew what?"

"That you were important to me."

It wasn't the answer she expected. "Why?"

He considered her question. "Do you need a reason? Because I don't have one. I just know. You're the most wondrous thing I've ever seen."

"Thing!" she scoffed, pretending to be insulted, appalled she was blushing again.

He tried again. "You are the most wondrous creature I've ever seen."

"Creature?" she glowered, reaching to poke his ribs.

Zizi caught her hand and placed it on his chest. The beat of his heart was steady and strong, a melody she could listen to forever. She didn't want to spoil the moment, though she wasn't entirely sure if what was happening *was* a moment. But Madam Meng's words were troubling her.

"Your grandmother told me to stay away from you."

Zizi's expression turned lukewarm. "My grandmother sees the past and the future. She says many futures are possible, depending on the actions of individuals. If she told you to stay away from me, then it's probably for your own good." He let go of Rui's hand, as if assuming she would do just that.

But Rui kept her hand on his chest. "You fool. To hell with fate."

There was only silence as they stared at each other.

Then, Zizi grinned. "To hell with fate."

It sounded like a promise.

They lay on their backs, staring at the ceiling of false stars and dreams, of a heaven that did not exist, and a future beyond this moment, neither feeling the need to say anything aloud.

Rui wasn't sure how much time had passed when Zizi reached over. His eyes were anxious, uncertain in a way she had never known him to be. His fingers grazed her lips. "May I kiss you?"

She nodded, forgetting to take her next breath as he leaned in. But he tipped his head up, pressing his lips gently on her forehead like she was something precious.

He drew back, wincing slightly, his hand going to his temple.

"Are you all right?"

"I thought I saw—" He blinked a few times. "Never mind. Must be the migraine."

"You should go back to your grandmother and figure out what's wrong," Rui said, though she didn't want to let go of him just yet.

"I'll do that." He smiled and pulled her closer. "But first—"

Footsteps were coming closer.

Someone else was in the library.

"Rui? You in here? Zizi?"

Yiran didn't look at all surprised to see them lying next to each other on the floor, faces inches away from each other.

Zizi groaned. "Excellent timing, Mochi."

"What are you doing here?" Rui spluttered.

Yiran yanked them both up. From his expression, she knew something was amiss.

"What's wrong?" she said.

"We need to leave right now."

Zizi protested, "Hang on, you can't just barge in here and ruin our moment and—"

Yiran silenced him with a glare. "I don't care about your moment; reenact it later. There's trouble in the city. We need to leave now."

32
Rui

Rui hit redial on Yiran's phone. She chewed on her nails, waiting. "Ash isn't picking up."

Yiran snapped, "Try again. Why are you giving up?"

"I'm not. This is the fifth time I've called. Maybe Ash is busy with the situation. I'm sure we'll get more news once we get back to the Academy," she said, peevish.

Yiran floored the accelerator in response.

Rui slumped against the seat and stared out the window. The roads were empty save for a few emergency vehicles that zoomed by with their sirens wailing. A pall had fallen, and the streets took on an eerie feel.

Zizi's fingers grazed her wrist, and she turned to him. The light from outside bathed the car's interior in shades of gray and grainy sepia like a vintage photograph, framing his face in alternating shadow and light. She'd thought he should have stayed at The Reverie, but he'd insisted on coming along. Truth be told, she was glad he did. They still didn't know what had happened to the missing mages, and she wanted to keep him close.

Yiran smacked the steering wheel. "How could it even happen? How could those brainless monsters plan an ambush?"

"Ever heard of Hybrids?" Zizi said.

"Not that again. Hybrids don't exist, even I know that."

"How are you so loud and so wrong? You're not exactly the best source of what's fact or fiction when it comes to Revenants."

"Didn't all our troubles start with you and your stupid spell?" Yiran lashed out. "If you didn't create it in the first place, if you didn't give it to Rui—" He halted abruptly.

"Go on, tell me how this ambush on your brother is all my fault," Zizi shot back. "I'm impressed by the mental gymnastics you just did there."

Yiran brought a fist down to the horn. The deafening sound dragged on.

When he finally lifted his hand from the horn, Rui said, "I told you, Hybrids do exist."

"You're jumping to conclusions without evidence," Yiran muttered as he took the next turn. "The both of you."

Rui seethed. "I was there; I know what I saw that night."

"But—"

"*You* weren't there," Zizi snapped. "Don't tell her what she did or did not experience."

Yiran's eyes flicked to meet Rui's in the rearview mirror. She could sense his confusion, his desire that the world he understood remain as it was. The link between them felt stronger than ever.

"If there's even a possibility that Hybrids might exist, why would the Guild keep it a secret? Why wouldn't my grandfather tell everyone?" he finally said.

Why indeed, Rui thought. She could think of a few answers, none of them favorable to the Guild. The tension in Yiran was pulled so taut it felt like he might break if she provoked him, so she said nothing.

After some silence, Yiran said, "Do guests at The Reverie have to be invited to stay there?"

"It's like any other hotel, you make a booking, you get a room, and you pay up," Zizi replied. "Why?"

Yiran faced the back seat. "There was a little girl in the garden looking for her brother. I thought she was a guest, so I told her to go inside, but she said she had to be invited."

Just then, something ahead in the otherwise empty sky caught Rui's eye. The thing was swooping through the air in a way that didn't feel birdlike.

"There was something weird about her," Yiran continued. "She said her name was Seven, and she did this thing with a rose—magic or maybe it was a trick—sucked all the color out of its petals. Totally creepy."

Rui grabbed the front seat. "What did you say her name was?"

"Seven. Why would parents name their kid after a number?"

Rui's blood ran cold. Another King from the underworld was roaming in the human realm, and this King had made a connection with Yiran. What did that mean?

"What did Seven talk to you about?" she asked.

"What's that thing in the sky?" Zizi said at the same time.

Yiran peered through the windshield. "What thing—"

The thing descended onto the road in front of them and stood up.

It was a person.

Running toward the moving car.

"Watch out!" Rui yelled.

Tires screeched. But Yiran couldn't stop in time. The impact flung them against their seats.

Rui's stomach somersaulted as Yiran wrestled for control of the wheel. The car swerved, coming to a stop on the road shoulder.

Groaning, Yiran unbuckled his seat belt. "Is anyone hurt?"

Rui untangled herself from Zizi's arms. "I'm okay, just shaken."

Zizi gave his shoulder a few rolls. "Nothing's broken. What the hell happened? Did we hit someone?"

"Why were they running at us?" Rui said, rubbing a tender spot on her back.

"I don't know. I'll go check." Yiran opened the car door and staggered out.

Rui watched as he jogged toward the body lying in the middle of the road. The car hadn't hit the person hard enough to kill them . . . right?

Feeling helpless, she picked up Yiran's phone and dialed a few numbers in succession: Ada's, Ash's, her dad's.

No one picked up.

Zizi pressed up against her.

Rui stiffened in surprise. "What are you—"

"Shush." He was staring out the window. "Something's not right."

Outside, a fog had rolled in. Chilly air seeped into the car. In the distance, Rui made out the faint silhouette of Yiran crouching on the ground. He seemed farther away than she thought he would be.

Zizi wound the window down. "Get back in the car!"

Yiran remained in the same position.

Zizi shouted again, but Yiran did not respond.

"It's like he can't hear us," said Rui, uneasy.

"Does he have a weapon or talismans on him?"

Her throat tightened. "No."

"Do you feel it?"

"Feel what?"

Zizi didn't answer. Instead, he opened the car door and scrambled out. "*Song Yiran*—get back here!"

It was the first time Zizi had ever called Yiran by his actual name.

Something was very wrong.

Zizi slammed the door in Rui's face and stuck a hand in to press a button. The window started to wind up.

"What's going on?" she asked. "What are you doing?"

Then she felt it. A kind of shiver down her spine like something unholy was scuttling across her ancestors' graves. The same feeling from four years ago, the same from outside the karaoke club.

Hybrids.

Zizi was whispering something she couldn't hear.

Was he casting a spell?

"Zizi, wait—"

But he'd taken off into the night.

Rui tugged at the door handle. Stuck. The window wouldn't wind down either. She crawled to the front and tried the doors. Nothing budged. Zizi must've used a spell to lock her in.

Rui punched the seat in front of her. How could he leave her here like this? She wasn't some helpless damsel to be hidden away at the first sign of danger. With or without her magic, she was still an Exorcist-in-training.

A protector instead of the protected.

She grabbed one of her swords, turned the pommel around, and smashed it into the window.

"Come *on*." She bashed the window again and again, half cursing at Zizi, half swearing at Yiran—what kind of windows were these? She should've known that any car owned by the Songs would be reinforced for security.

Gradually, cracks formed on the thick glass. Rui dropped her sword and stuck her legs up, anchoring herself with her palms on the seat. She took a breath—and kicked as hard as she could.

The glass broke. Small pieces fell to the ground.

"Yes!" she grunted, prepping for another kick.

She might not have magic anymore, but sometimes all you needed was brute strength.

33
Yiran

The cold night air woke Yiran up from the daze of the accident. He shivered and zipped his jacket, turning up the shearling collar for warmth. In the fog, the light from the streetlamps dimmed to a hazy rust orange. Everything felt surreal, like he was underwater. Dark and misty, the road seemed to stretch on and the distance to the body on the road felt longer than it should.

What if the person was dead? *Then you'd be a murderer, dumbass.*

Yiran swallowed, his throat suddenly parched. He would get kicked out of the Academy. He'd get kicked out of life. This wasn't a minor traffic offense. His grandfather wouldn't and couldn't get him off a manslaughter charge, and Commissioner Senai was kind, not corrupt. *Young, rich, bastard, no-good grandson of the Song family . . .* The headlines practically wrote themselves. With the media circus that would surround his case, some district judge would want to make an example of him. They would try him as an adult. He would go to jail. And he would deserve it.

There.

The body was in front of him.

His heart sank. It was a boy no older than himself, someone with a full life ahead of him. A life Yiran had possibly cut short.

The boy's dark hair fanned out on the tarmac, and one of his legs was bent at an angle that turned Yiran's stomach. He was wearing a flimsy ivory shirt with billowing sleeves and loose pants. His feet were bare as if he'd woken from sleep and wandered onto this highway. There was no blood on his clothes or the ground.

Bending over, Yiran reached a shaky hand to the boy's neck, fingers meeting skin as cold as ice.

A pulse.

Yiran reached into his pocket, only to remember he'd left his phone with Rui.

"Call an ambulance!" he shouted back at the car.

The fog was thicker now, and the headlights were diffused orbs like the eyes of a demon. He couldn't see Rui or Zizi.

"Rui?" he shouted again.

There was no response.

Should he pick the boy up and carry him to the car? But moving him might worsen his injuries. He glanced back at the boy.

Goose bumps erupted on his arms. Was that lock of hair always across the boy's cheek? Was the angle of his broken leg different?

Panic crawled up Yiran's vertebrae and nestled in his head, its worm-like fingers wriggling in his brain. He was underwater again, pressure in his ears, in his head. Maybe it was delayed shock. Maybe this was all a dream, maybe—that sound, like the scratch of nails on a chalkboard—was it coming from the boy?

The panic worms in Yiran's brain squealed and squirmed. Shakily, he pushed to his feet. He had to get back to the car.

Something cold wrapped itself around his ankle.

He looked down.

The boy's eyes were open.

Yiran's entire body screamed.

Next thing he knew he was flat on the ground, the wind knocked out of his lungs. He could smell it—that miasmic mix of flowers and nightmares. How had he missed it before? So much for his training. He didn't have a weapon with him, not even a talisman. His body was gripped with fear, unable to move. He was nothing but a tasty snack for a Revenant.

The Revenant boy stood over him now, one leg still bent at a horrific angle. He wasn't snarling like the wild monster at the Night Market or morphing into distorted shapes. The boy's slender eyes sparkled with intelligence as he gazed through long lashes, and when his lips curled back,

Yiran noticed that his front teeth were slightly crooked in an altogether too-human way.

He was beautiful.

"Where do you think you're going, handsome?" the Revenant boy said.

"You can talk."

"How observant of you." There was a series of cracks as the Revenant straightened his broken leg. He pouted at Yiran. "That really hurt."

"You ran at a moving car. What did you expect?" said Yiran's asinine mouth.

"Ha ha. Let's see if you're just as funny when you're dead."

The Revenant's hand was at Yiran's neck, cold fingers digging in, pulling Yiran to his knees.

"You're an Exorcist, aren't you?"

"Cadet," Yiran choked out stubbornly. He was getting lightheaded, which might explain his stupid and petty urge to argue with a Revenant.

To his surprise, the Revenant boy loosened his grip.

Yiran gulped air into his lungs.

"What are you? A sixth-year?"

Yiran wheezed, "Enrolled a few weeks ago."

The Revenant raised an eyebrow.

"I'm a special case."

"You should've stayed away from that place and all the lies they feed you. This world is full of useless fools. There's no need to save them all."

"What are you talking about?"

The Revenant's lips curled with pleasure. "Don't worry your pretty little head over it. I'm only making polite conversation over dinner."

"Seems a bit rich for you to tell me not to worry, seeing that I'm the meal," Yiran retorted, giving him a humorless grin in return.

Keeping his smile, the Revenant licked his lips suggestively.

Yiran felt a shiver of anticipation. "Do you have a name or something?" he asked, suddenly curious. Maybe too curious.

Confusion flickered in the Revenant's eyes, as if he never thought someone would ask a creature like him something so courteous.

"Yuki."

"Well, Yuki, can't say I'm pleased to meet you under such circumstances. I'm Yiran."

"Enough with the attitude." Yuki rolled his eyes, muttering, "If only you knew."

"Knew what?"

"Aren't you a nosy one?"

"Aren't you a tease?"

Yuki pressed his full lips together, seemingly unwilling to say more. But Yiran could tell he wanted to. It struck him that Yuki might be enjoying their conversation. The cold hand around Yiran's neck was relaxed now, as if Yuki had left it there because he wanted to touch rather than to hurt. But Yiran had a feeling any sudden moves from him meant a certain and swift death. He needed to play for time, to draw things out until Rui and Zizi came looking for him.

"You're interesting." Yiran kept his tone conversational, as if the two of them were hanging out together on a coffee shop date and one of them didn't have his hand wrapped around the other's throat. "I didn't know Revenants could speak. The last time I met one, all it did was growl at me. It had these scary red eyes and it turned into a tentacled monster and tried to kill me. You're different, you look different—I mean, no tentacles, which is awesome. You seem so . . . you're not like—"

"Not like other Revenants?" Yuki scrunched his nose and made a face that Yiran thought was unfairly cute. "You're so transparent. If you think flirting with me in such a pathetic manner will stop me from ki—"

"Human. I was going to say you seem so human."

Yuki went so still it felt like time had stopped. Emotion crept across his face in a slow, painful way.

Yiran saw a kind of wretched yearning for impossible things, things beyond Yuki's reach now, a melancholic longing for lost hopes and wasted wishes.

Yuki's hand fell from Yiran's throat, hanging limply by his side. "What makes you think I'm not?"

It took a full second for everything to sink in.

Yiran breathed out. "You're a Hybrid Revenant."

Yuki smirked. "Took you long enough."

Shaken, Yiran couldn't make sense of anything. *A Hybrid, he's a Hybrid*, his mind kept repeating. Rui and Zizi were right. Hybrids *did* exist. Surely the Guild knew? Why had he never been told or warned about them?

"Don't look so worried," Yuki said. "The first kill is always the clumsiest, but I have better table manners now. Unlike some of the others, I don't play with my food. Your death will be painless, like falling into a deep sleep."

"Wait! Tell me more," Yiran said, desperately grabbing onto anything he could think of to delay his imminent demise. "I want to know more, I want to know about you."

"About me?" Yuki was surprised.

"Yes, you. There're other Hybrids like you, right? You must have a hideout. Where is it? How many of you are there?"

"Fishing for information? It doesn't matter how many of us there are— there's no hope for you. I'm tired of being hunted; the only hope is in building a new world for *us*."

"A new world for Hybrids? The Exorcists will stop you—" An iron grip choked off Yiran's words.

"Then we'll create a world *without* Exorcists. I've had enough of your questions," Yuki hissed. He leaned in, dipping his head, lips a breath away from Yiran's, almost like he was about to kiss him. At the last moment, Yuki turned his head, and all of Yiran's questions disappeared.

A quick shot of pain. Cold spreading through his body. The wet trickle of blood down his neck. He'd learned about the *drinking* in his lectures, but this felt nothing like what the professors had described. His body relaxed, a heady sensation spreading through his limbs, a kind of perverse euphoria. Was this it? Was this how he would depart this world?

It's not a bad way to die, he thought vaguely.

Something flickered.

Through half-closed eyes, Yiran saw ... *fire?*

34
Yiran

Yuki shrieked. Crimson fire was engulfing his shirt. He released Yiran and retreated with a cry.

The uneven tarmac cut into Yiran's palms as he collapsed. His lungs filled with air, and the heady feeling dissipated. Through the fog, a thin figure emerged, his black coat rolling behind him like a storm. His eyes were dark and wild, his lips muttering a string of spells. He stopped a few feet away and turned to Yiran.

Zizi.

Yiran didn't think his heart could pound harder or faster, but it did. Why was he suddenly more afraid of the mage than the Hybrid standing right next to him?

"Stay out of my way," Zizi commanded, as if Yiran were an ant to be crushed under his unforgiving boot.

The flames around Yuki had died down. He was largely unharmed and very pissed off. "Who are you?"

Zizi grinned. "Your worst nightmare."

"Another Exorcist?" Yuki snarled.

"*Please*, don't insult me." Zizi wriggled his fingers and several talismans appeared above his hands.

"You're the mage," Yuki said. "Seems like you're going to be more trouble than I thought."

Teeth bared, Yuki tilted his head to the night sky. There was a sound of bone breaking, bone growing, bone forcing itself out in ways it should not.

Violet shards sprouted from Yuki's spine like panes of broken glass. They melded together into two separate wings, one on each side of his spine, the left smaller than the right. Unlike the mutated Revenant at the

Night Market with its slimy tentacles, Yuki's jagged wings were beautiful—and deadly.

Zizi tilted his head, fascinated. "What are you?"

"He's a Hybrid," Yiran said. *He's still human*, he almost added. No. Yuki wasn't human. He was a Revenant.

He was the enemy.

"Shut up." Yuki growled. But he didn't attack. Instead, he reared up and flashed his wings.

Yiran had seen this sort of posturing in schoolyard fights; Yuki was afraid.

"I've never fought a Hybrid before," said Zizi, looking a little feral himself. "I'm dying to have a go."

"If you wish to die, then your wish is my command."

Yuki flung his wings back. Violet spikes burst from them, hovering in the air above him.

Yiran covered his head and face with his arms as spikes rained down in staccato flashes of light. But the glass-like bullets never reached him.

Yuki was only aiming at Zizi.

The mage had spread his arms. A glowing circle three times the size of his body formed in front of him. The spikes fizzled when they touched the shield, but not before they burned holes in it.

Yuki launched into the air, twisting his wings. Another hail of violet bullets shot down. Again, Zizi braced with his shield.

"Is that all you got?" Zizi called out.

Yuki cackled. "Seems like more than what you can handle."

Yiran glanced at the mage. Sure enough, Zizi had taken damage. A few stray bullets containing Yuki's yinqi had burned through his shield, slicing through his clothes. Blood seeped from a gash on his leg. Yiran had no idea how good of a fighter Zizi was. Exorcists worked in teams, each member a complement to the others. If Zizi's main mode was defensive spells, it was Yiran's role to back him up on offense. But here he was, sniveling on the ground like a useless hack.

Yuki swerved right, prepping for another attack. "Let's see how long you can hold out."

"That depends on who's the one-trick pony here." Zizi laughed. "Is it me? Or is it you?"

In response, Yuki spun in the air, throwing momentum into his attack. The night sky lit up in violet as a hundred jagged pieces burst from his wings.

Every single fragment was pointing at Yiran.

Before he could react, the violet shards assailed him.

Yiran shrunk back. A crimson shield appeared in front of him—just a second too late. He felt something hot on his face and smelled his own burning flesh. He yelped in pain, curling into a terrified ball behind the shield.

Moments later, the attack stopped. Zizi's shield had taken most of the damage, but the heat on Yiran's cheek was almost unbearable.

"You okay?" Zizi asked. His shield shimmered and disappeared.

Yiran nodded, not daring to touch the part of his skin where Yuki's yinqi had torched.

Zizi shouted at the Hybrid, "That was dirty. Leave him alone—*I'm* your opponent."

"There is no fairness in the fight for survival," Yuki said, breathing heavily from the effort of his attack. "You are both my enemies."

"In that case, let's end this."

Zizi threw off his coat and extended his left arm, dragging his right hand down pale skin. Something emerged when his hands met.

His spiritual weapon.

It was a thin sword that looked like the night on fire. The steel was pure black, its edges gleaming red. But the weapon was unfinished; the top part of it was serrated like it'd been sawn off, and it was only half the length of Zizi's arm.

A broken sword.

If a spiritual weapon reflected the wielder's character and ability, what did that say about Zizi?

"A new toy?" said Yuki. "What other secrets do you have?"

"If I told you, it would ruin the surprise." Almost leisurely, Zizi pointed his sword at Yuki. "Any last words?"

Seething, the Hybrid flared his wings.

Zizi rolled his eyes. "Not that again." He whispered two words under his breath.

There was a sharp whistle of metal slicing through air.

Yuki cried out. Half of his left wing had shattered, the violet spikes strewn on the road, fizzing out.

Yiran hadn't seen the blow coming either. It was as if the other half of Zizi's sword had appeared from nowhere, slamming down with a force so large, there was a split in the tarmac.

"Surprise!" Zizi whooped, brandishing his broken sword.

Yiran gawked at him. "What the hell?"

Zizi grinned. "Told you I was gifted." He lowered himself, whispering quickly, "Each hit takes a lot out of me. I can't keep this up for long. You should run if you can."

But Yiran stayed where he was. He wasn't helping the fight, but he couldn't abandon Zizi.

Sweat dripped down Yuki's face as he strained to re-form his wing. He barely made any progress when the sharp whistle sounded again.

Yuki sprang aside.

But he miscalculated the direction of Zizi's blow.

He collapsed as Zizi's sword took out his other wing.

"Say your prayers," Zizi sang, flinging his sword arm out.

Yuki struggled on the ground, writhing in pain. It was becoming clear that he would not win this fight.

I'm tired of being hunted.

Instead of relief, Yiran felt a pang in his chest, even as his face was still hurting from Yuki's assault. The Hybrid boy had seemed so alone, so bitter. And he would disappear from this world, just as alone and bitter.

Yuki's eyes found his.

Yiran didn't, *couldn't* look away in Yuki's last moments. Yuki seemed to smile at him, and just when Yiran thought it was the last time he would ever lay his eyes on this beautiful Revenant boy, the night sky exploded with light.

35
Rui

The air crackled.

From the car, Rui heard a sharp whistle.

A force shook the ground, and the vehicle rattled loudly.

Zizi.

He'd told her he only used his spiritual weapon when he had no other choice. He'd also shared that the nature of his attack allowed for three strikes before he needed to recover from the exertion.

Another whistle.

Another blow.

Rui clambered out of the broken window, wincing as tiny bits of glass cut her palms. *Hurry,* she urged her legs. If whoever Zizi was fighting hadn't perished from the first two strikes, it meant that he only had one more chance to finish the job.

But before she could get any closer, violet and crimson light burst into the sky, like lightning from another world.

Rui sprinted, then skidded to a stop, shocked by what she saw.

Yiran was hunched over, but he seemed largely unhurt. Near him, crumpled on the ground, was a waiflike young man with violet stubs sticking out of his back.

A Hybrid.

He wasn't the only one.

Spiky hair, callous eyes, and a sadistic smile—if you could call it a smile. The other Hybrid was built like a tank. Growing out of his back were eight violet spinal blades, each with a point ready to inflict pain. They arched over his head and around his body, sharp ends crisscrossing like the teeth of a Venus flytrap. Ensnared in those blades was a boy, his arms limp, head lolling to the side.

"Zizi!" Rui shrieked.

"Come any closer and he dies," the Hybrid growled.

A violet blade slid out, agonizingly slow, just under Zizi's left collarbone. Red seeped into the white of his T-shirt, spreading fast.

Rui cried out. It felt like she had been impaled along with him.

Zizi opened his eyes and found her. "I thought I told you to stay in the car," he rasped. His tone was so utterly normal, like he was telling her about a new set of pajamas he'd bought instead of bleeding to death in front of her.

"Why did you run off without me?" she screamed.

"I didn't want you to get hurt."

"I had to smash the windows to get out of the car."

"Should've known there was no stopping you." Zizi managed a crooked smile. His teeth were stained with blood.

"Enough of this lovers' chitchat," the hulking Hybrid snapped. "I thought you'd put up more of a fight, mage. I was hoping to have some fun tonight."

Zizi coughed. Blood dribbled down his chin. "I was distracted by your friend. Two against one seems kind of unfair, don't you think?"

A sound of pain came from the other Hybrid. Smoke rose from the violet stubs on his back. They were disintegrating. It looked like something had been chopped off.

His yinqi. It was depleted. Which meant they stood a chance.

Rui caught Yiran's eye. The skin on his cheek was a painful red and blistering, but he could fight if he had her sword. He could take the weaker Hybrid out. Yiran nodded imperceptibly at her. He understood. All she needed was an opportunity.

"What are you doing here, Aloysius?" said the Hybrid boy, looking dazed as he struggled to his feet.

"Yuki, Yuki, oh sweet little Yuki. Did you think they wouldn't send me to check up on you?"

Rui's ears pricked. Who was Aloysius referring to?

Yuki lowered his eyes. "I had it under control."

It wasn't fear Rui sensed in his words, but anger.

"If you say so. This was a simple job. This was your chance to prove yourself, and you screwed up." Aloysius cackled, seemingly reveling in making Yuki feel small. "They're not going to take kindly to your failure."

Yuki sneered. "They're not going to take kindly to you running your big mouth either."

Aloysius looked confused. "Eh?"

Zizi's T-shirt was turning redder by the second. Rui didn't want to find out how much blood a human body contained. "Let him go," she said.

"Don't tell me what to do, little girl." Aloysius dismissed the weapon in her hand, turning his attention back to Yuki instead. "Look at her, do you sense her qi levels, Yuki? She's just an ordinary human, and you couldn't even kill her first? You're a waste of space."

Yuki glared at Aloysius with deep hatred.

"Leave the two of them alone," Zizi said, staring at Rui. She knew he'd come to the same conclusion as her: the target of this ambush was *him*. But it was clear the Hybrids wanted him alive, otherwise Aloysius would've finished him off.

Aloysius snickered. "Trying to play the hero?"

"I'm not the hero type." Zizi's grin was turning into a grimace. "I just enjoy being a know-it-all. That boy over there is Song Wei's grandson. If he dies, you'll have the Exorcist Guild devoting every resource they have to hunting you down. I'm guessing you don't want that."

"Let them come." Aloysius snarled, driving his blade in deeper through Zizi.

Blood flowed from the curved end sticking out of Zizi's chest, dripping down to his feet. He looked like he was about to faint, but he kept talking.

"You're ruining my shoes, *Aloysius*. It's going to be a pain to remove all that blood from leather."

"Shut that mouth of yours."

Aloysius rotated his blade.

Zizi blew out an agonizing breath. His eyes were glazing over. Rui couldn't stand to watch this. She moved her arm by half an inch, ready to throw her sword over to Yiran.

A violet blade shot out from Aloysius.

Yiran gasped. The blade was pressed against his jugular.

Rui met Aloysius's glare, cursing silently. His reflexes were too fast. They had to find another way.

He spat at her. "Sneaky brat! Try that again and your boyfriend dies. And you! I don't care whose grandson you are. I suggest you stay down like a good dog before I put you down."

"We're supposed to be lying low," Yuki said. He stole a glance at Yiran. Rui could've sworn there was a shadow of concern on the Hybrid's face. "We have who we came for. Let's go before their reinforcements arrive."

Aloysius shot Yuki an irritated look, but he retracted his blades.

All of them.

The night trembled with Zizi's scream.

The Revenant flicked his blade clean. Blood splattered everywhere. Zizi dropped to the ground, his body lying motionless in a growing pool of red.

Flashes of a different body, a different time, exploded in Rui's mind.

Something inside her caught, like the teeth of a key latching. A snarl rose from the depths of her being. It grew louder, hungrier, bursting forth like a primal scream.

Fire erupted from her hands, pluming like a celestial halo.

She stared, shell-shocked. Blue and brilliant, the flames were neither hot nor cold. They crested over her arms, spreading to her body.

"Stop!" Aloysius shouted at her, dragging Zizi with him as he retreated. "Stop or I'll kill him."

But Rui's feet continued to move. Her body had a mind of its own, held hostage by something she didn't understand. She stared at the blue fire blazing from her hands. Fascinated. Horrified. At her next exhale, her spiritual weapon lit up with the same flames.

This wasn't her magic. This wasn't *her*. But did it matter? All she wanted was to save Zizi, and this, this *thing*, this blue fire—it could work.

"That magic can't hurt us," Aloysius said, still backing away. "It draws from the darkness, just like ours."

Was Aloysius telling the truth? Was the blue fire truly useless against him? He didn't look as sure as he sounded. If the blue fire came from the darkness, it would harm Zizi. But if Aloysius was bluffing, then maybe it would pass *through* Zizi the same way yangqi had no effect on magic practitioners who used it.

But even if Rui wanted to use it on Aloysius, there was no opening she could detect; Aloysius was using Zizi's body as a shield.

As if she'd said her thoughts aloud, Zizi opened his eyes.

He winked.

And nodded.

Rui gritted her teeth and plunged the flaming sword right into his chest.

36
Rui

They locked eyes as her blade ran through him.

In that moment, Rui realized Zizi hadn't been completely sure if he would survive her attack. She wanted to weep at his daredevil stupidity, but she held her sword in place, willing him to stay alive.

Behind him, Aloysius convulsed. His flesh was smoking where the blue flames had touched him. But he wouldn't let go of Zizi.

Somehow, Zizi found the strength to pull away, even as the Hybrid's spinal blades pierced his arms. Even as Rui kept her sword firmly in his chest.

"Do it," Zizi gasped.

Rui saw her angle just over his shoulder, a breath away from his cheek. She reached over with a hand.

Blue fire torched Aloysius's face. With an anguished roar, he finally released Zizi and turned on his heel.

Rui pulled her sword out and leaped in pursuit. She didn't have to go far. The flames proved too much for the Hybrid. He collapsed, making strangled, high-pitched sounds that shook Rui to the bone. The smell of burning flesh tainted the air, and soon, there was only silence.

Aloysius was wrong. Whatever magic Rui wielded wasn't from the darkness. It had, after all, killed him.

The taste of victory salted her tongue. But the body on the ground didn't look like a monster. He looked like a man. Slowly, he turned gray like a stone statue, features crumbling to fine ash.

Rui dropped her sword, the clang of metal dull against the tarmac. Her blue flames had extinguished as mysteriously as they had appeared. But the shock of what happened had not worn off.

She stumbled back to the boys, falling to her knees next to Zizi's prone body.

"Is he . . ." She choked on her words, unable to continue.

Yiran grabbed her arm. "He's alive. I checked his wounds—I think the bastard tried to heal himself."

"Zizi?" Rui touched his face.

Zizi inhaled sharply and opened his eyes, like he'd just come back to life. Groaning, he rolled onto his side, spitting out a black substance.

"Didn't heal . . . completely," he wheezed. "But I'll live."

Rui wanted to hold him. But she didn't move. "What were you thinking? How could you gamble your life like that? You didn't know for sure if the blue fire was safe, did you? I could've killed you."

"We both took a calculated risk." Zizi ran the back of his hand over his bloody lips. "You knew it was possible I'd die, and you still did it."

His words were a knife. Rui wondered if he'd meant to make the cut.

I did it because I trusted you, she almost said. But that wasn't it, was it? Deep down she knew that no matter how she felt about him, she would do whatever it took to kill a Revenant. The moment they shared in the library of The Reverie felt like a lifetime ago. Maybe Madam Meng was right: Rui was bad news.

Maybe I should stay away from him. "Pull that on me again and you might not live the next time," she said coldly.

Zizi gave her a bloody grin.

"Where's Yuki?" she asked, suddenly noticing his absence. It was disturbing to call a Revenant by a human name.

"Never mind him, never mind that freaking Hybrids really do exist," Yiran said, raising his voice. He was staring at her like she was an alien. "What the hell was that? I thought you lost your magic!"

"I . . . I don't know." Holding out her hands, Rui switched up her breathing pattern, trying to channel her magic, or at least the blue flames again.

Seconds passed. Nothing happened.

"I can't summon anything."

"Which means your magic hasn't returned, and the blue fire is something else," Zizi deduced.

"What is it then?" Yiran said. "How did she manage to kill Aloysius?"

That magic can't hurt us. It draws from the darkness, just like ours.

Aloysius cackled in Rui's head. But it was Ten's face she saw. Ten had claimed she'd been touched by death. Was this what he meant? Was she somehow connected to the darkness because of that? But the blue flames killed Aloysius in the end. Hybrid or not, he was still a Revenant, a creature of the dark.

Nothing made sense.

Rui stuck her hand into her pocket, fingers closing over Nikai's mirror. The Reaper might know something, but she had to wait until she was alone to contact him.

She wished she could tell all her secrets to the two boys in front of her. They were staring, one at the night sky, the other at the highway. There were lights from vehicles drawing near.

Yiran turned from the road. "Why is it that when something bad happens, it's always the three of us?"

"The hell would I know," Zizi muttered. His skin had a sickly tint.

"We need to find out what's wrong with Rui," Yiran said to him.

"You're right, we do."

Since when did they get along well enough to agree? And since when was *she* their joint responsibility?

"What we need to know is why the Hybrids tried to kidnap Zizi," she said. "What if the missing mages were hired by Hybrids to create the spell and that's why they're after you now?"

"The man who hired me wasn't a Hybrid," Zizi said.

"And now he's dead. The Hybrids could've used normies to hire the mages, and then killed them to cover their tracks. The other mages might be missing because they succeeded in creating some type of separation spell like you did, and the Hybrids took them."

Zizi shook his head, wincing as he checked his chest wound. "More likely the mages failed and that got them killed. Aloysius was only toying with me. He wanted me alive, and I think I know why—the Hybrids want me to re-create the spell."

Yiran raised his hand. "Wait a minute, I'm not following any of this."

"A man came to my shop asking for a spell that could split a Revenant's spiritual energy from itself," Zizi said. "I told him it wasn't possible, but he said to try anyway, that he'd double the price if it worked for even a few seconds. I took the job as a challenge, thinking I would fail. But I succeeded, and now you and Rui have proven the separation can last longer, that it could be permanent. The Hybrids must want to exploit this somehow."

"Yuki said something about creating a new world for Hybrids," Yiran recalled with a shudder. "A world without Exorcists—"

"Where Hybrids and Revenants can feed on humans freely," Rui finished. "What else did Yuki say?"

"Not much." Yiran touched his cheek gingerly. The patch of skin was raw and red.

"You warned me, Zizi," said Rui, nauseated by the thought that came to her. "You said if I touched a Revenant after casting the spell, its qi might affect me, and the hunger will possess me. What if the Hybrids want your spell so they can create more of them?"

Yiran blanched. "Is that even possible?"

"Maybe," Zizi said. "These Hybrids want to survive, like any other living organism. If the spell works the way they want it to, they don't have to wait for the Blight to randomly infect humans. They can make it happen themselves. And if there're more of them, they can overpower the Exorcists. Take over the city. Feed on anyone they want."

Yiran pinched the bridge of his nose. "We have to tell the Guild—we have to tell them everything."

"We can't tell them everything," Zizi said.

"Then what do you propose?" Yiran shouted. "That we do nothing about the Hybrids? Should we wait until they have a chance to kidnap you again?"

"They can't force me to do anything," Zizi insisted stubbornly.

"You don't know that," said Rui.

"Whatever it is, we shouldn't tell the Guild about the blue fire. We don't know what they might do to you."

Even though he was seriously injured, Zizi was only worried about her. The guilt Rui felt for risking his life gnawed at her and she broke his gaze.

Yiran glared at the both of them. "At the very least, we should get back to the Academy and tell the Guild about the spell and what it can do."

"If we do that, your grandfather will know how *you* got your magic," Rui said quietly. "Are you ready for that?"

"I don't know." Yiran punched the tarmac. "But we should tell them about the Hybrids."

"The Guild says Hybrids don't exist, remember?" Zizi mocked.

"That's because they didn't know—" Yiran began.

Rui cut him off. "How can you still believe that?"

The sound of approaching car engines was growing loud. They'd been too busy arguing to notice three black SUVs drawing closer to them.

Zizi squinted. "Well, look who's here."

"Exorcists," Rui said, recognizing the hood ornament on the cars. "How did they find us?"

"They must've tracked Mochi's phone."

Yiran scrambled up. "At least we're getting help."

The SUVs stopped. The doors opened and an Exorcist stepped out from each car while the drivers remained seated. The two men and lone woman were dressed in the signature black trench coats of the Guild. One of the men wore his hair in a ponytail while the woman had a bleached-blond buzz cut and heavy eyeliner. She and the other man had the Captain's lapel pin on their coats.

Rui didn't recognize them.

"I'm so glad you guys found us," Yiran said. "We were just—whoa!"

The blond Exorcist grabbed his arms, twisting them behind him, securing his wrists together with a zip tie. "What's going on? Why do I feel like I'm being arrested? Not that I've ever had the pleasure of that experience."

The Exorcist looked unamused.

"I don't think my grandfather would appreciate me being manhandled this way." He continued, "Could you maybe lay off the zip tie? It's cutting into my wrists."

The Exorcist didn't reply, and she didn't loosen his restraints.

If this was how they were going to treat Song Wei's grandson, it was best not to protest.

Rui pointed to Zizi. "He's injured and needs a healer." She offered both her wrists to the ponytailed Exorcist.

After securing her, he walked over to Zizi and lifted his T-shirt. Zizi looked on unhappily as the Exorcist examined his wounds.

"This one has magic too." The Exorcist added, "He's human."

Rui exchanged a look with Yiran. She wondered who or *what* they'd expected to find here.

Slinging one of Zizi's arms over his shoulder, the ponytailed Exorcist got Zizi to his feet. He wasn't bothering to be gentle or careful. Zizi said nothing, allowing himself to be led to one of the cars.

"Get in." The blond Exorcist nudged Yiran toward another vehicle.

"Where are you taking us?" Yiran demanded.

She shoved him into the back seat in reply, then motioned Rui to the third SUV.

"Why are you separating us?" Rui said as she got into the car.

The young woman surprised Rui by answering, "We need to question you."

Of course. The three of them had to be questioned to see if their stories matched up.

"You'll heal my friend, right?"

"Sure."

The answer didn't inspire confidence, but there was nothing Rui could do. She wondered what other unwanted surprises the night might have in store.

The door slammed shut. The divider between the back seat and the front seats rolled up. Something misted onto her face.

"What was that?" She coughed and waved the air. "Hello? Hey!"

When no one answered, she banged on the plastic divider. But quickly, she felt her limbs relaxing. It was getting hard to stay awake. She heard the hiss of the mist again and held her breath as best as she could.

But soon, everything went dark.

37
Yiran

The door creaked open.

Yiran raised his head from the cold metal table. Whatever drug they'd sprayed on him to knock him unconscious had lost its effect. He had woken alone, sitting in muted darkness with his thoughts. They weren't pleasant ones.

Yuki's sad smile kept appearing in his mind. The Hybrid's revelations about an impending new world order, the blue flames that ascended erratically from Rui . . . Ever since magic entered his life, it'd felt like he'd been treading water in the deep end of the pool, his feet unable to find solid ground.

The lights flickered on.

Yiran rubbed his eyes. A small square room. Unnaturally bright walls and ceiling. Another chair across the table from him. Empty.

A tired-looking Ash walked in. His clothes were caked with dirt and dried blood.

Yiran rose to his feet. "Where are we? What's going on? Where are Rui and Zizi?"

"Sit down."

Reluctantly, Yiran obeyed.

"Your friends are fine."

Ash stripped off his coat and torn shirt and unbuckled his holster, laying his pistols on the table before sitting down. An old scar ran down his side from the top of his ribs to his hip bone, long healed but vicious looking. A newer scar, curved like a crescent moon, joined it across his chest. It was fresh and pink, recently worked on by a healer.

Yiran had never seen that second scar before. His voice was softer when he said, "Are you all right?"

Ash sank his head into his palms, then scrubbed his eyes with the back of his hand. "We lost three of our own tonight."

"I'm sorry." Yiran didn't know what else to say. He knew there was always a risk of casualties during a Night Hunt. But his eyes had glazed over the statistics that popped up in the news off and on, desensitized and indifferent. They were just that, numbers without faces or names. But it hit him now that they were numbers with families and friends, with hopes and dreams.

Ash lifted his head. His eyes were bloodshot and wet. "This is how it is. There will be victory and there will be loss. We can plan everything down to the smallest detail, and people will still die. Sometimes it happens right in front of you and there's nothing you can do."

He reached over and ruffled Yiran's hair the way he used to when they were kids, before Yiran started to squirm away from Ash's attempts at affection. This time, Yiran didn't move a muscle.

It could have been Ash who died tonight.

Briefly, Ash's gaze shifted behind Yiran's head like he was checking something. *The walls.* Were they being watched?

"I have some questions for you," Ash said. "It seems like you left the house with your two friends, went to a hotel—The Reverie—and then on the way back, your vehicle was involved in an incident with some Revenants."

There was nothing accusatory about his tone, but something about it felt too rehearsed. Best to proceed with caution. "We were attacked, ambushed by two of them," Yiran said, giving nothing away.

"Let's start from the beginning. Tell me everything that happened after you left Song Mansion. We need as much information as possible on the Revenants you encountered. Leave nothing out."

It sank in then that he and Rui and Zizi were witnesses to a secret the Exorcist Guild had painstakingly kept from the public. They had seen the Hybrids; Rui had even killed one. They'd been zip-tied, drugged, and separated. Somewhere else in this compound, Rui and Zizi were being interrogated by other Exorcists too.

This wasn't a friendly conversation between brothers. The Guild must have sent Ash specifically to loosen Yiran's tongue. Manipulating a subject's emotions before interrogation was merely Ash's job. That was why he'd shown Yiran his scars, why the first thing he brought up was the death of his comrades in combat. Brother or not, this was what Ash was trained to do. The thought sat uncomfortably on Yiran's chest.

Yiran weighed his options. He saw no choice but to behave like he was cooperating. Deliberately, he told Ash everything that happened, what Yuki revealed and the fight that ensued. But he was careful not to use the word *Hybrid*, and he didn't reveal the dark stains on Zizi's hands or the separation spell, nor the blue flames that burst out from Rui like she was possessed by something beyond this world. And he didn't breathe a word about Seven, the child who could suck the color out of a rose.

Ash listened closely, riveted by everything he said. "You've done well to remember all this. But there's one thing I'm not clear about. Are you certain Cadet Lin killed the second Revenant with her spiritual weapons?"

"She had only one sword with her at the time."

"Our healers have examined her. Her spirit core is still in recovery. In her current state, it would've been difficult for her to kill that Revenant by herself."

The easy thing to do would be to spill everything. But throwing Rui and Zizi to the wolves was no guarantee that Yiran would get to keep his magic. More importantly, his gut told him to protect Rui.

"Difficult but not impossible," he said. "Rui's the best at the Academy."

Ash made a skeptical sound. "The details are important. Try to remember *how* she did it. Walk me through what you saw step by step and leave nothing out."

Something clicked in Yiran's head.

"You want to know how she killed a *Hybrid*. Specifically," he said, finally revealing his card.

Lips thinning, Ash picked up his pistol. He started to clean it with the hem of his shirt, his admission so obvious Yiran was surprised.

This was what the interrogation was all about. The Guild must've been battling Hybrids in secret for a long time. As evident from tonight's ambush, they were having trouble dispatching them. They wanted to know how Rui had done it so easily. Zizi's intense dislike for the Guild was making more sense by the minute.

"You've known all along Hybrids exist. That's why you're not surprised by anything I've told you, about the weird things growing out of Yuki's and Aloysius's backs, about what Yuki said about them banding together. You know they're out there and they're planning something."

Ash continued to clean his weapon.

The truth sank in even deeper. Yiran raised his voice. "The Guild has *always* known, hasn't it? Your old scar came from a Hybrid—I've always wondered why it looks like that. It's because you were burned by yinqi." He raised a hand to touch the fresh dressing that covered the wound on his own cheek. "Your new scar is also from a Hybrid, and your Exorcist friends died tonight because you were ambushed by *Hybrids*, because those monsters can think, plot, and scheme, just like humans. Am I right? Tell me—"

Ash's pistol clattered onto the table. He stood and made a slicing motion with his hand. The unnaturally bright walls dulled. The sour taste in Yiran's mouth grew. Someone had been watching and recording their interrogation.

"What do you want me to say?" Ash asked.

Yiran met his weary gaze. "Respect me. Tell me the truth the same way I told you everything. Stop treating me like I'm a kid."

"But it's my job to protect you," Ash said fiercely. "You *are* my kid brother."

"Half brother."

Ash flinched like he'd been slapped.

Yiran looked down. They hadn't let him wash his hands yet, and Zizi's dried blood stained the lines on his palms. He heard a sigh.

"You're right," Ash admitted. "We've known for a while that Hybrids exist."

It was a confession Yiran didn't want to hear. What other secrets were the Guild and his grandfather keeping?

"You shouldn't hide the truth from the people," he said.

"We shouldn't hide the truth?" Ash scoffed. "Don't be naive, Xiao Ran. You've seen the Hybrids, they look like normal human beings until their weapons come out. Do you want to live in a society where everyone is suspicious of their neighbor? Of their family and friends? People will be policing each other, pouncing on anything that seems a bit different, even if it's nothing. What do you think life will be like?"

"But if they knew about the Hybrids, maybe less people will be killed. If people knew what to look out for, how to identify one, how to . . . I don't know . . ." Yiran clenched his fists, hating that Ash was right. Fear and paranoia would run rampant. The city would dissolve into chaos.

"There're already people out there questioning the Guild; we can't let that snowball," Ash said. "We can't change the fact that our presence draws Revenants and Hybrids, but no one must think *we're* the problem. We need people to know we're doing our jobs and doing them well, that we are their protection. We may have magic, but we still bleed when their bullets strike us."

What will happen if they decide we're no longer doing our jobs well? That we're redundant? Or worse, that we are dangerous? This was what Song Wei was worried about, what he harped on whenever he disciplined Yiran.

"Things are never so simple," Ash continued, sounding brittle. "Nothing is ever black and white, and we fight and survive by working in the gray. *You* are a part of this too. You're one of us. Never forget who you are, Song Yiran."

You're one of us.

For as long as Yiran could remember, this was something he wanted to hear. What he wanted to feel. It wasn't his grandfather saying it, but for a moment, it felt almost enough.

Was it so bad that the Guild was hiding things? It wasn't like they were leaving ordinary people to fend for themselves. The main goal was to rid the world of Revenants, and extraordinary circumstances required difficult decisions. Maybe some lies had to be told. Maybe the lies kept everyone safe.

Ash gripped his shoulder. "Soon you'll be an Exorcist. You'll fight by my side, and we'll make Dad proud. I need you with me."

You'll fight by my side, and we'll make Dad proud.

The light in Ash's eyes broke through Yiran's last defense. It didn't matter whether Ash had been sent by the Guild to interrogate him; Yiran knew Ash meant what he said. Drowning in the well of emotions, Yiran was tempted to confess everything: how he'd gotten his magic, how Rui actually killed the Hybrid, how Zizi might have accidentally made a spell that could turn the tide of the war in the Hybrids' favor.

It wouldn't be an act of betrayal. He never made a promise. He would be doing the right thing. But the confession stayed stuck in his throat.

. . . deep inside that soul of yours, you know what's right and that makes you a good person . . .

Zizi was wrong.

Yiran wasn't a good person. A good person would put everyone else ahead of his own desires. But Yiran couldn't bear to lose his magic and his chance to belong.

"Are you with me?" Ash asked, in a tone that was soft but heavy with meaning.

Yiran nodded. He would be complicit in hiding the truth from the public. "What happens now?" he asked.

"You keep training, I'll keep hunting Revenants. Life goes on."

"Just like that?"

"Just like that."

"What about Rui and Zizi?"

"Well," said Ash, looking uncannily like their grandfather. "I guess it depends on whether their stories match up with yours."

38
Rui

Rui had fallen unconscious, but her body retained impressions of the car ride. It was smooth and winding, slowing down at turns that felt too narrow to be city roads. The Exorcist Guild headquarters was in the middle of downtown. Everyone knew that. Where Rui had woken wasn't the headquarters.

The blond Exorcist—she'd said her name was Surin—was sitting across the metal table. Dressed in a black tank top that showed off her impressive biceps, she was filing her nails with the blade of a large butterfly knife. From the way she handled it, Rui guessed it was likely her spiritual weapon. It was unusual to say the least; you had to get *close* to a Revenant to use it. She placed Surin to be around Ash's age. Pretty impressive to be a Captain too.

Surin smiled. White teeth. Friendly eyes. Dimples. She'd kept up a chummy attitude throughout the interrogation. Rui wasn't convinced.

"Anything else you'd like to add?" Surin asked.

Rui folded her arms. "No. Are we done here? Where are my friends?"

"We'll be done once you tell me everything that happened tonight."

"I told you everything."

Whistling, Surin flipped her butterfly knife between her fingers, rotating the handles rapidly. The blade flashed in the light as it moved quickly, up and down and sideways. Rui stared, entranced.

Surin's smile deepened, a hint of bite behind it. She flicked her wrist. Her knife closed with a snap. "Maybe you told me everything, maybe you didn't. I'm going to go with *didn't*. I'm still stuck at the part where you said you killed the Revenant by yourself. The healer said your spirit core isn't fully healed. No way you could've done that."

Rui lifted her chin. "*Hybrid.* Go on, you can say it. I promise I won't freak out."

"Call it whatever you want. Doesn't change what I'm saying."

"I told you. I used magic and stabbed it with my sword." It wasn't technically a lie. Rui had merely left out what kind of magic she'd used. It wasn't like she knew the source of her blue fire anyway. Aloysius's face flashed in her mind. The triumph of the kill had long vanished. All she had left was a sick feeling that she might've killed something closer to a human than not.

Surin tutted. "That's the story you're sticking with?"

"That's the truth. There's nothing I can do if you refuse to believe me." Rui slumped in her chair.

Abruptly, Surin turned her head, touching the earpiece in her left ear. "Now? I'm not done yet." A pause. "He wants to talk to her about *what*? Are you sure?" Surin sounded surprised. Another pause. "Fine. I'll wrap up." She put on her sunglasses and said to Rui, "Let's go."

"Where are we going?"

"Kids these days, always asking questions."

"I'm not a kid," Rui said. "I'm eighteen, and you're not much older than me."

Surin looked at her sideways.

"I'm *eighteen*," Rui repeated, her cheeks warming.

"And I'm not interested," Surin snickered. "Got a girlfriend already. Come along now."

Rui got up and followed her out of the room. Everything outside was stark white. Just corridors and closed doors.

When they got into the elevator, Rui asked, "Is this the Guild's secret facility?"

Surin slapped her thigh, laughing. "Is that rumor still going around at the Academy?"

Rui scowled at her. But it only made Surin laugh harder.

As the elevator car soared sharply, Rui's stomach dropped. Her legs went soft, and she steadied herself against the wall. They were going up. A long way from the feel of it. Was the interrogation room underground? What would Rui find above?

The doors opened.

Craggy peaks and old pine trees greeted them. Warmth spilled from the rising sun, and the air was fresh and thin. In daylight, the events of last night felt suddenly far away.

There was something familiar about the place, but Rui wasn't sure what. The edge of the cliff beckoned. Curious, she walked over and looked down.

Sprawling out in the distance was Xingshan Academy and its odd collection of buildings. Rui could see the green splotch of the field in the middle, a smaller splotch of the secondary field, the reddish-brown ring of the running track, the gleaming white building with the Simulator. Four years at the Academy, and she'd never paid much attention to the old mountain range that ran to the north, the one the Academy was named after.

Xingshan: the mountain of stars.

"The secret facility is next to campus?" she said.

Surin sighed. "There's no secret facility. This is a sacred place."

"What do you mean?"

Before Surin could answer, Rui heard footsteps behind them.

Song Wei.

Surin acknowledged him with a bow. Rui followed suit, albeit unwillingly. He had fallen in her eyes, a false idol she no longer worshipped.

Song Wei wasted no time for pleasantries. "We meet again, Cadet Lin. I commend you for your actions last night," he said. "Taking down a highly dangerous Revenant by yourself . . . impressive as always."

Ironic how she'd spent years proving herself worthy of joining his elite ranks. Now his praise had no effect on her at all. Her heart pounded, but her voice rang loud and clear in the crisp mountain air. "It wasn't a highly dangerous Revenant. It was a Hybrid, just like the one that killed my mother four years ago. The Guild has been lying to everyone."

Song Wei didn't deny it. He stared at her with a shrewd expression, a powerful man with an even more powerful presence. Rui could feel his qi, the strength of it, as if he were sucking the life from the sun above and the very mountains and trees that rose behind him.

"Do you feel it, Rui?" he asked.

For a moment, she was confused. Then her senses focused. She *could* feel it.

This is a sacred place.

The qi she detected wasn't Song Wei's qi, but the vital force—the *essence*—of this place. It was full and vibrant, rolling with the breeze, leaping from the rocks and leaves and waterfalls. Unlike the layers of magic in The Reverie pressing down like a heavy shroud, this was light.

This was *life.*

"You are standing in the birthplace of Exorcism," Song Wei said, as Rui looked around in sudden awe. "Many, many years ago, a group of individuals came together here in secret to train their minds and bodies, honing their vital energy, forging weapons that allowed them to conduct their life force. They did all this to keep their villages safe from Revenants, and they made a pact to defend those who were not born with the same gifts as they had. But in those days, Exorcists moved in the shadows, no different from their enemy. Many generations ago, the Exorcists slowly moved out of the shadows, working to assimilate into normal society. Their wish then, as is ours now, is to be accepted. You may wonder why all of this isn't public knowledge, why the Academy does not teach you this history. Our roots began in a secret society, and not everything is meant for the ears and eyes of others, especially those who do not possess the same gifts as we do."

"Why are you telling me this now?"

"The time is right to offer you the courtesy of knowledge, Cadet Lin. The fact remains that although we have evolved, so has our enemy. You killed a Hybrid last night, and you did it easily. *That* is valuable to us. The first known encounter with a Hybrid occurred almost eighteen years ago—we don't believe they existed before. We have been trying to study them ever since—"

"Eighteen years?" Rui shouted, voice distorted, hands shaking. "You knew for eighteen years, and you kept it from everyone?"

"To minimize the impact on society."

She stared at the old man in horror. At its heart, the Exorcist Guild was a shady, secretive society that pretended to be respectable. It didn't care about others, only their own and their survival. No wonder Zizi hated them.

A dam broke. Fury gushed through her. Grief flooded her senses. *The Hybrid's face . . . His voice luring her in . . . Her mother pushing her away . . . The sudden bright flash of light . . .*

Her mother was killed by a Hybrid four years ago. But the Guild had known for much longer. If only they had informed the public. If only they'd warned everyone.

If only Rui had known.

"How about *me*?" she screamed. "No one believed me, no one took me seriously when I told them how my mother died!" Hot, angry tears blurred her vision. "You were at my mother's funeral. I saw you in your car. Why did you come? Were you feeling guilty?"

"I was not there for your mother or you," Song Wei said without any hint of emotion. "And I will not regret a decision that was made for the greater good. Your mother was collateral damage—"

Snarling, Rui plunged forward, fingers clawing at Song Wei's face.

Arms wrapped around her at once, yanking her back.

Surin hissed in her ear, "Control yourself."

Rui kicked out. "She wasn't collateral damage—she was my *mother*!"

"You will come around when you understand what is at stake," Song Wei said coolly.

A throttled cry erupted from Rui's throat. She struggled to break free, but Surin was too strong. Helplessly, she watched as Song Wei walked away with barely a glance at her.

The elevator doors closed, camouflaged against rock.

He was gone.

"Let go of me," Rui said through her teeth.

"Only if you behave yourself."

"I will."

Surin released her, and she crumpled in a heap.

The sun shone on Rui's back, but she was still cold, still hollow inside. She imagined herself in a white room with nothing in it. She didn't want to care about anything or anyone anymore. Caring brought pain and she had enough of it to last a lifetime.

After what felt like forever, she raised her head.

"When did you know about the Hybrids?"

"About three years ago," Surin said, "when I was on track to being Captain."

"How do you sleep at night, doing what you do? Knowing what you know?"

Surin gave her a quizzical look. "How do I sleep? Like a baby full on her mother's milk."

Brown skin gleaming in the sun, Surin stretched, confident and collected. This was how Rui had pictured herself in a few years' time. A Captain. Someone strong and powerful, someone others would depend on and look up to. Once, Rui had thought herself wise beyond her years. Now she knew it was merely youthful hubris. Maybe she wasn't so sure what she wanted in life. Maybe she wasn't sure about anything at all.

Rui sank her head into her hands. "All this time I was so sure that Hybrids existed. But now that I know it's true, why do I feel worse?"

Surin had crouched beside her. Her warm brown eyes were frank and kind. "Because this is how it feels when your elders turn their backs, when institutions fall from grace, when the world moves on even as you're standing still, when something you believe in turns out to be a lie. Because you're no longer a child, and you're realizing the world you live in operates in shades of gray. Sometimes, there isn't a right or a wrong—there's only doing the best you can in spite of the odds stacked up against you and forgiving yourself when you fall short."

Rui stared back, uncertain of how to feel.

"I know you're angry, Rui," Surin continued. "You feel cheated, you feel wronged, even when you've just been proven right. It's the worst kind of vindication. It feels personal because it makes you question yourself, makes you wonder what you would've or could've done differently. Your feelings are valid. But this isn't about you or me or Master Song, or even the Guild. This is about the bigger picture. The fight's not over yet. I don't know how you managed to kill that Hybrid when your spirit core is all messed up, but you're obviously gifted and I respect that. *You* can make a difference. Don't waste your chance. Don't let the lives that were lost be meaningless."

Once, praise and advice from a Captain would have filled her sails. But the wind had changed Rui's course, left her out in open ocean with no land in sight. She nodded, but she didn't know if she believed or agreed with Surin's words.

"On your feet, Cadet Lin."

Unsteadily, Rui stood.

"You need to move on from whatever's holding you in the past," Surin said. "The second-worst thing in life is having regrets."

"What's the first?"

Sadness flashed across Surin's face, and she looked away. "I hope you'll never find out."

"Rui!"

Yiran was jogging toward them, a beaten-up-looking Ash following behind.

"Are you all right?" Yiran asked.

She could feel his concern. "I'm okay." She touched his cheek gently, feeling the ridge of skin. A healer had worked on the burn left by the Hybrid boy, but the wound remained angry and red. "Are you?"

Yiran turned his scarred cheek from her and nodded.

"Where's my grandfather?" Ash asked Surin.

"The Guild Council is meeting inside. They're deciding what to do about the mage."

"Zizi?" Rui said, heartbeat tripping. "What does the Council have to decide? What's going on?"

Yiran looked just as worried. "What's going to happen to Zizi— and us?"

"Seems like your friend confessed to something," Surin said. "I expect we'll get more answers in a while."

Rui shared a look with Yiran. *He* wouldn't reveal anything she didn't want revealed. She knew that.

In the end, out of the three of them, the wild card was Zizi.

39
Rui

They were summoned to a large room shaped like a decagon. A flickering screen sat on each wall, projecting the shadowy image of a Council member. All ten were present. But apart from Song Wei, who was Head of the Council, the identities of the other nine were unknown to anyone.

Zizi was standing in the middle of the room. Someone had thrown an Exorcist's overcoat over his bare shoulders. The coat fell delicately down to his shins, like an outer robe, pewter in color with silver and gold embroidery. The fluid fabric was finely spun to accommodate an Exorcist's movements and imbued with protective magic that acted as a temporary shield or armor during combat. Rui was surprised that a mage from the underground magic community was allowed to wear the crest of the Guild, and she wondered how Zizi himself could bear to have the Guild's mark on him.

As she and Yiran moved to stand beside him, she saw that Zizi's bare upper torso and left shoulder were wrapped in bandages. His skin still had a sickly hue, and there was something different about him, a lack of the usual humor in his posture, a new stoicism in the slant of his brows. At once, she knew he'd gone ahead and done something big and irreversible.

And she had a feeling she wasn't going to like it.

"Now that everyone is here, let us speak frankly." The Councilwoman's voice was proud to the point of arrogant, and her shadow seemed to loom larger than the rest. "None of you are to speak of this place, what has happened here, and any conversation you may have heard or taken part in. Neither will you share the details of last night's incident with anyone outside this room, nor are you allowed to reveal the Hybrids' existence. Since Lin Ru Yi and Song Yiran are cadets at Xingshan Academy, they are bound by their oaths." She addressed them: "Break that oath, and I do not need to explain how harsh the consequences will be for the two of you. As for the mage, *Zizi* . . ." She paused.

Zizi shoved his hands into his pockets, the jut of his chin stubborn.

Rui bit the inside of her cheek so hard she tasted blood.

The Councilwoman continued, "He has confessed to dabbling in unorthodox magic, and while what he did is not akin to sorcery, such dangerous behavior must still be punished. But he has also given us valuable information about the Hybrids and what they seek, and we acknowledge the talisman he created no longer exists. The Council is fair. Full punishment will be tabled for now. In return, we seek his cooperation. He will remain here in isolation and under guard. Indefinitely. This is for his own safety—"

"How is this fair? You can't lock him up here," Rui interrupted heatedly. The Zizi she knew wouldn't have confessed. He wouldn't have accepted the punishment without a fight. He would hate to be stuck here, his every movement watched, his freedom taken. It would be his personal hell.

"You have not been called upon to speak!" a thin voice reprimanded. The snakelike aura coming from this Council member was so strong, Rui could feel it through the screen. "You have no influence on our decision. Do not interfere."

But Rui's mouth was running before her brain could catch up. "You coerced him to make a confession, didn't you? It doesn't count! If you imprison him, I'll tell everyone about the Hybrids."

Did she just threaten the Guild Council? Was she botching her chances of being an Exorcist? She decided she didn't care. Out of the corner of her eye, she saw Surin shaking her head.

"Be careful what you say, Cadet Lin," said the first Councilwoman. "Zizi offered us information voluntarily in return for amnesty for you and Cadet Song. Since neither of you knew what Zizi was doing on the side, the Council agreed, and we have come to terms. He has taken responsibility and avoided a harsher punishment. Unless *you* would like to throw a wrench in our agreement?"

The threat was clear.

Zizi spoke calmly. "Cadet Lin is speaking out of turn. It doesn't affect what I have agreed to."

"Do you have anything else to add, Cadet Lin?" asked the Council-woman.

Zizi was shielding her and Yiran, allowing them to exit the situation unscathed. She caught Yiran's look of relief, felt it run through him. A sick feeling pooled in her stomach. If she overturned the agreement, she wouldn't be the only one in trouble. She had to choose, and she owed it to Yiran after putting his life at risk. Reluctantly, she shook her head, hating herself.

Ash stepped up. "Council, if I could have a word?"

There were quick murmurs of permission.

"It seems to me we're missing an opportunity here." Ash had looked tired before, but now his eyes glittered in anticipation. "Zizi is someone of immense talent, with healing powers the Guild could use, should he be willing to help us. Perhaps we should be asking him to lend his services to atone for his mistakes."

There was a sharp hiss.

It'd come from Zizi. His expression was murderous, but he said nothing.

"Excellent idea!" said the Councilman with the snakelike aura.

A few other shadows chimed in with their approval.

"With the Council's permission, I would like to have custody of Zizi until the situation calls for a different solution. Captain Surin Woo and I will vouch for his safety, but I alone will take full responsibility of his actions during this time."

Lowering his eyes, Ash bowed like he was asking for permission. But Rui caught the satisfaction in his expression. He had the Council eating out of the palm of his hand.

Surin didn't look happy about being dragged into Ash's scheme, but she inclined her head.

"If the Head of the Council has no objections?" the Councilwoman said.

The shadow of Song Wei replied, "None."

"In that case, consider this matter closed for now. Keep us informed of any new developments. You are all dismissed."

The screens flickered, turning black.

Ash swiveled around to face Rui, Zizi, and Yiran. All three stared back, expressions varying from suspicion to disgust to anticipation.

He clasped his hands together. "Ah, my precious little ducklings, it's time to bring you back to the nest."

40
Rui

An inauspicious chill in the air heralded an early winter. As light receded, an ominous pall fell over the city, and the days were getting darker by four.

Clusters of Revenants popped up all over town. Even though the Exorcists were dispatching *most* of them, Rui knew the Hybrids were the real issue. The public was still kept in the dark about their existence, but the news headlines shifted in tone, questioning the aptitude of the Exorcists, demanding answers for the spike in victims.

Back at the Academy, the old rumor about Hybrids resurfaced, only this time, the whispers in the hallways were taken more seriously. Whenever Rui was within earshot of a conversation, she'd bite her tongue, turn away, pretending she knew nothing. The secrets inside her festered, a different kind of infection.

She stared out at the sun setting over the horizon of water now, as she sat on the bench by her favorite spot on campus. Waiting. Restless, she picked up a pebble and flung it into the sea. It made a sad plop, and she felt worse. She wondered if it was because this place reminded her of her encounter with Ten.

Her own hubris had resulted in their deal. Thinking she could do anything; thinking she could do everything by herself. But she was still no closer to finding Four or taking her revenge. And she was still without magic.

Rui stared at her hands, clenching and unclenching them. She'd tried to channel her magic time and again. But no matter how hard she pushed, she came up with nothing. None of that strange blue fire either. She was still damaged.

Maybe something worse than damaged.

The sound of familiar footsteps turned her head. Rui looked up at the tall boy who was bundled in a thick gray hoodie and leather jacket.

"Hey," said Yiran, turning his cashmere baseball cap around.

"Heard anything new?" Rui asked immediately. They'd taken to meeting here, sometimes sitting together in silence, sometimes talking about anything and everything. Maybe the empathic link had something to do with it, or maybe it was because they shared both history and secrets, but his presence made her feel less alone and their connection felt stronger than ever.

"Nothing much," Yiran replied. "They're increasing the frequency of Night Hunts again, and there's some talk about recruiting cadets for missions."

Rui bit her lip. "Anything about him?"

"Only what we already know. He's been on Hunts, but they're still mostly having him assist the healers. He hasn't called you yet?"

She shook her head. She wasn't counting on it. "I think they took his phone away," she said. "The number's been disconnected."

Yiran removed his cap, running his fingers over the fabric. "Look, Rui. Zizi made a choice. He decided to protect us. Just . . . respect that. He wouldn't want you to worry."

"No one asked him to protect us," she said, stubborn.

Yiran shrugged. "I don't see the point in being angry with him."

But Rui wasn't only angry with Zizi for striking the bargain with the Guild Council alone, she was mad at herself for standing by and letting him make that sacrifice. "You don't understand how much he hates the Guild," she said. "He must be miserable right now, working for them and being ordered around by Exorcists."

Yiran looked like he was about to argue, but he shrugged again and put his cap back on. "The wizard can take care of himself." He took Rui's hand and pulled her up from the bench. "Come on, I want to show you something—a surprise. But first, I'll buy you a mint-chocolate ice cream cone."

Rui arched an eyebrow. "Are you bribing me to go with you?"

Yiran replied without missing a beat. "No, I'm cheering you up, silly. Friends don't have to bribe friends." He smiled.

We really are friends, Rui thought. She smiled back. "In that case, make it a whole pint."

Located behind the Simulator building, the north field was close to the edge of the campus and less well-lit. It was dark by the time they arrived after Rui demolished her pint of ice cream. She could see the twinkling stars, wisps of clouds, and the serene face of the waxing moon. The night breeze from the sea over Xingshan Mountain brought the subtle scent of snow and a hint of something more. Something that refreshed her senses. She faced the mountain range, thinking about what had happened there.

"Do you feel it too?" Yiran asked quietly next to her. She nodded, and he said, "Ash told me the mountain was sacred."

The birthplace of Exorcism. Rui suddenly wished Song Wei had told her more. What had it been like all those years ago? Who were the founders of Exorcism and the original secret society? Rui realized there was so much she didn't know.

"We're here!" a husky voice called out.

Rui turned.

Mai, Ada, and Teshin were strolling over.

"I heard you're too shy to demonstrate your spiritual weapon in front of everyone, so it's just us tonight," Mai said to Yiran.

Rui shot a puzzled look at Yiran, but he didn't notice. Spiritual weapon? Was this the surprise he was talking about? She knew he'd made friends with Tesha Mak and she was helping him train on the side. But how was it possible for him to have a spiritual weapon when it was *Rui's* magic that he was using? The only spiritual weapon he could match with was her dual swords.

"Always good to get a boost of confidence from my most ardent fans before I unleash my greatness on the locals," Yiran quipped.

"Whoo-hoo," Teshin said monotonously, pretending to wave imaginary pom-poms in the air. "Hang on, Tesha and I need a favor from all of you." They pulled out several small velvet pouches from their backpack and distributed them.

"What's this?" Rui asked, flipping the pouch. Tiny coins rolled out onto her palm. They shimmered with a faint crimson light.

"Qi bombs," Teshin replied. "Tesha's new incendiary weapon. Could you test it and give her feedback?"

Ada was rolling one between her fingers. "They look more like qi pennies."

"Sure, we'll test it," Rui said, stuffing the velvet pouch into her pocket.

"Well, what are you waiting for?" Mai grumbled at Yiran, pulling her coat tighter. "I'm freezing. Quick, show us."

"Patience is a virtue." Yiran smirked. He removed a slinky glove from his pocket. The material shone under the field lights. It looked metallic, but light and malleable like silk.

"A *glove*?" Mai exclaimed. "I don't think I've ever heard of anyone having a glove for a spiritual weapon."

"Technically, it isn't a spiritual weapon," Teshin revealed.

"What do you mean—" Rui asked.

"True," Yiran said at the same time, "but it allows me to do *this*."

He stuck his hand out and channeled.

A large, glowing crimson circle appeared in front of them, the size of a truck.

"A defensive shield this big?" Ada gushed. "That's upper-level magic."

Mai let out a low whistle. "Well done, er shaoye."

Rui stared at Yiran's shield, a confusing mix of emotions rioting in her. It was *her* magic that was doing this, her magic that was impressing her peers.

Seemingly unaware of Rui's feelings, Yiran kept on grinning. He didn't seem to mind Mai's use of the honorific either.

"This shield is stronger than the ones cast from talismans because it doesn't need a secondary diversion of magic," Teshin said. "And guess what? He can make even bigger ones."

"Really?" Ada's eyes sparkled. "That's incredible. The Exorcists could use someone like you on their Hunts, Yiran."

Yiran laughed nervously, but his shield remained bright and strong. "I'm not sure about that. I've only done a giant shield once."

"Practice makes perfect," Teshin said. "Think of what else you could do when Tesha gets the second glove ready."

"You're not usually this modest, Yiran." Mai laughed. "You're sustaining this shield so effortlessly; I can't believe everyone thought you were a normie just months ago. How did they miss your potential with that spirit core of yours and all the energy swirling inside?"

A small, surprised sound escaped Rui as a sudden realization hit her in the gut.

"I—I have to go—remembered something—" she said. Heart pounding, she spun around and ran across the field.

"Rui? Rui!"

She heard Ada calling out, but she ignored her best friend and kept running.

Rui slammed the door to her dorm room shut and locked it. Her pulse was still racing, and she had a stitch in her side. Shakily, she sat on the floor and pulled out the shard of glass Nikai had given her.

All you need to do is say my name.

Rui had not used the mirror before. Would it work?

"Nikai? Nikai, are you there?" she whispered. "It's Rui."

The glass shimmered like liquid mercury, turning black and then clear again.

The Reaper appeared.

Rui was relieved the mirror had worked, but Nikai's hair was disheveled, his tie crooked, and he seemed out of breath.

"Is everything all right in the underworld?" Never in a million years did Rui think she would ever ask a question like that.

"Hello, Rui. And yes—well, actually no. It's a mess, everything's a mess." Nikai batted at something above him, outside of the screen. "The Tenth Court's still standing—thank goddess—but the Nothing appeared in the outskirts of the Third Court yesterday. We've lost two towns to it and hundreds of souls." He looked at her, suddenly hopeful. "Do you have good news? Is that why you're contacting me? How is the search going?"

"It's not going. They've been keeping us on the island ever since the Hybrid ambush, so I can't leave campus. I've been researching vessels in the library, though, but nothing has come up so far."

Nikai's face fell. "I see."

"I contacted you because I have a question." Rui hesitated.

With all that spiritual energy, Mochi's spirit core should've burned out, but it didn't. Look at him, he's perfectly fine.

How did they miss your potential with that spirit core of yours and all the energy swirling inside?

The only person Rui had ever felt a connection with was Yiran. She'd dismissed it, assumed it was the effect of the spiritual energy transfer from Zizi's spell. But that was only because Yiran had told her he was born with an ordinary spirit core.

What if he was wrong?

After all, he'd been training hard, refining the yangqi inside him and using it for magic. An ordinary core wouldn't allow for all that, would it? Tonight, she'd seen him cast a high-level defensive shield effortlessly. He'd been doing all this with his supposedly ordinary spirit core, and it was still intact. It made no sense. But it *would* make sense if Rui cast aside all assumptions and came to one logical conclusion: *Song Yiran always had an extraordinary spirit core.*

That was why he could hold Rui's spiritual energy in the first place, and why he'd absorbed all of hers. That was why, despite everything, he was still alive. And if Yiran could hold energy that *wasn't his*, if he could *store* it, could he have some kind of ability like that of a vessel?

You will be able to sense him.

What if the connection between them was due to something other than the spiritual energy transfer?

"Rui?"

She startled.

Nikai was looking at her through the mirror, anxious and waiting. "What's the question?" he asked.

"What's going to happen to the person who houses Four's soul?" she said. "What's Ten going to do with them?"

Nikai frowned. "What do you mean?"

"I mean, sure you'll get your King back, but what happens to the human he used to contain his soul?" said Rui.

"I assume we would extract Four's soul and bring him back to the underworld, where he belongs. I'm not familiar with how we would do it."

"Will the human's life be endangered in the process? Will they die?"

"I don't know. There is no guarantee of anything," Nikai said. "But you are weighing one human life against the entire underworld, against the lives of other mortals in your realm. You're weighing it against what *you* want, your revenge, your magic."

Rui felt her jaw tensing. "That sounds like something Ten would say."

Nikai looked away, shoulders sagging. "You have made a deal with a King, Rui. It is binding."

Ten is a King, and all Kings are dangerous. "I'm aware of what I did," she said.

"Do you feel a connection to someone, Rui?" Nikai asked quietly, avoiding her eyes. "Is that the reason for your questions?"

Rui wasn't sure about her theory of Yiran yet, and Nikai didn't have the answer she needed. There was no point in giving Nikai a name. She kept her voice steady. "No. It was just a thought I had."

She couldn't tell if he believed her, but he nodded.

"Can you find out what will happen to the human that houses Four's soul?" she said.

Nikai nodded again. "Is that all?"

"Not quite. Something weird happened to me." She told him how the blue fire had burst from her hands during the altercation with the Hybrids. Nikai's expression grew grimmer and grimmer as she went on. "I haven't been able to summon the blue fire since that night," she finished.

Nikai opened his mouth. Closed it, seemingly rendered speechless by her revelation.

"I wanted to tell you earlier," she said, "but it didn't happen again, so I thought maybe it was a weird one-off thing." *I didn't want to tell you because I was scared*, she thought, as Aloysius's face appeared in her mind. When Nikai stayed silent, she said, "One of the Hybrid Revenants said the blue fire draws from the darkness. I thought you might know what it means."

"The darkness?" Nikai seemed paler than usual, but it was hard to tell from the small piece of glass.

"Does it mean anything?"

"I'm not sure, but I think—"

There was a loud knocking on her door.

"Rui? You in there?"

Ada.

"Rui? We have to assemble in the hall now—the Exorcists are here," Ada said, sounding urgent.

The Exorcists? "I have to go," Rui told Nikai, scrambling up. "If you discover anything, let me know."

"Wait, Rui—" Nikai called out.

"Be right out, Ada!" Rui pushed the mirror under her pillow and went to the door.

41
Nikai

"Wait, Rui—"

Nikai gestured for her attention, but the mirror had gone dark. He was left standing in the throne room of the Fourth Court, trying to make sense of what he had heard.

"Blue flames, blue flames . . ." he repeated to himself.

His spine pulled taut. He could *feel* the Tenth King's presence before he saw him.

Knees suddenly weak, Nikai turned around.

Ten was sauntering into the throne room, shuffling a pack of cards. His hair was disheveled, fair strands escaping from the now-loose ponytail. Once a rich red, his robes had turned drab. Even his skin looked stretched and sickly.

Ten never visited, choosing to oversee the Fourth Court from his own kingdom. But today he passed Nikai and draped himself onto the throne. Nikai's hands tightened by his sides. The throne belonged to *Four*.

Reluctantly, Nikai bowed. "What brings you here, Your Majesty?"

Ten lowered his chin, peering at Nikai in an unnerving manner as he continued to shuffle his cards. "Was that Rui's voice I heard coming from the mirror?"

Nikai sensed a layer of hostility under Ten's lazy purr.

"I instructed you to keep an eye on the girl," Ten continued, "but I do not remember telling you to contact her directly. Yet here you are, talking behind my back, exchanging information, and hiding it from me? You have broken my trust, Reaper. And that is a dangerous thing to do."

Nikai gulped. "I'm not hiding anything. I'm only trying to help with the search, Your Majesty."

"Go on then, tell me what you learned," Ten said generously, but his eyes glimmered with malice.

"Why did you lead Rui to believe she only needed to look for a human with a strong spirit core? Why didn't you tell her that Four would store his power in a vessel from the start?" Nikai said instead.

Ten's lips stretched into a serpent's smile. "Call it . . . a hunch."

"It seems like you were the one hiding something all this time, Your Majesty."

Ten's smile twisted. "How bold of you, Reaper."

He approached, looming over Nikai. There was something quietly unhinged in the King's eyes. He flicked a card at Nikai's face. It hit his cheek. Landed on the floor. The king of spades.

"Have you heard of this game humans play—poker?"

"Y-yes."

"Then you must know that you should never show your hand until the right time. And you must know cards can be replaced, especially when they may spoil your hand."

Nikai heard the threat in Ten's words. "Rui can conjure blue flames," he said quickly.

To his surprise, Ten did not react. "I already know."

"How?"

"I have made some associates. Very useful associates."

. . . let me make the deals I need to . . .

"That's why you've been visiting the human realm so often—who have you been making deals with?" Nikai demanded.

"Oh? Someone's been *spying* on me." Ten smiled coldly. "I guess the trust never went both ways in the first place. Pity. You see, Reaper, I must be careful with every step I take. I mustn't scare my brother away. Those who seek him shall never see him, remember?" Ten patted Nikai's cheek. "I am afraid I no longer have a need for you. I cannot take my chances with a Reaper I cannot trust. I will send you away for a while."

Fear filled Nikai's soul. "I'm sorry, Your Majesty, I didn't mean to—"

"Quiet." Ten cupped his chin. "Do not worry, *Nikai*. The place I am sending you is not *too* dark."

As Ten's fingers closed in on his throat, Nikai's breaths hitched. He was shaking uncontrollably. "The blue flames, the blue . . . it's power from the depths of Hell."

"More specifically," Ten whispered in his ear, "it is the power of a King."

42
Yiran

Yiran scanned the grand hall for Rui. The other seniors were standing around, but he didn't see her. She had run off earlier when he was demonstrating his new glove, and he had no idea why.

The latest iteration of the glove worked much smoother than Tesha's initial prototype, which meant there was a high chance of her eventually crafting him a proper spiritual weapon. It also meant Yiran didn't have to steal Rui's, and he was glad for that. And with Zizi taken away by the Guild, Yiran didn't think there could be anyone else who could help her reverse the magic swap anyway. He'd won in a way, but he felt far from victorious. He was getting to keep his magic, and he didn't even have to do anything. It'd fallen into his lap because of someone else's sacrifice.

He craned his neck again, finally spotting Rui and Ada slipping in through the side entrance. They made their way to where he, Teshin, and Mai were standing. Yiran smiled at Rui, but she didn't return it. He sensed she was hiding something from him. Something big . . . something *bad*.

Ash stepped in, and all chatter in the hall ceased. He was flanked by two Exorcists, Surin and the ponytailed one from the highway. A shadow skulked in behind them—a young man with sharp cheekbones, his light blue irises startling against the dark circles under them.

Zizi.

But it wasn't his looks that caught the other cadets' attention.

It was what he wore.

His Exorcist coat was thrown over a white tank top, black sweater, and jeans. But there was a large hole in the flowing fabric of the coat where the Guild crest would normally be. Yiran couldn't help but smirk. At least the mage was wearing boots instead of flip-flops.

Zizi retreated to the corner, slanting against the wall, hands tucked into pockets to hide the ink-like stains Yiran was certain were still there. When Zizi caught him staring, he tilted his head, *Mochi*. Yiran arched an eyebrow in return, *Wizard*.

Mai jerked her head in Zizi's direction. "Who's that?"

"Rui, isn't that your friend from outside the karaoke club?" Ada whispered, nudging her.

All color had left Rui's face. She didn't seem to hear Ada's question; she was staring at Zizi like he was the only person in the room.

Ash stepped forward, clearing his throat. The hall became pin-drop silent.

"This isn't a social visit, so I'll get straight to the point," he said. "We're in a difficult situation with the Revenants, and we need more of our people on the streets. The Academy has given the Guild permission to bypass the usual protocols for recruitment, so from tonight, all of you seniors will have assignments from the Guild. Some of you will be in the field, others will provide support. Assignments will be distributed on a rotational basis. Cadets Song, Senai, and Mak—you're coming into the field with me effective immediately. The rest of you will have your turn, but for now, Lieutenant Shuang will assign you to other areas accordingly."

Anticipation hummed in Yiran's veins. He couldn't believe he'd been picked for a field mission so fast.

You'll fight by my side, and we'll make Dad proud.

Ash was making good on his promise. He gave Yiran a curt nod. If anyone saw this exchange between the Song brothers, no one showed it. The cadets remained at attention as the ponytailed Lieutenant Shuang rattled off a list of names and assignments, dividing the cadets into groups.

"Everyone but the field team follow me. I'll be briefing you in the next room," he finished.

Rui spoke up, "I haven't been assigned anything, Lieutenant Shuang."

"Stay here, Cadet Lin; you're about to be," Ash told her. He waited until the rest of the cadets and Shuang left the hall. "Listen up. The three of you assigned to the field will have your first mission tomorrow. Think of it as an evaluation of your readiness."

Ash paused to give them a once-over. The cadets straightened. "Transportation arrives tomorrow morning at dawn. You'll be given more details shortly." He waved Zizi over. The mage sidled up to the group, standing as far away from Rui as possible. "This is Zizi, a healer."

A glimmer of the old Zizi shone through. "I hope this will be the last time any of you see me," he drawled, "because otherwise it'll mean something terrible happened to you in the field."

Ash's jaw muscles twitched. Between the hole in Zizi's Exorcist coat and his wayward mouth, it was clear Ash couldn't fully tame him.

"We may need the extra beds in the infirmary in the next few weeks," Ash said, his expression somber. "Zizi will be stationed here on campus. Cadet Lin, since you're still not at a hundred percent, you'll remain here to assist him."

"But, Ash—" Rui protested.

"Captain."

"But Captain Song, you know I'd serve better in logistics or strategy. Why have I been assigned to help a healer? I don't have the skills."

"So learn them."

"But—"

"Do you intend to be useful to the Guild or not?"

"I assure you, Cadet Lin," Zizi interrupted, finally looking at Rui, "that despite my forbidding appearance, I'm lovely to work with. I'm sure Captain Song can attest to that. I look forward to having your assistance."

Rui stared at the floor like she wanted it to swallow her up. The tension between them was palpable. It was obvious they knew each other, and Rui's objection had more to do with the person than the assignment itself.

Yiran wanted to shake some sense into the both of them.

Meanwhile, Ada and Teshin were watching the whole exchange, one with great interest and the other with great confusion.

Surin stepped in. "You two can come with me," she told Rui and Zizi. "Let's look at the setup in the infirmary."

After they left, Ada leaned in, asking Yiran in a low voice, "Something's going on there. Know anything about it?"

Yiran shrugged.

"Listen up," Ash said. "Tomorrow's mission is a simple one, but there's always a chance things might turn dicey. Be prepared. The three of you will be sent a code to view your assignment details."

Yiran wondered if the mission would involve Hybrids and if Ash would reveal their existence to Ada and Teshin. Yuki's face flitted in his mind, followed by an uneasy feeling. The scar on his cheek reminded him of the Hybrid every time he looked in the mirror, and he'd been spending too much time thinking about the cold touch of Yuki's fingers around his throat.

"Go through everything before you leave in the morning," said Ash. "Absorb every single detail—the document disappears once you're done reading."

That drew a look of surprise from Teshin. "That only happens when the information is highly classified."

"Every mission we do from here on is highly classified." Ash's expression darkened. "Sleep well tonight. It may be the last time you'll ever have a good night's rest."

43
Rui

An herbal scent lingered in the infirmary, but it didn't cover the stronger smell of regularly sanitized floors. It reminded Rui too much of waiting outside doors, of a flurry of strangers in white coats telling her there was nothing else they could do.

She threw an irritated look at Zizi, unconsciously tracing the planes of his face where moonlight skimmed it. His hair had grown longer, wilder. She wanted to run her hands through it; she wanted to throttle him. She didn't want to be near him; she hated his absence even more.

Rui moved farther from him, hoping the distance would quell the turmoil inside her.

As if feeling the same way, Zizi edged to the wall. Hands in his pockets, he stared out of the window stiffly.

Shaking her head at them, Surin said, "Considering what's going on, we think this is the best place for Zizi. Like Ash said, we might be needing the infirmary beds soon. A powerful healer will be useful here."

"Is it the Hybrids?" Rui asked. "Are they the ones causing trouble?"

Surin nodded. "It's clear they've been organizing." She sighed, rubbing the short blond hairs on her buzzed head. "There've been reports of other creatures as well."

"What other creatures?"

"Things that have been touched by too much yinqi," Zizi replied, still facing the window. He didn't elaborate.

Rui shivered as a chilly silence fell on the room. What other vile creatures were out there?

"Everything looks good here," Surin said. "The infirmary's well-stocked, so there isn't much we need to do right now. You'll both be on call. Go get some rest tonight. I'll check in with you tomorrow."

After switching the lights off on her way out, Surin headed down the hallway.

Rui hurried after her. "Surin!"

The Captain halted.

"Has he been okay?"

"Zizi?" Surin gave her a look. "Why don't you ask him yourself? I don't know what's going on with you two, but I know he's happy to see you. I thought you'd be happy to see him."

"I'm glad I can be of service to the Guild," Rui said, keeping her expression blank.

She marched back into the darkened infirmary. Zizi was still standing by the window.

"Your hands."

Resolutely keeping them in his pockets, Zizi said, "What about them?"

Rui grabbed his wrist. She pushed his sleeve back and sucked in a sharp breath.

The black markings raced up his forearm, reminiscent of veins or tattoos. If this went on, they'd be full sleeves soon.

"It's gotten worse," she said.

Zizi snatched his hand back.

"Did your grandmother figure out what's wrong?"

"Haven't spoken to her."

"Why not?"

"Been busy. Lots of Revenants and their buddies running around these days, in case you haven't heard."

Rui glimpsed a shadow of his teasing smile, and she was struck by how much she missed his annoying face.

"Besides, I defected. I can't face her," Zizi said, dark brows meeting again in an angry line.

Giving up all pretense of a civil conversation, Rui backed him against the wall until there were only inches between them.

"Why are you helping the Guild? You hate them."

"It's part of the deal, remember?" he said, sounding tired. His clothes seemed to hang looser on his frame.

"Nobody told you to make any deal," she said. "No one made you confess that day; no one asked you to protect them."

"*No one* wants your opinion." Zizi was still refusing to look at her.

"You've been using too much of your spiritual energy, haven't you?" Rui said. "It's making those things on your hands worse. They're working you too hard; they're exploiting you. I'm going to talk to Ash about this."

She turned to go, but Zizi caught her arm and whirled her around.

"Do I have to spell everything out? It's because of *you*."

He was facing her now, eyes blazing. Rui didn't understand the look on his face.

Because of you.

He was mad at her for putting him in this position. By working with the Guild, he was going against his principles, betraying his friends. He was right to be mad. It *was* because of her. Rui was too cowardly to reveal she'd lost her magic. Instead, she forced everyone to lie for her. She had put other people at risk: first Yiran, then Zizi when she took the chance to kill Aloysius. She'd gambled with their lives, weighed them less worthy than her own desires.

She backed away from him. "I know it's my fault. This all started because I cast the separation spell on myself. I shouldn't have dragged you down with me."

"That's not what I meant at all. I never said it was your fault—it's not." Zizi closed the distance between them. "The Guild has resources, ancient magical texts, rare ingredients—working for them means I've some access to all of that. I've been researching, trying to re-create the separation spell in a different way so I can reverse it without causing any harm to you."

Relief washed over her. He sounded like his normal self, the one without the cold walls around him. He wasn't angry at her, but still, she didn't want him to risk more than he already had.

"Does the Guild know you're doing this?" she asked.

"No. I let them believe it was impossible to re-create the exact spell. That's probably true, but there might be another way to go around it. I just have to find it."

"What if you get caught?"

"I've been discreet," Zizi said. "But Ash might suspect I'm doing something. That man has an uncanny way of sensing things."

"If Ash thought you were doing something suspicious, he would stop you."

"You fail to understand what kind of person Song Lan Xi is."

"But all this is affecting your spiritual energy, making you sick, making those black veins worse. You need to stop," she said. "It's not worth it—*I'm* not worth it."

Zizi shook his head at her. "The Rui I know wouldn't say that. She wouldn't give up. What happened?"

What happened? Rui wanted to scream. Everything unraveled with the loss of her magic. For so long, it'd been her compass. Now she was caught between two crumbling worlds and trying not to drown in an ocean of secrets and lies. *That* was what happened. All the times she had to stand and watch when Yiran channeled magic, knowing that he was using *hers*. He always looked so proud of himself. So *happy*. She didn't want to take that away from him, but she wished, each time she *wished* it would be the last and he could never use it again. *That* was what happened.

Frustration welled up in her. But the words stayed stuck in her throat, and she found herself on the verge of tears.

"I know what magic means to you, Rui," Zizi said softly. "Not having it makes you unhappy, and I don't like it when you're unhappy. I told you I would fix it. I'm keeping my promise."

"Many things make me unhappy. The *world* makes me unhappy, Zizi. You can't fight everything and everyone for me," she rambled. "And you can't . . . you can't always be the one who saves me. I have to—"

Her breath caught, her thoughts floating away.

Zizi was cradling her face in his hands, gently wiping her tears. "That's the difference between you and me, Rui," he said, voice rough. "You want to save the world and the innumerable fools in it, whether they deserve a chance or not. But I—*I* would give up this entire world for a single breath to leave your lips again. And I don't need you to feel the same way about me to do it. Do you understand what I'm saying?"

All the times he had tried to reach out and she held back. All the times he'd asked her to stay and she pretended not to hear. All the times he looked at her and she turned the other way when she knew.

She *knew*.

He repeated, "Do you understand? You don't have to be afraid; I'm here."

She stared into his pale blue eyes. She didn't want to pretend anymore.

I don't need you to feel the same way about me.

But she did.

"I understand," she said, brushing her fingers across his lips. "Can I?"

"Always." He smiled and dipped his head.

Rui stood on her toes, arms wrapping around his neck, threading her fingers through his hair—and kissed him.

She had thought kissing him would be familiar, like returning home after a long absence. But it was that—and more. It was being one with the world, and the world was just the two of them, and *they* were one, the missing pieces of one soul filled by the other.

It was magic.

A low sound rumbled at the back of Zizi's throat as her teeth found his lips and her hands smoothed over the soft fabric of his sweater and the hard muscle under it. She pushed the Exorcist coat off his shoulders. She wanted him without his shackles.

Just him. Only him. Always him.

At first, Zizi was hesitant, respectful, his movements asking, not demanding—until he realized she wasn't going to be gentle with him. He matched her need with his own, as if suddenly set free. A vague thought about how anyone might walk in on them surfaced in Rui's mind, but

Zizi's mouth and hands proved too distracting for reason.

Somehow, when they drew apart, Rui found herself sitting on the nearest bed with Zizi kneeling in front of her.

He was looking slightly dazed. "Wow, did you . . . did you *feel* that? I can't believe we waited so long—"

"Shhh," she murmured. Sadness flickered in her chest. He was right; they had lost so much time. She shrugged off her jacket and reached for him again, fingertips grazing his kiss-swollen lips, deciding she wanted to ruin them just a little more. As if he knew what she was thinking, Zizi grinned, face a little feral, teeth a little too sharp.

"To hell with fate," she said, and yanked him close.

Their next kiss was like sparring: anticipating an opponent's next move, shifting into a better position, surprising them with a feint—testing their resolve. Rui discovered that Zizi was very, very good at sparring.

She didn't know how much time had passed before he finally pulled back. His cheeks were flushed, and she lost herself in the pale fire of his eyes.

"What?" Rui whispered, suddenly shy.

"I like looking at beautiful things."

She made a small noise of complaint and tugged at his clothes. "So do I," she said, her eyes sweeping over his bare skin as he pulled his sweater and tank top off.

Moonlight shone through the windows, illuminating his cheekbones, his chest, the hard lines of his body. Still kneeling before her, Zizi tensed at her touch, his gaze growing hungrier as her fingers followed the tattoo just inches below his left collarbone, above his heart, the tattoo she had been longing to see.

Two butterflies.

Their loveliness contrasted with the many wicked scars on his chest and arms from Aloysius's blades. Rui felt a sudden spiteful pleasure for killing the monster.

The blue fire she'd driven into Zizi left the barest trace of a burn. The skin around the area was unblemished, except for a thin ridge of skin, about two inches long, where she had stabbed him with her sword.

"I'm sorry I hurt you," she whispered. She felt his breath catching as she leaned in and touched her lips to the scar.

Zizi was looking at her like he was memorizing every detail for one of his charcoal sketches. Rui wondered who he saw, if he recognized the angry, frightened girl who spoke only with her blades.

"I've missed you," he said.

"It's only been a few weeks—"

"But it *felt* like years. I was a man in the desert dying of thirst; only your presence could quench my—"

Seized by laughter, Rui buried her face into his neck. She felt him shiver as her breath tickled his skin. "How do you even come up with such lines?"

"I enjoy the occasional romance novel. Something about the way they're written, so compelling and—"

The next word stayed in his throat as Rui clapped her hand over his mouth. His lips were so soft. She wanted them on her.

"Shut up and kiss me again."

Zizi laughed. "Bossy."

He placed a hand on her cheek, and she leaned into his touch, brushing her mouth against the edge of his palm. Suddenly his lips were claiming hers again, more demanding than before. She matched his urgency, sensed his desperation, felt his need to be with her.

Rui's lungs were heaving. The ache, the *want* was too strong. She yanked her top off.

Zizi hesitated. His pupils were blown wide, his irises just a rim of blue. "Are you sure?"

She nodded, blushing furiously.

Whispering her name with a reverence that made her gasp, he trailed kisses from her bare shoulder across her collarbone, lips lingering on skin.

A jolt of pleasure shot through her, and when he skimmed the sensitive part of her throat—

Her veins—*something was moving in her veins.*

Rui shot up, gasping for breath.

"Rui? What's wrong?"

She heard the panic and worry in Zizi's voice.

"I . . . I don't feel—" She couldn't complete her sentence.

She was drowning. She was ice but on fire. The room spun. Her vision blurred and came into focus and blurred again. Darkness fell.

She was alone.

Lost.

She heard Zizi's voice from a distance. Muffled and echoey. He was swearing, asking her questions she didn't understand.

"*Rui.*"

Surfacing, she blinked hard. Moonlight flashed. The world zoomed back into focus.

Zizi's face was white. "Dammit, Rui! Breathe."

She sucked in. Choked on air.

He squeezed her shoulders, the pressure grounding her. "Listen to my voice; stay with me."

He counted, slow and steady. Rui forced herself to listen to his voice, to breathe. When her chest finally loosened, she followed his gaze down to her hands and understood why he had that look on his face.

Blue flames danced across her fingers, glowing in the dim room, like prayer candles for the dead.

44
Yiran

Yiran lay on his dormitory bed, half wishing he were back home on his own larger, more comfortable one with its soft sheets and down duvet. He'd memorized everything in the brief for tomorrow's mission. He was to be part of a team inspecting a neighborhood that had previous Revenant activity, escorting a technician who was doing maintenance work. It seemed fairly straightforward, almost too straightforward. The Guild wasn't about to send cadets out on anything too dangerous—or exciting—for their first mission, he supposed.

An hour passed, feeling like it'd dragged on for days. His eyes were still open. Insomnia had crept in. The more anxious he was about sleeping, the more awake he felt. Finally, he threw off the covers, put on his glasses, and started doing pull-ups on the bar he'd installed in the bathroom doorway to tire himself out.

At the thirteenth pull-up, something hit the window.

Yiran paused, hanging on the bars, listening.

Clink. There it was again.

He went to the window. There was no one on the grounds outside. Weird.

Something creaked. A pair of legs dropped down in front of him.

Yiran cursed in fright.

An upside-down face appeared next.

Yuki.

Yiran's room was on the highest floor of the dormitory. The Hybrid had to be hanging from the rooftop deck right above.

Yiran slid the window open. "What the hell are you doing here?" he whispered. Why was he whispering? He should be sounding the alarm.

Yuki smiled and disappeared.

Dammit. Yiran put on a pair of jeans, pulled a hoodie over his head, and stepped out on the narrow window ledge. The chilly air gave him goose bumps. Praying the ledge wouldn't break under his weight, he felt for a secure spot to haul himself up.

There was a weather-beaten couch left on the roof deck by a previous batch of cadets, and some odds and ends like old sparring sticks strewn in a corner. Yiran had only been up here once, when Mai decided to have an impromptu campfire. It was always cold and windy on the deck, and he didn't care for the view.

Yuki plopped onto the couch. He didn't seem to mind the dirty upholstery.

If anyone knew Yiran was up here with a Revenant, he'd be in trouble. But inexplicably, it wasn't himself he was worried about.

"You do know this is a training school for Exorcists, right? You'll get killed the moment someone sees you and recognizes you for what you are."

"And yet, I'm still alive. I thought you might start screaming to wake everyone up." Yuki cocked his head. "But you didn't."

It sounded like a question, and it was a logical one. Why was Yiran up here, unarmed and talking to the enemy? He didn't have an answer.

"How did you know where my room was?" he said.

"Luck? I was in the trees when I saw a light in a room and someone who looked like you."

"Unintentional stalking, I see," Yiran said in half jest. More suspiciously, "What do you want?"

"Company."

"You wanted company, and you came *here*? Do you know how ridiculous that sounds?"

Yuki flung his head back on the couch. "I was bored, okay? I wanted to see if I could break in, so I did."

Yiran didn't know whether to believe him. But what else could Yuki want? If he intended to harm Yiran, he'd already have done so.

"Relax, I didn't have to kill anyone to be here," Yuki said. "Xingshan needs to do something about its security."

"Thanks for your advice."

"You're welcome."

"I'll notify the administration."

"As you should." Yuki patted the spot next to him. "Now stop pretending that either of us is going to attack the other and come sit with me."

Against his better judgment, Yiran did so. Up close, Yuki's gray eyes twinkled with amusement. Without the killer wings at his spine, he looked like an ordinary teenager. Yiran gave himself a mental shake. If he wasn't going to sound the alarm, *if* he was going to keep talking to Yuki, he would wheedle information out of him.

"You've recovered from your injuries," he said, trying not to stare at Yuki's smooth skin and elegant neck.

"Perks of being a Hybrid. It takes quite a bit to kill us," Yuki said dryly.

"Aloysius was killed."

"Good riddance. He was an abusive jerk when he was human and stayed one when he changed. The world will not miss him." Yuki smirked. "I should thank that girl if I see her again."

"Did you get into trouble when you went back empty-handed? Were *they* upset with you?"

"I don't want to talk about that."

"What do you want to talk about then?"

"Do you like Exorcist school?"

"Why do you care?"

Yuki looked amused. "I'm curious about you the way you're curious about me."

Yiran wasn't sure what to make of that. He stuffed his hands into the pockets of his hoodie, shivering as a gust of wind blew by.

"You know, I don't feel the cold anymore," Yuki shared. He was staring at the moon, and his skin seemed to glow in its light. Dressed in white billowing clothes, he resembled an ethereal prince from a long-forgotten tale. Not a knight in shining armor, but the one who was locked up in a tower, waiting to be freed from a curse.

"Good for you. I'm freezing my butt off." Yiran pulled his hood over his head and blew into his fingers.

"Isn't this nice though?" Yuki said with an impish grin. "Us sitting on this crummy couch, chatting as if we aren't about to be mortal enemies in the near future?"

In spite of himself, Yiran smiled.

"You know, I lost all my friends when I changed."

"Can't be friends with someone who wants to eat you."

"*I* was the one who stayed away," Yuki told him. "I hid myself from my family and friends because the hunger was too much and I didn't know what to do at first . . . I think they thought I ran away from home or something."

"How did you become like this?" Yiran asked, noting the sadness in Yuki's eyes. It was strange to see such a human emotion in a Revenant.

Yuki stretched his arms out and sighed. "About a year ago, I was on my way home from a movie. There was no moon that night and no curfew either. Everything seemed fine. I remember taking my usual shortcut home from the subway, down one of those side alleys. I felt something sweep over me, like a thousand needles poking my skin. Next thing I knew, I woke up in a different neighborhood. Alone and cold and hungry. There was blood all over me, but it wasn't mine."

The Blight got to him, Yiran thought. It was bad luck, nothing more. It could happen to anyone. "What happened after that?"

"I met some . . . friends. They helped me acclimatize." Yuki looked coyly at Yiran. "I can control myself better now. It's the reason why you're sitting next to me and still breathing."

"Is it difficult? To be here beside me?"

"Yes." Yuki raised his hand suddenly, fingers grazing the scar on Yiran's cheek.

Yiran flinched, and his hood fell off. The Hybrid's touch was cold, but it had sent a bolt of heat through him.

"The mage made me angry. I never meant to hurt you."

"As I recall, you made it plain you wanted to kill me," Yiran reminded him.

"Did I?" Yuki laughed. Then a genuine look of regret appeared. "I'm sorry it left a scar."

"Takes more than a scar to diminish my good looks."

Yuki laughed again. There was no reason for his laugh to sound so melodious to Yiran's ears.

"The glasses suit you." Yuki made a square with his thumbs and index fingers of both hands, and pulled back, framing Yiran's face as if he were taking a picture of him. "The perfect college boyfriend vibes."

"Flattery doesn't work on me," Yiran quipped. But he felt his pulse speeding up. "You said you could control yourself, your hunger . . . how?"

"The Blight turns spirits into ghoulish things—the original Revenants—but the strain that infects humans causes people to react differently to it." Yuki paused to stare at him, as if deciding whether to go on.

Sensing this could be valuable information to the Guild, Yiran said, "What happens to the infected humans?"

"Always digging for information, aren't you?"

"Maybe that's what you're here for too," Yiran countered. He didn't want it to be true.

Yuki held his gaze. "It would be stupid for either of us to trust the other."

"Never said I trusted you."

"You shouldn't." Yuki glanced away. "Anyway, as I was saying, some infected humans die immediately because their bodies can't handle the change. Others starve to death because they refuse to feed." He side-eyed Yiran's grunt of disgust. "Don't judge—feeding is a natural instinct. Sometimes, the infected person changes entirely, becoming totally unrecognizable, something more grotesque like the original Revenants."

Yiran remembered the first Revenant he had encountered at the Night

Market, how it'd started off looking more human before morphing into a monster, how it'd hardened and turned to ash when he killed it, just like Aloysius's corpse. That first Revenant must've been a Hybrid. A human whose body reacted badly to the infection.

"And then," Yuki continued, "there are those like me."

"Meaning?"

"Like you said, I'm not one of those mindless monsters. Sometimes I think it's a disease and I need a cure. Sometimes I think it's just evolution. Human food is tasteless to me, and the sun saps my energy, but I've retained most of what you'd call my humanity—my thoughts, feelings . . . I'm aging every day, but it's slow, so I look the same." Yuki made a face. "Maybe I'll be stuck looking nineteen for a long time. I heal faster, and I'm stronger, my senses better attuned to my surroundings. Take away the aging thing and the inability to taste food, it's kind of like being an Exorcist, don't you think?"

Yiran recoiled. "We're different—"

"Are we?" Yuki said bluntly.

"Yes, we—"

"What you mean is you're *better* than me because you think you picked the right side."

"That's because I *did*."

"We're only trying to survive, like all other living organisms," Yuki argued. "What makes it wrong? Aren't you doing the same? Aren't you training to survive? It's the law of nature—eat or be eaten."

"It's not the same," Yiran said.

Defiance flashed in Yuki's eyes. "How is it different? Tell me."

"First of all, we're not trying to *eat* people—your kind kills them. We save them—"

"Why do you care about the normies?"

"I—what?" Yiran was confused by the question. It was a simple one, but he was struggling to find a good answer.

"I was a normie once," Yuki said. "I know how they can be. Ungrateful creatures. They fear what they don't understand. They're weak. They require protection from the strong, from Exorcists. But somehow, they think they're superior, they think they're better because there are more of them and that's what makes them *normal*. Why are they worthy of saving? Shouldn't they bow to superior beings like us?"

Freaks. The normie man from the karaoke club had called Yiran and Zizi and Rui that. He'd even suggested *feeding* those with high spiritual energy to the Revenants, as if they were lesser beings undeserving of life and dignity. Yiran recalled the shock and rage that had pulsed through him when he heard the man's words. Was that Yuki's point? The man was dead now. Good riddance—*no.*

No.

Yiran was appalled by his own thoughts. He couldn't think like that. He couldn't save people unequally. He couldn't decide who was worthy and who was not. He had no right. He couldn't be like that man. He shook his head. This was ridiculous—the entire conversation, him sitting here next to Yuki—Yiran pushed himself off the couch.

"I should get some sleep."

Yuki got up too. "Got an early day tomorrow? The Guild planning something?"

"I'm not telling you anything. You're my enemy."

Yuki blinked. "I know."

And then he moved closer.

Yiran felt the chill of Yuki's lips before his brain could register what was happening. His body reacted, leaning into the kiss, his hand instinctively reaching for the small of Yuki's back.

He had kissed before, and been kissed, but this was different. It should've felt wrong. Should have been foul and monstrous. Should have made him sick.

But he wanted it, and it scared him.

Yiran pulled away, breathing heavily as he raked a shaky hand through his hair. He could feel the flush of his own cheeks while Yuki's remained pale and cold. There was a frenzied look in the Hybrid's eyes. Yiran wondered if it meant he was *hungry*. If he was using Yiran to test his resolve.

"I should have asked," Yuki said. "But I was afraid you'd say no and it would make me sad. Don't worry, it won't happen again."

The wind picked up, ruffling his hair and billowy shirt. Something stirred in Yiran. He wasn't looking at some monster, he was looking at a boy drowning in a white ocean, waiting for someone to save him.

Yuki stepped backward to the edge of the roof, his gaze never leaving Yiran's face as if he was committing it to memory.

"Why did you come here?" Yiran asked, unsure if he wanted to know the real answer.

With a small smile, Yuki turned and disappeared over the ledge.

45
Rui

A light breeze came through the windows in the infirmary, and the blue flames flickered toward Zizi. But he didn't move, didn't even flinch. He wasn't afraid of her fire.

Wasn't afraid of *her*.

"Does it hurt? Is it burning you?" Zizi asked, still holding her hands away from her body.

Rui shook her head. The flames on her hands were small, a little warm, almost tickling her fingers. "They're . . . different this time. It felt like it came from a place of anger on the highway, like a scream in my head. Right now, they're just . . . here."

"This doesn't make any sense." Zizi looked confused, but also relieved. "Maybe it's a sign you're adapting to them."

Somehow it didn't feel that way. Rui shivered, a raw catch in her voice. "What's wrong with me?"

With no regard for himself, Zizi wrapped her up—fire and all—in his arms.

Rui struggled, but he held firm. "It's okay, the flames don't hurt me either, remember?" he assured.

She softened, allowing him to hold her. The steady beat of his heart centered her, and slowly she felt the thing inside her subside.

When she pulled away, the blue flames were gone.

Zizi helped her with her clothes, wrapping his own sweater around her like a scarf. "I'm taking you to your room," he said, scooping her up in his arms before she could protest. "Grab that, will you?"

She snagged his tank top, but when she reached for his Exorcist coat, he shook his head.

"Leave it."

"It's freezing outside."

"The cold doesn't bother me much."

Pressed against his bare chest, Rui directed him to the dormitories, trying not to feel mortified as he carried her across campus. It was late, but several cadets were still around, and they gawked at the half-dressed boy swaggering down the hallways of Xingshan Academy with its star cadet in his arms and a shit-eating grin on his face.

She was never going to live this down.

With the door to her room firmly shut, Zizi settled her onto the bed. His nose was pink, and his skin looked as chilly as she felt. As he pulled on his tank top, Rui stared at the sprawling tattoo of wings on his back. They moved as his muscles tensed.

"Ash said there's a room for me on campus, but no one bothered to tell me where." Zizi shrugged. "I'll stay the night to make sure you're okay; I'll be outside your door."

"If you're staying, you're staying in the room." It would be against the Academy rules, but Rui had already broken so many tonight, she didn't care anymore. "Ash would be upset if he knew his prized healer was sleeping out in the cold. I don't want to be responsible for that."

"Lan Xi does take care of his people," Zizi admitted with a frown, reluctant to praise the man who'd maneuvered his way into recruiting the mage for the Guild. "We should have a hot shower to warm up." When Rui stared, Zizi added, "*Separately*. Get your mind out of the gutter, Rooroo."

"I wasn't—" she started to say, then shut her mouth. Zizi grinned as she felt her cheeks burn.

"You can go first," he said with a gracious gesture.

Rui kicked his shin and he yelped. "I hate you so much," she said fondly.

"You must be feeling better to kick so hard," he said, rubbing his leg.

She almost laughed. She wasn't better. They both knew that.

"I'm too tired. I'll save the hot shower for morning." She could barely get under the covers by herself.

"Rest is good," Zizi agreed, flicking the light switch.

The room plunged into near darkness. He sat on the floor next to the bed, leaning his back against the frame.

Rui tapped the top of his head lightly. "You don't have to sleep there."

Zizi looked up over his shoulder. Half his face was in shadow, but she could see the dubious arch of his eyebrows. "Looks like you have a twin-sized bed. I'm six feet tall and—"

"You sleep on a crappy mattress on the floor of your shophouse," Rui reminded him. "I'm sure my Academy-issued bed is fine."

"—a gentleman."

She sighed. "Oh, just get in."

Zizi shook his head with amusement. "This wasn't how I imagined our first night together."

Rui's jaw dropped. "Have you actually imagined—"

He pressed a finger to her lips. "Didn't mean to say that out loud. I must be tired too. Please ignore whatever I just said—thank you, I will join you in your tiny and uncomfortable Academy-issued bed."

She laughed and made room for him to climb in. Draping an arm around him, she rested her head on his chest.

Zizi's hand found hers immediately, his fingers stroking her knuckles absently, like a habit so ingrained it'd become a natural part of him. Rui smiled. It felt *right*, like they'd always been together, lying side by side, fingers interlaced, two pieces of the same puzzle created for the sole purpose of fitting together.

"If your spiritual weapon was a conduit for the blue fire, then isn't the fire also a form of spiritual energy?" he said suddenly. He must be thinking of the first time her blue flames had manifested on the highway, when she drove her flaming sword through Aloysius—and him.

"Aloysius said it was similar to yinqi." Rui shivered. She didn't want to think about the Hybrids.

"That's impossible." But she thought she heard a hint of doubt in Zizi's voice. "Anyway, it's late," he said, holding her tighter. "You should get some rest. We'll talk tomorrow."

Rui nestled into him, wishing the night would last forever, that she could lie in his arms, the two of them hidden from the rest of the world.

The pitter-patter of rain against the window woke her. Stretching her stiff limbs, Rui found herself alone in bed.

Something scratched her skin. A pink sticky note on her arm. She recognized Zizi's slanted writing.

Went to the hotel. Didn't want to wake you. Back soon!

Rui smiled at the comically large heart drawn over the last two words. Had he gone to ask his grandmother about her blue flames? Or did his head hurt again? Either way, she wished he had taken her with him.

She frowned at the red thread looped a few times around her wrist. It looked like the one Zizi always wore. He must have taken a length from his own and tied it there. Was it meant to be a romantic gesture? Smiling to herself, Rui found her phone and checked the time. It was almost noon. Crap. Too late to see Ada off on her mission.

She tramped into the bathroom. The hot water from the shower was a welcome reprieve from the cold weather and the lingering chill in her bones. Trying to absorb all the warmth she could, she stayed in there until the skin on her fingers puckered. She was pulling on a sweater when she heard a noise.

A whisper.

Was someone in her room? She stuck her head out of the bathroom. The room was empty.

But there it was again. The same childlike voice.

"Hello? Hel-looo!"

It was coming from her bed.

Rui tipped the pillow over.

Nikai's mirror.

"Nikai?"

A face appeared in the glass, but it wasn't his.

A young girl was staring back at Rui, her large brown eyes looking too big for her face. The ends of her dark brown curls were ashy, like the color was fading.

"Hello," she said.

"Hi? Who are you?" said Rui, noticing the skull print on the girl's purple dress. Was she a Reaper too? "Where's Nikai?"

"Nikai cannot speak at the moment."

"Did he send you? Does he have an update? Has he found out anything about the blue—" Rui bit her tongue. Why were the words spilling out of her mouth? Even through the mirror, she could feel a force pushing her to speak.

Rui had a sudden inkling who this girl might be.

The little girl quirked her head. "Show me your blue fire."

"I can't—it bursts out of me randomly. I can't control it."

"Randomly?" The girl seemed disappointed. "There should have been a pattern. But maybe you fail to see it."

"There isn't. It comes out of my hands, but I've used my sword with it once. I think it was a fluke and—" Rui cursed angrily. "I will speak because I want to, not because you're making me. I don't know how you're doing it through this piece of glass, but I know what you're doing, *Seven*." Damned if she addressed a little girl with *Your Majesty*.

She felt the force releasing her.

Seven giggled. "Clever . . . what a clever little bug you are. You're pretty, too. I can see why he likes you."

Was she talking about Nikai?

"Why did you contact me?" Rui asked. "Do you have a message for me?"

"I guess." Seven made no move to elaborate.

Rui's patience was wearing thin. The Kings of Hell were an annoying bunch. "Out with it," she said sternly.

Seven widened her eyes. "Nikai has discovered who contains Four's power."

Who? Was Seven saying that the other vessel was a person, too? What were the odds of Four choosing two different humans; one to contain his power, one to house his soul?

Suddenly, Seven made herself small, pulling in her arms and legs like she was afraid. "The Nothing is coming," she whispered. Her lips lost their color, and her face was pallid. She looked like she was fading, just like her hair. "You must save us, Rui. If the underworld ceases to exist, there will be nowhere for the souls to go. They will not be collected, they will wander aimlessly in your realm, and the Blight will take them."

The glass flickered, and the edges of Seven's face blurred. She was still mouthing something.

"What are you saying? I can't hear you," said Rui, picking up the mirror.

". . . is waiting . . . will tell you . . ."

"Is Nikai waiting for me? Does he want to meet to tell me who the vessel is?"

The glass flickered again.

Seven's face vanished, and Rui was left with a disembodied whisper.

". . . he is waiting beneath the stairway to heaven . . ."

46
Yiran

Yiran listened to the rhythmic tip-tapping of rain splattering off zinc roofs and onto potholed roads as he trudged down the uneven path. He was cold and wet and miserable. This wasn't how he thought his first mission would go.

They had split into two groups when they arrived: Yiran, Ada, and Eddy heading to the sensors first, while Ash and Teshin did a ground sweep. There weren't supposed to be any more Revenants left in the area, but Ash had wanted to be sure.

"Ever been here?" Eddy asked. He was an apprentice in the Guild's technology department. Only a couple of years older than Yiran, he had a mop of curls and an affable, self-deprecating air about him.

"Nope, I've never been here," said Ada, looking extra zippy. She'd downed a can of double espresso in the car.

"Neither have I," Yiran said. The squelch of his boots on muddy ground was starting to annoy him. He glanced at his surroundings.

This old neighborhood had nothing to offer. It was near the city margins, run-down and close enough to the marsh to smell funky in the summer. The real estate company in charge of the redevelopment project here had gone bankrupt the year before, and illegal squatters moved in.

The Guild's new spiritual energy sensors had recently detected unusual activity within its borders. That's when the dead bodies were discovered. Since the squatters were destitute, no one knew they were missing in the first place. Yiran wondered how many others had perished the same way, their absence unreported and unnoticed because they had become an invisible part of the city through some misfortune.

"It should be in and out for us," Eddy said as he scanned the desolate half-finished blocks of apartments and the ramshackle huts that sprouted beside them. "Just need to make sure those sensors are working. Maintenance work, really. That's why they sent me."

He nodded at Yiran. "I heard you joined the Academy not too long ago, but you're already on your first official mission. You must be really talented. Must run in the family, huh? The great gift of magic."

"It only means I've a lot of catching up to do," Yiran said lightly.

"You've been doing fine," Ada said. "You wouldn't be here if Ash didn't believe in your abilities. He's not the sort to risk things."

She was probably right. But Yiran's impostor syndrome was alive and well.

"Captain Song's a good man," Eddy said.

Yiran couldn't help but smile. "He is."

"I'm not good at magic myself," Eddy went on. He seemed the sort who enjoyed striking up conversations with strangers. "My spiritual energy level's right on the border. Can't really fight either. I'm just glad the Academy took me in. Taught me how to manage myself. Plus, it pays the bills. My younger siblings are normies, and I can help put them through school. You know, give them the normal life I can't have."

Yiran hadn't given much thought to people like Eddy. Borderline cases whose spiritual energy didn't allow them to wield a weapon or cast spells well enough to become full-fledged Exorcists. They didn't attend Xingshan Academy, studying at an affiliated school in the city instead, learning the technical skills that made them the support network for Exorcists who went into combat. Their jobs weren't flashy. No one knew their names or faces, and they would get no accolades or glory if a Hunt went well. No normie would know to thank them for saving lives. But they were the backbone of the Guild. Ash was right; Yiran needed to pay more attention to the people who really mattered.

"What song is that?" Ada asked suddenly.

Eddy stopped humming. "Sorry, got an earworm. It's my kid sister's favorite song—something about a super fish. Tuna, I think. Drives me up the wall when she plays it, but here I am, singing it all the time myself."

They all laughed.

As they walked on, Yiran decided to put his new glove on. He flexed his fingers, marveling again at Tesha's craftsmanship. It fit like a second skin, allowing for dexterity. She'd promised that the other would be ready in a few weeks to complete the pair, and he couldn't wait.

Minutes later, Eddy stopped at a tree, pulling out a meter-like contraption from his backpack. "Here's our first."

Yiran looked at the ground. "Where's the sensor?"

"Up in the tree. There—right by that branch. See it?"

Yiran spotted the slim device. It was a few inches long, attached to a branch and camouflaged to look like tree bark. "Uh huh."

"I'll do a test, check if it's functioning. They're temperamental things, but hopefully the upgraded versions will work better. It'll take a few minutes, then we'll go to the next one. We've got about nine of these." Humming the super tuna song, Eddy fiddled with his machine.

Ada nodded at Yiran. "Stay alert, Cadet Song." Hand on her whip, she paced in an arc around the area.

Yiran wiped the rain off his face, scanning the area for anything unusual. At least it was only a drizzle now, though it was misty because of the wetlands nearby.

They moved on to the next few sensors, going farther away from the buildings and closer to the marsh. Eddy continued his work, always humming the same tune.

The light dimmed as the day wore on, and it seemed to make the work duller. The comms remained quiet. Yiran wondered why they hadn't run into Ash and Teshin yet.

He was starting to lose focus. Starting to think about narrow gray eyes sparkling with intelligence, an elegant neck he longed to trace with his own fingers, the cold touch of full lips—

Stop.

The line between fear and desire had blurred last night.

It won't happen again.

Why did those words disappoint him?

He needed to clear his head. "I'm going to do a few sprints to wake myself up," he said.

Ada hesitated.

"I won't go far," Yiran assured.

Before she could say anything, he took off.

The wind sang in his ears as he ran. But when he stopped and turned around, the mist had swallowed up his crew. Still, he thought he could hear Ada's footsteps and the faint humming from Eddy.

The cold had woken him, but it didn't put to rest the ghost of Yuki's kiss. It lingered on his lips, haunting his thoughts. He wanted to scour the feel of it from his flesh, exorcise the thought from his memory. Why hadn't he reported Yuki's trespassing? Was it the guilt of letting the Hybrid leave unscathed that was stopping him? Or was it the shame of wanting to see Yuki again?

Yiran wrinkled his nose. The smell from the marsh was getting stronger. Maybe he'd wandered farther than he thought.

It took him a second to notice it had gotten quiet. Eerily so.

And it took him the next second to realize he could no longer hear Eddy's song.

47
Rui

. . . he is waiting beneath the stairway to heaven . . .

There was only one place in the city that fit that description: the new office tower at Outram. And the only thing *beneath* it was the old subway station. Nikai had picked a strange meeting place, but maybe he had his reasons.

The shuttle off the island came quickly, and soon Rui was on her way into the city. She had studied the network of subterranean tracks once when she got curious about the underground magic community. An easier way to Outram would be to take the train to the stop after and backtrack on foot, but the faster way was going through the tunnel itself. Nikai was waiting for her with news of the vessel—news that could help her fulfill the end of the bargain with Ten. She wasn't going to keep him waiting.

Rui sprinted to the subway gantry and slipped into the train as the doors were closing. It emptied out at the next stop. Stroke of luck. No one to witness what she was about to do.

She made her way to the door between compartments, waiting anxiously as the train rumbled on for the next few stops. As it curved between stations, she pried the door open and jumped. Dusting herself off, she crept northward alongside the tracks. Gradually, her eyes adjusted to the orange light cast from occasional lamps attached to the graffitied walls.

There. A fork in the path ahead.

The stench of sewage was strong, and the old tracks damp. Water from small puddles splashed beneath her boots, wetting the hem of her jeans. Rats and other creatures scurried out of her way as she crashed through, not bothering to hide her presence. Something caught her eye. She shone her phone light at the scratched-up metal sign hammered to the wall. She was almost there.

Another left turn and Rui found herself at the abandoned station. Built in a time when subway trains had fewer cars, the platform was shorter than what she was used to and there was no barrier between the tracks and the platform. Panting, she heaved herself up from the tracks.

"Nikai?" she shouted. "I'm here!"

The place was in a state of disrepair. Dirty scuffed-up floors, tiles falling off in places to reveal concrete, mildewed ceilings dripping with runoff . . . But the electricity was still running, and half the lights were flickering.

Rui peered into the broken windows of the stationmaster's office. There was nothing but old cabinets and machinery and what looked like a decades-old burger wrapper.

There was no sign of the Reaper.

"Nikai?" Her voice echoed. Did Seven send her to the wrong place, or had Rui misunderstood her instructions?

Something red edged into her vision.

Rui looked up.

A tall, slender figure was moving gracefully toward her. But in that grace, something darker lived.

"Nice to see you again, Rui," said Ten. His flaxen hair had lost its shine, and his robes were dull, the edges colorless the way Seven's skin was earlier. "I see my little sister led you here. Well done. Is she not lovely?"

Rui shrank back instinctively. "I thought I was meeting Nikai."

"I'm afraid he's unavailable right now." Ten pulled a sad face. "And is this how you greet an old friend?"

"You're not my friend."

"And you would be wise to remember that, rude little mortal. How long has it been since we met? I do not pay attention to how time passes in the mortal realm, especially when I have been *so* busy."

It was best to be upfront. "I haven't found your brother yet," Rui said, trying to calm her racing heart. "But Nikai found the vessel, didn't he? If he tells me, it'll help me with my search for Four's soul."

"Nikai this, Nikai that . . ." Ten shook his head, feigning disappointment. "Did you forget your deal is with *me*?"

"No," Rui stammered.

"Good." Ten bared his teeth. "Because I have come to collect."

"But I just told you I haven't found—"

"Hush. He's here."

"Who?"

"Someone waiting to make a dramatic entrance, as one does in these situations." Ten clapped. "Come on! Do not keep us waiting."

Rui spotted shadows shifting at the far end of the tunnel. A few silhouettes were coming forward.

Human-shaped.

Gooseflesh sprouted on her arms when she sensed them for what they were. This was a trap. Ten must be punishing her for not fulfilling her end of the deal. Death seemed extreme, but he was a petty god from the underworld. Anger overcame her fear. Of all the ways he could have killed her, she couldn't believe he chose *this*.

"You can kill me yourself," she said. "No need to get *them* to do your dirty work."

"You misunderstand me, Rui," Ten scolded, a hand to his chest as if she'd wounded him deeply. "Our contract binds us, remember? I am not here to kill you; I am here to deliver a gift."

The Hybrids walked out of the shadows, climbing up from the tracks onto the platform. There were five of them, a ragtag-looking bunch. Rui was struck by how young they looked.

A sixth figure came forward into the light and pulled himself up next to them.

Numbness pooled in Rui's legs. Time buckled and warped. Pressure in her ears built up, and it felt like her head would explode.

Her mother's murderer was standing right in front of her.

Not a test, not a simulation. Just as real as she was.

"You're all grown up now, but I know you," said the Hybrid Revenant.

"The little girl who got away. The little girl who gave me *this*."

He raised his shirt to reveal an ugly scar running across his chest.

Rui remembered him.

She remembered the cruel curve of his smile, his hypnotic voice, the way he held her attention like a snake charmer, except *he* was the serpent.

But she didn't remember giving him that wound.

Every cell in her body was screaming to kill him now. Her hands itched for her swords. But without her magic, the steel on her weapons would only make the Hybrid bleed. It would not destroy him.

Quickly, she calculated the distance between them, turning slightly so the length of her coat hid her hand. Her fingers found the soft pouch dangling from her belt, and she filled her palm with its contents.

The Hybrid was eyeing her hungrily. "Are you sure I can't have some of her yangqi?" he asked Ten. "A little sip for old times' sake?"

"Mind your manners, Feng," Ten said. "Besides, you are here for a different reason." He turned to Rui. "One condition has been fulfilled. I have brought you your mother's murderer. Now, we have other things to—"

"Wait a minute, what's he going on about?" Feng interrupted, glancing nervously at the other Hybrids.

The five stayed silent, their expressions blank. But Rui noticed they were now blocking Feng's path if he wanted to leave.

Or escape.

Clearly, Ten had struck more than one deal. What had he promised the Hybrids in return for surrendering their comrade?

Ten sighed. "As I was saying before I was so rudely interrupted—"

Rui flung her hand up.

Tiny coins shot in the air.

All eyes focused on the shiny balls of light.

Rui slid forward. Swept her leg across, catching Feng's ankle. He stumbled. She rammed into his chest, knocking him off the platform.

The Hybrid slammed onto the tracks below. Foul-smelling water splattered everywhere. She heard Ten's squeals of disgust, punctuated by small blasts of qi bombs exploding. Shrapnel filled with yangqi pierced the Hybrids' flesh. Screams echoed.

But Rui was focused on only one thing.

She jumped onto the tracks, knifing a knee into Feng's sternum, pinning him down on the dirt. With a snarl, she caught his throat and squeezed. His jaw opened—just enough—and she shoved a handful of fizzling coins in, forcing him to swallow.

Rui didn't know if the qi bombs would kill him. But his life was in her hands, and as she looked into his once-arrogant eyes, now filled with fear, she let herself enjoy the moment—however brief.

"Enough of this!" Ten raised a hand.

A force threw Rui off. She hit the wall. A broken tile sliced her forehead. Blood ran down her face. Dazed, she saw Feng spitting the crimson coins onto the ground.

"You little bitch—" Feng wheezed, clutching his chest.

Rui laughed hysterically. A few qi bombs must've gone off inside of Feng. He was shaking uncontrollably and the skin on his throat was splotchy purple.

But he wasn't dead. Not at all. She would kill him with her bare hands if she had to.

She hurled herself at Feng.

Ten moved his fingers almost lazily.

This time, the force caught Rui in midair, flinging her back onto the platform. She landed on her side. Pain exploded in her shoulders and neck. Black spots appeared in her vision. She tried to stand, but she only got to her knees before collapsing.

"Stay down, Rui," Ten said. "I do not wish to hurt you more than I must. All I ask from you is a bit of patience. You will have your revenge."

"We should kill the brat," said a Hybrid in a green bomber jacket. She was about Surin's age, with dark hair piled on top of her head in a ponytail. Her forehead and neck had been burned a painful red by the qi bombs.

The other Hybrids growled in agreement, each showing varying degrees of damage.

Feng hissed, "She's mine."

"Know your place, fool," Ten said calmly. "She is nobody's. I tire of you and your nonsense, human." He spat the last word like an insult.

Rui tried to focus, her breath ragged. Why did Ten call the Hybrid *human*? Feng wasn't—

Twisting his wrist, Ten clawed his fingers into a fist.

Lifted by an unseen force, Feng rose in the air. His limbs dangled helplessly as he yelled, "Put me down!"

"As you wish." Ten dropped his arm, and Feng came crashing onto the platform at the King's feet. Ten gripped his face, sharp nails piercing skin. "I would kill you for your insolence, but your life belongs to the girl."

Ten let go.

Feng covered his eyes, emitting a high-pitched shriek that went on and on as he writhed on the ground. What terrible visions was Ten putting in his mind? Feng shook for a few more moments before going still. His eyes were open and vacant, a look of utter fear frozen on his face. He was living whatever nightmare Ten had trapped him in.

Green Jacket gasped, taking a step forward as if to help her comrade. But Ten threw her a warning glare. "Do not forget about our agreement."

Green Jacket paled, and she stayed where she was. The rest of the Hybrids exchanged uneasy looks. Rui had a feeling they'd gotten more than they'd bargained for.

"We'll fulfill our end of the deal and complete our task," said Green Jacket. "We won't get in your way, Your Majesty." She motioned. "Bring the rest out."

The other Hybrids scattered onto the tracks and into the dark.

Rui focused on Green Jacket. Could this Hybrid be their leader? She seemed competent, but Rui had a feeling there was more to their hierarchy. Green Jacket had reacted to Ten's torture of Feng; she had wanted to help her comrade. She couldn't be the mastermind of this scheme.

Someone else—someone who wasn't here—was leading the pack. Rui promised herself that if she survived this, she would track down the real brains behind the Hybrids and make them pay.

As Rui slumped against the dirty walls of the station, thinking of how she could end Feng's life for good, a peculiar change was coming over the Tenth King. He paced back and forth, smoothing out his low ponytail, neatening his robes. Rui sensed his anticipation. But she couldn't think of anyone Ten would care to impress.

There was movement in the tunnel. Footsteps. Low grunts. Three of the Hybrids reappeared, each with a body slung over their shoulders. They dropped the bodies unceremoniously onto the tracks. Normies. They were unconscious, not dead. Why were they here?

The last Hybrid was wrestling a young man with a hood over his head who was very much not unconscious. The Hybrid caught an elbow to the jaw, and he snarled and hunched over. Something violet began to grow from his spine. But a look from Green Jacket, and the Hybrid straightened, his violet spikes receding.

The other Hybrids went to help him. Together, they threw the young man to the ground, where he lay, catching his breath.

"Free him," Ten commanded.

Green Jacket didn't look happy, but she yanked the young man up anyway and untied his hands. She pulled off the hood and removed the gag from his mouth, giving him a vicious kick in the back.

The young man stumbled into the light. Barely able to walk, he fell hard to his knees onto the train tracks.

He looked up, and Rui found herself staring into eyes, blue like the hottest part of a flame.

48
Yiran

Had he wandered too far? In the heavy mist, everything felt farther apart as Yiran sprinted back. Half-built buildings in the distance rose like giant tombstones amid the gray and brown landscape.

A flash of pink. Muffled sounds of a fight.

"Eddy? Ada?" Yiran shouted, pulling out his talismans. "Ada?"

Tiny explosions. Bursts of light. Then a big one, cutting through the mist.

He finally saw them: Ada twirling her whip, fighting two Hybrids who were tag teaming her—and—

Eddy impaled to a tree.

Eddy bleeding.

Eddy dying.

Yiran flung a talisman in the air, yelling out the incantation. It burst into flames. Crimson arrows shot across the air.

The taller Hybrid screamed as three arrows found their target.

The other Hybrid—a young man with a shaven head and tail-like thing sticking out of his back—screamed with her. "Ling! No!"

Ada snapped her whip at him, pulling him back into the fight.

"Yiran—again!" she yelled.

Another talisman. Another slew of arrows.

Yiran's insides were heating up, but he didn't care. He recited the incantation again.

More arrows shot through Ling. The Hybrid writhed as yangqi burned into her flesh.

"Felix, Felix—it hurts . . ." she gasped as her jaw started to melt.

"Ling!" Felix dashed to his comrade.

But he was too late.

And Ada was too fast. The deadly hook of her whip pierced Ling's chest. Ada channeled a blast of magic.

And pulled.

Felix screamed. He lurched, falling onto the ground, crawling to Ling. She was turning to ash, and he cradled her crumbling body with a tenderness that felt wrong.

He's a monster. They both are. They shouldn't feel anything.

Yiran turned from them and ran to Eddy.

The violet spikes pinning him to the tree were disappearing. They must have belonged to Ling, and with her death, the yinqi ceased to exist.

Yiran caught him as the last spike holding him up vanished, and laid him gently on the ground. Blood leaked from the many puncture wounds.

"T-told you not good at . . . magic," Eddy wheezed. "Can't fight . . . either." He was clutching a small metal device tightly in his trembling hand. "Tried to steal s-sensor . . . they want . . . they want our tech—can't let them know . . ."

"Shh, stop talking, you're okay." Yiran pressed his hands on Eddy's stomach, trying to stem the flow of blood. "You're going to be okay." He repeated the words again and again, willing them to be true.

"Yiran." Ada was limping toward them. Her clothes were torn and bloody, one of her eyes bloodshot and swelling. "Yiran, we have to finish the job."

"He's going to be okay," Yiran told her. "He's going—"

Behind them, Felix let out a feral roar.

He was standing, face distorted with anger and anguish. The tail-like thing behind him rose like a serpent. He flung his arms out. Hundreds of violet spikes fanned out from his tail in a semicircle on either side, like the hood of a cobra. He drew his arms close, fingers pointing at the three cadets.

The spikes detached.

Yiran had seen this attack before. He knew what would happen next.

"No!"

He punched the sky with his gloved fist.

Crimson light exploded from it, forming a massive dome over the area with Eddy and Ada and him in the center. The Hybrid's spikes pelted down like a torrential downpour.

But Yiran's shield held.

A searing heat was spreading throughout his legs, his torso, his arms, his *mind*. But Yiran gritted his teeth, channeling everything he had into his shield.

And still the violet spikes came raining down.

And still his shield held.

His world went white. He couldn't see anything, couldn't feel anything. The heat was unbearable.

Gunshots rang in the air. Shouting and the clang of metal.

Through half-closed eyes, Yiran saw two familiar figures sprinting toward him. Felix turned his spikes on Ash and Teshin, but he was swiftly overwhelmed.

Yiran released his shield and pressed his hands on Eddy's stomach again. The red pool around him had grown.

"Eddy . . . Eddy? Hang on, we're getting you help," Ada whispered, kneeling beside them.

Eddy's face was so pale, it was almost translucent. His eyes fluttered open and found Yiran's.

"That was . . . a-amazing . . . Yiran. Must be nice . . . your gift of magic."

He made a sound, like a soft sigh, and closed his eyes again.

49
Rui

Zizi.

Fear tightened its grip on Rui. What was he doing here? Did the Hybrids catch him on his way to his grandmother's? His sweater was shredded, revealing cuts and bruises on his arms and torso. Dried blood stained the side of his face. He looked dazed, like he'd been drugged.

Blinking rapidly, he took in his surroundings. He saw her.

"Rui? Who did this to you?" Zizi demanded, glowering at her injuries. He was up on his feet at once, settling on Ten as the likely suspect. "Was it *you*?"

Zizi ran a hand down the length of his arm. The black hilt of his spiritual weapon appeared.

Ten rolled his eyes.

Pain shot through Rui's nerves. She cried out, staring at her hand in horror. Her index finger was bent wrong.

Zizi stopped in his tracks. He lowered his arm slowly, his spiritual weapon disappearing.

Ten quirked his head, observing the mage. "I see you are quick to pick up on things. All I need is a small favor. If you agree to do it, nothing else will happen to her."

"Who are you and what do you want?" Zizi said.

"You will soon know who I am. But first, re-create the separation spell for them." Ten pointed at the Hybrids, not bothering to hide his distaste for the creatures.

"No! Don't you dare!" Rui shouted. "Don't listen to Ten—"

Another finger twisted.

She clapped her uninjured hand over her mouth to stop her screams. Fury burned through her. One day, she would give this god a taste of his own medicine. One day, she would bring him to his knees.

As if he heard her thoughts, Ten smiled at her. A suffocating weight pressed down, and she whimpered.

Zizi roared, "Stop!"

Ten's spiritual pressure lightened, just a little. "Yes?"

"The spell was a one-off thing. I can't do it again," Zizi said, his eyes never leaving Rui. She wanted to reassure him, but she was in too much pain to speak.

"That is not what you told us, Your Majesty!" Green Jacket looked mutinous. "We know this is the mage who created a successful separation spell, but we failed to capture him the first time because of *her*." Green Jacket glared in Rui's direction. "*You* came to us, Your Majesty. *You* told us you had leverage and a way to make this work. We made a deal, and now he's saying he can't do it?"

"Relax," Ten said, looking almost bored by Green Jacket's tirade. "I will hold up my end of our bargain. He can do it. He just doesn't know it yet."

Ten pulled out a dried branch from his robes. He closed his fist, and the branch crumbled to dust. He went to Zizi. "Give me your hand."

Rui shook her head, but Zizi stuck his hand out and Ten poured the crushed remains into his palm.

"Perhaps you have tried to create the spell again and failed," Ten said. "But you will not fail this time. The artifact you hold," he paused, nodding at the dust in Zizi's palm, "it may not have the power it used to, but it will be enough."

Zizi stared at the brown mound.

"You feel its power, do you not?"

Zizi nodded, looking both intrigued and repelled by what was in his hand.

"This time"—Ten tossed his ponytail—"make sure the spell can be cast an infinite number of times."

Zizi's jaw dropped in shock. He hesitated, fighting with himself.

"Don't do it," Rui pleaded. "You know what the Hybrids will do with that spell."

"Oh, but you *love* her, don't you?" Ten crooned. "And love is what makes you weak and pathetic, and a fool."

He glanced in Rui's direction, and she felt the weight of the god's power again. It snaked into her, squeezing from the inside, the pain radiating from her stomach and up her spine. She gasped, barely able to stop the scream rising in her throat.

"Stop hurting her!" Zizi shouted.

It was the first time Rui had seen him this afraid. And he *was* afraid—of losing her.

"I am impatient by nature," Ten said, "and we are running out of time. She feels a little fragile at the moment. I am afraid her spirit core is not doing so well. I suggest you act quickly before I slip and kill her by accident."

Green Jacket threw a sheaf of yellow parchment at Zizi. "Hurry up. Any one of us would be happy to finish her off if we don't get what we want."

No. Rui shook her head at him. He couldn't re-create that cursed spell just to save her. One life was not more worthy than the rest. She tried to speak, but the words jammed in her throat as Ten's spiritual pressure crushed her.

Zizi cast her one last desperate look, and she heard his words from the night before echoing in her head.

I would give up this entire world for a single breath to leave your lips again.

And then she watched the boy she loved doom the world she had sworn to protect.

50
Yiran

The car sped down the highway back to the Guild headquarters with Ash at the wheel and the three cadets behind. Ada's eye was swollen shut, and she rested her head on Yiran's shoulder, exhausted from the fight. On his right, Teshin was polishing their blade with a stony expression.

Yiran's insides hurt. Every breath took effort, and he wanted to lie down and sleep forever. He'd also wanted to ride with Eddy's body in the other transport, but Ash had put his foot down firmly.

Yiran clenched his hands. "Why didn't you bring a healer?" he demanded. He felt Ada tense beside him. "Last night, you said things might get dicey—why didn't you plan for this?"

Ash replied tightly, "The area was already cleared. This was supposed to be a routine task." Then, quietly, "I thought I'd made sure of it."

Had they been assigned to this low-stakes mission because Ash wanted to keep *Yiran* safe? The thought only made Yiran angrier. "Maybe this wouldn't have happened if you told everyone on the team about the Hybrids." When no one responded, he fumed, "Come on, aren't either of you angry that you've been lied to?"

"I've always believed Rui," Ada said. "But I didn't expect Hybrids to be so powerful."

"Exactly my point! If we knew—"

"Stop throwing a tantrum," Ash said.

"I'm not throwing a tantrum." Yiran punched the back of the seat in front of him.

Teshin put their blade down. "Why weren't you there, Yiran? Why did you wander off? Ada was alone with Eddy when the two Hybrids snuck up on them."

Teshin's bluntness was a cold slap to the face. Their implication was clear.

This was Yiran's fault.

He remembered Rui's disdain when she found out he'd driven his car to campus so he could zip in and out whenever he wanted to.

This isn't fun and games, not when lives are at stake.

She was right.

Lives *were* at stake. This wasn't about him and how he wanted magic for himself. This was bigger than him. He thought of Eddy and how he'd clung on to the stupid sensor, how he'd staked his life for it because he knew the consequences of the enemy getting their hands on it. How he'd sacrificed himself without hesitation.

Exorcists worked in teams. Yiran had abandoned his. He had left Ada to fight alone; he had left Eddy to fend for himself. And yet here he was, taking it out on Ash when the only one to blame was himself.

Ada squeezed his hand. Yiran wondered what his face was telegraphing for her to be looking at him like that.

"It's not your fault," she whispered, so soft only he could hear it. Then, louder, for the rest, "You did the best you could in the moment. You saved me. I would've died if it wasn't for your shield."

But it is my fault, Yiran wanted to say. *I was daydreaming about kissing the enemy while you were fighting for your life, while Eddy was dying.* Guilt was an iron weight on his chest, something he would bear for the rest of his life.

"It's been a difficult day," Ash finally said.

Both of his hands were gripping the steering wheel, knuckles white. He sighed, the sigh of someone who had seen too much but who was forced to keep his eyes open. How many people had died in front of him? How many people had he failed to save? Yiran didn't know the ghosts that haunted his half brother.

"It's not what I wanted you to experience on your first mission," Ash went on, his voice toneless and hollow. "But the sooner you know what it means to be out in the field, the faster you'll learn and adapt." He glanced briefly at the back seat. "Ada's right, Yiran. You did what you could. It was an impressive defensive shield. I've never seen one so large."

This wasn't the praise Yiran wanted. Not like this.

There was a cackle of static.

"Captain Song? Come in, Captain—"

Ash picked up his comms set. "Yeah?"

"The qi sensors in sector twelve have picked up some abnormal activity. A unit is heading that way, but we'd like to send more backup."

"Sector twelve?" Ash said. "Is that Outram?"

"Affirmative, Captain."

"I'm with some cadets, but I can be there after I drop them off at HQ. ETA twenty minutes."

"Very good, Captain." There was a blip of static, and the comms went silent.

"You have to bring us along," Yiran ordered.

"Oh I do, do I?" Ash snorted. "Look at Ada, she needs a healer."

"I see fine with my other eye," Ada declared.

Yiran said, "You want us to learn and adapt fast? Throw us in the field. This isn't a choice, Ash, we're going with you."

"And you, Cadet Mak? It's obvious you're the only rational one in the back seat," Ash said, shaking his head. "What do you have to say about this?"

Teshin shrugged. "It's three against one, whether it's a vote—or a fight. We'll also get there faster without the detour to the headquarters."

Ash considered their response. "Fine, but only if the three of you follow everything I say." He glared. "I should charge the three of you with dissent."

But Yiran caught his faint, proud smile as he floored the accelerator.

51
Rui

The flickering station lights cast an eerie greenish tint on the unconscious humans, the Hybrids, the death god who stood in his flowing robes—and the figure kneeling in the middle of the train tracks.

Sweat broke over Zizi's brow as he worked. He spoke, so softly Rui couldn't make out the words, his fingers moving quickly over a rectangular piece of yellow parchment. Faint red lines began to form on it. The characters of a spell. With a trembling hand, he held the crumbled remains of Ten's branch over the talisman.

A coppery-gold trail of dust rose from those remains, floating in the air, swirling for a moment, then swooping toward the parchment, disappearing into it.

Energy crackled around them.

Darkness surrounded Zizi. Unseen, but felt. He raised a hand, and Rui saw that the black veins had climbed all the way up his arms to his collarbone and the base of his throat. Seconds later, he gasped in pain.

The talisman fluttered to the ground.

Zizi tipped over, bracing himself with a hand. He glared sideways at Ten. "Take it."

One of the Hybrids picked the talisman up instead. "How do we know if it works? How do we know if it can create more of us?"

Rui shuddered. This was the culmination of the Guild's fears: a world overrun by monsters.

"We need to test the spell," said the Hybrid. "You're the mage—cast it." Zizi didn't move.

The Hybrid nudged one of the unconscious bodies with his foot. "We brought guinea pigs. Come on, show us that it works."

Zizi stared. "Fuck you."

"That's it, we're taking him with us," the Hybrid said to Ten.

"That is not part of the agreement, I am afraid," Ten said coldly. "You will have to take my word for it. The spell works."

The Hybrid's eyes darted to Green Jacket for confirmation. She gave him a curt nod.

"Are we done?" Zizi said, looking murderously at Ten.

"Not quite. We are waiting for someone else to arrive." Ten turned to the Hybrids. "Shoo. Our deal is complete. Take your spell and leave."

Rui caught him exchanging a secretive look with Green Jacket. Green Jacket cocked her head, and the other Hybrids took her lead, walking away into the dark tunnel, dragging the unconscious bodies with them.

Rui felt the slightest touch of relief. At least Zizi would not be forced to do anything more. But who was the *someone else* Ten was waiting for? She felt his spiritual pressure lifting from her. Ignoring her injuries, she scrambled down to the tracks to Zizi.

But as she hobbled past the Tenth King, she heard him say, "I am truly sorry that this will hurt."

A violet spinal blade shot out from the tunnel.

Something warm and wet splattered on Rui's cheek.

She saw Zizi's hand go to his neck. Saw the shock on his face, the red rivulets dripping—down his fingers, his collarbones—the fast-spreading stain on his clothes.

Zizi staggered, one hand reaching out to her, the other hand still at his throat, covered in his own blood.

His eyes rolled back.

And he fell to the ground, silent and still.

52
Yiran

There was a slew of activity when they arrived in Outram. Traffic had been halted for several blocks, and impatient honks and shouts filled the air. Closer to the old subway station, squad cars were lined up by the roadside, and a blockade had been set up. Beyond the barricades, a team of Exorcists were assisting the police with civilian evacuations from the nearby office buildings. The main area of interest seemed to be the old subway station built underneath a spanking new office tower, a spiral-shaped monstrosity that Yiran thought was an eyesore.

This is big. He hadn't expected a full-scale expedition. What was happening?

They hurried out of the car.

Ash pointed at a small makeshift tent. "Take Cadet Senai to the healer over there. I'll be back after I get briefed." He jogged to the group of Exorcists gathering by a fire hydrant.

Yiran waited outside the tent with Teshin as a healer attended to Ada's eye and the cuts on her arms. He turned to Teshin, wondering what to say. There was a new awkwardness between them, and Yiran hated it.

But Teshin spoke first. "I'm not mad at you. I just thought better of you."

Yiran felt their disappointment. It seeped into his bones in a different way than his grandfather's disappointment. With the old man, all Yiran ever felt was anger and resentment in response, the fervent and unreasonable desire to dig in and continue on the wrong path. Teshin's disappointment hit in another way, more painful because Teshin had treated Yiran as his own person from the start.

"I have no excuse," Yiran confessed. "I wandered off because I was distracted, because I didn't take the mission as seriously as I should have.

I thought it was whatever it said on paper. Check the sensors in some old neighborhood. It wasn't a proper mission in my stupid head—it wasn't a proper mission because there weren't supposed to be any Revenants. It was . . . logistics." He felt like a complete ass.

"No fight, no glory," Teshin said. "Just like Rui."

Two different faces, two sides of the same coin.

"Except Rui cares more about other people."

Shame flooded Yiran's gut. "I . . . I won't let you down again," he said.

"It's not me you should be making promises to. Ash is right about your shield, though. The way you've been using your magic from the very beginning—it's unusual. Have you heard of Amplifiers?"

"No. What are those?"

"I'm not entirely sure. My grandmother used to talk about people who were born gifted with innate traits that gave them the ability to use magic differently. The Academy doesn't teach this at all. It's lore I learned from her. Maybe we should ask Tesha . . ." Teshin broke off.

Ash had come up to them. He stuck his head into the healer's tent briefly before coming back out. "The sensors are buzzing. Everything up here seems fine, so we think the disturbance is coming from underground, which means we're going down there. We're entering from two points, with the third team as backup on the surface. The healer says Cadet Senai's out of commission. Are the two of you sure about coming along?"

They nodded.

Ash asked Yiran, "Think you can cast that shield again if we need you to?"

Ignoring the echo of pain in his chest, Yiran nodded.

"Good. Come with me."

They joined the other Exorcists. Yiran spotted a familiar face.

"Didn't expect to see the both of you here," Surin said, smirking at the teens.

Ash raised his voice. "Civilian evacuation?"

"Complete," an Exorcist confirmed.

"The cops?"

"At the far perimeter. They've been instructed to let us handle this alone."

"All right," Ash commanded, "barrier up."

Two other Exorcists threw up their spells. The air shimmered and a large translucent dome rose around them and disappeared.

"Everyone in your teams. Shuang, circle us. Surin, you're descending first." Ash glanced over his shoulder. "Yiran! Teshin! You're with me. We'll head down once we get the all clear."

Adrenaline coursed through Yiran's veins as he hastened forward. The Exorcist standing next to Ash gave him a curt nod, and Yiran stiffened his spine.

"Thanks," he said to Ash, "for trusting me."

Ash grinned. "I'll always bet on family."

Yiran tried to smile back, but the feelings he had were too complicated.

They watched as one team of Exorcists went into the subway station. At the other end, Surin's team dislodged the cover of a manhole. She cracked a glow stick and threw it down. Moments later, all three members of her team descended.

As they waited, Yiran felt the tension in the air adding to the heavy pressure that shrouded the area. It was a strange *spiritual* pressure, dark and otherworldly.

But there was something else, too. He concentrated. A hint . . . a feeling of—*Rui.*

He could sense her.

Worse. He could sense her *fear.*

Something was happening beneath their feet. Something that involved Rui.

He grabbed Ash's arm. "They're down there."

Ash threw him a sharp look. "How do you know?"

"I just do." Yiran didn't know how else to explain. "We have to go down—now."

Before Ash could react, Surin's blond head popped out of the manhole. "Jackpot."

"Okay, gather! We're going down!" Ash called out.

The Exorcists who had flanked out to survey the area jogged back. Everyone had their spiritual weapons drawn.

Yiran took a step, and the ground beneath him began to shake.

53
Rui

A sound grew in Rui's throat, a wail so sorrowful her world shook.

Blue flames raged out of her hands, illuminating the far end of the tunnel. One of the Hybrids was trailing the rest of the group, and she could still see the violet blades protruding from his spine.

He did this. He killed Zizi.

Lips pulled back in a snarl, Rui flung her hand out.

Fire slammed into the Hybrid, engulfing him quickly. His screams echoed in the semidarkness.

But something else was happening.

The flames.

They were flowing out of her like running water, swirling in the air, blue tendrils undulating toward Zizi's prone body.

Stunned, Rui could only stare as the fire grazed him and disappeared. His body didn't burn. But there was no movement, no rise and fall of his chest, only stillness.

Slowly, the fire dampened to a trickle, then vanished from her hands completely.

Every muscle in her body shrieked in agony. But her only thought was Zizi. He looked so peaceful, like he was fast asleep. He couldn't be gone. He *couldn't*.

The pain in her heart was infinite.

She lashed out at Ten. "He did exactly as you asked—why didn't you stop that Hybrid from killing him?"

"Everything is going according to plan, Rui," Ten replied. "Did you forget? Each condition of our deal must be fulfilled accordingly. The Hybrids and I have our own agreement. What just happened is the conclusion of that deal. *Our* deal is only just beginning to move forward. I have brought you your mother's murderer." He gestured at Feng, who was still catatonic. "That is one condition. Soon you will have the rest of what you desire, and so will I. Like I said, I am a god of my word."

"You're not making any sense!" Rui screamed. "I haven't found Four, I haven't found the vessel, I—"

"Oh, but you have, Rui."

"*What?*" She collapsed on her knees, shocked and confused.

"You are quite right that Nikai realized *who* the vessel containing Four's power is. And fortunately, so did I," said Ten. "Four could have found a magical item or relic—but he decided to use a *human* with a suitably powerful spirit core. One who could hide his power, mask it, and keep it safe inside them. Whether it was fate or a fool's luck, Four chanced upon a child who could do that on the same night he stole a powerful artifact from my realm. And you, Rui," Ten said, stooping to cup her chin, "*you* are that child."

Rui pushed his hand away, recoiling. Ten was lying. This was impossible.

"Believe me," said Ten, standing again. "I had my doubts. How could it possibly work? How could such a human vessel exist? But the spiritual energy transfer between you and the other human boy triggered my interest. And when I met you, I felt a trace of my brother's power. You *have* been touched by death, just not in the way you thought. Of course, the trace could have been there because he saved your mother's life and yours. But when the Hybrids told me one of their brethren was killed by blue flames that came from *you* . . . that is when I knew. After you lost your earthly magic, that power from the depths of Hell became unstable, and it began to escape."

Rui heard every single one of his words, but none of them made sense. Everything felt like a terribly made-up joke, and *she* was the punch line.

"Eighteen years ago, the First King followed a sign from the fates and sought to save your life," Ten continued. "Four took advantage of the situation. He saw in you a living vessel, someone he could use to fulfill his goal. It is the only reason why he let your mother live that night. It was a selfish reason, and it is Four's selfishness that has caused chaos in both our realms."

"But what does all this have to do with Zizi?" Rui choked out. "Why did he have to die?"

Ten smiled. "The boy is not dead."

What? Was Ten telling the truth? Her heart stuttered and flailed. She fell upon Zizi's body, checking for signs of life. He was still warm, but she couldn't find a proper pulse, just a disturbing feeling of *something* under his skin.

"What did you do to him?"

"Not me, Rui," Ten replied. "*You.*"

"I don't—I don't understand."

Ten came closer. "When did the blue fire first appear?"

"We were ambushed by some Hybrids. Zizi was badly hurt—"

"How did you save him?"

"I . . . I used my sword, drove the flames into him to get to Aloysius."

"And when else did the blue fire appear?"

Tonight, when I thought he was dead.

Unbidden, an image from last night flashed in Rui's head: Zizi holding her in the infirmary, the blue flames never harming him.

Seven's thin voice whispered in her ear, *There should have been a pattern. But maybe you fail to see it.*

The blue flames . . . she couldn't summon them at any other time. They had only appeared when *Zizi* was in danger. Although he wasn't in danger when they appeared the night before, he'd been *close* to her, intimate. And the flames had taken a different form. They didn't rage out of control, seeking to devour what had hurt him.

"Finally starting to use this?" Ten said, tapping his head lightly. "I see you are making connections. The power from the underworld recognizes its master, and it seeks to protect him. It is inevitable that the two of you are drawn to each other. Whatever you think this boy feels for you, it is a lie. You were merely a host, a convenient coincidence."

Haven't you ever felt like that? Like you're searching for someone out there who's just right *for you—someone who completes you.*

When I saw you that night, I knew.

Rui clutched her face. "I don't believe you. I don't."

"It does not matter what you believe, Rui. The truth still stands. How did you meet?" Ten quirked his head. "Didn't this boy save you? Just as the power in you seeks to protect its master, the vessel must be protected too. That scar you left on Feng—it was the blue fire that protected you that night."

Rui didn't remember that. She'd fallen unconscious right after her mother died. She only remembered a bright light. Was it the blue fire? She couldn't be sure. There wasn't a coherent thought going through her mind, just a constant stream of anguish.

"I feel almost sorry for you, Rui," Ten said, but he showed no sign of sympathy. "It must be devastating to know you were used this way, to have thought the boy's feelings toward you were true."

Did Zizi know? Had he been pretending all this while? Befriending her and keeping her close because she was the vessel . . . He'd told her he was an orphan, that he didn't remember much of his childhood . . . Was it all a lie?

A gasp came from behind.

Rui turned to the boy lying on the tracks, covered in his own blood.

Zizi drew a shuddering breath and opened his eyes.

They were no longer a pale blue, but dark like the deepest night.

"Behold," said Ten, overcome by sudden emotion, "the Fourth King of Hell has arrived."

54

They say each King is born without a heart.

But when Four sees her body lying motionless on the softly fallen snow, he knows it is a lie.

Four sits in the Garden of Tongues, eyes fixed on the night sky. He presses a hand to his chest. If he presses hard enough, he thinks he can feel a beating heart.

As he gazes at the stars, yearning for things lost, he sees the spirit trail of a dying star, its green light moving eastward. An anomaly is about to happen in the mortal realm, he thinks.

The spirit trail descends rapidly, but it does not hold his interest—

—until another, fainter trail appears where the dying star once hung in the sky.

Four stands up now, curiosity stirring inside him as his eyes follow the second light. Barely visible, the green light flickers, streaking in the opposite direction of the first.

Upon its death, the star had split into two.

Hell is a never-ending night.

The shadows are long and sharp when Four finally arrives at Wangyi Lake. Its silvery-gray waters are pristine; looking into them is like looking into a mirror. Except instead of his own image, he sees strangers.

Human faces, disturbingly real in detail, drift in the water, swirling like koi in search of food. Four wonders if the faces belong to people who have lived, or if they represent the hordes of souls that populate the kingdoms.

Or perhaps, they are the faces of the living.

Despite existing in the underworld for so long, there are so many things about his realm that he does not understand.

A hexagonal pavilion stands in the middle of the lake. Its sloped roof is ivory-tiled, its pillars made of equally fair stone. Inside, a solitary figure sits. A woman. Beyond the pavilion, the faint outline of a bridge stretches far into the horizon.

Four has never been here. None of the Kings have any real business in a place where souls begin their journey back to the living world.

He takes a tentative step onto the lake.

A lotus flower, slightly larger than the size of his foot, springs up from under the water and meets his weight. Each step he takes is greeted by another flower until he reaches the pavilion.

The woman inside stands and bows. Her robes are white silk, the fabric so seamless he cannot tell where it starts or ends. White hair, almost translucent, flows down her back, loose and free. She is ageless, her face easily forgettable. But the more Four gazes upon her, the more familiar and beautiful she becomes. Still, he knows that once he departs, he will be unable to describe her, and he will not recall any detail of her person.

Such is the way of the Pavilion of Memories.

"Greetings, Lady Meng." Four bows, unable to shake the feeling that she has been expecting him.

"I am pleased to see you are well, Your Majesty." The Lady of the Pavilion waves her hand, and a stone stool appears next to him.

"My visit will be short," he says, taking a seat. "Every soul in Hell must go through your tea ceremony before being reborn into the human realm. I want to know if your tea will work on a King. I want to know if drinking it will allow me to forget and cross over."

There is no change in Lady Meng's expression when she replies, "Your Majesty knows my nature does not allow me to lie. Yet you insist on asking me things a King should never need to know."

Four tugs at the black strip of silk around his neck. It is suffocating him, always suffocating. "I did not take this crown myself. It was placed onto my head before I could even conceive of what a crown meant. Tell me, will your tea work on me?"

Lady Meng remains silent.

Four knows his questions are dangerous. There are good reasons why no King has drunk her tea or crossed the bridge. It is said that if the underworld is even one King short, chaos will ensue.

Four places the willow branch on the table in clear view. "I intend to use this."

"A wish?"

Four nods.

"You will bind me to it," Lady Meng said. It was not a question.

"I am sorry, but it is necessary, and you are the only one who exists in both realms."

Lady Meng regards him. Her milky-white irises focus, seeing nothing and everything at once.

Four gasps.

It feels like his chest is being ripped open. She digs and digs. Clawing, raking, until she finds what she is looking for.

Then she withdraws.

Four's breaths are shaky. He feels torn apart and put back together carelessly, his insides no longer fitting.

"That was a taste of what you want," Lady Meng tells him.

Four shivers.

"What you want can be achieved under the right circumstances," she continues. "Certain conditions must be met when a soul partakes in my tea ceremony. First, it requires them to forget."

"I am willing to sacrifice anything," he replies hoarsely.

"It would mean forgetting the reason why you are doing this. It would mean forgetting her."

How did Lady Meng know he was doing this because of her?

She is the reason why he must do this. Why he must escape from this life of shadow. The time they had together was brief, for she left him too early. He has existed for so, so long; an endless stretch of days and nights—but every moment with her was a moment he felt truly alive.

He wants that feeling again. Knows he can never get it back. Even if he did become human, it would not be the same. Not without her. But he cannot forget her, he cannot forget what he did to her. And maybe . . . he wants to. Maybe it is relief he feels, now that he knows there is a way to put his memories to rest.

"I am willing to sacrifice anything," he says again. "I was never given a choice to be a King. Now I will make my own."

"Very well," said Lady Meng. "But your power and your soul are eternal and tied to this realm. If you wish to exist in the human world, you must separate them. This cannot work without the appropriate vessels: one for your power, one for your soul."

Four swallows, wondering if it is fortune or fate at work. Unaware that the dying star had split into two, One followed the first green light to the site of that accident, and they had asked Four to help save a baby's life.

But Four had seen the second light, the other spirit trail of the dying star that had split into two. He chose to follow it and was shocked to discover what—or who—was at the end of it.

As far as One is concerned, only one anomaly exists. But Four knows better. And he knows, for his plan to succeed, none of the other Kings must ever find out.

"Two anomalies occurred in the mortal realm at the same time tonight, and that is why I am here," he tells Lady Meng. "I have found two suitable vessels. Human ones; a boy and a girl."

Lady Meng's eyes widen, her hands clasping together. "Yuanfen," she whispers. "A fateful coincidence. The universe conspires, and so, it is inevitable." Then, knowing what is to come, she draws a long breath and nods.

Four places a hand over the willow branch and closes his eyes. "Those who seek me shall never see me; only you alone will know my fate and protect my secret, but to others you may never speak a word of your duty."

In the end, the darkness is lonelier than expected.

He is tired, so tired. But he continues, following his instinct. Following that tug pulling him forward ever since he broke free.

The ragged piece of silk, once tied around his throat, is clutched in his hand. This tether to his kingdom is the only thing that remains of his previous existence. His grip on it loosens as he walks. Already, he can feel the change inside him.

He is weak. He is cold. He is vulnerable.

He is becoming mortal.

He wonders if this is what freedom feels like, if this is what it means to live.

The bridge seems to stretch on forever. The rope burns the flesh on his palms, and the wooden planks beneath his feet feel like mud. Should he fall, there are sharp knives below to catch him.

He was a King the last time he ventured near this space between worlds. Searching for hope. Searching for her. But he found neither. Just a soul in the Nothing, unable to cross over.

Nikai, he remembers. The name brings comfort. But he can feel his memories slipping.

"Nikai," he says out loud.

Another step, another tug. And the image of his friend vanishes from his mind.

He shudders. What was he thinking of? Who was he thinking of? It wasn't her. That he knows. Her face is still clear to him. Her voice. Her laugh.

Her touch.

But soon. Soon. He will forget.

And he does.

He walks on and the darkness grows.

Somewhere along the way, he forgets his own name.

Finally, he forgets himself.

The darkness takes him in its arms, folds him into itself. Slowly, gently. Until he can see nothing. Until he is part of it.

And it is dark. So very dark.

Darker than black.

* * *

Zizi opened his eyes.

He was covered in blood. He couldn't tell if he was dead or alive or something else.

Astonishingly, he felt fine. But he had depleted most of his spiritual energy in creating that wretched separation spell. He had no reason to feel fine.

He blinked, focusing on Rui.

She was looking at him in horror. No. Worse. She was looking at him like he had betrayed her.

He tried to speak, but his throat refused to work.

"Behold, the Fourth King of Hell has arrived," said the man with the flaxen hair and red robes.

The man snapped his fingers.

Everything went silent and still. Everything except Zizi and the man.

Ten, Rui had called him. At first, Zizi thought he was a mage, but his aura was all wrong and no mage could stop time.

"What are you?" Zizi rasped, finally finding his voice.

Ten smiled. He reminded Zizi of a spider, or a snake. "Do you remember who *you* are?"

Zizi shook his head carefully. Based on the new memories in his head, he had a hunch. But it was so absurd he refused to accept it.

"My dear brother," Ten sighed, "I see you are in denial."

"Those are not my memories." Zizi was sure of it. "I don't know what you did, and I don't give a shit about what you believe or say. I'm not your brother."

"I suppose it will take some time for you to remember everything, and for you to revert to your actual self instead of"—Ten gestured at him, wrinkling his nose with distaste—"whatever *this* is. I much prefer my brother's original face, but at least your eyes have changed."

What does he mean? Zizi didn't want to *change*; he didn't want to be someone else. *This* was him. Teeth gnashing, he scrubbed at his face in panic. *No, no, no.* He felt a weird push-pull sensation in his body, like his insides were having a tug-of-war.

Lines creased on Ten's forehead. "Interesting," he said, staring hard. "Your eyes . . . they are blue again. *How?*"

"I . . . I don't know."

"No matter." Ten dismissed it with a swing of his sleeve. "All things will be restored when we return to the underworld."

But Zizi had caught the confusion and displeasure in his expression. Ten wasn't expecting this. He didn't think Zizi could push back against the change. *Can I stop it?* Zizi wondered, his panic subsiding. If two souls existed in his body somehow, did it mean that one soul could dominate the other? Could *his* soul keep Four's at bay like he had for the last eighteen years? Could he remain the human he'd been and wanted to be?

"I'm not going anywhere with you, asshole," he said. "I'm staying right here." *With Rui*, he thought.

"Ah, the name-calling. I forgot how fond you were of that," Ten groused. "Though I must say, it was seldom directed at me."

Ignoring him, Zizi went to Rui, his pulse racing the way it always did when he was near her. Her expression was stuck in a moment of despair, her body frozen in time. He touched her cheek gently, just to be sure. It was warm, and he breathed a little easier.

"If you are concerned about the girl, you should know that this is what she wanted."

Zizi twisted around in disbelief.

Ten was examining his ruby-stained fingernails. "Rui made a deal with me to get her magic back and to save the life of the other boy. What was his name? Yiran?" Ten smiled coyly at Zizi. "I see you are surprised. I guess she kept it a secret from you. This is all part of the plan so she gets what she wants."

You're wrong, Zizi wanted to say. But he didn't. While he was sure *this* wasn't what Rui had in mind when she tried to get her magic back, he was just as certain she would always choose herself. It was one of the things he admired about her. But in this case, it seemed she had chosen Yiran too.

"I sense your doubt, dear brother—"

"Stop calling me that," Zizi snapped.

Before he could get another word in, Ten drew a circle with his finger. A small black dot appeared in midair. It grew bigger and bigger, a dark hole forming out of nowhere. An abyss to somewhere Zizi would rather not know.

Something black flew out from the portal and wrapped itself around his neck.

It burned.

"Get it off me!" Zizi pulled at the fabric, but it only tightened. It felt like it was strangling him.

"Alas, I cannot remove that," said Ten. "It binds us to the underworld. Each King has one." Ten pointed to the leather harness around his waist, incongruous against his silk hanfu. "Don't fight it," he advised.

Loosening his grip, Zizi tried his best to breathe normally. The burning sensation tapered off, and he let go of the collar. But that tug inside him shifted instantly. For a moment, he felt like he was losing his balance and falling, but the descent was happening in his *mind*, like something was dragging his consciousness down into the dark.

Breath ragged, Zizi floundered.

Ten quirked his head. "Black again? I see. There is a fight going on inside you, and it explains why your eyes keep changing. But understand that you have no choice but to return with me to the underworld. Know that your presence will mend the rift between the realms and restore balance. The Nothing will retreat to its confines, and the underworld will be safe. When that happens, our realm will stabilize, and the Blight will stop mutating and infecting *humans* in this world. And the girl will not be in danger."

His grandmother's words came to Zizi suddenly, spoken four years ago on a cold winter's morning after he had found Rui that fateful night.

Your story will not end well. The girl must be left alone, Madam Meng had said, in a voice that sounded barely human. She wasn't a kindly relative who had taken him in after all, but someone he had bound to himself. Someone who made sure he drank his tea so he would forget. So he would keep forgetting.

When Rui lost her own spiritual energy, the power of the underworld must have surfaced, yearning to return to its master. The strange episodes of Zizi losing pockets of time, appearing in different places without knowing how he got there—it was all linked to the awakening of that power. But now, equilibrium was restored. The black lines on his hands and arms had vanished, and he could feel that power coursing through his veins.

Zizi clenched his fists. In the end, Madam Meng's words did ring true. She had warned him to stay away from Rui. He had refused. And now, Rui was paying the price.

Ten was right. There was no other choice.

"I won't go without saying goodbye," he said. "Unfreeze everything."

"There is no time for silly farewells," Ten mocked. "You will soon forget your life here and you will be forgotten, too."

Zizi shot him a deathly glare. "You're wrong. I will never, *ever* forget her."

"You think you are in love with her, but it is false, merely something you feel because she held the power that belonged to you." Ten scoffed. "You do not love her. You *cannot*—you are a King."

Anger throbbed in Zizi's veins at that thought. He felt a rush of something big and unknown surging through his body. He flung out a hand by instinct.

Time flowed again.

Water dripped from the cracks in the ceiling, and musty air filled his nostrils.

Rui was staring at him in horror.

Ten cackled. "Oh my, getting reacquainted with your power so soon, brother?"

55
Rui

The world had reeled out of control. There was a black vortex across the width of the tunnel spinning impossibly fast. The ground beneath her was shaking, throwing her off balance. Pieces of debris were falling from the walls and ceiling.

But Rui's attention was fixed on the boy standing in front of her with his new eyes, so dark against his pale skin.

Zizi looked otherwise the same. But she wasn't sure if she recognized him. If she knew him.

"Rui."

He even sounded the same.

"Rui," he repeated, with more emphasis, with more meaning.

He stepped closer, but she shrank back. "Stay away from me," she said, trembling with anger.

Hurt flashed across his face. Grunting, he clutched his head like it hurt or like he was trying to squeeze something out. He let go, panting heavily, turning to her—

His eyes. They were pale blue again.

"Who are you?" Rui shouted. What was going on? Was he Four? Or was he—

The walls around them creaked loudly, lines forming on the cement, the fractures spreading.

Ten made an impatient sound. "We do not have time! I have opened a portal to the underworld. The longer it stays open, the more destruction it will wreak in both our realms. Come with me, brother."

But Zizi didn't move. He was still staring at Rui, stricken.

She forced herself to look away, turning on Ten. "If you knew it was *him*, why go through the charade? Why didn't you grab him from the start?"

Zizi spoke before Ten could answer. "Those who seek me shall never see me."

"What?"

"Ten didn't know. It was part of the spell, the wish the Fourth King made with a powerful relic from the underworld. Anyone who was looking directly for him would not see him for who he is. They wouldn't recognize him." Zizi continued, "The only way to find Four was to go around his spell."

"How do you know all this?" Rui demanded.

"He remembers what he did eighteen years ago," Ten said with a smug smile. He extended a hand to Zizi. "We must leave now."

Zizi ignored him. "I won't leave without saying goodbye."

He took a tentative step toward Rui, but there was another groaning creak in the walls.

Asphalt crashed down between them, the thunderous sound echoing through the tunnel. Cables dropped from the damaged walls, sparking and fizzing with live electricity. The air was hazy with dust.

Knocked to the ground, Rui cried out in pain. Her leg was stuck under a block of cement, and her ankle felt twisted. She could hear cars honking, shouts and sounds of panic from the streets above.

"Rui!" Zizi called.

She couldn't see him. Couldn't see Ten. Rubble stood between them.

"Rui!"

"Zizi," she groaned. Her lungs felt soggier with each inhale. She thought she heard other voices. She craned her neck. Cement and rock piled up behind her, blocking that path too. The voice called out again from behind the debris. *Surin?* No, it didn't make sense; the Exorcist couldn't be here in the tunnel.

Rui closed her eyes, exhausted and ready to give up. But the rubble in front of her moved. In moments, Zizi was standing before her. He flicked his hand. The cement block lifted off her leg, crashing to the side.

"Your leg—" he said, crouching down.

She felt her ankle and shin, turning her foot slightly. Nothing was broken, but her leg was bleeding and sore.

Zizi helped her up, brushing hair off her face, looking at her with such tenderness, it hurt.

"All this time," Rui couldn't help but ask, "did you know?"

"Of course not." His anguish was sharp and clear. She wanted to believe him.

"Everything you said, everything you told me—about me, about *us*—did you mean it? Was it real? Or were you only drawn to me because you're . . . you're *him*?" She couldn't bring herself to say his real name.

"You're asking me a question I don't know how to answer. I don't even remember *who* I am."

But Zizi had hesitated for the briefest of moments before saying that, as if a different answer had come to him first.

"*What* are you?" she whispered.

"Lost." Then, for some reason, he grinned in that same off-kilter way he always did.

And it broke her.

Rui clung onto him. He folded her in his arms and lifted her chin. His eyes had regained their kind glimmer. But now they also held a profound sadness.

"And what am I?" she whispered.

"Only human." His fingers grazed her cheek in the barest of touches, wiping her tears as he leaned in, murmuring four words in her ear.

She smiled, even as she felt a part of her die.

He pressed his lips to her forehead for the last time.

And then, he let her go.

56
Yiran

The ground continued to shake.

Yiran fell onto his knees.

"Is it an earthquake?" Teshin shouted above the noise, helping Yiran up.

"I don't think so."

The ground gave another sigh—

And broke.

There was a loud crack, then more. The asphalt was splitting, the cracks radiating out.

"Move, move, move!" Ash yelled, shoving Yiran forward.

Everyone ran desperately for safety as the road tore apart.

Yiran scanned for Teshin; they'd separated in the mayhem. He spun around, spotting a pink-haired figure instead, crawling out from the crumpled heap that was the healer's tent.

"Ada!" he called out. She waved weakly. He wanted to go to her, but she was on the opposite side of the giant crevice in the ground.

Just then, Teshin appeared next to her. "I got her!" they shouted. "Get out of there, Yiran!"

Yiran realized he was one of the unlucky few stuck on the wrong side of the crevice. The ground around him was unstable. He staggered as it started giving away completely, sinking beneath his feet. *Move. You'll fall in if you don't move.* He scrambled toward the blockade.

A few steps later, a metallic sound screeched in his ears. He glanced in its direction. The tower crane next to the office building was creaking menacingly, the slabs of concrete hooked onto the trolley swaying as the structure shook and groaned. Gulping, Yiran ran faster. The creaking grew louder, like a piercing roar.

There was a violent lurch, and the base of the crane tilted into the asphalt. The concrete slabs slid off, crashing down.

Yiran was thrown forward into the air. He braced for impact, hitting the ground, rolling over coarse debris. Gingerly, he lifted his head. There was a ringing in his ears, and he was bruised and battered, the cuts on his arms and legs bleeding freely.

But he'd been fortunate, thrown clear onto the stable ground.

Dazed, he struggled up and stood in the chaos of sirens and screams and rubble and dust. He was strangely numb. In shock. The late-afternoon sky had turned orange, and the large sinkholes that had appeared looked like sinister portals to another world.

"Yiran!" Ash was suddenly next to him, holding his shoulders. "Are you okay?"

"You're bleeding—"

Ash swiped at his head, his hand coming away wet with blood. "It's nothing. Let's get you somewhere safe."

They had barely taken a few steps when Yiran felt it happen. Something *tearing* inside him. His chest seized. He crumpled to his knees. Grabbing at air, grabbing nothing, grabbing Ash's leg.

"Yiran! Yi—"

The sky above him was so orange. The world so silent. He didn't feel anything. Was he dying? *This isn't so bad*, he thought.

Suddenly, he felt Rui. Her fear, her anger—her sadness.

Stabbing pain. A shock of ice.

Then nothing.

And he was dying he was dying he was dying—

Air rushed into his lungs. Sounds blasted his ears. The world was in motion again.

"Yiran? Yiran, what's wrong?"

Worried faces surrounded him. He couldn't see them. Everything was a blur of gray. His insides *burned*.

"Hang on, Yiran—help's coming." The voice was distorted, far away and frightened.

It's too late, Yiran tried to say. No sound came out of his mouth.

Someone gripped his arm. "What? What are you saying?"

Yiran closed his eyes . . . and the hollowness seeped into him again.

57
Rui
THREE DAYS LATER

"That's right, Peter. As you can see behind me, multiple large sinkholes appeared three days ago during a fierce fight between members of the Exorcist Guild and a nest of Revenants."

Rui's eyes fluttered open.

She was startled to find herself staring at a blank white ceiling. For a moment, she thought she was back at the Guild's secret facility, but the lighting here was soft and warm.

The clipped voice of the news reporter went on: *". . . after a preliminary survey of the area, authorities say that the damage to power lines and nearby buildings, while severe, can be fixed. A one-mile radius has been cordoned off while construction and recovery take place . . ."*

Groaning, Rui tried to sit up.

A nurse hurried over. "You're awake!" she exclaimed. "Was the TV too loud? I can turn it off."

"Leave it on," Rui mumbled. Her words came out heavy and slurred. Her throat was dry, her tongue lethargic. Thankfully, the nurse understood her.

Rui peeked under her blue hospital gown. Bruises stamped her torso, along with signs of magical healing. But there was only so much the Guild healers could do, especially if they were dealing with other casualties among the Exorcists. Rui's broken fingers were taped up, her left arm was in a cast, and her head felt woozy in a way that made her certain she'd been given painkillers.

Something was thrumming in her veins . . . something familiar.

Rui took stock of her surroundings. The hospital room was large. A coffee table in the middle, a small sofa beside it, a plush armchair next to her bed, and a flat-screen television on the wall. She was the only patient in here. A private room with her own dedicated nurse? She couldn't afford this.

She reached for the cup on the side table and came up with a fistful of air and a whimper.

"Here, let me." The nurse set the cup carefully in Rui's hand. "You've been unconscious for a few days. They gave you something for the pain. Everything will feel a little strange while your body adjusts."

The nurse watched as Rui gulped down as much water as she could stomach. There was something odd about the way the nurse was looking at her. It gave off a sense of admiration bordering on reverence, and it made Rui uncomfortable. In the background, the news coverage droned on.

"... thank the Exorcists for their work. As you recall, three civilians were rescued from the scene due to the quick actions of Xingshan Academy's top cadet, Lin Ru Yi, and dozens more were saved in the vicinity. We're told Cadet Lin is currently recovering from her injuries ..."

Rui dropped her cup. Water splashed onto her blue hospital gown, leaving an embarrassing splotch down the middle.

"... is the daughter of renowned biology researcher Dr. Matthias Lin, who is most known for his work on ..."

Her face was on the screen.

Her *face* was on the screen.

They had used a photo from an old yearbook. Rui stared, not quite recognizing the smirking girl with long black hair. That girl looked a lot more confident than she ever remembered feeling.

"That's you, isn't it?" the nurse said, her excitement barely contained.

Rui made an incoherent sound.

The machines' beeps sped up, and the nurse jerked into action. "No, no, you mustn't get up."

"Turn it off!"

"Okay, there," the nurse said, hitting the switch for the television. "Better?"

Rui thought quickly. She had to get rid of this woman. She pretended to settle down. "Yes, better. Sorry, I was just confused. I didn't expect to see myself on the news."

"I can't imagine how frightening it had to be, but you were so brave."

Rui avoided eye contact. She didn't want the woman's sympathy or admiration.

"It's a miracle you survived," the nurse went on. "I heard the entire subway tunnel caved in."

It's because he saved me . . . again. Rui wasn't sure how Zizi had done it. The tunnel had collapsed further when Ten closed the portal. But none of the rubble had fallen on her. She touched the red string tied around her wrist. It'd stayed on throughout everything somehow. The only piece of him she had left.

"We couldn't get that thread off," said the nurse. "Couldn't cut it for some reason. Do you want me to try again?"

"No!" Rui pulled her arm back, almost snarling. The nurse looked at her funny. Rui tried to smile. "I'm hungry. Could you get me something to eat, please?"

"You poor thing, of course. I'll get you some hot soup."

The door closed.

Immediately, Rui bolted upright. She yanked out the needles and tubes connected to her arm. The machines went silent. Already fearing what the hospital bill would be, she swung her legs over, shivering when her bare toes touched the cold floor.

There was a sharp knock on the door.

A man wearing a white doctor's coat and polished shoes stepped in. He took one look at her and chided, "You can't be discharged yet. Please, lie down."

"No, I can't—" Her legs shook, and she lost her balance. Just as she was about to hit the floor, someone caught her fall.

"Don't you know, Doctor? She's very bad at taking advice and very good at doing whatever the hell she wants."

"Ash?" Rui said, staring at the newcomer who had swooped in to help her. He was wearing his noncombat Exorcist suit and a faded bruise on his angelic face. The right side of his head was shaved, and he'd flipped his gray hair over to cover it. He laid her back gently onto the bed. When he turned to talk to the doctor, she saw that his hair was hiding a fresh scar on his scalp.

Ash smiled, charming as always. "May I speak with Cadet Lin for a few moments in private, Doctor? Guild business—you understand."

The doctor glanced at the red pin on Ash's jacket lapel. "You have fifteen minutes. We must get her hooked up again, and she needs to rest."

Ash shut the door firmly after the doctor and sat in the armchair.

"I'm probably not the person you want to see, but I'm here nonetheless. Don't worry, I won't stay long. Your father's been here every day, and Ada visits too. But no one else has been allowed into your room yet. Guild's orders," he said, almost apologetically.

They don't want anyone to talk to me before you do, Rui thought, swallowing painfully. Her throat was still parched. "Why did they put me in this room?"

"Because I told them to. We take care of our own, and as a valuable member of the Exorcist Guild, we're making sure you're in the best environment for your recovery."

A valuable member of the Exorcist Guild? That was news to her.

"Why are they saying I saved all those people?" she asked, even though she had a hunch.

"Because you did." Ash steepled his fingers together, elbows on the arms of his chair. "You're a hero now; you helped us wipe out a nest of vicious Revenants in our planned Hunt. Everyone knows this. More importantly, everyone *believes* this."

The Guild had already planted the "truth" about what had happened, and the media was spreading it to the public. Whether it was true or not, they'd molded the narrative to their advantage. Rui could speak up, give her version of things, tell everyone what had really happened in the tunnels. But would they believe her? And what would she gain from telling the truth?

"You and I will be chatting in the next few days—private conversations," Ash continued. "And by the way, you have a guaranteed spot in the Guild—Captain track."

A bribe to keep my mouth shut. The thin hospital gown bunched up in Rui's fists.

"You're clever, Rui," Ash said, observing her intently. "Don't mess up. You have an important role to play."

Maybe it was the shock of it all. Maybe the doctor was right, and she needed more rest. Maybe she was simply too broken inside. Rui felt the fight go out of her. She was tired. Her hands unfurled, falling limply to her side.

"I'm glad you understand." Ash looked at her pointedly, lowering his voice. "I have two questions for you today. We know you went after the Hybrids because your mother's murderer was part of that group. I want to know how you knew that."

Rui kept her expression dazed, pretending the sedation had not worn off fully and her mind wasn't already lucid. "I wanted him dead." She paused. "Zizi told me." It hurt to say his name.

"Which brings me to my second question—where is Zizi?"

A dull ache began at her ribs, spreading up to her chest. "I don't know."

Ash sighed, shaking his head. "He must've known he'd be in bigger trouble with the Guild Council for this. I guess he found an opportunity to slip away during the chaos."

Rui didn't correct him.

"You know, I really thought better of him." Ash didn't hide that he was upset. Maybe he'd been genuinely fond of the mage. "You should rest. We'll speak again soon." He got up and walked to the door. "I'll send word to your father and Ada. They can see you tomorrow."

"Ash."

His hand paused on the doorknob.

"Are they really dead?"

"Our team went down, and we found the Hybrids trapped in the rubble when we found you. I took care of *him* myself," Ash said quietly. "They're dead. It's as if they never existed."

There are others out there, and they have a leader, Rui wanted to tell him. She was sure of it, and she was sure that he knew it too, and that their future conversations would focus on this. But instead, she said, "I wanted to kill him with my own hands."

"True revenge is surviving. Remember that." Ash gave her a nod. "I'm glad you're alive, Rui."

The door opened and closed and opened again.

The doctor and nurse came into the room, fussing over her. Needles and tubes went back into her arm. Hot and salty soup filled her mouth and stomach. When they were satisfied she wasn't going to do anything foolish, they left her alone.

Pulling the IV pole with her, Rui made her way slowly to the window, wincing with each step. The painkillers had worn off, but she had refused more. She stared at the impossibly blue sky and bustling city streets below.

Ten Kings reside in the underworld again, she thought.

He was gone, never to return. And the world had simply moved on.

Rui crept back into bed, curling up on her side, pulling the covers over her head. She could feel her own breath fluttering against her cheeks, the wetness of her pillow. The low thrum inside her grew louder, begging for her attention. Her magic . . . it was back, just as Ten said it would be. But a different sort of emptiness had formed, a void that would never be filled.

She closed her eyes, remembering his soft, gentle voice, repeating those four words in her ear, over and over again.

Sometime later, she woke with a start. It was night. Someone was in the room with her.

"Who's there?"

A click.

The lamp on the side table lit up, casting shadows on Yiran's face, slicing it into sharp angles.

Rui propped herself up. Her eyes felt puffy from crying and her head hurt, but she was glad to see him.

"Why are you creeping around like some stalker?"

She expected a smile at least, but Yiran remained stone-faced. Faint circles ringed his eyes. It'd only been days since she last saw him, but there was something different, like he'd grown older. Harder.

"Are you . . . okay?" she asked in a small voice.

"Why did you do it?" She couldn't sense his feelings anymore, but his distress was obvious.

"Do what?"

"It's *gone*." Yiran was looking at his hands. They were shaking.

"Yiran, what's wrong?" She started to get out of bed, but his vicious glare froze her in place. "Yiran?" she said, suddenly afraid.

"My spiritual energy is normal again. My magic's gone. You got yours back, didn't you?"

"I . . . I just woke up today . . ." Rui couldn't go on. Her magic *was* back, which meant his was gone. Which meant his spirit core was safe, that *he* was safe. But she felt no elation, no relief. Only dread, the heavy sense of things ending.

Yiran's eyes glittered feverishly. "You feel it inside you, don't you?"

She hung her head.

"Do you know what he said to me?" Yiran was talking about his grandfather. "He said he was glad. He was *happy* that I lost my magic."

Rui felt the pain in his voice.

"I played by the rules, did everything I could to please him, to show him I could achieve something, to prove that I could make him proud. Should've known . . . and *you*"—Yiran turned sharply to Rui— "you didn't ask the first time, so why would you ask the second? You used me. I tried to protect you, I lied for you, but you *used* me."

All the reasons, all the excuses, died in Rui's throat. She couldn't defend herself. Couldn't meet Yiran's eyes. He was right. Her own actions were no different from Four's. Four had used her as a convenient vessel, and it was what she had done to Yiran. She'd cast a spell on him without consent, giving him a taste of something he had wanted so desperately, only to snatch it back.

It was cruel.

The hurt on Yiran's face was unmistakable. "Don't call me. Don't look for me. I don't ever want to see you again."

"Yiran . . ." She faltered. She had already lost one, she couldn't lose the other. "I'm sorry. I'm sorry, Yiran—stay, please. Don't go."

But he was already at the door.

He opened it, and his body split in half. A boy in the light; a boy in shadow. He gave her one last, lingering look.

"I wish I'd never met you that night."

Five Three, Five Four

ONE MONTH LATER

The apartment smelled of ginger rice and steamed chicken. The floor was vacuumed, the shoe rack tidy, and a stack of laundered clothes rested neatly on an armchair.

Rui fought the urge to pinch herself awake. This was a normal she'd forgotten, but it was the new normal her father had promised. The sight of her in the hospital, beaten and bruised, had shaken him to his core. He'd said he couldn't lose her too, and he'd vowed to clean up his act.

He was busying in the kitchen now, his eyes sober behind his new glasses. "Hmm . . . it's been a long time since I cooked this. Think I forgot my secret ingredient."

Rui said, "More garlic?"

Her father laughed. "Yup."

The doorbell rang, and they both froze.

"Matthias? Matthias, are you home?" It was only Auntie Chen.

Her father shook his head with a resigned smile. "Bet she needs help with her computer again. You don't have to do anything. Sit tight and rest, I'll be right back, okay?" He'd taken on the tone he'd used on her when she was a little girl, but Rui didn't mind.

"It's not like I can do much anyway," she said, sticking her hand up. It was still in a cast.

Worry lines deepened on her father's forehead, but he managed a smile. "You got pretty banged up, kid." He opened the front door. "By the way, something arrived from the hospital. It's in the bedroom. Guess they sent it here instead of the Academy."

After he left, Rui poured herself a glass of grape juice and shuffled to the bedroom. A small ziplock bag was on her father's desk. They had given her the essentials when she was discharged—a ratty wallet and a broken cell phone. These must be the other things they'd found in her pockets. She put her juice down and fiddled with the bag with her good hand. Old receipts, a gross stick of gum, bobby pins, a jade rabbit, and some bits and bobs she didn't care about.

Light flashed.

Nikai's mirror.

Carefully, she slid it out of the bag. There were hairline fractures in the fragile glass.

"Nikai? Seven?" she whispered on impulse. But her heart cried out a different name.

The glass remained dull, and as she held it in her hand, it turned gray and crumbled into ash, leaving behind only a small shard.

Whatever magic the mirror had was gone.

Rui clutched the remaining piece, remembering the legend Zizi had told her at The Reverie, about the beings who were born paired, then separated by wrathful gods, doomed to live their lives apart, always seeking to find their matching half. She thought she understood the story now.

The Tenth King had kept his word. She'd asked for her vengeance, her magic, and Yiran's life, and she'd gotten it all. Even her father was coming around. But Yiran was no longer speaking to her, and Zizi was gone, and there was a new hole inside her to fill.

Sighing, Rui slipped the shard of glass into her pocket. As she picked up her grape juice, she noticed something sticking out from the corner of her father's desk drawer.

An old photograph, furled at the corners like it'd been stuffed somewhere, forgotten, then dug up again.

She tugged the photograph out.

A group of teenagers in their Xingshan Academy uniforms with wide grins and messy hair stared back at her. They looked young—third-years, maybe. Two boys at the back of the group stood out because of their height.

The photograph shook in Rui's hand, and the juice spilled from its glass when she put it onto the table.

"How . . . what?" she breathed.

There was no mistaking who the bespectacled boy on the left was: a teenage Matthias Lin.

But as far as she knew, her father had ordinary levels of spiritual energy. He'd never told her he'd gone to Exorcist school.

Heart racing, Rui opened the drawer. There was another photograph. It was faded like the other. Her father was older in this one, in his early twenties. The photographer had caught him in deep conversation with the same tall, handsome young man he'd stood next to in the other photo, their heads bowed close together.

The longer Rui stared at the handsome young man, the clearer his features became, and in them, she recognized the face of a boy she once knew.

Song Yiran.

The penthouse lounge in Theo's condo was getting on Yiran's nerves. The fireplace was fake, the plush decor screamed nouveau riche, and the cloying scent from the reed diffusers was giving him a headache. He was dying to get out of here. But he said nothing, waiting patiently for Nick Cheng to draw a card.

A smile broke on Cheng's face.

"Got a good one?" Theo nudged.

Cheng ignored him.

Theo shrugged. He and Sweets had already folded. The game was once again to be decided between Yiran and Cheng.

"My turn." Yiran swiped a card off the deck and threw it carelessly onto the table. The jack of hearts stared back at him balefully. "Bust," he sighed.

Cheng punched the air. "Winning fair and square like a man."

"I agree in principle but find fault with your gender dichotomy. Good game, Cheng."

"Give me back my watch, asshole."

"Easy with the name-calling, babe," Yiran said without ire. He stuck his wrist out and Cheng unbuckled the watch.

Cheng gave an ironic little bow while flipping them off. "So long, suckers."

Everyone laughed.

Sweets rolled off the sofa. "I'm heading off."

"Me too. Time for dinner." Theo glanced at Yiran. "You'll let yourself out?"

Yiran nodded.

After they left, he sat there, delaying his return to Song Mansion. The house felt colder these days, and he no longer thought of it as his home. He couldn't forget Song Wei's reaction when he found out Yiran could no longer practice magic. He'd looked *victorious*, and it had killed any love Yiran might have had for the old man.

Something flickered against the windows. Snow.

Yiran opened the heavy glass doors and walked out onto the terrace. The air was brisk, and he could hear the faint honking of the cars from the streets below. He shivered in his thin T-shirt.

It had been weeks since he last saw Rui. She had looked so small and fragile in her hospital gown. He hated her. He missed her. He knew it wasn't her fault, but he needed someone to blame. It was too painful to be around her, to be reminded of what she had done and what he had lost.

He'd heard that the stupid wizard had disappeared. Ash assumed Zizi left the city to hide from the Guild and his punishment. But Yiran knew Zizi would never abandon Rui. *Fuck*, Yiran thought when he realized he missed the annoying mage too. He was getting soft.

Something stabbed his palm. The jack of hearts card was crumpled in his tight fist.

"If you're not careful, you're going to catch a cold."

Yiran felt his heart stop.

He recognized the voice. Hated that he recognized it. Hated that his immediate thought was *Thank gods he's not dead*. He couldn't bear to turn around. Couldn't bear to see that beautiful face and those sad gray eyes again.

"Are you finally here to kill me now that I'm defenseless?" Yiran asked.

"No, silly. I'm here to ask you a question."

"Go ahead."

Footsteps coming closer. A soft laugh. A cold breath ghosting against his ear. A voice sending shivers down his spine as it said:

"Do you want your magic back?"

The darkness was lonelier than expected.

Hell's dungeon was cold and damp and silent as a graveyard. *A graveyard.* Zizi almost laughed at that thought. Except laughing would hurt.

He could barely raise his head or move his fingers. It felt like a ton of bricks was sitting on his shoulders, pressing against his spine. There was a constant pulling in his brain. His mind was fighting with itself—with Four.

Everything was pain, *pain*, and more pain.

The first few days in the underworld had been bearable. Weirdly ordinary. He had a nice room in one of the Fourth Court's villas. It reminded him of a five-star hotel, except room service was a bunch of souls taking care of your every need.

He wasn't allowed to leave, obviously, but they had kept him well fed with food from the human realm. He spent his time missing Rui, which was a different kind of torture. To torment himself even more, he'd asked for paper and some charcoal. He sketched her face endlessly, trying to forget how she'd looked at him the last time he laid eyes on her, wishing he had told her the real answer to her question.

Everything you said, everything you told me—about me, about us*—did you mean it? Was it real? Or were you only drawn to me because you're . . . you're* him?

No matter what they told him, no matter what they did to him, Zizi *knew*. His feelings for her belonged to him and him only.

Soon enough, a slow trickle of eager visitors curious about the new Fourth King arrived.

Zizi made his stupid jokes, got a few laughs. Eight was a man who reminded him of one of those finance types in the human realm. Arrogant and tedious to talk to. Five was extremely shy. Seven was a little girl who sang Zizi a lullaby about spiders and ate his food. Zizi liked her best.

Zizi never saw Ten. He wondered if the bastard was being punished for his transgressions in the human realm.

The Kings who did show up were excited to meet Zizi, until they realized he wasn't some death god brother coming back into their fold. He didn't remember anything apart from the few memories that returned in the tunnel. He didn't understand the things they were saying to him. It felt like he'd failed a test he didn't know he had to study for.

Eventually, an old crone dressed in tattered gray robes appeared, her wizened face half hidden by a hood. She was the Second King, and she'd asked to see his hands. He'd given them to her, palms faced up, and she held them in her withered ones.

"His soul is still asleep."

"Well, that sounds ominous," Zizi said, with a humor he didn't feel. "What does that mean?"

"You are here to keep the balance of the Ten."

"So I've been told." A safer human realm meant *Rui* would be safer. It was the only thing keeping him sane.

"But as of now, the balance is still tipped," said the crone. "First, you must remember."

"Remember what?"

"Everything."

"You're not being helpful," Zizi scolded lightly.

The old crone leaned her head back. Her hood fell, revealing a skeletal face. Where her eyes should be, two black holes stared back at Zizi.

He'd shuddered, but he couldn't look away.

"Time is running out," she'd said. "You house the soul of a god, but

390

this body is that of a boy. It is human and mortal, a vulnerable vessel that will age and turn to dust. In our realm, this body cannot survive. You must not fight the change; you must let it happen."

"What if I don't want to change? Can't you pull Four's soul out of me and send me back to where I belong? I'm *human*, not a god."

"Alas, we cannot extract Four's soul from its vessel, not when his power now resides there too. They are fusing, even as we speak. It is too dangerous to separate them. Further chaos across the realms may ensue."

"How lovely."

"You are afraid," Two murmured. When Zizi stared defiantly back at her, she whispered, "Wake up, sweet prince."

After she left, Zizi looked in the mirror and saw that a lock of hair on his head had turned silvery white.

That very night, the black collar around his neck started to burn. It made his skin itch, and he'd tried to rip it off. Two men in expensive-looking suits appeared the next day. One was built like an ox, the other had a long face that reminded Zizi of a horse. They removed him from the Fourth Court and brought him to a dank cell and clamped thick manacles around his ankles and wrists.

"For security," Ox-Head had said.

Zizi laughed bitterly. "Afraid I'll escape again? Why can't I stay in the villa? You can chain me up there."

Horse-Face gave a snort that sounded more like a neigh. "This is the deepest part of Hell. There are ancient forces alive in here; it will help you remember."

A while after, a visitor arrived. A young man, barely older than Zizi. He had large, haunted eyes, like he'd seen the worst of the world and beyond. The red candle shook in his hand as he held it up to his face.

"Do you remember me?" he asked.

"No," Zizi replied.

"I am Nikai, a Reaper from the Fourth Court." The young man hesitated. "They released me so I could come here to jog your memory."

"I don't know you."

Nikai looked wounded by Zizi's words. "You're not him," he whispered, a catch in his voice.

As Nikai retreated into the shadows, Zizi couldn't resist calling out, "What was Four like?"

He heard a small, strangled sound from Nikai.

"He was my friend."

The silence that followed told Zizi that he was, once again, alone in the dark.

Soon the tug-of-war in his mind began again. In between wretched sleep and wakefulness, he writhed in endless pain.

Then, dreams started.

Laughter. The starburst scent of wildflowers. The taste of something sweet like honey. A young woman's voice. Stars. Blood on snow. The young woman, with her back turned to him.

Delirious and lost, Zizi whispered to the dark, "Who are you?"

But the dream only repeated.

Laughter.

The starburst scent of wildflowers.

The taste of something sweet like honey on his tongue.

Her voice.

Stars.

The woman.

Blood on snow. A body, cold.

Then one day, it changed.

The young woman was standing by an ancient wisteria tree that reminded Zizi of his own back in his shophouse. Her purple hanfu flowed to the ground, black hair cascading down her back.

Turn around, please, Zizi said in his dreams. *Let me see who you are.*

He asked again and again, until his voice was hoarse.

Finally, she did.

Do you remember me? said the woman, who was wearing Rui's face.

Author's Note

TETRAPHOBIA

In various Chinese languages, with a slight change in intonation, *four* (四) sounds like *death* or *die* (死). Thus, tetraphobia (the aversion to or fear of the number four) is a phenomenon common in East Asian countries and countries/societies with significant Chinese diaspora communities.

NUMERONYMS

Due to the tonal nature of Chinese languages, wordplay often occurs in colloquial speech and interaction. The title of this book, *Darker by Four*, is a reference to tetraphobia and a play on the sound of the number four in Mandarin and Cantonese.

The number five (五) sounds like *I* or *me* (吾). *Five* can also sound like *no* or *none* (无). The title of the prologue, "Five Four," is a play on this and can be interpreted as "My Death" or "No Death."

The number three (三) is interesting, as it can sound like *life* or *to live* (生) and also *to split*, *to separate*, or *to part ways* (散). The title of the epilogue, "Five Three, Five Four," is a play on all of this and can be interpreted in various ways—for example, "My Life, My Death" or "No Life, No Death." The epilogue title also alludes to the parting of ways between characters.

Pinyin tonal markers, or diacritics, have been left out of this book to facilitate the above wordplay. Pinyin markers have also not been used for honorifics and terms of address between characters to retain consistency.

YUÁNFÈN

While it is sometimes simplistically translated as *fate*, the concept of yuánfèn (缘分) refers to a karmic relationship between people who have been brought together (or separated) through an affinity that is predestined. It is important to note that the past plays a role in yuánfèn, as this karmic relationship between two people is affected by their past actions in a previous life or incarnation. The one instance where yuánfèn is mentioned in the book refers specifically to this concept.

Acknowledgments

Writing this book was weird. I started drafting bits and pieces in the middle of chemotherapy, through brain fog, memory loss, and days of being bedridden, in an emotional haze, not always aware of where the plot was going or what the character arcs would be. I only knew that it was an escape and a distraction from my existential crisis. The story was then revised and edited during a global pandemic, where life as many of us knew it had changed.

So, forgive me if I decided to indulge myself with this story and have a *little* fun. But I lie; I threw it all in . . . the BTS mint-choco ice cream debate, Namjoon's wisdom, Jin's "Super Tuna," TXT's "Blue Orangeade," references to various anime and manga I enjoy (you can guess which!), the superstitions and customs from my childhood and home country, my fascination with Haw Par Villa and the Ten Courts of Hell, hints of the cities I adore, my love for soulmate-reincarnation tropes in xianxia C-dramas (done here with a modern twist), and the cultural legacy of tragic, forbidden love stories from classic Chinese romances . . .

In other words, I wrote this for me and hoped that other people would love it too.

Happily, I'm in remission now. As for whether the characters in my story are bestowed their own *happily ever afters*, well, I guess you'll have to read the sequel to find out lol. In the meantime, please enjoy character art, playlists, and more from the world of *DB4* at junecltan.com/darker-by-four 😊

My deepest, most heartfelt thank-yous to:

Laura Rennert, my phenomenal agent, whose fierce support keeps me afloat. The wonderful team at Andrea Brown Literary Agency, and the amazing Taryn Fagerness—it's an honor to be represented by you.

Alice Jerman, my brilliant editor, whose sharp eyes and big brain made me a better storyteller.

Clare Vaughn, Mikayla Lawrence, Gwen Morton, Anabelle Sinoff, Nicole Moulaison, Catherine Lee, Jessie Gang, Lisa Calcasola, Lauren Levite, Kristin Daly Rens, the Epic Reads crew, the school and library team, as well as the sales team and everyone at Team HarperTeen. Thank you so much for all your hard work behind the scenes.

Molly Powell, Kate Keehan, Claudette Morris, Callie Roberston, Sarah Clay, Natasha Qureshi, Sophie Judge, and the incredible Team Hodderscape. A special shout-out to designer Natalie Chen and artist Yingting (@cyt_draws) for the beautiful cover!

The lovely Anissa and Team FairyLoot. Team Pansing for bringing my stories home, and all the international teams.

The authors who took the time to read my book and offer their kind words. The tireless booksellers, librarians, teachers, champions of and in the book community. Every reader on the clock/camera/bird/threads apps and irl who yells about their love for stories—you have my utmost gratitude and appreciation.

Friends who were there from the beginning of this wild publishing/author journey—Hd, word warriors, goosies, and many more—I am forever grateful.

My family and friends in my first home, Singapore.

And, as always, C & Z.